The award-winning author of **The Reunion** *continues her dazzling new series with a novel of one woman's fall from saint to sinner . . .*

Lucy Betancourt's future looks bleak. The daughter of an ailing vicar in a village with no eligible bachelors, her only hope is to find employment as a governess or companion. As she helps her childhood friend, the new Duchess of Worley, through her pregnancy, the ever-practical Lucy makes her plans. But life—in the way of the dashing Bex Brantwood—has something else in store for Lucy...

Upon meeting Bex, the duke's cousin, Lucy offers herself up to him. But Bex is no family man looking for a governess. And Lucy is not exactly mistress material. Still, the misunderstanding ends in a kiss neither can forget . . .

Bex finds the proper vicar's daughter and her most improper proposal endlessly amusing—and attractive. But, saddled with debt, he's in no position to keep a woman, much less marry one, which is what a woman like Lucy deserves. Little does he know that even with her reputation at stake, Lucy will take the biggest gamble of her life by following her heart—straight into his arms . . .

The Offer

Brides of Beadwell

Sara Portman

LYRICAL PRESS
Kensington Publishing Corp.
www.kensingtonbooks.com

LYRICAL PRESS BOOKS are published by

Kensington Publishing Corp.
119 West 40th Street
New York, NY 10018

All Kensington titles, imprints, and distributed lines are available at special quantity discounts for bulk purchases for sales promotion, premiums, fund-raising, educational, or institutional use.

Special book excerpts or customized printings can also be created to fit specific needs. For details, write or phone the office of the Kensington Sales Manager: Kensington Publishing Corp., 119 West 40th Street, New York, NY 10018. Attn. Sales Department. Phone: 1-800-221-2647.

Lyrical Press and Lyrical Press logo Reg. U.S. Pat. & TM Off.

First Electronic Edition: October 2017
eISBN-13: 978-1-5161-0050-7
eISBN-10: 1-5161-0050-6

First Print Edition: October 2017
ISBN-13: 978-1-5161-0053-8
ISBN-10: 1-5161-0053-0

Printed in the United States of America

Also by Sara Portman

The Reunion

Chapter One

February 1818

There were times in which one could be cognizant that one's perspective on a situation was at once both absurd and entirely sensible. As Lucy watched her dearest friend retch violently into a chamber pot, she held back pangs of envy even as she held back her friend's thick, plaited hair.

Lucy did not normally desire to toss up her breakfast, of course, but Emma's uneasy stomach was in fact an unmistakable sign that she was expecting her first child. Envy, as it happened, was an unfamiliar and awkward-fitting cloak for Lucy. She flushed with shame for the feeling, grateful Emma could not see her face and, as dear friends are capable, divine her thoughts.

No matter how much one envied the situation of another person, Lucy reminded herself while handing her friend the damp cloth she held at the ready, one should always be conscious that no situation was entirely free of difficulty. Certainly, this wisdom applied most fittingly at the present. Just as dismal circumstances often held silver linings, so did the sunniest of situations possess the occasional black cloud. Were these *black* linings?

Perhaps.

Emma was recently married, and to a duke, no less. She was deeply in love with her husband, she was the mistress of a stately manor, and she had recently learned she was expecting the first of likely many children from her marriage.

She was also violently ill on a daily basis, and the illness had not subsided as her pregnancy progressed.

Black linings.

Lucy, by contrast, was unmarried with no prospects and no connections other than the recent elevation of her childhood friend to the rank of duchess. The plans she was currently making for her future meant she would likely never know motherhood. She did, however, feel quite well at the present. She'd only moments ago been contemplating her delicious morning repast. Breakfast at the vicarage with her parents was usually quite simple: strong tea, toast, a boiled egg. The elaborate meals served at the London residence of the Duke and Duchess of Worley had proven one of the great delights of the visit.

Silver linings.

It was as simple as that. She was ashamed to have experienced even a moment of jealousy. For all of Emma's happiness today, she had paid dearly for it, suffering the loss of her parents and the shame of society for a broken engagement. Lucy had never before compared her friend's circumstances, good or bad, to her own situation.

She should feel nothing but joy for her friend's expectant state and empathy for her present discomfort. And she did feel all of those things, but there was a tiny seed of a sinful voice that whispered, *This will never be me.*

She studiously ignored it.

"Oh, Lucy," Emma croaked. "I am so sorry." She rocked back on her heels and exhaled heavily.

"Do not apologize again," Lucy chided, taking back the cloth. "I shall be horribly offended if you believe we are not dear enough to witness the contents of each other's stomachs."

Emma grimaced toward the metal pot. "Will you help me to bed, Lucy?"

Lucy assisted Emma in rising to her feet and supported her as she walked unsteadily to the stately four-poster bed. Still holding Emma with one arm, Lucy used her free hand to pull back the delicately embroidered coverlet and plump the soft pillow in preparation for her friend.

"You are such a sport to care for me this way," Emma said with a sigh as she lowered herself into the spot Lucy had prepared. "I fear I am building a debt I shall never repay."

"Nonsense." Lucy helped Emma the rest of the way into bed and pulled the coverlet up to her gently rounded middle, smiling as she did so. "It's the reason I'm here, isn't it?"

Emma rolled onto her side and drew up her knees. "It was supposed to be a ruse. When I invited you to come, I knew you wouldn't agree unless you thought there was some greater purpose to your visit. I never truly expected to need so much help. I just wanted your company. The sickness was supposed to have ended weeks ago."

Lucy stepped back and stood, arms crossed, assessing her patient. "You are not as sly as you might think. I knew you were planning more for a companion than a nursemaid, but you will accept both graciously or I shall feel horribly manipulated."

Emma placed one hand on her stomach while she sucked in and expelled heavily a deep breath of air. "I daresay it's beginning to pass now." She took two more similarly deep breaths, as though testing this declaration, then rolled gently onto her back again, keeping her knees in their bent position. "Would you mind propping me up a bit? I seem to do better that way than lying flat."

Lucy obliged her. "Take care for your stubbornness, Emma. There is no need to push yourself to recover instantly."

Emma flashed Lucy a wide-eyed look of innocent confusion.

Lucy responded with a chiding grimace. "Do not pretend you've no idea what I'm about."

"Oh, be fair, Lucy, you're no less stubborn and independent than I," Emma said, beginning to regain her color as though by force of will.

"But I am not the one applying that trait to defy a present ill state," Lucy said, pulling the bell to have the soiled pot removed. "I've had no less than three letters from your sister-in-law insisting that I be particularly vigilant for your overdeveloped sense of independence."

Emma's eyes lifted heavenward. "It's lovely of Charlotte to be concerned, but she's just as mule headed as the two of us. She says she detests London so much, she will not come until I've provided a niece or nephew to visit, even though we have seen neither her nor Hugh since their wedding."

"With or without a visit, she has very strong opinions on the attention and care you are to receive and I will be quite unable to face her if I fail," Lucy said with a teasing smile.

"You are a tyrannical caregiver, Lucy, and I love you for it. I'm certain I shall be well by dinner. I was reckless to choose cake at tea. I've had a very tenuous relationship with sweet things of any kind. They always look so appealing, but are absolutely certain to turn my stomach of late." She released a wistful sigh. "It really is a wretched tease. I have never craved sweet things before. Now I want them more than ever, but am not allowed to partake without dire consequence."

"It is cruel, isn't it?" Lucy asked, taking a seat in the small chair nearest Emma's bed. "I promise you, once you have delivered this child into the world, you shall have all the cakes and sweet things you desire. For now, I shall kindly request your cook help you avoid temptation."

Emma reached out and placed a warm hand over Lucy's. "I am fortunate in my choice of caregiver, it would seem, even if it was not my intention that you should be called into service."

Lucy clasped her hands in her lap and spoke firmly. "I'm glad you think so, as I've made a decision, Emma, and I will need your help."

Emma's hands paused in the motion of smoothing her coverlet over her lap and she peered at Lucy. "What sort of decision?"

Lucy straightened her shoulders and fortified herself against Emma's disapproval. "A decision about my future," she said, with what she hoped was a convincingly decisive dip of her chin.

"You were always one for making plans, Lucy, so I cannot say I am surprised, but I will caution you, with myself as an example. You cannot always plan what your future will hold." She patted Lucy's hand. "But I am rambling. Go ahead, please. What have you decided?"

"I have decided that you have done me a great favor by bringing me to London as your companion. The particular recommendation of the Duchess of Worley will be invaluable in gaining another post as a companion or governess after the baby is born and you are no longer in need of my help."

Emma's distaste for the plan was evident a full breath before the peppering of questions began. "But what need have *you* of a post? Why would you want to be a governess? Has something happened to your father?"

Lucy shook her head. "Perhaps I should not have upset you while you are still recovering. We can discuss this later."

"Nonsense. You cannot make such an announcement and simply leave it alone. We'll discuss it now," Emma said, regaining possession of the full imperiousness that allowed her to appear every bit a duchess when she so desired.

Lucy, who had played with Emma as a girl and helped the woman after tossing up the contents of her stomach mere moments ago, was not so susceptible to the intimidating tone. "Don't play duchess with me," she said, leaning forward in her chair. "I'll have your rooms littered with cakes and see where you are then."

"But why, Lucy?" Emma asked, ignoring the teasing threat. "What has happened? Is your father ill?"

Lucy felt a pang of guilt at the worry that once again depleted the color in her friend's face, when she had only recently recovered it. "My father and mother are both well enough. There is no cause for concern."

"Then whatever has prompted this…this…preposterous idea?" Emma lifted her arms and dropped them to the bed again in a huff to punctuate her statement. "Positions as governesses and companions…these are for women in *need* of a position—women with no family support. You are not without a home. You are not without friends."

"The idea has been prompted by good sense," Lucy explained pertly. "My father is not ill, but he is aging. He has decided he is no longer able to proceed without the assistance of a curate. That will mean extra cost for wages, not to mention the addition to the household. It is past time I ceased to be a burden to my parents." She swallowed heavily. "And my father will not live forever. He will be gone someday."

My, but it was disturbingly final to say it aloud. She'd thought of it, of course, but when given a voice, it seemed so much more…imminent.

"Well, all men will someday be gone," Emma declared. "That was true of your father before you were even born."

"But he is older now," Lucy said with quiet resolve, "and I am grown. I cannot pretend that my future life has not arrived. I am four and twenty this year. My father will be nearly sixty years. One day, my father will be gone and there will be a new vicar, and *he* will live in the parsonage house with his family. I cannot remain there."

"Of course not. You will be married with a brood of children by then," Emma declared.

That seemed very unlikely to Lucy, as she had received no offers, nor encountered any likely prospects, in all her twenty-four years. Though her parents had not said as much, Lucy knew the decision to employ a curate changed their situation considerably. The expenditure would gradually whittle away any funds set aside for supporting Lucy or her mother once her father was gone. How could Lucy in good conscience accept a dowry of any amount if it left less for her mother in the event of her father's death?

She did not burden Emma with these details, but instead said, "Perhaps," with a shrug of her shoulders. "Taking a position as a companion or a governess does not prevent me from marrying someday, it simply provides a safeguard against the possibility that I do not."

Emma speared Lucy with a dubious expression. "You are not likely to meet any eligible gentlemen from a position caring for children too young or ladies too feeble to be out in society."

Lucy laughed. "I am no less likely to meet a man as a governess than I am hiding away in Beadwell, where all the gentlemen are either far too young or far too old."

Emma sighed, but she did not dispute Lucy's rationale. Both women knew well there were no eligible men of any station in the little village.

There was a knock on the door followed by the entry of a maid who, at Lucy's nod toward the offending pot, hurried to collect it and left the room with a promise to return shortly with a clean replacement.

"Still," Emma said once the maid had gone. "I repeat my point. All men will someday be gone. What has created the present urgency?"

"It is not so much urgency, as opportunity," Lucy explained. "Serving as companion to a duchess during her confinement will serve as a very high reference. Especially," she added, her eyes wide with meaning, "if I may rely upon said duchess to make a few useful introductions to those families who may be in need."

Emma sighed. "I'll grant your rationale is not entirely illogical. Still, I find I don't want to go along with it. Any of it. In fact, at the moment, I rather dislike this penchant of yours for forward planning."

Lucy stood and placed closed fists on her hips. "Must I remind you again you are being stubborn?"

"But I am stubborn for good cause, Lucy," Emma said from her bed, not in the least quelled by having to look up from her supine position. "I understand your desire to take responsibility for your future, but I don't believe you've sufficiently thought this through."

"But I have," Lucy insisted. "My circumstances are exactly the sort that lead a woman to take a position of employment. I am gently bred, but of little means. My prospects for marriage are slim, but I am respectable and well read. I've benefited from lessons alongside the daughter of an earl," she said with a pointed look toward Emma. "I am capable of conducting myself properly with the highest levels of society, and I play both the pianoforte and harp." Lucy lifted her chin. "When viewed objectively, I have excellent qualifications."

Lucy waited for Emma to rise to their debate, but she did not.

Instead Emma gazed up at her with such sorrow, Lucy could have just as well announced the death of a beloved mutual friend. "I beg you to reconsider. It is a lonely position in which to be in any household, Lucy. You will be neither family nor staff. Do you really want to take all your dinners on trays sent to your room and be left to yourself for long stretches of time when the family have no need of you?"

"I believe most women in service would consider long stretches of time to themselves a rather luxurious perquisite," Lucy pointed out.

Emma shook her head, having none of Lucy's rationalizations. "What a waste of your endearing personality, Lucy, to be shut up in a room and no one upon whom to bestow it."

"But you make it sound as though I shall be caged," Lucy said on a laugh. "I'm sure if I've the benefit of free time, I shall be allowed to leave my room." She put one hand to her mouth and whispered loudly, "They may even task a maid to walk me now and then. Pets do benefit, I understand, from the fresh air."

Emma pressed her lips together and shook her head. "Do not tease, Lucy. My concerns are for your happiness. I only mean to caution you of the consequences of your choice."

Lucy sat again. "And so you have, dear. And I am grateful for it, but I have been considering this with great care. It truly is the most sensible thing for me to do. You have provided me with an opportunity too convenient to dismiss."

Emma pouted. "I would much rather spend this time in London introducing you to eligible gentlemen."

Lucy laughed again. "Aren't we disregarding a rather obvious impediment to your sponsoring any debutantes this coming season?" She glanced meaningfully at the recently replaced chamber pot.

Emma scrunched her lips together. "Well the timing is poor, I'll grant you. , but Aunt Agatha could do it." She shrugged her shoulders. "And I would be there to…advise you."

Lucy laughed. "But you had a horrid debut season!" She sat down next to her friend. "Emma, your willingness to disregard all obstacles in pursuit of my happiness is why you are the very best sort of friend." She smiled, dreading Emma's disappointment. "You know this cannot work. Presenting me at society events full of lords and ladies will not make me any more likely to be married than I am today. I am not a worthy match for the sort of society you and the duke keep. I will be tolerated as your friend, but will otherwise be entirely out of place. That is all. No one would be queueing up to pay calls or make offers to *me*."

Emma opened her mouth, but Lucy stilled her friend's objection with a hand on her shoulder. "Besides," Lucy said, "Aren't well-bred ladies supposed to retire to their country houses when they're increasing?"

Emma sniffed. "Not this well-bred lady. John is anxious to take his seat in the House of Lords and do what good he can in furthering the reform agenda. And I am not keen to be apart from him. I can be perfectly respectable remaining here, in London. Besides," she said, displaying the first bright smile since she'd become ill that morning, "I've discovered the benefit of my rank is that I am less likely to be deemed 'not respectable' and much more likely to be considered merely peculiar."

"If London society considers you peculiar for preferring the company of your husband, I daresay I won't fit in at all." Lucy paused. She regarded her friend thoughtfully. "You know, I am rather surprised you would even propose I seek a husband here. You were miserable in your first season and you never seemed particularly complimentary of the set."

Emma nodded. "There are sharks in these waters, to be sure," she said, finally testing the strength of her legs to hold her upright. "But there are good people hidden amongst the awful ones. *I* was there all along. My aunt and uncle were there. So were several other friends who proved quite supportive and helpful when Charlotte needed them."

"Yes, well I am unlikely to marry any of the people you've just listed."

Emma reached out a hand to Lucy and spoke quietly. "Is it a matter of the dowry, Lucy? Because if it is, I know that John would not hesitate to—"

"No, Emma," Lucy interrupted. "You know it is not a matter of a dowry—not only. I would have to be an heiress of grand proportion for any of the titled gentlemen in your set to look my way. I love you, but you cannot find me a husband. And you cannot convince me that taking a post as a governess is the end of my happiness in life." She smiled to soften the rebuke. "Let us be reasonable, now, and talk about Lord and Lady Ashby, shall we?"

"What about them?"

"They are coming to dinner this evening, correct?" Lucy prompted.

"Yes."

"And you did say they have daughters, do they not?"

"You don't mean to find yourself a post now," Emma said, dropping back onto the bed to gape at Lucy. "The baby will not arrive for months."

"But you said just last week that Lord and Lady Ashby were seeking a governess," Lucy said with a gentle laugh at her friend's dismayed expression. "It was that conversation that prompted the idea. Of course I will stay with you until your child is born, but there is no reason why I cannot have an arrangement settled in advance for where I shall go next. You have always spoken so highly of Lord and Lady Ashby."

"I do think highly of them," Emma admitted, "but it is premature to begin pursuing posts right this minute." Lucy opened her mouth to respond, but Emma shook her head. "No, Lucy, I am quite firm on this. I know you are usually the practical one, but I am being practical in this instance. We have only just discussed this. The baby will not arrive for another five months and, frankly, you can stay on with me indefinitely after that. There is no need for haste. We should think on this more thoroughly before taking action."

Lucy sighed, recognizing the resolution in Emma's tone. The matter might wait for the present, but it would not wait long.

Chapter Two

Having instructed her friend to rest before the guests arrived for dinner that evening—advice Lucy was certain would not be followed—Lucy returned to the drawing room to recover both the book and shawl she had abandoned there prior to Emma's sudden malady. As she made her way through the halls of Worley House, she lamented the loss of the opportunity to apply for the position of governess to the Ashby girls. She had never met Lord or Lady Ashby, but if Emma considered them friends, they were surely good, decent people. Though Lucy was reconciled to taking a position, she most definitely wished to avoid one in which she would be ill treated.

Several days had passed since Lady Ashby had mentioned to Emma her intent to employ a governess. She may well have already begun assessing potential candidates. If Emma insisted upon waiting much longer to aid Lucy in finding a position, this particular post was sure to be already taken.

Lucy sighed loudly as she turned the handle and pushed open one of the painted paneled doors that led to the drawing room, noting that the household staff had efficiently whisked away the remnants of tea and closed up the room after she and Emma had fled so suddenly earlier. She crossed the room to retrieve the shawl and book and, as she did so, walked through a slanted column of light caused by the late afternoon sun shining through the windows. Each of the three tall windows opposite the door created such a column, giving the room odd, striped bands of shadow and light.

Lucy had not seen the room in such a state before. Sunlight saturated the room at midday, when it was commonly used, and by dinnertime lit tapers in the sconces would provide a weaker but equally warm source of light.

The household staff saw it this way. They saw it striped in fading afternoon sun, or fully engulfed in darkness before the sun rose or fires were lit. The tentacles of this thought took an odd, fixating hold on her. Was Emma right to caution her so sharply? Was she entering an entirely new realm? Lucy had never lived a life of privilege or luxury, but neither had she ever been a servant. Modest living and domestic service were two very different things.

It was only common sense to understand the lives of some occupants in this house would be unrecognizably different to the others depending on their station. Same house. Entirely different worlds.

She shook her head at the silly thought. She was already in a different world. She was a simple vicar's daughter. She was no duchess, nor the daughter of a peer. Her life would not be unrecognizable because she came into a household like this one at a lesser station. Life at the parsonage house had never been so segmented. She was both family *and* domestic there, as were her mother and father.

As she picked up the book and shawl, she looked down and noted how the line between light and dark slashed across the front of her dress.

Where had all this fanciful thinking come from? Emma, well intentioned though she might be, was wrong—Lucy was perfectly suited to a position as a governess. Yet, after one pleading conversation, here she stood, dancing in shadows, questioning her entire future.

My goodness. She shook her head. She was too practical for that.

She stared unseeingly at the shadow-striped floor and tapped her fingers on the cracked spine of her book. Emma would come around. She always eventually came around to Lucy's sensible view of things. It was one of Emma's best attributes, really. But would it be too late? Here—this evening—was a very good opportunity with a very good family.

Hmmm. She shifted her weight between her feet and continued the rhythmic tap of her fingers along the book in her hands. Perhaps all was not lost and she could at least build some sort of a start. She could not very well introduce the topic of needing a position at dinner, of course, but perhaps she could offer to play—exhibit her qualifications in pianoforte. Then the evening would not be a total loss.

"Are you lost?"

Good heavens.

Lucy spun about to discover she was not alone in the drawing room. She blinked. A man rose from a chair in the shadow-shrouded corner of the room and took several steps toward her. She could not make out all the details of his features, but he was tall and finely dressed.

She blinked again and looked back at the doorway through which she had come. Had he been there the entire time and she'd not even noticed him?

A heavy weight began to congeal inside her. She'd been staring at shadows and daydreaming like a ninny and had made a perfect idiot of herself in front of none other than Lord Ashby.

"I beg your pardon, my lord," she said in her most sensible tone, rushing to repair his impression that she must be a half-wit. "I was just retrieving my things. I had not realized the dinner hour was so nearly upon us."

"Oh, I don't believe it is upon us quite yet," he said. "Worley summoned me early so that we might meet before dinner."

His response was not unkindly given, and the tightness that had bunched around Lucy's neck and shoulders upon his greeting unwound a bit—though not entirely. Of course he had come early to meet with the duke. They were political allies, were they not? They must meet regularly. Where was her head? If Lord Ashby had arrived only for dinner, he would be accompanied by his wife.

"It appears His Grace is a bit delayed, however," he said, stepping forward into the slash of light.

She couldn't help but notice he was younger than she'd expected. How old were his daughters? Perhaps his wife was determined to raise virtuosos and wanted musical instruction to begin very early. *All the better,* she thought, *to secure a position for years to come.*

She smiled pleasantly at him. "I'm very sorry you've been made to wait, my lord. No doubt the delay was quite unexpected, as I've always observed His Grace to be quite considerate."

"Indeed," was his only reply.

"I apologize for disturbing you," she said, nodding politely and gathering her book and shawl more tightly to her. She was conscious of wanting to make a positive impression with Lord Ashby, but how precisely did one go about doing such a thing after he had caught her woolgathering?

"I have the sense it is I who has disturbed your private thoughts, rather than you disturbing mine."

Lucy groaned inwardly and felt the flush rising in her cheeks. "I do beg your pardon, my lord. It seems I was preoccupied."

"No apology is necessary."

He smiled at her. It was not a dismissal. It was…kind. Perhaps she *hadn't* disturbed him. Perhaps he had waited some time and was happy for the distraction, however insignificant. He stepped back slightly and, even in the dim light, Lucy could see it was to allow his eyes to drop all the way to her feet before returning to her face as he took in her full measure. She squared her shoulders and did her best to appear both pleasant and deferential, as she presumed one should when being evaluated by a prospective employer.

"Are you always such a daydreamer?" he asked finally.

"I am not," she assured him firmly. "I am usually quite sensible, as a matter of fact. I have always been reliable, I assure you. My mother has relied upon me from a very young age in aiding her in her work with parishioners in my village. I was never wayward or flighty as a child."

A smile tilted the corners of his mouth. "No?"

"No, my lord, not at all."

His only response was a mildly dubious lift of one brow. How was it that lords always managed to seem so...lordly? Lucy had simply stopped gaining height at the age of thirteen. She had felt small compared to nearly every person she had ever met, but compared to this broad-shouldered man who towered over her in heavy boots and dark coat, she felt positively elfin. How did one project competence and sensibility under these conditions? Heavens, but this was an unfortunate beginning. She had to salvage this somehow.

"You are probably wondering who I am," she said. "My name is Lucy Betancourt. I am..." She paused. She had begun to say she was a friend of the duchess, but amended her words. "I am at Worley House as companion to the duchess during her confinement."

"I am sure she is quite grateful for your companionship."

"Thank you, my lord." Perhaps because he seemed so kind, or perhaps because his expectant look demanded some continuation of the conversation, she added, "I am sorry to have intruded upon your wait, my lord, but perhaps it is fortuitous that I have done so." Lucy smiled brightly at him, then faltered. Would Lord Ashby would prefer a stern governess? She amended her expression to a more neutral, less happy one. It would not do to appear overeager, after all.

She thought idly as she stood, not quite smiling at the man, that Lady Ashby must be a particularly lovely woman. He was handsome enough to have set thousands of lashes fluttering across London before he was married, and with his title to match, he would have had his pick of ladies. His eyes were the dark gray of smoldering coals.

Those eyes, she realized, were staring at her in patent confusion. "Fortuitous in what manner?" he inquired.

She immediately regretted her choice to speak boldly, though the quirk of his brow did appear more amused than annoyed. There was no help for it now.

In for a penny, as they say...

"I am so terribly sorry to be presumptuous, my lord. I mean only that I am...that is, circumstances are such that I find I must..." Lucy's flush deepened, and she understood quite clearly in that moment why one should wait to be introduced. She looked up at the imposingly tall man with dark eyes and hair too perfectly unstudied to be accidental and knew without question that she was making an absolute fool of herself.

She had to get through it, now that she had begun. *Pleasant, but not eager,* she reminded herself. Serious, but not stern. "As a matter of fact, I had been hoping for an introduction as…well, you see, once I am no longer needed here, I will be in need of another position."

Her revelation did nothing to remove the confusion from his expression. A startling thought occurred to her. Did gentlemen even become involved in the selection of a governess? Would Lady Ashby handle the entire matter without ever even consulting her husband? Oh, why hadn't that occurred to her earlier? Why had she even spoken?

She felt the heat in her cheeks concentrating into burning splotches. Even as she knew she appeared more foolish with every word, she continued speaking, somehow unable to stop. "My lord," she said, stepping forward, "I apologize. It was very unconventional and impulsive for me to approach you in this manner, and I am sorry for it. It was poorly done of me, but I assure you I am not usually impulsive. I had hoped to make a positive impression when first we met." She smiled bravely up at him, wishing fervently that he would somehow at least see the good intention behind her error.

Again, the eyebrow danced. This time his dark eyes danced as well. "Did you, now?" he asked, seeming just a bit more curious than before she'd explained.

She relaxed just a bit. At least he could see the humor in it. She considered it a boon that she had not been summarily dismissed. "Of course, my lord. I'm sure you can understand my desire to gain your favorable opinion."

"You desire *my* favorable opinion?"

"Certainly." She tilted her head to the side and peered up at him. "On what other basis would you select me, my lord?"

Chapter Three

Select her?

Bex Brantwood peered down at the pixie-sized person who stared back up at him with wide frost-blue eyes that matched her frock and decided he must have misheard the girl. "Select you?" he asked.

She bit her lip, drawing his gaze to her mouth, which was just as sweetly pink as her cheeks at that very moment. It was quite pretty, that blush, on an angelically pale complexion underneath a halo of silver-blond hair. She looked like a fairy sprite—an odd, nonsensical fairy sprite who had wandered distractedly into the room and then calmly requested that he *select* her.

Select her for what?

Her brow furrowed in consternation and she wrung dainty hands. "I'm making a mess of this, aren't I? I've never pursued anything quite like this before and I'm afraid meeting you unexpectedly prompted poor manners on my part. I should have waited until we were properly introduced. Normally my manners are quite respectable, I assure you. My parents do not move about in society much beyond our small village, but I have been a longtime companion to the present duchess and am quite capable of presenting myself well in all levels of society; you would have no need for concern there."

"I assure *you*, miss, I was not at all concerned regarding your manners." He did, however, have grave concerns regarding her mental state. What the devil was going on here? She seemed to have no shortage of words, yet somehow the more she spoke, the more muddled the entire situation became. The girl—no, woman, he corrected, taking in her full appearance as his eyes adjusted to the dim light—behaved as though she were interviewing for a post. And cocking it up a bit in the process.

"You seem to know considerably more of me than I know of you," he observed.

"Oh, of course, my lord," she gushed, clasping her hands in front of her. "How thoughtless of me." She ran her hands down the front of her frock and took a deep inhale of air before beginning. "I am the only daughter of the vicar in the village of Beadwell. I am, as I said, a longtime friend of the Duchess of Worley. I play both the pianoforte and harp and am widely read. At four and twenty, I have recently concluded that it is well past time I cease to be a burden to my parents and make some arrangement for my future, so you can understand how fortuitous it was to learn that your visit to the duke and duchess would be coinciding with my own."

She exhaled. Good lord, how did she have breath left after that soliloquy?

He said nothing, but considered her. So that was it. The poor vicar's daughter from the local village had decided to arrange for her future and was importuning *him* to become that arrangement. So much boldness for such a little thing. At least she was honest. That was a bit braver than most girls who might have tried to lure him into a situation that compromised her and forced his hand.

Honesty or not, she had chosen the wrong mark. Security was the last thing he had to offer anyone. All attempts at marital arrangements concerning Bexley Brantwood had come to a definitive halt the previous year when his cousin, the true duke, had returned to claim the title. Clearly this poor girl was too naïve to realize Bex's only remaining friends were gamblers, ladies of the night, and unscrupulous moneylenders.

"I applaud you, dear, for your sensibility in addressing your future. You are young and pretty. Marriage to some stable young gentleman is, of course, what you should consider. For precisely that reason, I am unable to be of any assistance to you. I do wish you success in your pursuit." With the briefest of smiles meant to punctuate the end of their conversation, Bex stepped aside so that she might be allowed to exit the room.

She remained standing in place, her eyes growing large as she comprehended his response. "Oh, no, my lord. I understand you might have concerns about taking me on if you believed I intended to marry, but I am much more...practical...than that." Her cheeks flushed again and her smile took on a self-deprecating asymmetry. "I am well aware that without any family connections or dowry my marriage prospects are dismal indeed. When added to the fact that I am limited to my small village with no gentleman of marriageable age and the lack of funds for even a local season…I…well, I am resigned to my circumstances, sir." She averted her eyes, but he could see the way her cheeks flamed to be laying bare these truths of her situation. "I understand I must be practical about my future and pursue other arrangements."

Other arrangements? *Christ.* What had he stumbled into? Was this angelic sprite of a vicar's daughter actually offering herself up to him as his mistress? Bex had received such offers in the past, but they were veiled invitations from the jaded London set, not blushing, flustered proposals from the daughters of country gentlemen.

Bex pivoted and allowed his gaze to travel more slowly over the woman in front of him. She was becoming in the way of a china doll—all pale porcelain and disastrously fragile. Her frost-blue eyes were anything but cold, however. They were quick. They darted everywhere and expressed everything. They had none of the veiled mystery she would need if she truly expected to spend her prettiest years moving from one protector to the next based upon their pocketbook rather than their likability.

Her shape was intriguing. He could understand why some men favored petite women who fed their need to feel large and, well…masculine. He could probably reach his hands entirely around her trim waist.

He tilted his head to one side. "So you've given up entirely on the prospect of marriage, have you?"

She nodded vehemently. "I have, my lord, and I assure you, I am quite enthusiastic about this next endeavor."

Bex couldn't help it. He threw his head back and laughed aloud. This was becoming absurd. If he were a good man—a truly good man—he would pat her on the head, send her on her way, and perhaps even have a good talk with her father once he'd done so.

Thankfully, he was not a good man. Frankly, whatever she thought she knew of his reputation was inflated and he couldn't afford her anyway, but still his conscience could not find any objection to at least humoring the girl for a few more minutes just to see what else she might say. She'd told him about her skill at the harp, for God's sake. Who gave a fig whether their mistress could play the damned harp?

He stepped more closely. "What did you say your name was again, dear?"

"Miss Betancourt, my lord. Miss Lucy Betancourt."

He would have sworn she nearly curtsied. And why was she calling him lord? The only people who called him that were too uneducated to understand he wasn't lord of anything—save poor decisions.

He crossed his arms in front of his chest and peered at her. "I will admit to a great curiosity as just what your friend the duchess thinks of your intentions, Miss Betancourt."

Her bold gaze faltered at his question, eliminating any point in voicing a lie. No self-respecting peeress would encourage another woman into such an arrangement.

Had she come up with it all on her own, then? "You're a bold bit of cake, aren't you?"

She managed to look genuinely confused at his question. She took a small step backward. "I...I apologize," she said. "I realize it was unforgivably impertinent of me to approach you."

Don't back away now, you little minx, he thought. *Not now that you've put the proposal to me and I've not yet answered.* She bit her lower lip and the action again caught his attention. She was lovely. He had never been particularly drawn to the sweet and innocent, but never had it been offered up to him so audaciously. He regretted that he could not afford her in that moment, watching how her pink lower lip slid teasingly from the hold of white teeth. If only he could, he would be quite tempted to accept.

Of course, she may not be as innocent as she appeared. It was very likely, he reasoned, that she was ruined already. That would certainly make a respectable marriage unlikely, wouldn't it? He looked at her again, hints of her dainty shape visible beneath her prim pastel gown. He wondered whether her boldness would manifest itself in the bedroom; then the unexpected thought captured his imagination.

His body heated at the visions that assailed him and he stepped toward her. "I respect your self-sufficiency and...shall we say, ingenuity... Miss Betancourt. I cannot in good conscience deny you without a fair trial," he coaxed.

She eyed him warily. "A fair trial? I'm not sure what you mean."

"A sample of your skills, perhaps?" he said, warming more and more to the idea.

"My skills?" she asked, her eyes wide with uncertainty. "I...I could play for you, I suppose."

His grin widened. "I do not require a musical audition." The more wolfish he felt, the more visibly apprehensive she became. She had approached him, had she not?

"There are more applicable skills to consider," he said, and catching her around her doll-sized waist with one arm, he dropped his mouth to hers in a searing kiss.

He felt her stiffen and heard the outraged squeal muffled by the contact of his mouth on hers. She placed both hands on his chest and pushed.

She wasn't strong enough to push him away, but he voluntarily complied, pulling his mouth from hers and stepping back. He was not a paragon of virtue, but neither did he force himself on unwilling women.

Her eyes were wide and her chest rose and fell as she attempted to recover herself.

"Lord Ashby, how dare you?"

Bex stopped. He stared. "Lord Ashby?"

Lord Ashby? Bex let this revelation settle over him. She was throwing herself at the wrong man? Of course, he thought ruefully. If she were going to ruin herself to become a mistress, why choose a man with nothing? Clearly she had aimed much higher in trading her virginity.

She puffed up what bit of height she possessed and glowered at him. "Lord Ashby, clearly there is a misunderstanding here regarding the sort of governess I would be. I apologize for taking your time, but surely you and *your wife* must seek to fill the position elsewhere, as I don't believe we should suit at all."

Bex threw his head back and laughed loudly. Well, damn and blast. *A governess?*

"I don't believe this is humorous in the least, my lord," she said in a scolding tone.

"Calm down, Miss Betancourt," he said once he'd recovered his ability to breathe. "There has been a misunderstanding here."

"That, my lord," she clipped, "is quite evident."

He shook his head, still shaking with his laughter. "I am not Lord Ashby," he said once he was able. "I do not possess a wife or children and certainly would have no need for a governess."

She gaped up at him. "You...you are not Lord Ashby?"

He shook his head. "I am quite certain I am not."

Her brow furrowed in confusion. "Who are you, then?"

Bex stepped back and bent forward into a dramatic bow. "Mr. Bexley Brantwood, miss, insignificant cousin of the Duke of Worley."

For a fleeting moment, the poor girl appeared as though she might become physically ill, her hands rising to her crimson cheeks, but the expression passed almost as quickly as it had come and was replaced with a sagging relief. "Oh, thank heaven." She said it toward the floor, as though the observation were not intended for his ears at all.

Then she lifted her head again and peered at him for a long moment. "If you have no children, what sort of position...did you...you thought..."

She stared, eyes widening as understanding dawned. "You thought I was importuning you to become your…your…" She completed the sentence with a look that implied he was welcome to fill in the missing bits on his own.

"It was a rational conclusion if you see the situation from my perspective," he said. "Pity we can't share the story, eh? Ah well. No harm done."

She crossed her arms and shifted her weight to one side, one dainty toe sliding forward, as she stood peering at him. "Sir, you are being very cavalier about taking liberties with a virtuous young woman."

"Oh, come now, there's no need for prudishness. It's just a harmless kiss, love, and barely one at that. Your virtue is intact."

She stiffened. "Contrary to your impression of me, I am not in the habit of engaging in casual kissing, harmless or otherwise. As a matter of fact, I have never been kissed."

She announced it as though it were an achievement worthy of a medal. He studied her. "No, you haven't, have you?" That much had been clear to him. But why not? She was lovely. She'd already given her age as twenty-one or -two or something. She was certainly old enough.

"Why haven't you been kissed?" he asked.

"You heed no attention to manners, do you? That is a very impertinent question."

He grinned languorously at her. "You claim to be scandalized by my liberties and my manners, but you haven't scampered off yet, have you?"

Her mouth quirked. "I am not a rabbit. I don't scamper anywhere." She eyed him more closely and stepped forward rather than away. "I may not be experienced in the area of kisses stolen by libertines, but I am not a child and you don't frighten me. You've already explained that you kissed me in error, due to the mistaken understanding of our conversation. Now that our misunderstanding has been resolved, there is no reason to believe you would take inappropriate liberties again."

Hmmm. She should not be so sure. He would rather like to attempt it again. She hadn't really given the thing a fair try. Why hadn't she been kissed plenty?

He repeated his prior question. "Why haven't you been kissed?"

"I beg your pardon?" she asked, but she didn't puff up in indignation. She laughed.

Thank God. He would have been so disappointed in her if she had resorted to missish dramatics.

"I find it very hard to believe you haven't been kissed, or for that matter why you're seeking a governess post instead of planning a wedding and a brood of children. What's wrong with all the gentleman in this village of yours?"

She shook her head. "Thank you for your flattery, but there is no need to be charming. The error was mine, not yours."

"I'm not particularly known for my charm."

Her eyes flew to his and stayed there just long enough to cause the heat to rise in her cheeks again. "Well, then," she said. "I wouldn't say there is anything particularly wrong with the gentlemen in Beadwell, except there aren't any—none of an age to be married, anyway. My family hasn't the funds for any sort of a season and I don't have a dowry to offer anyhow. I believe I explained this before, but your focus may have been a bit distracted at that point in our conversation."

In all honesty, he was distracted now. His imagination had produced all sorts of interesting thoughts when he thought she offered herself as his mistress. He found he was quite unable to make those thoughts disappear now that he knew her to be a virginal governess instead. He valiantly attempted to ignore them. "So that is why you seek a governess post?"

"Yes. I do not wish to be a burden to my family." She smiled at him and the expression was startlingly open and bright. "I gather I have not yet mastered the art of seeking such a position, as the first step would be to apply to the correct prospective employer."

Bex nodded. She was being a rather good sport about the whole thing. He liked her. He really did.

"And this lack of neighboring men," he asked, because his curiosity weighed on him, "this is why you've yet to be properly kissed?"

She cast him a baleful glance. "Among other reasons, yes."

"Well, my dear, I have no children nor elderly relative, therefore I cannot offer you a post."

"I understand that quite clearly now, Mr. Brantwood. Again, my apologies."

"I can provide some assistance, however, due to the uniqueness of your circumstances."

"And what assistance is that, Mr. Brantwood?"

He could tell her, but he decided to show her. In one quick motion, he stepped forward and snaked his arm around her waist, drawing her closer as he lowered his mouth to hers.

Chapter Four

He was *kissing* her. Again!

Oh, goodness.

Then he wasn't. He pulled away from her and looked down at her with a chiding expression. Her cheeks felt like fire.

He shook his head. "I'm trying very hard to be helpful to you, Miss Betancourt, but you are wasting your opportunity."

Her eyes darted to his. "What?"

"I'm trying to remedy a lack in your twenty-two-year-old life by kissing you properly."

"Oh." She swallowed. "I'm twenty-four," she added, as though that had any bearing on the situation at all.

Just what did "properly" kissing entail?

"What if someone saw us?" It came out as a whisper and she knew herself enough to admit she wasn't trying to decline. Was it so sinful, really, to allow this man to kiss her? His point was well made, after all, that her opportunities would be rare.

And he was so...so...well, the sort who seemed to know what kissing was about.

"I think it's past time to worry about someone coming along, don't you? Besides, some feel fear of discovery adds to the fun."

"Really?"

He chuckled low in his throat at the innocence of her question and she immediately regretted voicing it.

"Yes, really," he confirmed. "Why do you think forbidden loves are so tempting? Kisses shared between husbands and wives are so very ordinary." He pressed closer. "But secret kisses, shared in stolen moments, arranged with a cryptic note or a meaningful glance—there is where the excitement happens."

Lucy experienced a horrendous, stomach-twisting guilt at his words. "And you would know the difference," she asked, her eyes downward, "because you are married?"

He laughed. Or almost laughed. It was no more than a cynical smile accompanied by an amused exhale of air. "Married? Me? God, no. I believe I already mentioned that."

Had he? Relief surged through her that she had not—even unwillingly— participated in marital infidelity. She looked defiantly up at him. "How would you know, then, if kisses among married folk are no better than ordinary?"

"My dear, one does not have to observe London society for long to arrive at that conclusion," he said, lifting one finger to tap it on the tip of her nose as though she were a child and he the teacher. "Nothing ruins passion so well as a marriage. The marriage mart is a game and when the game is done, the fun is over."

Lucy had heard the rumors of the scandals rampant in London society, but surely not all married couples in London were jaded and unfaithful. What of Emma and her husband? She cocked her head at him. "You take a very cynical view of marriage, Mr. Brantwood."

"I take a practical view, Miss Betancourt. Now, dear, is it your intent to have a conversation or a kiss?"

At his words, Lucy's eyes involuntarily fell upon his mouth. A feeling of anticipation started low in her belly and spread through her until it tingled at her fingertips. Dear Lord, she had already decided, hadn't she?

She lifted her eyes to his, feeling very small and very, very inexperienced. She gave a slow, slight nod.

His mouth curved just at one corner to show his pleasure at her response and his eyes—his dark eyes gleamed wickedly. He placed a hand on either side of her waist and drew her forward until the lace on her bodice nearly brushed the front of his waistcoat.

Her head fell back to look up at him, for the difference in their heights was surely a foot or more. She stared, waiting for whatever was to come next, until he laughed softly. She was near enough that she felt rather than heard it—not much more than a vibration in his chest topped with a wry smile.

"Why don't you close your eyes, Miss Betancourt?" He paused. "No. Tell me your full name." He lifted his hand and drew his thumb along the ridge of her jaw, from just under one ear to her chin. She felt each spot on his path become individually aware as he touched it.

After his thumb traced along the other side of her jaw, his fingers cupped her nape and supported her there as she remained tilted up to him.

"Well?" he asked.

She swallowed. What had he asked again? "Lucy," she said, barely recovering her wits. "My name is Lucy."

"Ah. Pure, saintly Lucy." His fingers kneaded at her nape, while his other arm drew her fully up against him. "Tell me, Saint Lucy, would you like your first real kiss to be sweet, or more dangerous?"

Dangerous? Her eyes widened. What did dangerous kissing involve? She tensed. That her mind wasn't imaginative enough to put specifics to his meaning did not appear to matter to her body. As soon as he had spoken the word, tiny darts of anticipation had traversed to all of her extremities and back again to her very core.

His questioning lips slowly widened into a devilish grin. "Excellent choice."

"But I…I haven't answered yet," she breathed.

"Yes, dear. You have."

He lowered his mouth then, not to her lips, but to her ear. "Dangerous kisses," he whispered, brushing his lips across her lobe, "can start anywhere."

His hot breath brushed her neck and she shivered before she could help it.

"Like here," he said, taking her earlobe in his mouth and dragging his teeth across it before releasing it, dampened, to the cool air. "And here." He kissed a spot below her jaw.

Lucy stood frozen in stark contrast to the hot chaos of sensation moving within her. He lifted his mouth from its branding of her throat and gazed hotly down at her for the briefest of moments before he dropped his lips to hers.

This was no gentle press of lips to lips. As soon as his mouth met hers, his tongue probed until her lips parted and the kiss became devouring. She didn't know what to do. Wasn't even sure what she *was* doing, but she was responding. Without even knowing, she was responding.

It was not sweet. What a silly, benign word to be connected to this assault of mouths and hands and sensations.

Yes. Hands. The arm at her waist had become exploratory, moving up and down her back in an ever-lengthening line that inevitably included long, squeezing strokes of her backside that pulled her into him in the most intimate way.

She should protest. This was more than a kiss. He was groping her. But...

Hmmm. That was the part that made it so…so…*good.* Every time his hand moved upward from her backside, she felt its loss. And when it trailed back down to cup her again, she melted just a little bit deeper. His hand veered off course to splay across her rib cage before passing lightly, but slowly, across the peak of her breast.

And that was good too.

All the while, his mouth held hers, their tongues dancing while her own hands traced his muscled back.

When had she begun her own exploration? She didn't know when, but she knew why. The need to touch him was too tempting—too seductive.

And there was the danger. This was no kiss. This was seduction. Even as it happened, she knew what place these new sensations were occupying in her. They were occupying the places happily vacated by her good sense.

Dangerous, indeed.

She muttered an objection, but it came out only as a breathy groan that he swallowed with his deepening kiss.

With Herculean effort, she tore her mouth from his and turned her face away, taking in greedy gulps of air. She felt his breath rise and fall with the same labor, but she did not look at him. She could not.

"I...I think I have the way of it."

She kept her eyes to the floor and hurried from the room, knowing even as she did so that she was, in fact, scampering away like a frightened rabbit.

Chapter Five

Bex stared at the door through which she'd fled—fled as though her very life were at stake.

What the hell just happened here?

The vibration began as a slight contraction of his midsection, but it grew strength as it traveled through his chest. When it had coursed upward far enough to match itself with his widening grin, he had no choice but to release it. He threw his head back and laughed. He laughed in such loud, roaring bellows, he had to take in great gulps of air. He bent and clutched his gut from the force of it. Lord, he'd not laughed with such abandon since he was a boy. The entire household probably could hear him. Certainly, *she* could probably hear him, but he could not keep it from happening.

Eventually his breath became more steady as the spasms subsided and his guffaws lessened to sounded sighs.

It was only then he became aware of a particularly coarse clearing of a man's throat behind him and swung around to face the doorway.

The butler made no effort to disguise the haughty disapproval that seemed the particular training of butlers in great houses—like they were the bloody enforcers of decorum of all who passed through their domains.

Let him disapprove, thought Bex. What would the man do? Turn him out? He was here on the duke's summons.

Bex took two more large, deep breaths and raised questioning eyebrows at the crusty old man.

"His Grace will see you now, sir," the man said in a carefully dignified tone, surely meant to school Bex in the correct manner of conducting oneself. If only the old man had come a little sooner. What would he have thought of Bex's conduct then?

With a smile at the thought, Bex followed the butler from the room. As it was, the brief interaction was nothing but a comedy of errors leading to a bit of fun. There had been no real harm done. The thought of having been caught in his interlude with Saint Lucy of Beadwell by the officious butler was certainly diverting, but he was not callous enough to truly wish for it.

What a scrape that would be for poor Saint Lucy.

Not for him, of course. No one cared a fig for who he was or the state of his reputation. Besides, even if they did, men always seemed to overcome these things. Women like Miss Betancourt—vicar's daughters in need of employment—they did not.

It seemed rather uneven, now that he thought of it. A man must be very, very bad to have his reputation cause him any serious trouble, particularly if there was any wealth or title to shield him. He had only to consider himself to know this was the case. He'd treated a certain Miss Mary Huxley unconscionably, but that hadn't mattered to anyone once he was suddenly in line for a dukedom.

The memory sobered his laughter. Why had he thought of her? It was of no matter to anyone now. The girl was already married. She likely had a brood of children. He was not married to Miss Huxley, nor was he in line for a title of any sort. The entire circumstance was long past.

As his thoughts completed their inevitably fitting journey from the diverting to the unpleasant, Bex followed the disapproving butler around the final corner and into the duke's study.

Damn.

The duke rose from behind a massive desk, but the bow of deference Bex gave was a distracted one. He'd met the present duke twice before, and briefly at that. He had no complaint with the man.

It was the man who did not rise—who remained seated facing the duke's desk—who received the full venom of Bex's glare.

As though finally unable to hold his resolve against the loathing emanating from Bex upon his arrival, the man finally faced him. The look they exchanged was cold.

The duke spoke first. "Please come in, Mr. Brantwood."

Bex stepped forward. "Your Grace," he said with a deferential nod. He crossed the remaining space from the doorway to the vacant chair and lowered himself into it. Then he slowly turned, just enough to direct his greeting, but not enough to fully face the occupant of the other chair.

"Father."

"Bexley."

"I was not aware, Your Grace, when I received your message," Bex said, working to keep the disgust from his tone, "that my father was to be here as well."

The duke looked curiously at Bex. "I invited you here in response to the request for a meeting I received from your father—a request on your behalf as well as his own. Were you not aware of it?"

"I was not."

The duke's sharp eyes darted between the two men "Do you not reside together?"

They did for the time being, though Bex had become particularly adept at never encountering his father. He preferred things that way.

"Allow me to apologize, Your Grace," the elder Mr. Brantwood purred. "I did not explain to Bexley my purpose for requesting our meeting."

Ah. So it would seem, then, that Bex's father had not only the advantage of knowing the full list of attendees for their discussion, but the agenda for it as well. How considerate.

Bex watched carefully as the duke's discerning gaze settled upon his father's practiced expression of earnest humility.

"We are all here now, per your request," the duke pointed out. "Is your father unwell?"

To Bex's knowledge, his grandfather—the man who would have been the seventh Duke of Worley, had John Brantwood never reappeared—was happily situated at Oakwood Lodge with his daughter-in law. He was elderly, but Bex had not heard from his mother of any decline in the man's health.

Edward sat forward in his chair. "He is as well as can be expected, Your Grace, given all the dramatic events to which he has been exposed at his advanced age. You can imagine what a blow it was to believe he would be elevated to the peerage only to have it snatched so suddenly from his grasp."

The duke did not bother to meet the other man's eyes, instead relocating a stack of correspondence on his desk as he responded. "I've had a letter from your father—several, in fact, over the past year. He indicated his great relief, not only for my safe return but also for his rescue from the burden of assuming the responsibilities of the dukedom."

Edward did not hesitate in his retort. "I'm sure he saw no cause to spread ill will. Most men aspire to some elevated status of authority or wealth for which they will be remembered after their death."

"Yes." This time the duke's direct gaze cut to the man opposite him, his blue eyes becoming cold and wary. "Some men do."

Silence settled on them following the duke's statement, and Bex granted his titled cousin a measure of respect for recognizing his father's ploy.

Edward had not yet revealed his purpose for the meeting, but Bex had his suspicions. He sincerely hoped they were incorrect.

Edward finally cleared his throat, piercing the quiet. "My father's health is not the purpose for requesting your time, Your Grace." He shifted in his chair to lean conspiratorially forward, as though defending the words from unintended ears, yet oddly spoke loudly enough for Bex, the only other occupant of the room, to hear quite clearly. "I understand your years away prevented you from benefiting from your father's mentorship and I'm sure you are quite overwhelmed by the responsibilities you face." He sat straight again. "I applaud you for your very wise marriage, but there are countless other matters requiring your attention. As I am among your nearest living family and am decades your senior in age and experience, I would be remiss in not offering my wisdom and aid until you have gained your footing."

The duke rested one elbow on the velvet-upholstered arm of his substantial chair and regarded Edward coolly. He said nothing.

The older man squirmed under the duke's stare for a few moments before launching into his true purpose. "It still remains, for instance, to deal with the unfortunate consequences of your absence, Your Grace."

The duke gave no outward reaction to this claim. "Enlighten me as to the consequences most concerning to you," he calmly bade the other man.

Edward adjusted himself in his chair yet again. His face had turned ruddy, his eyes dark with disfavor for this duke who'd declined to grasp at the offer of counsel.

His father was a pompous fool.

"There are many, Your Grace," Edward began, more slowly and deliberately than before, "but perhaps the most urgent matter pertains to accounts that must be settled."

Ah. Disappointingly, Bex had theorized correctly.

"My father's secretary was dismissed," the duke stated, "but I have replaced him. The position was not vacant for long. I'm not aware of any delinquent accounts, nor have I been notified of creditors appearing to make such claims." The duke knew as well as Bex did exactly whose accounts the old man was here to have settled. Bex couldn't blame the duke for making him spell it out. He would have done the same, in the duke's position. If Edward Brantwood had come to beg for money, let the man openly beg.

"You understand"—Edward's voice was decidedly tighter—"there were expenses incurred by our family in preparing to take on the responsibilities of the dukedom while you were believed deceased."

Bex eyed the duke, who remained impressively devoid of any outward show of surprise or disgust at the claim. Bex didn't care if his own disgust was evident at this point, along with his rising anger at having been brought to Worley House under false pretenses.

"Perhaps I should understand what sort of preparations were undertaken," the duke suggested patiently.

Edward coughed. "As you can imagine, Your Grace, once everyone was convinced of your death abroad, it was incumbent upon my family to take our place in society and begin to move about in circles befitting a duke and his heir."

"But you were not, in fact, the duke or the heir. Were you, cousin?"

"My father was heir, but as you know he is quite elderly. He was unable to relocate to London on behalf of the family."

"I see."

Edward shifted uncomfortably in his chair. "Your Grace," he began, "I have for some months been considering the need for an indulgence of your time so that you might understand our present situation and your connection to it." He waved his hands and stammered, "Through no intention on your part, I am certain, Your Grace. I expect you will be dismayed when you learn the seriousness of the matter."

The duke's mouth tightened to a grim line. "Pray, elaborate."

To Edward's credit, he was not evasive. "We have exhausted all available funds, Your Grace, and unless we can make some payment on amounts due, we will not be extended further credit."

The duke was quiet for some time, propping his elbows on the desk and tapping his tenting his fingers. After a long moment, he released a fatigued sigh. "I gather by your reference to 'further' credit that you have already incurred considerable debts."

It was a statement, not a question, but Edward replied nonetheless. "We had necessities, you understand, for establishing ourselves in London. Moneylenders were happy to extend credit to a duke's heir."

"Or the heir's heir," the duke added wryly.

Edward did not dispute it.

Bex remained silent. He had no excuse whatsoever for hurrying to London five years prior and accepting all of his father's rubbish about why they could not simply continue to live as gentleman farmers until they actually inherited. The reasons his father had given then were the same he'd given the duke—they had to gain polish and build connections in society, lest they disgrace the dukedom with their provincial, unsophisticated ways. In hindsight, Bex did not see how spending money one did not actually possess on expensive clothing and card games was particularly sophisticated. He would wager as well that the dukedom found the present circumstance considerably more disgraceful than if they had simply remained gentleman farmers.

But they had not.

And Bex could not deny his participation. He had believed every encouraging word his father had said and arrived in London as a man barely twenty believing he would someday inherit a kingdom. It may as well have been a kingdom, compared with the small estate in Surrey. He had been young, naïve, and expected to inherit a vast fortune. He had been every moneylender's fantasy.

At least he had youth to blame. It was not much, but it was something. What had his father as an excuse?

"Do you not have debts as well?" the duke asked.

"I have my own debts, yes," Bex said. "They were no less foolishly acquired."

The duke released a burdened sigh. "I will require an accounting."

"With all due respect, Your Grace"—Bex lifted his chin and met his cousin's hard blue gaze—"no."

Surprise flashed through the intelligent eyes. "No? You'll not provide an accounting?"

"That is correct."

The duke leaned slowly back into his chair and peered at Bex. "That will complicate things, you understand."

"In what manner?" Bex asked stiffly.

"How am I to pay creditors for whom I have no names or amounts?"

Bex rose. He looked from his father to the duke. "If there has been a misunderstanding, allow me to clarify. I have not made any demands for financial support, nor do I intend to do so. I am no longer a duke-in-waiting, nor do I expect to live as though I am." Bex stepped behind the chair from which he had risen and gripped the back of it, certain his hands would quake with his anger if he did not steady himself. There were noises of objection coming from his father, but he ignored them. "My congratulations, Your Grace, on the pending addition to your family. Rest assured, I harbor no secret desire that you will fail to produce an heir. I shall live out the life for which I was always intended, benefiting from the modest portion set aside by my grandfather until such time as I inherit Oakwood Lodge and become a quiet, unassuming gentleman farmer." He meant the last for his father, who was finally quiet. "And I shall suffer the consequences of my own poor judgment by seeing to the settlement of my debts myself," he added.

The duke nodded and seemed to accept this declaration with some measure of respect. Bex finally looked to his father then, already preparing for the disgust and disapproval he would see there. His father would not understand his choice, and he did not much care.

When his eyes took in his father's expression, however, his pulse stilled, for what he saw was not disapproval. It was something far more worrying—guilt.

Any last vestiges of respect that Bex harbored for his father hardened as the significance of the man's expression registered. "There is more," he said flatly. As much as he knew his own name, he knew his father had not delivered the last of the disastrous news. "Tell the rest you have to tell, Father."

Edward adjusted his position in his chair, lifted his chin proudly, and demonstrated a maddeningly thorough lack of shame when he spoke. "Your inheritance is gone."

Bex did not speak. He could not speak.

"Explain yourself," the duke commanded.

"My father has been ill for some time," Edward clarified. "He entrusted to me the oversight of his financial affairs."

"A disastrously misplaced trust," Bex spat.

"What, precisely, is 'gone'?" The duke asked, making no effort to mask his impatience.

"All of it," Edward answered simply.

"Has the estate been lost, or only the funds?" the duke asked.

Edward had the grace to at least redden at this last question. He did not respond.

So it was gone. Oakwood Lodge was gone. The home Bex had known all his life—the small, insignificant domain that should have one day been his, would not be after all.

"I believe my father is quite thorough in all his undertakings," Bex observed bitterly. He turned to the man he had once desired to emulate and felt a shudder of revulsion. "You had no right to plunder my inheritance." But even as he spoke, he knew the point had no significance. What recovery could there be? He hated him anyway, as though hating him might somehow make the betrayal less of a blow.

Edward half stood then settled back into his chair. "What need had you of that pitiful sum, when *this* was to be your inheritance," he blustered. "We had every reason to believe the line continued with us! We could not assume the ducal title trussed out like poor farmers and unable to move about in society." He turned his red-faced explanations toward the duke. "Would you have us shame the family name?"

The duke interrupted. "Do I understand correctly that Oakwood Lodge has been sold? Where is your father? Where is your wife?"

"The farm was sold with a lifetime lease," Edward explained.

"Whose lifetime?" Bex asked, his voice cold and harsh even to his own ears.

"Your grandfather's," Edward answered.

He should have known. A lease that lasted his grandfather's lifetime would only minimally reduce the proceeds of a sale, whereas the deduction for a lease based upon Edward Brantwood's life would be considerable, as the man could live for decades yet. Of course, his father would have pursued the larger sum and disregarded the risk.

The duke sighed heavily and set his elbows on the desk, again joining his fingertips and thumbs into a contemplative triangle. "So the new owner of the house and lands will take possession upon your father's death," he said.

"Yes," Edward confirmed.

"Leaving your family without a home or income," the duke concluded.

"My son and I currently reside in London, Your Grace."

The duke considered this statement wearily. "In a house for which you have taken a lease."

Edward gave a slow nod.

"A lease that you will be unable to pay without an income."

Edward's second nod was more abbreviated. He was quick to defend himself, however. "Surely, you can understand that my family had no need for a farm in Surrey, when we were to inherit the Brantmoor estate. The advanced funds from the sale of the farm allowed us to take our position in society and to prepare for the great responsibility of the dukedom." Edward leaned forward, leaving no subtlety to his final comment. "But for the misunderstanding caused by your absence, Your Grace, it was a prudent arrangement."

Bex did not wait for the duke to respond to this open transfer of blame. He spun around to face his father, allowing all of the accumulated disgust of both the past few minutes and the past five years spill out of him. "You have wasted your life and mine counting unhatched chickens, Father, and you do not even have the decency to accept responsibility for your shortsighted actions. You sit in the pit of your own making and point the finger of blame at others. I will not join in your shame and disgrace."

Once more, Bex addressed the duke, his unrestrained anger clipping his words with bladelike precision. "I ask nothing of you, cousin, but that you will pass my felicitations on to your wife."

Bex strode from the room without a glance backward for its remaining occupants.

What a stroke of luck, he thought bitterly, that the vicar's daughter did not elect to ruin herself on his account. He could scarce afford a dockside whore.

Chapter Six

Bex sat quietly at a corner table and waited. He sipped his drink absentmindedly while he watched. The Birdcage was a busy place and there was plenty to attract his attention as fortunes changed hands at hazard and faro.

He took entertainment in watching. He could tell by the expression on each man's face whether luck had been kind that evening. Some were less subtle than others, he thought, as he watched a ruddy-faced man toss his cards to the table and stomp away. He turned to another group and his attention was caught by a man in a finely cut jacket of rich blue. The man's eyes subtly narrowed at the turn of the cards. His patrician features were otherwise expressionless. His eyes were sharp, rather than cloudy with drink, like so many of the others. He had the manner of a savvy cardplayer, one who played the game as though it were a sport, applying skill in the hopes of gaining an advantage.

"Always watching, never playing. You will put me out of business, my friend."

A shorter man with a build that spoke of manual labor and clothes that hailed from the finest tailors slid into a chair beside Bex and looked onto the scene with him.

"You're far too successful to need my meager contribution, Gibbs," Bex said, setting his glass to rest upon the table.

"But you set a poor example," his companion insisted. "If everyone came only to take in the view, my doors would be closed for good in a fortnight, and my poor family turned out on the streets."

"Fear not." One side of Bex's mouth curved upward. "The Birdcage will always attract a flock of enthusiastic pigeons."

"No one wants to come to a cage." Gibbs shook his head in reproach at Bex's use of the unofficial moniker. "We are humbly providing a service for all who desire it."

Bex turned to face Archibald Gibbs. The man was wrong on both counts and he knew it. No. 22 King Street, affectionately known among its patrons as "The Birdcage," was by no means a humble establishment. And if the doors ever closed for some unforeseen reason, the Gibbs family would in no way go hungry. The Birdcage might be the center of Archibald Gibbs's business pursuits, but his interests stretched far beyond cards, dice, and drink—as Bex well knew.

Bex gave no voice to these thoughts, however, but simply nodded at the other man. "You are a most magnanimous public servant."

"I do what I can." Gibbs waved a hand, and the motion brought a serving girl sashaying to the table. "Bring me a drink and send the Mathematician."

The girl nodded and left as she had come, never sparing a glance for Bex. So that was the reason.

Bex had suspected Gibbs had summoned him here to discuss his accumulated debt. If they were to be joined by the Mathematician, his suspicions were most assuredly correct.

It seemed Bex was being summoned everywhere of late. The insistently polite invitations to Worley House had come with weekly regularity since his last disastrous visit there and were exceeded in number only by the less polite demands from his father. Bex disregarded both of these and had done so for nearly two months, though avoidance of the fatherly demands required greater skill, given their shared residence.

Bex had no interest in hearing whatever dictates his father had for him. His father was responsible for the dire circumstances in which Bex now found himself. And damned if he would appear for a family dinner at Worley House, despite the invitations that arrived weekly. They were only sent out of obligation anyway. He would not accept funds from the duke to pay his own debts, and he could not show his face to the duchess, who most certainly despised him after his ill-advised encounter with her friend.

A summons from Gibbs, however, could not be avoided. He owed the man a significant sum, and only by the grace of their amiable relationship did Bex escape the less civilized methods of collection that Gibbs could employ.

He wondered how much Gibbs knew. Everyone knew Bex would never be a duke, but did Gibbs know the extent of it? Bex would never be anything. He currently lacked funds, but the truth was so much worse.

Bexley Brantwood lacked an identity. He had been lowered to a state in which he subsisted solely upon the grace and favor of others. He was a beggar, despite his gentleman's clothes. Today, he needed the grace and favor of Archibald Gibbs to continue for just a bit longer.

"There is no need to summon the Mathematician," Bex said in a carefully congenial tone. "I have a full reconciliation of my accounts. This scheme in Hertfordshire seems very promising."

Gibbs nodded slowly. "There may yet be cause for optimism in Hertfordshire," he said, but there was no confidence in the statement.

"I received the information your man delivered on Birmingham," Bex added.

Gibbs ran his hands from his thighs to his bent knees as he sat looking at the crowd. He sighed heavily. "Yes, well, we may be unable to pursue Birmingham."

Bex took another sip of his drink and slowly lowered it to the table before asking, "Oh? And why is that?"

Gibbs eyed him steadily. His drink arrived and he accepted it without acknowledgment to its deliverer. "Hertfordshire," he said, setting the beverage on the table, untasted, "has taken considerably longer than anticipated. When we sent you the information regarding Birmingham, it was with the expectation that there would already be progress in Hertfordshire."

Bex searched his companion's expression, but Gibbs had the eyes of a cardplayer and they revealed nothing. He turned to the room and gave an easy shrug. "These things require patience."

"Patience becomes thin as interest remains unpaid." There was more truth than menace in his tone, but Bex knew better.

He met the other man's steady, dark gaze with an unflinching stare of his own. Mentally, he calculated. If Gibbs was unwilling to advance further funds, he possessed sufficient information regarding Birmingham to pursue it on his own, provided he could borrow the capital elsewhere. He let his eyes fall and gave another shrug. "Then we don't pursue Birmingham. I am still bullish in regard to Hertfordshire, despite the delays."

"Optimism does not feed my family in the meantime. More importantly, optimism is no guarantee of collection in the end."

Bex shifted in his seat to face Gibbs more directly and spoke firmly. "I am confident. Confidence is a measure above optimism, wouldn't you say? And your fee is collected regardless, if you recall our arrangement."

"Therein lies the challenge to my patience. If there is only failure in Hertfordshire," he said, with a smile that did not reach his eyes, "the fee is still owed, but from whom will I collect? Who will pay the other amounts owed?"

Bex understood the implications of the man's questions. He understood them certainly better now than he had as a young pup first arrived in London. The consequences of failing to repay debts to men like Archibald Gibbs could be far more disastrous than any debtors' prison.

"I have invested considerably in you," Gibbs continued, calmly surveying his domain as he spoke. "I felt much more secure in my investment when I believed it was backed by the wealth of a dukedom. Then your cousin returned and now I understand there is an heir on the way. Your family's ascension to that title becomes more improbable by the day."

Bex's jaw clenched, despite his best efforts to project an unconcerned air. "The balance you are owed is not so great that only a duke's wealth will repay it."

"It is great enough."

Bex tilted his head in acknowledgment. He couldn't very well dispute it.

"I was rather heartened," Gibbs continued, still surveying his domain rather than meeting Bex's eyes, "to learn that the duke had been generous with your father." His hand lifted then to stroke the underside of his chin. "I understand Worley has settled a number of his accounts around town."

Bex stiffened. The man was well informed. It should not have been a surprise, he supposed. Gibbs's business depended upon it. Bex had not remained to participate in the arrangements after his father had shamelessly demanded a financial rescue from the duke, but he knew it had been granted—though to what extent and for how long, he could not be certain. Although Bex had very clearly declined any direct assistance from the duke, it rankled him to know his cousin now paid the monthly rental for the London house.

"I had rather hoped you, and thus, I, would benefit from such generosity, but none has been forthcoming." Gibbs investigated the tidiness of his fingernails. "Though I understand, despite your family connection, you are not necessarily an intimate of the duke's."

Very well informed, indeed.

"On the contrary," Bex said with as much of a casual tone as he was capable. "The duke and duchess are not hosting much, given the duchess's condition, but I am regularly invited to family dinners and attend when I can." He looked out over the gaming tables. "I will be dining at Worley House in two days' time, as it happens."

One fastidiously trimmed eyebrow lifted dubiously. "Is that so?"

"It is."

Damn. Now it would have to be so. Bex cursed his rash speech. "I am on quite good terms with the duke and duchess," he lied, just to settle a little more quickly into his sinkhole.

"I am very glad to hear it."

Bex gave a clipped nod in response, not wanting to commit beyond what he'd already implied—that payments from the duke might be expected shortly.

"Did you have need of me, sir?"

Bex lifted his eyes to a tall, gray-eyed man of indeterminate age and an ill-fitting jacket. His complexion bore the look of one who kept indoors to an unhealthy degree.

The Mathematician.

If the man had a true name, Bex did not know it and Gibbs never used it.

"Ah. Your timing is exemplary," Gibbs said. "Please provide Mr. Brantwood with a current detail of his accounts."

"Of course, sir." The man gave a slight bow.

"Thank you," Bex responded with a nod, seeing no purpose in reminding them he already possessed a full accounting.

The Mathematician's eyes flitted over Bex, and he had the distinct impression there was very little this man failed to notice. Bex imagined behind every successful gaming operation there must be at least one such man—a man who was more interested in the numbers for the numbers' sake. When so many funds, cards, and dice moved freely around the room, with credit extended here and winnings disbursed there, any wise proprietor of a gaming hell must rely heavily on a man who excelled at sums and figures. But none other than the Mathematician did so with such spectacular memory and precision that his reputation exceeded his employer's. If rumor held true, he could recall every play, every card, every shilling owed, and his word was final in the settlement of any dispute. He was not a brash or forceful man, but at his quiet signal, other men—less intellectually inclined—could be dispatched with immediacy.

"Will you be staying longer, or should I have your statement sent around to your house, Mr. Brantwood?" the Mathematician asked.

"No need for the trouble of a courier," Bex said, rising from his seat. "Perhaps I'll see what is happening at the card table this evening while I wait."

"You don't play cards, Mr. Brantwood." The man's response was not a question. It was a fact—noted by a man who specialized in factual details.

"I no longer play cards," Bex confirmed, "but I find still I enjoy observing cardplayers."

The tall man nodded stiffly in acceptance of this explanation and departed their company.

Gibbs rose as Bex had done, smoothing his hands down the front of his thighs as he did so. "You won't be harassing my cardplayers, will you, Brantwood?" he asked, his voice congenial and light despite the unpleasantness of their recent business. "They're a superstitious lot. A loitering observer may put some off their luck."

"No need for concern. I'm simply an interested spectator. I won't linger overmuch near any one player."

"If you want to observe without discomfiting anyone, perhaps I might draw you to the hazard table. It's an intriguing game. You might find yourself drawn in."

Bex looked across the room to where a crowd gathered around the hazard table, a group large enough to include both players and observers. He would much prefer to observe cardplayers this night, but his position with Gibbs was precarious enough, so dice it would be. "Indeed," Bex said. "Perhaps I can watch and learn. But tell me," he said, "who is the cardplayer at the far table? The serious fellow in the blue jacket? He has drawn my curiosity."

Gibbs followed Bex's line of sight to the man in question. "Ah. Lord Ashby. He does take his play quite seriously."

Ashby.

The name tugged at him with a distant familiarity before he remembered. Lord Ashby had daughters in addition to a penchant for cards. Bex's interest was only in the latter, so he resisted the smile that tugged at the corners of his mouth. He did not inquire further. Gibbs would have too much discretion to clarify whether "serious" play translated to skill and thus success at the tables. "That was what drew my notice," he said. "Good luck to him."

Bex said nothing further of Lord Ashby and compliantly followed Gibbs to the hazard table, setting a mental reminder to accept the duchess's invitation to dinner. He wondered idly just how much time could pass following that dinner before Gibbs realized Bex had not used the opportunity to pass his statement of account on to the duke for payment.

* * * *

"I've decided to undertake a course of self-instruction," Lucy announced to Emma as the two sat quietly together in the smaller, west sitting room of Worley House. The comfortable and less formal parlor had become the location in which the ladies spent most afternoons, now that Emma's pregnancy had progressed and visiting was rare.

Emma paused in her needlework to glower at her progress. "What sort of instruction?" she asked.

Lucy closed the novel she'd been reading, using a finger to hold her place. "If I am to be the best sort of governess," she said, "I will likely take my charges on educational outings. We could examine historical artifacts at the British Museum, or discuss botany at Kew Gardens. I cannot authoritatively conduct such outings if these places are as unknown to me as to my charges."

Emma set her sewing on the sofa next to her, then pushed it even farther away with a temperamental shove. "I think that is an excellent thought," she said, turning back to Lucy. "Only...I couldn't possibly accompany you."

"I would never dream of allowing you to do so," Lucy declared. "What sort of caregiver would I be if I dragged you all over the city in your condition?" She shook her head. "No, I thought perhaps the maid, Agnes, could accompany me."

"But you're not familiar with the city," Emma protested. "I would never dream of sending you to wander London by yourself. What sort of friend would I be?"

"Not by myself," Lucy corrected. "With Agnes. And I shall only embark on these outings when you are resting and not in need of my company."

Emma shook her head remonstratively, setting to motion the chestnut curls that framed her face. "Lucy, you are not my paid companion. You are my friend and houseguest. You are not required to spend every moment by my side." She looked pointedly down her nose at Lucy in a teasing scold. "I will not participate in this scheme to make you a governess if you insist on being one around me. I've done with governesses, thank you."

"And you detested them," Lucy said with a laugh.

"I didn't dislike any of them personally," Emma corrected. "I simply preferred to be out of doors—on my horse or in the garden."

"In addition to outings," Lucy added, "I thought perhaps I should look for books that might provide some guidance or instruction for governesses."

"Yes, I suppose someone must have written a book for governesses," Emma said, then turned to look at her needlework again with a defeated expression. "What sort of mother is unable to make any useful contribution to her own child's layette?" she asked.

"A mother who is better able to love than sew," Lucy assured her. "And one who is fortunate enough to be able to hire a horde of seamstresses if need be."

Emma smiled ruefully at Lucy. "But there should be something meaningful, shouldn't there? Something crafted with love?" She sighed. "Perhaps Aunt Agatha can produce something."

"I'm certain she would be quite thrilled by the request," Lucy said. "Will she and Lord Ridgely be joining us for dinner this evening?" Emma's aunt and uncle had habitually dined at Worley House once or twice weekly for all of Lucy's visit thus far. Lucy quite liked them both and hoped for their company.

"Yes," Emma said, holding up the oddly shaped child's bonnet and peering at it. "As will John's cousin, Mr. Brantwood."

Lucy's breath caught. "Mr. Brantwood?" she asked, sincerely hoping her voice was steadier than her heartbeat.

"Yes, the younger Mr. Brantwood," Emma clarified, turning the bonnet over in her hands. "You have met the elder Mr. Brantwood. The younger didn't stay for dinner that evening." Emma looked into the distance as though searching for a memory. "I suppose that was some weeks ago, wasn't it?" She shook her head. "Anyway, I've sent countless invitations since, and he's finally accepted one."

"How nice," Lucy said, though she wasn't certain it was nice at all. Thank heaven he had not stayed for dinner that evening. She might have behaved as an utter idiot if he had. Lucy felt her cheeks warm at the memory and was grateful for Emma's preoccupation with the malformed bonnet.

"You'll remember the story, of course," Emma rambled, snipping at threads to undo the morning's work. "The Mr. Brantwoods, elder and younger, are distant cousins and were in line for the dukedom during the years John was believed to have died in the war."

Lucy nodded. "Yes, I recall."

"It is an unfortunate consequence of the whole situation," Emma continued, still plucking stitches from the tiny white scrap. "I'm riddled with guilt and have no way to assuage it but to encourage the family connection. I haven't met him, actually, but I'm hoping he's a bit more pleasant than his father. I hate to say it, but I found the father a little…off putting, I suppose." She lowered the project to her lap and looked at Lucy again. "What did you think?"

"I…um…yes, I suppose," Lucy said, recovering her wits enough to respond.

"I didn't like the way he reprimanded the footman over the soup," Emma continued. "Mine was not too hot. And I think it was bold of him to reprimand our footman—especially when we don't make a habit of speaking to the household staff that way."

Lucy nodded. "Of course you wouldn't." Lucy had felt very scandalous through dinner that evening. Ever since, she had vacillated over how harshly she should judge herself for her participation. Just that morning, however, she had concluded the event had been a *good* thing. Without it, she'd have been left to wonder her entire life about the experience of being kissed.

Would all kisses feel the same? Mr. Brantwood had said stolen, indecent kisses were more exciting. Or was the reason simply her inexperience? Or perhaps—and this was the question that plagued her most of all—was her reaction specific to the man? If some other man had kissed her, would she have reacted in the same way?

"Do you think," Emma asked, brow furrowed in thought, "that I could purchase a few plain items and add some stitching or decoration myself?"

"What?" Lucy asked, turning to her friend in confusion.

Emma stared at Lucy and held up the deconstructed bonnet. "The layette," she said. "For the baby."

"Oh, yes. I'm sure that would be very nice," Lucy said. "Very nice."

Heavens. She was already a flustered ninny.

If she behaved so in his company, he would no doubt find it very entertaining. Imagine his amusement at knowing she had been thinking of him nearly every day for two whole months.

No, not him, she corrected. *The kiss.* That distinction was quite important.

Oh, but she could anticipate very clearly the tickled expression on his face as they were introduced that evening.

Lucy's eyelids closed briefly. What if he spoke of it? What if he was reckless and unthinking enough to reveal they had already met, or worse, what they had done? He had been reckless enough to kiss her, after all. He could not be so foolish—could he? He would ruin everything. Why, Emma would likely never let her out of her sight again. Lucy could not predict how the duke would react, but it would certainly create some sort of family rift.

If anyone outside the family learned of it…

Well, that would bring a swift end to her plans.

Chapter Seven

Lucy was already dressed for dinner and quietly reading in the drawing room when she heard the voice of the butler on the ground floor below, answering the door to arriving guests. Though she strained to hear, she could not identify the number of voices. She hoped fervently for a single guest, as opposed to a pair. She would only have an opportunity to speak privately with Mr. Brantwood if he were the first to arrive and, even then, only for a few brief minutes. If Lord and Lady Ridgely arrived first—well, she wasn't certain what she might do in that case.

She concentrated on the sound of footsteps on the stairway and hoped she would not have to face that particular dilemma. She reminded herself, as her heartbeat seemed to gain strength with the ever-nearing steps, that she was only conspiring to speak privately with him because of the very great need for discretion. Her preoccupation with their dalliance and her great curiosity to see him again were of no significance at the present.

No bearing whatsoever.

The door opened and the butler stepped into the room, facing the arriving guest. "I shall inform His Grace of your arrival, sir." He did not even look into the room to notice Lucy.

Sir.

Lucy's pulse quickened.

Mr. Brantwood entered and the butler efficiently departed. Unlike the butler, Mr. Brantwood did not fail to notice her presence. Surprise and something else—*pleasure*, she thought—flitted across his features at finding her there.

"Miss Betancourt," he said, with a generous display of teeth and charm, "how do you do this evening?"

All at once, her miscalculation occurred to her. She had been very forward in conspiring to create a few private moments with him and she had allowed him to kiss her the last time they'd met. Could he assume she was hoping for some repeat of their prior encounter?

Heavens. Would she never get this right?

She rose from her seat, setting her book on the side table as she did so. "I am fine, thank you," she said, hoping that her tone was polite without being overly encouraging. She cleared her throat to say all of the very important things she meant to say, but somehow could not seem to find the precise words on which to begin.

She tried to search for the words, but found herself studying him instead. He was just as tall as she remembered. His eyes were indeed gray, though she'd been unsure as to whether she'd recalled that correctly. He had a very square jaw, which she found interesting, as she had no particular memory of his jaw. His hair seemed a bit tidier than she remembered, but not perfectly tidy. It was just a bit too long—grown a few days past a needed trim.

How very surreal it was to see him as the stranger that he was, to recall what she could about him with no greater familiarity than any other person she had met only once before.

He had kissed her—held her in his arms, stroked his hands along her backside, and kissed her—but he was still a stranger whom she had only met on one brief occasion. She mused at the contradiction of it.

He coughed.

Drat. She was staring. When had she become so unable to behave like a sensible person? "Mr. Brantwood, I am so very happy that we have this moment in private to—"

"I couldn't agree more, Miss Betancourt," he said, stepping toward her.

"You do?" She blurted, panic rising. But he didn't know what she was going to say. He'd interrupted her. She felt quite certain what she had intended to say and what he thought she'd intended to say were vastly different ideas.

"Indeed," he said on a laugh. He stepped closer. "I think we may have some unfinished business from the last time we met."

She swallowed and stepped back. "Unfinished business?" Her voice came out as a squeak. An unwanted thrill accompanied the anxiety that gripped her at his words. He was bearing down on her and there was so much of him, all towering height and broad shoulders. Every part of her body was aware of his approach. Did she need to be kissed so badly? Was she going to forever be undone by his presence?

"I didn't...that is to say, rather, that I..." She was suddenly quite unable to draw upon her vocabulary. At least, she could not seem to push the words out of her throat and toward him.

"Although I enjoyed our first meeting immensely," he said, his lips curving as to give truth to his statement, "I would suggest perhaps it is best for everyone else to believe that this evening is, in fact, our first introduction."

Discretion. He wanted discretion. That was good.

"You wanted to speak to me privately, to recommend we not speak of...before?" she asked, desperate for the clarity that seemed so unattainable with this man.

"Precisely. No need to upset anyone, is there?"

His words drained Lucy of her tension so completely that she went limp from the loss of it, collapsing onto the sofa in undignified relief. "Oh, thank heaven."

He laughed then. "May I assume by your reaction that you agree?"

She sat up properly, recovering her posture, her wits. "I am in complete agreement," she assured him.

He grinned again, crooked and teasing. "Then we have found yet another point of compatibility, you and I."

She cut him a look. She did not want to think of their compatibilities. "Please know," she added, pointedly ignoring his comment, "that I am usually scrupulously honest. It is only that...well, I don't see any benefit in divulging information that would just cause harm or upset."

"I would expect no less from Saint Lucy of Beadwell."

She looked sharply up at him. He remembered her name. He remembered her home. Even as she knew he was teasing her, pleasure threaded through her at the thought.

Because it was quite certainly wrong for her to be pleased, she said, "Using my given name is too familiar, Mr. Brantwood, even if you are using it to mock me."

"I would argue that we have been quite familiar with each other, wouldn't you agree?"

It did seem a little odd to insist on formality when they were well past observing proprieties. "It is too familiar in the hearing of others, then," she said.

"So when we are not," he said, "you may call me Bex."

Before she thought better of it, Lucy blurted, "That is an odd name."

He only smiled. "Indeed. My name is Bexley. It is my mother's family name."

"Ah," she said. Bexley did not seem so odd as a surname, after all.

"You were truly worried, weren't you?" He asked. He stepped closer and seated himself in one of the chairs flanking the sofa. "Did you really think I would tell our story to the others?"

Our story. She was surprised to think of it as such, so used was she to thinking of it as hers alone. She looked at him and again considered how less and less like a stranger he seemed. They had shared a kiss and now they shared a secret. Yet she knew virtually nothing about him.

"I don't know you," she answered honestly. "*You* believed it necessary to ask for *my* silence."

One shoulder rose in response. "Women are prone to sharing secrets with their friends, I believe. At least some women. How was I to know you would not?"

Lucy nodded. "So you understand my similar concern. Discretion is the most sensible course, but I had no way of knowing if you are a sensible person. It's the reason I was waiting for you."

His brow lifted at her admission. "And here I had flattered myself that you were impatient to see me after our last encounter, when in fact you feared I may be an idiot. How lowering."

She smiled halfway despite her best efforts to quell the expression. "As it appears you are not an idiot, we are saved."

He leaned his head to one side and grinned at her again, the expression warming her when she knew it should not. "I am happy to help."

She lost the battle with severity and her half smile became whole.

"You're very practical about the whole thing, aren't you?" He peered at her. "No romantic fantasies fit for ladies' novels?" He pointed toward her book, still sitting where she had placed it on the side table.

"I try to be practical about all things," she said, suddenly feeling the need to defend herself. "And that book is not a novel."

He flashed her a dubious look as one long arm reached out to snatch the book from its resting place. He opened the book to its title page and read aloud. "*The Governess, or The Little Female Academy, Calculated for the Entertainment and Instruction of Young Ladies in Their Education.*" He lowered the book to his lap, looking at it as though it were a threat to him. "Good lord, was that the title or the first chapter?"

Lucy felt an undignified giggle rise at his scandalized expression. "I have found it to be an inspirational text."

He looked uncertainly at the book and then at her. He lifted it again and turned the page, skimming the book.

"I believe you will recall I am preparing to take a post as a governess. This is the first useful book I have found on the subject."

"This book was printed nearly seventy years ago," he said.

"It's the second edition," she countered.

He shook his head, smiled at her in a way that was somehow both teasing and warm. "I'm sure it's quite riveting."

So very true, she thought, her gaze riveted to his wide mouth. Curiosity tugged at her again as she was drawn back to the memory of his lesson, but voices sounded in the hall, saving her from her ill-advised imaginings.

Mr. Brantwood—Bex—rose and held the book out to her. She rose as well and took the proffered volume.

He winked.

She smiled.

And so they were accomplices.

* * * *

"I find myself in a bit of a dilemma," the duchess announced to the dinner party after the soup had been cleared, "but a lovely compromise has occurred to me."

"What is that, my dear?" the duke asked.

"It involves Mr. Brantwood," the duchess continued, drawing Bex's undivided attention. "The duke and I have been invited to an event Saturday next and I would very much like for Lucy to accompany us. It would make things much more convenient if you would agree to accompany us as well."

"More convenient?" Bex asked, more to forestall his intended denial of the request than out of actual curiosity for her meaning.

"I am quite certain Lady Ashby will extend the invitation to include Miss Betancourt as our close friend and houseguest, but it would be so much less of an imposition if I am able to propose an additional gentleman as well so as not to set her numbers askew. Lady Ashby is such a stickler for propriety and etiquette, you see—so much more so than I. Seating and the like can be such a headache for these things."

Bex considered. *Ashby.* He'd identified Lord Ashby at the Birdcage as just the sort of gambler who might be persuaded to a different sort of wager. Was it possible that just as he'd been puzzling how he would create an opportunity to speak to the man, one was being tossed into his lap so easily? He leaned back and smiled amiably at the duchess. "I would be happy to help in any way I can," he assured her, curiosity growing as to how Miss Betancourt would view his compliance. "What sort of event?"

"It is dinner, followed by dancing, probably cards for some of the gentlemen. I don't know if it will be a large group, but provided I'm able to keep her seating balanced for dinner, I am certain Lady Ashby will welcome two more. My aunt and uncle will attend as well," the duchess said, with a nod to Lady Ridgely.

"I am not otherwise committed that evening and would be happy to ease Miss Betancourt's introduction to society in any way that I can," Bex said, turning to the young lady in question.

She smiled happily at him. "It is very kind of you to be so helpful, Mr. Brantwood."

He grinned affably back. "It is hardly a kindness to spend time with good company."

"I'm so glad you think so, Mr. Brantwood. You see, Lucy and I were just discussing this afternoon her great desire to see some of the city, as this is her first time in London. Unfortunately, my condition prevents me from accompanying her. I have a little apprehension and considerable guilt in sending her out into the city with no one but the maid, Agnes, as her guide."

"That's sweet of you, dear," Lady Ridgely interjected.

"The duke's schedule is so occupied, we couldn't possibly impose upon him," the duchess said; then she turned wide eyes and a sweet smile toward Bex. "Perhaps you would be kind enough to show Lucy some of London while she is here, Mr. Brantwood? You must be familiar with so much of the city, and even a walk in the park would be a more exciting excursion than I am able to provide some days."

Bex turned to Saint Lucy to gauge her reaction to this suggestion. She blushed, clearly interpreting the duchess's intent much the same as he did—a blatant attempt at matchmaking.

Bex looked to the duke next and caught the quelling look sent from husband to wife.

The duke was right to ward her off. He, at least, knew with miserable detail just how ineligible a match Bexley Brantwood would be.

Apparently, the duchess did not, for she soldiered onward despite her husband's attempted warning. She addressed Bex directly. "Lucy has graciously agreed to be here in London with me until the birth of my child. We are very unfashionable, you see, in that I prefer to remain in my husband's company rather than retire to the country during this time." She glanced around the table as though visually surveying the response to this statement. "I shouldn't speak of such things so directly, but Mr. Brantwood is family, is he not?"

The duke looked to Bex with an unreadable expression. "He is indeed, but we cannot demand all of his time, dear. I'm sure he has other commitments."

"Of course he does," the duchess said. "Forgive me, Mr. Brantwood. I may have been inconsiderate in asking so much of you. I believe Lucy intends to begin her tour with an outing to the museum. Could we impose upon you, then, to accompany Lucy on this one outing? I do so worry, as she does not know her way in London. There are so many unsavory parts of the city."

"Indeed," he commented. He looked to Miss Betancourt then. Perhaps if she did not appear quite so embarrassed by her friend's attempts at matchmaking he would have answered differently. As it happened, he found himself saying, "I am quite knowledgeable of the museum exhibits, actually, and would be happy to accompany Miss Betancourt there sometime soon."

The duchess beamed at him. "How wonderful. You have my sincere gratitude, Mr. Brantwood."

"And mine," Miss Betancourt added. "I plan to visit the museum because I have adopted a goal of self-education. You see, I have decided to pursue taking a post as a governess."

He nearly laughed as she pursed her lips primly at the end of her speech. He was certain she was trying very hard to appear a proper governess. He thought governesses were supposed to be dowdy and harsh looking, of a mannish height perhaps. He did not think it appropriate for governesses to look like little fairy sprites, but he did not point that out.

"Self-education. That is very admirable," Lady Ridgely offered.

Bex grinned at Saint Lucy of Beadwell and could not resist asking, "Do you enjoy lessons, then, Miss Betancourt?"

She blushed prettily, but did not retreat from his question. "I am most grateful for any opportunity to become informed regarding a useful topic. My education attentions at present are therefore engaged with those skills that may enhance my capabilities as a governess."

And as such, not kissing. He could practically hear the words completing her thought.

"What about you, Mr. Brantwood?" she asked. "Are you the sort of man who believes in continual self-improvement?"

Bex coughed. She could not have realized how truly apropos her question was. He met her questioning blue eyes without guile. "I find I am the sort of man for whom self-improvement has become a necessity."

She lifted one dainty brow at his comment, but did not inquire further.

Chapter Eight

"You will not avoid me."

Damn.

Bex halted and released a defeated exhale of air. He was caught—mere feet from the door leading out of their rented London townhouse and into the freedom of the city.

"I know your game."

Bex faced his father. "There is no game."

Edward Brantwood glowered. "Do not lie to me. Do you think I don't know you have been avoiding me?"

Bex shrugged. "If you are here and I choose to be elsewhere, where is the game in that?"

Bex watched with surprisingly little feeling as his father, face purpling with rage, bore down on him.

"I am your father and you will show me respect."

Bex remained silent. He stared, unaffected, by the bluster and fury. He felt little for his father in that moment—certainly not respect. Disgust, perhaps, but even that was a bit strong. He looked at his father—really looked. The wrinkles webbing outward from his gray eyes looked deeper than the last time he'd noticed. His hair was more solidly white than before. His sneer was the same—very much the same as it had always been.

Bex's lack of reaction only served to deepen the shade of his father's complexion. "Answer me," he bellowed.

Bex crossed his arms and regarded his father coolly. He was no longer capable of rising to the bait of his father's temper. He felt nothing—not the shame in his father's displeasure that his much younger self had experienced and not even the fiery defiance of more recent months. It was as though all of his ire had been spent and he felt only a cold annoyance at the inconvenience of having to remain in his company. "I am here now," he said on a burdened sigh. "Is there a matter to discuss?"

Edward glared at his son, nostrils flaring with the exertion of restraining his temper. "You should not play the idiot unless you wish to be seen as an idiot. We will have our discussion over breakfast."

The elder Brantwood pivoted abruptly and stalked heavily away with no backward glance. Bex contemplated. His father was certain he would follow. Bex was not. He could just as easily turn the opposite direction and depart their shared townhouse before his father even realized he was gone.

Yet, as tempted as he was by the gratification of an eloquent display of independence, he would only delay the inevitable. Besides, the man might have an apoplexy if he walked out. He did not need a death on his conscience.

In the end, he chose to follow his father down the hall and into the small breakfast room. Deciding he should at least derive some benefit for enduring the pain of a fatherly lecture, he began filling a plate from the noticeably abundant sideboard. In the effort of avoiding familial company, Bex hadn't breakfasted at home in some months. Was this much food laid out each morning? It seemed an extravagance ill fitting for a man so recently begging relief from the burden of his debts.

Bex seated himself at one of only two place settings arranged at the circular table and faced his father. "Are you expecting others for breakfast?"

"Does it appear," his father asked, "that I am expecting others for breakfast?"

"The quantity of food seems extravagant for only two men who should be observing economies."

The elder Brantwood's open palm slapped the table. "Do not lecture me on economies. You do not pay for this home or this food."

Bex stared levelly at this father. "*You* do not pay for this home or this food."

Edward's mouth tightened to a grim line as he glared back across the table, then looked meaningfully to the manservant who stood at attention in one corner of the room, ready to see to their needs.

Pride can be such a petty thing, Bex thought. Of course this man, dutifully serving his master, did not know it was the Duke of Worley who now paid his salary, not Edward Brantwood. He also did not know that neither Edward Brantwood, nor Bex himself, knew precisely how long that beneficence would continue. As soon as it ceased, these roles would no longer be preserved. Edward Brantwood, playing lord in a house for which he could not pay, would then be no better than the very man he employed. Worse off, likely, as the footman boasted an employable skill, whereas the Brantwood men did not.

Accusations of gamesmanship seemed a bit hypocritical in the light of all this playacting, didn't they?

"What shall we discuss, Father?" Bex didn't bother to keep the impudence from his tone.

Edward turned to the manservant—one of two employed at the house—and indicated with a jerk of his head the man should exit, leaving them to discuss in private. Once the man had discreetly complied, he turned his full attention onto Bex. "You will defer to me as your father, or you will leave this house."

Bex had expected a lecture. He had been shortsighted not to expect a threat of some kind. Had he shown more willingness to be controlled without the use of threats, perhaps they would not have been required. Bex had no desire to remain in his father's false palace. He had personally refused the duke's offer of financial rescue, but he still lived under the favor of the duke and control of his father and both chafed uncomfortably. For the time being, however, he found the accommodation decidedly more comfortable than sleeping in the street. As he could spare no funds to pay for his own accommodation, he dipped his chin in silent acquiescence, conscious that he had only agreed to the vague commitment of deference. No specific demand had been made of him.

He knew well enough, though, to expect one.

At least one.

"You will need to marry."

And there it was.

"You forget, Father, that I have nothing. No home, no property, no income. Without our cousin paying for this house and, I imagine, this breakfast," he said, indicating the half-eaten toast on his plate, "I would be left to beg on the streets, and so would you. Who would possibly consent to marry me, and how precisely does an extra mouth to feed solve these problems?"

"Don't be obtuse. You will marry a woman of wealth."

Bex shook his head. "You are living in a fantasy. Any father with an heiress for a daughter intends to purchase *something* with all of that wealth—usually a title or connections, of which I have none."

"You are the cousin of a duke," his father said.

"My grandfather was the cousin of a duke. He is, I think, the third cousin of the present duke, so I believe I would be"—Bex paused a moment to consider—"fifth cousin? Is that correct?"

Edward chewed a bite of ham, and stared at Bex as though carefully choosing what he would say next. Bex took it as a clear warning that he would not like it, whatever it was.

"There is always a way to accomplish something, if you are sufficiently determined to see it happen," Edward said, raising a pointed finger as he spoke. "It is a matter of opportunity and creative thinking. You may not be the particular choice of ambitious parents, but young girls are not always so calculating in where they choose to direct their affections. If such a girl believed herself in love with you, the relationship could progress to a point in which marriage became more likely—necessary even."

Bex eyed his father with distaste.

Edward shrugged. "But you are correct. That may prove difficult. A more mature woman, however, could have her own wealth and social standing. The attentions of a young and virile suitor may prove quite appealing."

"A mature woman?" Bex asked. "If she is old enough not to care about connections, or titles, or wealth for future generations, then she is too mature for me."

"Not necessarily. I have heard gossip of a widow recently returned from France. The Comtesse de Beauchene. Englishwoman, married to a French comte, but an English lady in her own right. She has set herself up rather smartly here in town. Took a large house in Mayfair."

"How did she manage to marry a French comte while we were at war with France for more than a decade?" Bex asked, with a suspicion he knew the answer.

Edward's gaze was suddenly consumed with examining the striped wallcovering. "She was married some time ago."

"How much time?"

"I understand she was married before Napoleon came to power." He shared this bit of information as though it were of no significance—as though he'd said two or three years, instead of ten times as many.

"Before Napoleon? You cannot possibly be serious. I would have been a child when she married."

"She may have been very young when she married," Edward said hopefully. "By all accounts, she has taken society by quite a storm. It appears she's got some life in her yet. I have heard rumors, in fact, that she has had dalliances with younger men." An unpleasant smile tilted one corner of his mouth. "If one managed to be persuasive enough, he could tempt her into marriage."

"No."

Bex did not provide any more explanation or reasoning. As far as he saw it, the bloody reasons were self-evident.

"It's not as though she's elderly," Edward said scornfully. "She's like any other bored widow in need of something to do and somewhere to spend her wealth. And she's accustomed to the forwardness of French society. They are not so constrained there."

"I was not aware you had traveled to France."

"Of course not," Edward snapped. "Everyone knows the French are more promiscuous."

Bex did not, in fact, know this to be true, but chose not to dispute it. "If that is the case, why would she even consider marrying? Why not take to bed any man who strikes her fancy and exchange him for a new lover when she becomes bored again?"

Edward glared at Bex. "I'm certain you could convince her of her undying love for you."

Bex returned the glare with equal disdain. "I'm certain we shall never know."

The two men sat, gazes locked in challenge over a dueling field of linen and silver and half-eaten toast.

Edward spoke first.

"You will do as I say, or you will be cut off."

Bex rose on a bitter laugh. "Cut off from what? You have already squandered my inheritance."

Two clenched fists landed upon the table with enough force to rattle the silver. "You are a fool for wanting that life. I have given you a gift by forcing you to seek better. You dined at Worley House this week. Every opportunity is open to you. You have the connections to better yourself. I have given you that. You waste your time mourning the loss of something that should never have been enough to satisfy you."

Bex stiffened. "Do you speak of Oakwood Lodge or of Miss Mary Huxley?"

"All of it. That life is gone and good riddance. You will have better unless you are too stubborn to take it."

"Better?" Bex gripped the back of the chair from which he had risen. "Better? Yes," he ground out, "it is much better to have trampled the heart of a young girl in order to grasp at the chance to trick an old woman into marrying me so that I might take control of her fortune. Never mind that I cannot stand to lie with her, so long as I can support my noble father in his quest to pretend he has inherited a peerage after all."

Edward rose from his own seat. "You think I am so shallow, but what will you do? Will you go hungry and die on the street? I think you will not. You will take what you have and use it in the best way you can."

"And you have nothing. So you will use me. Let us not pretend that this is fatherly concern for my future. You wish for your own comfort, not mine. Your ambition to rise above the station to which you were born has only served to bring you lower and now you look to me to rescue you from your own disaster."

"Don't be righteous with me, son. You have nothing and no one without me. At least I have considered what you might do next."

"Yes. I am a lucky son, indeed."

The anger left Edward's face, but it was replaced by an expression that was no less malevolent. He lifted a shoulder in an unconcerned shrug. "You need not pursue this widow. It will be your choice." His head tilted to one side then. "Only take care you are thorough in packing your things. I can't say how considerate the servants would be in taking them to the street for you."

Chapter Nine

The real Lord Ashby, Lucy noted upon their introduction, was a stiff and somewhat distracted gentleman who gave the impression of having decidedly more important things to do elsewhere. Having met both Lord Ashby and his wife, she wasn't entirely certain the man even knew he possessed daughters. She couldn't imagine he bothered himself with their education. She could well imagine that approaching him in the way she had mistakenly approached Mr. Brantwood would have been a thoroughly humiliating disaster.

She made every effort not to think about the encounter that had ensued instead as the duke presented Mr. Brantwood to Lord and Lady Ashby. Lucy's efforts to ignore the curiosity inspired by said encounter were, of course, complicated by the very close proximity of the man who had incited it.

Even as Mr. Brantwood greeted their host and hostess, Lucy could feel his unspoken taunt as though he had flung it at her. She knew at some basic, instinctual level that he was taking the measure of the man for whom he'd been mistaken and was no doubt thoroughly entertained at being reminded of the entire debacle—at knowing *she* had been reminded.

True to his promise, however, he said nothing—not even to Lucy—when the introductions were complete and their small party continued onward into the parlor. She could have sworn, however, that a quirk of amusement hovered at the corner of his lips when he briefly met her gaze.

She turned away, dismayed at having been caught watching him. Why should she be looking at him, anyway? All was well, was it not? They had agreed. They were confidants.

She sighed, then immediately chided herself. She hated dishonesty, even to oneself. She knew very well why she was looking at him. She had thought of very little besides Mr. Brantwood in quite some time.

She would not be so intrigued by him, but for the fact that she could not know for certain whether it was the simple matter of the kiss, or with whom she had shared it. *That,* she thought with an inward sigh, *is the consuming question.*

The parlor at the Ashby townhouse, Lucy noted once she'd plucked herself from the depths of her preoccupation, was quite crowded.

"So many for just a dinner?" she whispered quietly to Emma, feeling unsophisticated even as she voiced the observation.

Emma sighed. "It is a greater number than I expected. Lord Ashby is quite well connected. I imagine it is rather difficult to keep the attendance reasonable when one cannot invite Lord A without offending Lord B, or Lady X without inviting Lady Y." Emma leaned more closely. "Lady Ashby is much better at this sort of thing than I will ever be. I avoid the entire situation by mostly inviting only family to dine. Anyone who is not blood has no reason to be offended."

"But I am not blood," Lucy couldn't help pointing out.

Emma gave a beleaguered eye roll and whispered, "Apparently, you're the hired help."

Lucy giggled.

"What are you two finding so entertaining?" the duke asked, looking indulgently at his wife.

"Only that I suffer from utter lack of ambition as a hostess," Emma said, smiling back at him.

The duke laughed. "One of the myriad of reasons we are perfectly matched, my darling."

Lucy felt a warming in her heart to see the two of them so enamored of each other. Emma deserved her happiness.

"You are a perfect hostess, my dear," Emma's aunt assured her.

"Ah, Your Grace," a shrill voice carried in their direction. In the manner that lightning is followed by thunder, the voice was followed by the presence of a lady who managed to appear as threatening as a storm despite her diminutive height. The cluster of menacingly sharp feathers protruding from the woman's hair contributed to her fierce demeanor, as did her resolute expression—that of a hunter charging to intercept her prey.

Emma smiled at the woman, but Lucy easily recognized it for the obligatory expression that it was. "Lady Grantham, how very nice to see you."

"And the same to you, Your Grace. Felicitations on your happy news," she effused.

Emma's chin dipped in acceptance of the kindness. "Thank you, Lady Grantham."

The older woman simpered as though she knew the gratitude was her due. "Why I was only just saying to Mrs. Woodley," she continued, "how surprised I was that you are even attending this evening. I told her I was certain you would be too cautious with the duke's heir to be concerned with social invitations." Her smile was tepid and did not reach her eyes. "But I was wrong and here you are."

"Yes." Emma's eyes narrowed. "Here I am."

Lucy thought the woman could not have been more cutting in her remarks, but she was mistaken.

"My own daughter, Lady Welton," she said, stressing the title as though it might otherwise go unnoticed, "is spending her confinement in Kent."

"Is she?" Emma asked, all false interest and excessive politeness. "How restful that must be for her, to be away from…town."

Lucy nearly laughed aloud at the collapse of Lady Grantham's expression. At least the woman had been clever enough to catch the subtle barb.

Emma's aunt, Lady Ridgely, stepped forward into the rapidly deteriorating exchange. "How very pleased you must be for your daughter's happy situation, Lady Grantham. I know I am anxiously awaiting the arrival of my grandniece or nephew."

"Of course." As Lady Grantham turned her attention to Lady Ridgely, her expression recalibrated to one of pity—the type that was far more condescending than charitable. "I'm sure you are, poor dear," she said, reaching forward to pat Lady Ridgely's gloved hand with her own. "You were unable to have your own children, after all. What a burden that must be for you and the earl."

Lady Ridgely's delicate hand slowly but surely retreated from the contact. She swallowed, but gave no retort.

Lucy, astonished at the spiteful woman's remarks, turned to take in Emma's reaction. Not surprisingly, her expression was no longer restrained. If this was an example of typical behavior, Lucy could well understand why her friend had chosen to avoid London society for so many years. Emma no doubt would have given the horrid woman a thorough dressing-down in defense of her beloved aunt had they not been joined by their hostess.

"Ladies," Lady Ashby interjected, unaware of the simmering dislike thrumming in the group, "you must come and meet my new friend, Lady

Constance. She is the Comtesse de Beauchene, but prefers to use her English honorific now that she is widowed and returned from France."

"I have heard of the comtesse," Lady Grantham announced sharply. "I understand she arrived in town, immediately let the largest house available, and began planning dinner parties as though she had never left. Very presumptuous, I would say."

"Of course, that is only gossip. One must meet a person to know the real truth," Emma pointed out, and Lucy silently cheered her defense of the absent comtesse.

Lady Grantham pursed her lips skeptically. "She is French, after all."

"If I recall, Lady Constance is the daughter of the fifth Earl of Marbury," Lady Ridgely said, with more pique than she usually displayed. "She is very much English."

"But she has spent the past three decades in France," Lady Grantham insisted. "She is certainly more French than English now, and it appears she has adopted their manners."

"She may a bit outspoken," Lady Ashby said, in an obvious attempt to smooth the disagreement. "But she is quite gracious and thoroughly civilized, I assure you."

"I should be very pleased to make the acquaintance of the comtesse," Emma said.

"As should I," Lady Ridgely said, stepping forward once more into the fray.

"And I," Lucy added in solidarity, championing the woman she had never met.

* * * *

The Comtesse de Beauchene, as it happened, did not appear to be a woman who required champions. She was a handsome woman of indeterminate age—as the most lovely women always seemed to be—but Lucy guessed she possessed at least a half century of accumulated life. Life in years of age was not the kind that most distinguished the Comtesse de Beauchene, however. Her rarity was in the life—the spirit—she exuded from the moment of observing her. Her blue eyes sparkled with youthful mischief despite the creases that edged them. Her smile was wide, somehow both knowing and sweet. And she sat, tall and regal, in a delicately painted chair, surrounded by a rapt group of attendants, giving one the impression that she had crossed the channel from France to assume her throne, much as William of Normandy had done centuries before.

"Lady Constance," Lady Ashby interjected, drawing the woman's attention from her audience. "I have brought some friends I would very much like for you to meet."

"How wonderful. I should love to meet any friend of yours." She rose from her chair, as did others in the assembled group. Several pushed chairs back to make way for Lady Ashby and her newcomers.

Lady Ashby presented the duke and duchess. Emma then performed the introductions of Lord and Lady Ridgely, and next Lady Grantham, who had insisted on joining the group despite her unkind opinions. "Mr. Brantwood is my husband's cousin," Emma said, completing the lengthy list of companions, "and Miss Lucy Betancourt is my dearest childhood friend." Lucy curtsied to the comtesse and found it was easy to smile at the woman when her eyes possessed such laughter and she greeted without any sense of reserved judgment.

"How very charmed I am to meet you all," Lady Constance said, giving as much attention to Lucy and to Mr. Brantwood as she did to the duke and duchess. Lucy liked her very much.

"Lady Constance, I understand you are the daughter of the Earl of Marbury," Lady Ridgely said. "I believe we may have been introduced on one occasion before your marriage."

"Is that so?" the comtesse asked, brightening at the possibility. "You must remind me of the occasion."

As Lady Ridgely began her account of a years-past meeting, Lucy sidled toward Emma. She spoke quietly at her friend's side. "If you really intend to serve as a reference, you should probably be introducing me as your companion, rather than as your dearest friend."

Emma smiled and squeezed Lucy's hand. "I love you with all my heart, Lucy, but I will not introduce you as my companion."

Lucy squeezed back. "Why ever not?"

Emma tilted her head. "Have faith, Lucy. I fully intend to help you find a post, but I will not pretend *I* am employing you." She turned to face Lucy then. "I would gladly pay you, only I know you would not accept it. Or worse, you might accept it and then stubbornly insist on behaving as though you were a member of the household staff."

"I would not," Lucy said, but her denial lacked vehemence. She knew in her heart she could not shirk duties for which she was compensated.

"Mr. Brantwood," Lady Constance crowed, drawing Lucy's attention. "You are lurking in the back there. Come forward, don't allow me to frighten you."

He laughed and Lucy found herself watching him. Bex, she decided, was a fitting name, though she had not yet decided why. "I do not frighten easily, Lady Constance. I would never presume to interrupt ladies' conversation."

Lucy looked around at his words and noted that he was the only remaining gentleman. She had not noticed the duke or Lord Ridgely depart, but they must have done so following the introductions.

"Don't be silly, Mr. Brantwood, the interruption of a young and handsome gentleman is never troublesome for ladies, and as I am old enough not to be coy, I may readily admit it."

His laughter deepened, and she gestured to a vacated chair at her side. "Come and sit, Mr. Brantwood, and I shall dismantle all your misconceptions of proper ladies."

"How can I deny myself such an opportunity, when men have sought for centuries to understand the mysteries of ladies?" He moved to sit where she indicated.

Lady Constance laughed lightly. "I offered to reveal misconceptions, Mr. Brantwood, not mysteries. A lady never shares her secrets."

Bex murmured a response that elicited further laughter from the comtesse, but Lucy could not hear it, despite straining to do so.

"Come sit with us as well," the comtesse said, waving at Lucy and Emma.

Lucy's cheeks immediately warmed, fearful that she had been too apparent in her curiosity. Nevertheless, she and Emma pulled empty chairs into the conversational circle and sat. Lucy cast a brief glance at Bex and caught him watching her. He winked. *Winked.* How was she supposed to respond to that?

The comtesse turned her attention to Emma and Lucy. "I understand you are expecting, Your Grace. Congratulations to you and your husband."

Emma nodded. "Thank you, Lady Constance."

The comtesse leaned toward Emma and said, without any trace of malice or irony, "I believe this would be the moment when a matron would provide some tidbit of maternal advice, but as I am not a mother, I am not qualified to do so. I will simply wish you great happiness, and leave it at that."

Emma's eyes widened. "Oh…I…thank you."

The comtesse turned to Lucy next. "And you are Her Grace's longtime friend, if I remember correctly?"

"I am. We have been friends from the time we were very young. My father is vicar in a village where the duchess's family owned a cottage."

"So you are here for the birth of the child, then. Is this your first time in London?"

"It is."

"And how do you like it?"

"I have found it very interesting, Lady Constance, but there is much I have yet to see."

The comtesse nodded sagely. "Yes, it is always interesting." She turned abruptly then to peer more closely at Bex. "And you are the duke's cousin, Mr. Brantwood. Are you visiting the duke and duchess, as well?"

"I am not. My father and I have a townhouse here." He leaned comfortably in his chair with the air of a man who did not question whether he fit in. Lucy wished she could emulate that confidence.

The comtesse glanced at Lucy after his response, and she wondered again if she had been too transparent in her interest in him. She did not address Lucy, however, but turned back to Bex. "Why is it, Mr. Brantwood, that you are tolerating conversation with an old woman rather than talking with some nice girl your own age, or hiding in the card room with the gentlemen?"

"I never play cards, Lady Constance," he said, failing to provide an explanation for the first part of her question.

Simply noticing he had failed to answer a question, Lucy reasoned, did not necessarily imply she had an interest in the answer. She was, after all, an observant person.

"And you?" Lady Constance said, turning her attention to Lucy. "Why are you not off husband hunting with the other pretty young girls?"

Lucy smiled at the woman's candor. She would very much like to be so outspoken someday. "I am not on a 'husband hunt,' as you call it."

"And why is that?" Lady Constance asked. "Are you an independent heiress, then, and have no need for the security of marriage? Because, I would be quite happy for you, *ma petite*, were that the case."

"It is quite the opposite, I'm afraid," Lucy said without shame or hesitation. "I lack sufficient family wealth or connection to draw the attention of any of the gentlemen of this set."

Or any other set.

"Is that so? Wouldn't you at least enjoy dancing and flirting for an evening? There is no point in sitting in the corner when you've bothered to dress and leave home."

Lucy smiled and willed herself not to look in Bex's direction. "There would be very little point in dancing and flirting, just to become enamored with a gentleman far outside my reach. I would only arrange for my own disappointment. Or worse, draw the interest of a gentleman who would be disappointed himself upon making inquiries and learning he has wasted his time and attention."

"It is of no use, Lady Constance," Emma interjected. "I have tried on several occasions to encourage Lucy to be *less* sensible, but have had no success in encouraging impulsive behavior."

Guilt speared Lucy that she had not confided in Emma her recent impulsive behavior. She felt Bex's gaze on her but looked to Lady Constance instead, who peered at her with great interest. She had the distinct feeling the woman was taking her measure.

"You are an extremely practical sort, aren't you?" Lady Constance asked finally.

"I do try to be," Lucy replied. "It is kind of you to notice."

Lady Constance laughed at her reply. "You would take it as a kindness, whether I meant it as such or not, wouldn't you?" She leaned toward Lucy. "I approve. And there are not a lot of you, I imagine."

"I should think practicality a very desirable trait in a person. I imagine there are a great number of us wandering about if one takes the time to look."

Lady Constance nodded. "Perhaps you are correct, *ma petite*, and if I kept better company, I might have the same observation."

"I beg your pardon," Lucy rushed to explain. "I never meant to give offense to you or anyone of your acquaintance. On the contrary, I'm sure many are quite practical."

Lady Constance laughed in a pleasant way that made her surprisingly youthful eyes sparkle more brightly. "Oh, I am certain they are not, *ma petite*. I have spent the past three decades with the French."

"Yet now you have chosen to return to England," Lucy said. She knew the declaration contained an indirect—and likely impertinent—question, but she was intrigued enough to ask and somehow sensed the lady would not take offense.

"I have, *ma petite*. My husband is dead, I have no children in France, and I am, in my soul, English."

Lucy smiled. Most would not consider it very English to think of one's soul at all, outside of church. "Is that why you are introduced as Lady Constance, as opposed to your French title?"

The lady leaned in as if to speak confidentially. "Nobody likes the French, *ma petite*. It's perfectly acceptable to tolerate the French, even to emulate the French tastes, but it's not entirely acceptable to *be* French. Too many memories of lads lost. One must be sensitive to these things. The honorific reminds everyone that I was born English."

Lucy nodded, recalling Lady Grantham's comments.

Lady Constance leaned away again. She waved her hand in the air as though dismissing a thought Lucy had not yet voiced. "Do not mistake, I loved my years in France. So many wonderful things about the French."

"I should like to hear more about them someday," Lucy said, and she meant it most genuinely, but she had already taken up too much of the comtesse's conversation. "Why don't I fetch you a lemonade, Emma," she offered, "while you speak with Lady Constance."

"I'm sure I can get something to drink in a bit," Emma said. "There is no need for you to get it for me."

"Nonsense, I am happy to do it," Lucy assured her. "Stay just where you are and I shall return shortly."

She rose. As manners required, Bex rose as well. She realized once she began to walk away that he had not reseated himself, but left the group also. Was he following her? She glanced over her shoulder. He was two paces behind her as she walked. He *was* following her.

Whatever for? She turned again. He had stopped. He was not even looking at her.

"Do you know the direction of the card room?" he asked a gentleman she did not know.

Lucy watched as he was given the requested direction and, after expressing his gratitude for the information, walked away. He did not even glance her way.

He had not followed her after all. An oddly deflated feeling came with that knowledge, but she did her best to ignore it, instead allowing her curiosity to circle about the fact that he was looking for the card room. Had he not just insisted to Lady Constance that he did not play cards?

Before she could think better of it, Lucy abandoned her previous destination and walked in the same direction as Bex. Now *she* was following *him*. Why had he lied about playing cards? It was not as though such an admission would be scandalous. Card rooms were set aside at events like this for the very fact that many perfectly respectable gentlemen participated. The more she realized his lie made no sense, the more determined she was to follow, though to what end, she had no idea.

She bemoaned her small stature as she attempted to track his progress through the room. From what she could see, he was making his way toward the far wall, which contained three recessed archways. She lost him for a moment, but, rising on her toes, she spied him again, walking into the center archway. Even as she questioned what she might do or say if she actually entered the card room—and she suspected women did not—she lowered herself back onto her heels and made her way to the far wall.

She stopped when she reached it, because there were not, in fact, three archways. There were four. Which meant, of course, that either of the middle alcoves could be the one through which he had passed. Slowing to a more meandering pace, Lucy strolled past first one and then the other middle alcove. Both led to recessed doorways.

* * * *

She stood, frozen, between the two doors, obsessed with the choice of which one he'd used, despite knowing with absolute certainty the correct choice for her was neither door, but rather to turn around, find a glass of lemonade, and spend the remainder of the evening at Emma's side.

Though, perhaps, if she could manage to only peek without being seen...

As though she had intentionally set out to disprove Emma's description of her sensible personality, Lucy turned and ducked into the archway to her left. The alcove was not deep and, as she'd already discovered, it ended at a tall, heavy door. She reached out and gingerly touched the handle. Slowly, she grasped it more firmly and pushed.

The door did not budge. It could not be locked from the inside, if Bex had entered. She pushed one more time. Whatever prevented the door from opening with her first push must have come loose, because with her second push, it swung wide, pulling her with it through the doorway.

Chapter Ten

She was outside.

Conscious of being seen, Lucy pulled the door shut behind her, only to be plunged into blackness at the loss of the glow from the interior of the house. From the little she had noticed when she could see, she was in a small, walled garden. She dare not take a step for fear of stumbling in the dark.

Why did Bex Brantwood have the effect of inducing her to make ill-advised and impractical decisions?

She'd taken complete leave of her senses. The mix-up of archways was a blessing. Fortune had taken pity on her wayward soul and, for the second time, protected her from her own impulsive foolishness. How easily she'd lost sight of her purpose here.

Pay attention, Lucy.

Lemonade.

Governess.

Go back inside, she told herself. *Retrieve Emma's drink.* She should direct her attention to behaving as the perfectly respectable vicar's daughter that she, in fact, was.

She placed her fingers on the handle of the door and felt it turn within her hand, before she'd applied any pressure to accomplish the task.

She snatched her hand back.

She gaped at the door. As it moved slowly outward, a thin shaft of light began to slice into the darkness of the tree-shaded garden.

Oh, God. Someone is coming! She should not be here by herself. Respectable young ladies did not lurk in dark gardens at London house parties. When her mind could not immediately leap to a plausible excuse for her present location, she put her limbs into action instead. With an indelicate lift of her skirts, she darted behind the largest nearby tree with the sort of agility one only possessed in moments of panic.

Eyes wide in the steadily brightening garden, Lucy pressed her back to the large tree and silently blessed whoever had decided to leave the old thing where it stood and plant a garden around it rather than cutting it down.

The door shut again and she blinked, once again plunged into dark as her eyes failed to adjust to the abrupt changes in light.

Footsteps.

If you wouldn't mind, unknown intruder, could you please return to the soirée and allow me to do the same? If only she could will the request to the mind of her unwanted companion. *Go back inside. Go back inside.*

She briefly considered an attempt to sneak past and get to the door, but discarded the notion. Her presence would only be announced when the darkness was again brightened from the open doorway, as it had been moments ago.

Yielding to her frustration, she made a face in the blackness that, of course, no one saw. She could barely see her own fingertips.

"Mariah?"

Lucy froze. The masculine whisper came from much nearer than she had expected. She held her breath.

"Mariah?" The voice was closer still.

"There you are, sweeting." A large hand closed around her forearm and tugged her forward.

She tugged back.

A low chuckle came from dangerously near her left ear. An arm snaked around her waist. "You're not going to become shy now, are you?" The breath was warm, but thankfully free of the scent of liquor.

Or perhaps, drunkenness would be preferable. She did not want to be recognized, after all. Wouldn't an intoxicated man be less likely to have a clear recollection? It was a useless point, she supposed, as this man did not suffer from that particular affliction.

Why was it so dark? She couldn't even get her bearings.

Absent drunkenness, however, perhaps the dark was better. She hastily considered. What would she say? *I beg your pardon, but I am not Mariah.* He would be embarrassed, she would be embarrassed, and what of poor Mariah?

Often, when one hesitates in decision, one loses the opportunity to decide. This was startlingly clear when she was pulled firmly against the broad chest of a strange man and felt hands tilt up her chin.

"My love," came his whispered declaration. Then his lips fell on hers.

Sara Portman

Lucy was most definitely being kissed, by a man she could not see and surely had never met. She was too stunned to react immediately. By the time she was capable of reacting, she decided to push him away—only she didn't. Instead, it occurred to her that here was a man kissing her as though she were his sweetheart.

Since she was *already* being kissed, she supposed she could at least gain an answer to her most pressing question. Would his kiss feel the same as Mr. Brantwood's?

* * * *

It was gentle.

He was gentle.

He did smell nice—like leather and perhaps a hint of tobacco.

She supposed it was…nice.

She didn't kiss him back, precisely, but she did allow him to continue kissing her, his unfamiliar lips pressed insistently to hers, as she evaluated.

Then he ended it and pulled back, still holding her waist. "What's the matter?" he asked.

Mariah, she decided, must be more enthusiastic.

"Um…" She tried to step back. "We'll be caught," she said in a breathy whisper that she sincerely hoped would successfully disguise her voice. "I should go."

"But we've only just gotten here," he said without yielding his hold.

"They'll catch us," she said in the same gravelly whisper, taking a calculated guess that there was, in fact, a "they." There was always a "they," wasn't there? Parents, uncles, chaperones of some kind. Why else take the trouble of a secret meeting?

"I don't want you to be afraid," he said. He sounded so heartbreakingly sincere, she felt guilty for not *actually* being Mariah.

"I will go in first," he said, "in case anyone saw me walk out just now. I will make sure your father is nowhere near. Wait a few minutes, then come back inside yourself."

Well, he did seem rather solicitous. If not for the absolute absurdity of the notion, she might have envied Mariah her chivalrous beau.

His hand slipped from her waist. Her eyes were beginning to adjust to the light and she was curious—incredibly curious—to see what he looked like, but she kept her head down. If she could begin to make out shapes in the shadows, so could he. What if he realized hers was not a match for the shape he'd been expecting? What if her eyes were bright enough to reflect the light and appeared the wrong color?

She kept her chin firmly down and said, "All right," one more time in her throaty whisper.

He placed a kiss on the top of her head. "Until later, my love," he said and stepped away.

She exhaled. She had not realized how long it had been since she had fully allowed herself to breathe. She stayed in place as the light filtered over her, marking the opening and closing of the door as he went inside. She blinked, and, once more, she was sightless in the warm, damp evening.

"That was touching...*Mariah.*"

She spun. She recognized this voice. Bex.

"What are you doing here?" Unable to see, she shot the question accusingly in the direction of the voice.

"I might ask the same of you, Saint Lucy. I am here because I received some inaccurate instructions and exited the wrong door. I stayed because I wondered what sort of business would cause a perfectly respectable vicar's daughter to sneak into a dark garden in the middle of a house party. A moonlight tryst *and* a false identity? I am impressed. That is a great deal of shameful behavior for one evening." She could hear his voice drawing closer. "One might even call it impulsive."

"This was not a tryst," she declared, beginning to make out his shape as it moved toward her. "At least it was not *my* tryst. Why would I go about masquerading as this Mariah woman? I am only here because I walked through the wrong archway as well. I thought I was at the door to the card room."

She recognized her error immediately.

"A tryst, a deception, and a weakness for cards." He clucked his tongue in disapproval. "Saint Lucy, you shock even me, and I do not shock easily."

Even recognizing it for the trap it was, she could not help herself. "Why were *you* looking for the card room?" she demanded. "You lied to Lady Constance. You told her you don't play cards."

"Saint Lucy, were you following me?"

She bristled. "It doesn't reflect well on your character that you would lie so freely."

"I assure you, I do many things that do not reflect well upon my character. Lying is not among them."

"But I heard you. You asked for the card room."

"I did ask for the card room," he said without concern. "But does it necessarily follow that I intended to play cards? Perhaps I sought a cardplayer, not a card game." He was very near now. "My behavior is nowhere near as scandalous as yours. What a surprise you have turned out to be." She could hear his smile in the dark.

"I already told you, I took the wrong door. I came outside by mistake. "

"So Mariah is not a pet name from your sweetheart? You do not play games that involve adopting roles like governesses or sweet young girls?"

"No," she hissed, "Mariah is not a role or a pet name. She is clearly a real person and planned a clandestine interlude with her admirer. If you want to be scandalized by anyone's behavior, you can look to her. Although," Lucy amended, "she did not come after all, did she? Perhaps she thought better of it and changed her mind."

His laugh was soft and low. "You are too good, dear. It makes you horribly uncomfortable to speak ill of this woman who is nothing more than a name to you—the name of a woman who is behaving less than respectably, I might add."

She stiffened. "I am in no position to judge this girl. I have never met her and know nothing of her." She had also just allowed the other woman's beau to kiss her, but she did not believe that warranted reiteration.

"Except that she was conveniently absent, thus you decided to take her place," he said, obviously deciding the reminder was, in fact, necessary. "Did you enjoy participating in her tryst?"

"Don't be absurd." It *was* absurd. Not entirely untrue, however. "I was taken by surprise when that man kissed me."

"Of course. So, naturally, you immediately objected and announced your true identity."

"I didn't want to be caught here, and I didn't want him to know that he had been caught as well. I thought I could extricate myself from the situation more easily by...by...cooperating."

He was standing directly in front of her—near enough to touch her. He spoke very quietly, but she had no difficulty in hearing him, or even feeling his breath as he spoke. "So, allow me to confirm my understanding. In order to avoid being caught in a compromising and scandalous position, you decided to let a strange man kiss you."

"It seemed more rational at the time," she hastened to explain. "It all happened very quickly."

"I should have thought your curiosity already satisfied."

It was as though he could read her thoughts. His intuition when he couldn't even see her face seemed a wholly unfair advantage. She had no sensible response that wouldn't paint her as a reckless, naïve fool—which she supposed she was.

"You *were* curious, weren't you?" he asked, taking her silence as confirmation.

"It's not what you think," she blurted. "It was already happening. If I *was* curious, it's only because I needed to know if it would be different."

He was quiet.

Lucy felt her cheeks warm. Why, why had she said that?

"Was it different?" he asked. Had he just moved even closer?

She set her jaw. "I do not wish to discuss this with you."

"Was it?" he asked. This time his voice was low, insistent, no longer teasing.

She lifted her head, but her voice was very small when she answered. "Yes." She wished very much that she could have simply lied to him.

He was right there at her answer, hands closing around her arms, just below her shoulders. His grip was urgent, but not rough. "How?" he implored.

She stared up at his face in the darkness, feeling as though her inability to clearly see him made this moment somehow less real. Could she answer his question in the daylight? Would she answer it?

"He was kind," she said. "He smelled pleasant. It was nice."

His grip tightened.

Her voice dropped to barely a breath. "It was only nice…not…not…"

She couldn't even say what it wasn't. She didn't need to say it. He showed her. He showed them both. His grip clutched her and his mouth fell to hers and, heaven help her, he showed her everything the stranger's kiss had lacked.

The insistent pull that forced her to not only receive, but participate to the extent her inexperienced self could know how.

The urge to get closer—to create as many points of contact as they could.

The build of heat between them until she thought it might explode.

All of these things, and the strength of will it required of her—to hold back from complete surrender into the kiss and wherever else the kiss might take them.

His lips moved insistently over hers and she knew, in the most natural way of knowing, that nice would never be enough. A sound that barely registered as her own rumbled softly in the back of her throat.

It was not an objection, but it should be.

She knew it should be.

She pulled her lips from his. She tried to step back, but met the abrasive bark of the tree against which she had been hiding. She sidled left, freeing herself from the heady pull of his proximity.

"I will be missed if I don't return," she said with what little breath she could draw. "I trust you will not speak of this to anyone." She turned from him and fled, heedless of whether her reentry might be observed.

* * * *

When Bex found the actual card room, he was grateful for the distractions there. He found Ashby engaged in a game and had no trouble waiting patiently as he considered the other gamers, wondering which he might be able to interest in a partnership if Lord Ashby declined.

Even with all the cards moving on multiple tables and all the men to consider as they played, Bex still found it difficult to keep his thoughts from drifting back to kisses in moonlit gardens. She had wanted to *compare*, for God's sake. The woman would be in danger from all sorts of rakes in London—himself included—if she could not learn to be coy.

He didn't mean it, of course. He liked very much that she was not a sophisticated flirt. Only, he should not like it. He should not like her. He did, though. He liked her enough to be troubled by the risk that she might be developing a liking for him. He would have to put a stop to any of those ideas before they started. The duchess didn't know what she was about if she was steering her friend in his direction.

In his peripheral view, Bex saw Ashby lay down his cards and rise from his seat. He had lost—Bex knew it from his expression—but he did not lose his temper as others did. Bex respected that, but more importantly, viewed it as further evidence that Ashby played the game strategically, rather than emotionally.

Bex worked his way slowly but deliberately toward his prey. To his great fortune, Ashby did not immediately enter another game, but stood at the wall, sipping whiskey from a tumbler and watching the others play.

Bex reached the wall where Ashby stood, sidling close enough to be overhead, and said, "Poor luck in the cards today?"

Ashby turned and faced him, quizzical at first, but then recognition dawned. "You are Worley's cousin, aren't you?"

Bex nodded. "I am."

"Worley is not much of a gambler, but I gather that is not a family trait," Ashby said, turning back to survey the action at the tables.

Bex shrugged, biding his time. "I appreciate the fun of a wager, but I rarely do so at the card tables these days."

Ashby looked back at him and a flash of something—disapproval, perhaps—crossed his otherwise neutral features. "Are you for dice, then?"

Bex grinned wryly. "There is no skill in dice," he said, knowing Ashby would view pure games of chance with the same disdain. "Where is the challenge in that?"

Ashby nodded and swirled his drink. "If you do not play cards or dice, on what do you wager?"

He had taken the bait. "I speculate with small investments," Bex explained.

Ashby sipped. "Trading shares on the exchange can be risky at times, but I find there is not much entertainment to it. If I am going to invest enough to make it worth my while, I will make a sensible investment—hardly a wager."

"I don't mean the companies listed on the exchange," Bex clarified. "There are other ways to invest, if you are interested."

Bex waited, and Ashby was quiet for a long moment. Perhaps he was not interested. If so, Bex would have to seek another partner—find another connection.

Ashby sighed. "I suppose I am interested enough to hear your explanation, if you're of a mind to share it."

Bex resisted the urge to smile. "Are you familiar with Gibbs, owner of a gaming hell called the Birdcage?" Bex asked, despite knowing the answer.

"I am."

"Gibbs acts as a facilitator for men who wish to become merchants or tradesmen but have no funds to begin. There are manufactories popping up all over Britain, but they require iron for machines and wages for labor long before any profits are generated. These are the sort of men who cannot gain access to listings on the exchange. Gibbs aids them in raising funds and in return, both the tradesman and the investor pay a fee. There are opportunities for considerable profit, with the right investment."

Ashby pursed his lips. "What you are proposing is that I become directly involved in trade. Owning shares through the Royal Exchange is one thing, but direct ownership in a factory—I don't know if I have the time or interest for such things."

Bex persisted. "With all due respect, Lord Ashby, the speculative interests I'm discussing are in amounts no greater than you might spend in an evening wagering on card games. These are really just wagers of a different sort." Bex saw the intrigued light in Lord Ashby's eye and continued. "Factories are increasing throughout Britain. Many will fail, but a few—perhaps more than a few—will be successful. In those instances, a very small investment could reap great rewards."

Ashby did not respond, but had not turned away, either, so Bex pressed forward in his proposal. "You are a peer of the realm. You are the steward of your family's estate. You, and others like you, will take the majority of your family's wealth and invest it in the safety of the four percents, with the security of King and country. You might own shares in the East India Company. Those investments will produce income, but significant income requires a significant investment. Compare that instead to the wager you place on a roulette wheel. It could be a small amount of money, but if your number is called, you've won many times your wager."

"Only fools play games in which they cannot develop an advantage," Ashby said.

"I agree," Bex told him and did his best to paint a tempting picture for the seasoned gambler. "These factories are the best of both. Think of the factories like the numbers on the green field of the roulette table. If you wager on the correct number, the gains are significant. Only, unlike roulette, in this field you can apply skill. The factories have circumstances that you can study. A strategic man can improve his odds by eliminating those factories based upon unoriginal ideas, whose inventors are lazy or ignorant of the trade they seek to enter. The more understanding one gains, the better one is able to refine his wager and improve his odds."

Ashby's eyes narrowed and he was silent for a moment, but then shook his head. "You miscalculate, Mr. Brantwood. I have cultivated my card-playing skills over nearly two decades. I lost much more than I won at the beginning when my skills were underdeveloped. I am wise enough to know I don't possess the skill required to make the selections you discuss. Those choices require a merchant's knowledge, or a tradesman. We've already established I am neither."

"I am not a charlatan, Lord Ashby. I have no intention of manipulating you into believing you will inherently possess the knowledge to make these choices. I propose a partnership with a man who does."

Ashby eyed him skeptically. "And who is the possessor of this strategic mind with whom I should be partnering?"

"I am."

"You?"

"Indeed."

Ashby tilted his head to one side and peered at Bex. "If you are so gifted in speculation, why do you not fund your choices with your own fortune?"

"Because I, too, began from a position of ignorance rather than skill. I have not always wagered wisely, but with each loss, I gained insight and education."

"And now you've accumulated enough insight to gain the advantage?"

"I believe so."

Ashby's lips formed a grim line. "You must have lost a great deal."

Bex did not deny it.

Ashby was silent, considering, and Bex waited. He turned his attention back to the tables.

Finally, Ashby spoke. "I will consider it," he said, looking down at his glass, rather than at Bex. "How will I reach you?"

Bex stepped away from the wall and passed in front of Ashby, discreetly handing him a calling card as he did so. "I look forward to hearing from you, my lord."

Chapter Eleven

The following day was thankfully a quiet one for Lucy. Agnes had arrived with a tray in the morning, informing Lucy the duchess was tired and had chosen to take a tray in her room. Agnes had assumed Lucy would prefer the same.

Agnes was correct.

Lucy didn't know which had exhausted her more thoroughly, the drama brought on by her poor decision making, or enduring the polite exchanges for the remainder of the evening, in an attempt to be well mannered and memorable, but not too interesting.

She dressed for the day and did venture out once to check on Emma, but otherwise spent a reclusive morning in her room reading *The Little Academy*, a timely reminder of the proper focus of her attention.

In the early afternoon, there was a knock on her chamber door and Agnes entered again.

"I'm to tell you there is a caller, miss."

Lucy set her book on the bed and sighed. "The duchess is not taking callers today, Agnes."

"Yes, miss, but the lady has called for you."

"For me?" Lucy wasn't sure what to make of that. No one had ever called for Lucy at Worley House. Could Emma have spoken to Lady Ashby about her after all? She quickly dismissed the idea. Lady Ashby would expect a prospective employee to go to her, of course.

Curiosity overcame Lucy's desire for solitude, and she rose. "I shall be down shortly, Agnes. Thank you."

She was down very shortly, as she didn't see any reason why her simple day dress wouldn't suffice for whatever visitor waited. She was not a duchess and no one would expect her to be turned out as one.

She regretted this decision slightly, however, when she arrived at the drawing room and found the lovely and luxuriously clad Comtesse de Beauchene smiling brightly at her from beneath a bonnet decorated with silk blossoms and rich ribbons. Lucy felt very much the simple vicar's daughter when contrasted with such continental sophistication and finery.

"Lady Constance," she said, hoping her surprise at seeing the woman was not evident in her greeting. "How nice to see you again. I am sorry that the duchess is ill and unable to visit."

The lady dismissed this concern with a wave of her hand, sending a subtle scent of perfume wafting toward Lucy. "I would have very much liked to visit with the duchess, of course, but I am equally happy for your undivided attention, Miss Betancourt. I was thoroughly entertained by our conversation last evening and decided we must continue it today."

Bemused, Lucy studied the woman as she crossed the room toward her. By all measures, the comtesse's return to English society had been a smashing success. She had spent the past evening surrounded by a circle of devotees. She could have taken the time today to call on any one of the aristocratic ladies of social power and pedigree who had flocked to her side. Why Lucy Betancourt, vicar's daughter and would-be governess?

"I am flattered you recall our conversation at all, Lady Constance," Lucy said. "I enjoyed it very much, but you met so many people last evening. Surely your head is dancing with names today."

"Not at all, *ma petite*," the comtesse said with a wink and a laughing smile. "I only bother with the worthwhile names, so I never have too many to recall."

How did she do it? Somehow the comtesse managed to say the most outrageous and outspoken things without offending. Lucy would only manage to appear unkind if she said anything similar, yet the comtesse seemed universally adored.

"Won't you sit, Lady Constance," Lucy asked. "I shall ring for tea." Lucy had never before rung for tea in the Worley House drawing room, as she was always with Emma, but as she was receiving a caller—a French comtesse, no less—she decided she was not overstepping. She pulled the bell and made her request to the responding maid, but couldn't help the apologetic smile she gave at the end of the exchange.

"So," Lady Constance said, once she'd arranged herself on the sofa. "You are a vicar's daughter from the country. Tell me more about yourself, *ma petite*. Have you brothers or sisters?"

"I do not," Lucy responded, seating herself in the chair to the comtesse's right.

"And your parents? Are they living?"

"They are. My father is vicar in Beadwell, a small village in Kent."

"And you have known the duchess since childhood?"

"I have."

"Well." The comtesse sat back against the sofa and smoothed her skirts. "That may explain it."

Lucy laughed at her odd comment. "I beg your pardon. Explain what, my lady?"

The tea tray arrived then, delaying the response. Once the tea had been distributed and the cakes offered, Lucy repeated her question. "I'm afraid I don't understand. What have I explained?"

The comtesse gave a delicate shrug. "You move in a very highborn set for one of your station, but you don't seem intimidated at all."

Lucy didn't suppose that was entirely correct, but she did not dispute it. "Should I be intimidated?"

"Never," Lady Constance said, leaning forward to add vehemence to her declaration. "That is why I like you so much."

Lucy smiled. She rather liked Lady Constance as well. "There is very little accomplishment in birth, is there?"

The comtesse winked. "Indeed, but never let on that we know."

Lucy shook her head. "Oh, I wouldn't." Of course, she just had. "That is…I shouldn't have said it. It would not recommend me well to offend the very families I would like to employ me, would it?"

"Employ you?"

Lucy straightened. "After Emma's…er, Her Grace's child is born, I intend to seek a position as a governess." She fully expected the revelation to change the comtesse's opinion of just how interesting Lucy was after all.

Lady Constance made a face as though the very thought put a horrid taste in her mouth. "Why ever would you do that?"

Lucy was unable to prevent a laugh at the woman's theatrics. As Lady Constance was so direct, she didn't see any reason to be vague. "Marriage is not practical for me at this time," she said. "My father is aging. It is time I am no longer a burden to my parents."

"But that is easily accomplished with a marriage, *ma petite*."

"I am not in London for a season," Lucy said simply.

"Surely your friend, the duchess, would sponsor you for a season," she said. "After the child is born, of course. Next year, perhaps."

"There is more to it than that, I'm afraid," Lucy said, surprised that the comtesse would even discuss the topic. She had expected a hasty withdrawal, but instead the comtesse managed to communicate her abhorrence with Lucy's plan without making Lucy feel judged, or somehow less. "Even if I arrived in London dressed as royalty and attended every ball given, I would not become a desirable match. Without wealth or family consequence, I would not find a husband in London any more easily than I would at home."

The older woman pushed her teacup away with a wistful sigh. "Marriage is all too often a financial arrangement."

"But what else can it be," Lucy asked, "when a family must make a home, must have something to eat?"

"You are far too young and pretty, Miss Betancourt, to have lost all sense of romanticism. Has no man ever turned your head? Have you no remaining girlish fantasies?" The older woman's eyes glinted with excitement and mischief.

Lucy felt her cheeks redden. Unbidden, a memory of Bex Brantwood filled her mind.

Lacy Constance eyed her speculatively, but continued. "Your friend the duchess seems quite enamored of her husband."

Quickly, Lucy pushed the traitorous vision aside. She swallowed and smiled placidly. "You misunderstand. I am not at all cynical and I am love's greatest proponent. You are indeed correct that the duchess had the happy fortune to find herself in a love match, though the engagement did not begin so. Theirs was a marriage born of practicality, Lady Constance. Their companionship grew to love."

Lady Constance shook her head as though saddened by these revelations. "I see," she said. "And though you claim to be a proponent of love, you are champion greater yet of practicality."

Lucy smiled. "I fear love makes weak soup, Lady Constance."

"And so it does, *ma petite*. And so it does." The older woman took a dainty bite of a tea cake from a small plate and returned the plate to the table that sat between them. "So instead of having children of your own, you will find some family who will employ you to look after their children."

"I hope to find a position as a governess. If I am unable to find a position with one family, I will likely begin giving music lessons."

This seemed to intrigue Lady Constance. "Music lessons, you say. What do you play?"

"I am proficient enough to provide instruction in pianoforte and harp."

"Is that so?" She squinted at Lucy as if contemplating some significance to this information of which Lucy was not yet aware.

"Yes, ma'am. I have played all my life."

"Well, that may do nicely. That may do very nicely," she said.

Lucy laughed. "I feel as though I have just become involved in something without knowing it," she said.

"I do believe you have, *ma petite*. How would you like to play for a concert I will be hosting?"

"A concert?"

"I am hosting a performance of Madame Castellini, the Italian opera singer." Lady Constance picked up the small plate with the half-eaten tea cake, considered it, and placed it back upon the table. She smiled wryly at Lucy. "I am accepted in society because I am English, *ma petite*, but I am interesting to society because I am French. If I am to remain interesting, I must be a source of continental entertainments."

"I don't know," Lucy said, attempting to construct an appropriately grateful and polite denial. "You have never even heard me play."

Lady Constance waved this aside. "You strike me as a person who would more likely understate her abilities than the reverse. I expect your talents are considerable, but of course you shall have a rehearsal or two with Madame Castellini before the performance."

"I don't know that my talents are at a level to provide accompaniment to a famous opera singer, my lady. I am very gratified that you would ask, but…"

The comtesse leaned forward and lay a hand on Lucy's arm, halting her speech. "Miss Betancourt, did you or did you not just explain to me that you intend to teach music to the young ladies of the ton?"

Lucy swallowed. "I did."

"And do you think these families would want the very best for their blossoming debutantes?"

"Of course, but…"

The comtesse lifted a staying hand. "There is no 'but,' Miss Betancourt. If you want to be sought after by the families of the ton, you must become the thing for which they will clamor. Everything is a competition. Every mother wants her daughter to be more accomplished than the next girl. Today, that means learning to play an instrument, but once one mother can proudly crow that her little darling has been instructed by the pianist who accompanied famed soprano Madame Castellini, everyone will need a music teacher with such a pedigree. Play for my concert, Miss Betancourt, and I assure you, your value will rise considerably."

Lucy considered this quietly for a long moment. Anticipation and no small amount of panic threaded through her at the thought of performing at such a prominent event. Except for private groups of family and friends, Lucy had never played for any gathering more distinguished than the assembled congregation at her father's parish church. Yet the lady's reasoning was sound. If she could play well enough, the concert could serve as an audition of sorts to demonstrate her abilities for numerous families at once.

She turned to Lady Constance. "You were invited to Lord and Lady Ashby's home last evening. Will you be reciprocating that invitation by inviting them to the performance?"

"Of course."

"Then I will do it."

"Because of Lord and Lady Ashby?"

"They are seeking a governess for their daughters. I am hoping to be considered for the post."

"Perfect!" She beamed triumphantly. "You do entertain me, Miss Lucy Betancourt. Perhaps I shall not allow you to take a post with anyone else. I shall have to hire you as my companion instead." She smiled conspiratorially at Lucy.

"I'm afraid you are insufficiently feeble to require my assistance and I could not, in good conscience, accept payment. Besides," Lucy added, "you are far too in demand to ever be alone and will surely have no need of companionship."

"That observation, *ma petite*, is a shortsighted one. Never confuse the moods of the beau monde with true friendship. I know this well. The whims of society are not so different on either side of the channel. As swiftly as one can rise, one can easily fall. C'est la vie, no? Everyone will someday test the loyalty of their true friends. You should always seek to gain one when you may."

That seemed a cynical truth from one with such a bright personality. She couldn't quite tell if the comtesse was offering her such a friendship, or cautioning her not to make too much of their connection. Either way, Lucy was intrigued.

Chapter Twelve

"You should wear the blue."

Lucy gazed down at her bed, upon which Agnes had laid two dresses from which Lucy would choose for the day's outing to the museum. The day had arrived for Mr. Bexley Brantwood to fulfill his promise to Emma, thus saving Lucy and Agnes from certain peril while observing the sights of London.

Drat.

She wished Emma had not spoken. She had been leaning toward the blue, but had been attempting to convince herself that she had not done so because it complimented her coloring and drew out her eyes. The blue, she had reasoned, was the more practical choice.

She just hadn't decided why, precisely.

Emma was concerned with matchmaking, and sadly, matchmakers as a rule rarely applied practicality.

"The yellow is more serviceable," Lucy said, just to be contrary, though contrary to Emma or her own instincts, she couldn't say. Perhaps both.

"How so?" Emma asked.

"The blue has ruffled sleeves. It's too"—she searched for a reason—"frivolous for an educational outing."

Emma laughed from her seat in the corner, holding her rounded abdomen as she did so. "Are you suggesting that ruffles at your shoulders interfere with your ability to acquire knowledge? I wasn't aware information was absorbed through the shoulders."

Lucy cut her a look. "I am saying one should dress for the occasion. The proper clothing puts one in the proper spirit."

Emma cast her a withering glance. "That is only true to a point, Lucy, and you know it. "I'm not suggesting you wear a ball gown and feathers, only a pretty color that sets off your eyes."

Lucy turned and faced her friend accusingly, placing one fisted hand upon each hip. "You are matchmaking."

"I am only matching you to a dress, dear. The blue is more flattering. The yellow is too pale."

"Liar."

Emma, horrid actress that she was, deliberately mistook her meaning. "I swear I am being perfectly genuine when I tell you the yellow dress is too pale for your complexion."

"You should not play matchmaker, Emma. You shall only be disappointed."

It would not do for either woman to have unrealistic expectations where Bex Brantwood was concerned. Emma, lovely soul and loyal friend though she might be, was wasting hope that the duke's cousin would be the man to save Lucy from a life of educating children belonging to other women.

Bex had no interest whatsoever in the marital state, but she granted Emma did not understand the extent of his disinterest. As Lucy could not reveal her own knowledge of the subject without divulging other, more embarrassing secrets, she did not enlighten her friend. She said only, "I love you, dear Emma, and I love that you are so content in your state of marital bliss that you wish to impose such a state upon me. That day may yet come," she said, knowing the words to be false, "but that day is not today."

"You cannot predict the day, Lucy," Emma argued. "It could be any given day."

Lucy looked into Emma's eyes, saw the hope there, and was frightened of it. She did not want Emma to be disappointed, but far more worrisome was the knowledge that such hope could be catching. Hope could spread from person to person like a communicable disease, driving decisions filled with risk and uncertainty, and where would that leave her?

Heartbroken in a pretty dress without plans for her future security.

Resignation was the safer dress to wear, and this day, resignation was yellow.

Emma sighed loudly, the exhalation mirroring Lucy's thoughts as she lifted the yellow dress. Of a sudden, it seemed rather unattractive, though she'd never disliked it before. She'd always thought it cheery, the color the sunflowers.

And jaundice.

She shook the thought from her head. She was being a ridiculous ninny, as it seemed she was wont to do whenever the intriguing and irreverent Mr. Brantwood was about.

Emma released another exaggerated sigh and levered herself up from her seat using the covered arms of the dainty chair. "Wear whatever dress you would like, Lucy, as you'll do so with or without my approval. The trick of it is," she added, a victorious curve to her lips, "you are lovely in either dress. Perhaps I knew you would be contrary and wanted you to wear the yellow all along."

Lucy laughed. "Another lie. You cannot decide to be manipulative after the fact."

There was a rap on the door and Agnes entered, first dropping into a curtsy toward the duchess then smiling widely at Lucy. "Mr. Brantwood is waiting downstairs, Miss Betancourt."

Was everyone in this house a matchmaker? Did they not understand they could not make a man court her against his will? He had not called upon her voluntarily. "You would all do well to remember," Lucy said, as Emma crossed the room to take her leave, "that Mr. Brantwood is only here as a favor to his cousin who happens to be a duke."

"Of course, miss," Agnes rushed to say, quickly dousing her bright grin.

Emma only smiled knowingly and glided from the room, managing to do so despite her increasing middle.

Lucy turned back to the dresses. She did so hate being a ninny. She would wear the yellow, and it would serve as a reminder to her for the duration of the outing that she had a purpose—a much greater purpose than allowing her head to be turned by a man with no interest whatsoever in marriage.

The marriage mart is a game and when the game is done, the fun is over.

She wanted to hold his words like a warning to ward off hopeful, girlish thoughts.

"Mr. Brantwood is gracious to accompany us today as a favor to the duchess," Lucy said, as much to make the point to herself as to Agnes. "Come help me dress, so I do not keep him waiting."

"Of course, miss." Agnes rushed forward and began unfastening the buttons that ran down the back of Lucy's morning dress. "Shall you wear the blue or the yellow, miss?"

The question startled Lucy until she recalled Agnes had not been present for the debate. She glanced again at the two dresses, side by side, one more time and knew there was only one sensible answer.

* * * *

Bex stood at the window in the drawing room at Worley House and watched the street below, wondering who might have taken note of his arrival. Today would be his third opportunity in less than two weeks to demonstrate his good relationship with the duke and duchess. How many such visits would be required before word reached Gibbs and bought him the desired respite from collection efforts? The man had spies everywhere. How many after that before Gibbs concluded the visits would not result in debt repayments?

If he could bring about one more conversation with Ashby, perhaps he would not need so long. Ashby had balked, yes, but he was intrigued, Bex could tell. His proposal had brought the light of curiosity to Ashby's gambler's eyes. He'd spent enough time at the Birdcage to recognize it—the look before an intrigued spectator capitulated, reaching into his pocket to join the game.

He felt certain he only needed one more opening with Ashby to pull him in, and the duke was his best chance to create that opportunity.

He disliked knowing, one way or another, he needed the duke's help. He'd declined the duke's direct offer of funds and instead took help from his cousin in another way, without the man's knowledge or consent.

Somehow it was better, though. Somehow there was more dignity in simply using the connection—even dishonestly—as opposed to accepting direct charity. Taking the money would be simpler. If the duke repaid his debts, Gibbs would not hesitate to loan him the funds for Birmingham, but Bex could not do it. He could not grovel to the duke after his display of righteous indignation, but even more so, he could not stomach the idea of being rescued.

Whether or not his father shared in the blame, Bex had dug a considerable portion of his own pit. He could not sit at the bottom and allow himself to be lifted by a savior. Even if he did, what would he do next? He was not the distressed maid in a child's tale. He was a grown man. He would climb out of the damned pit grasping and fighting.

He stepped away from the window. Fighting was not so difficult when his battle consisted of an excursion to the British Museum with Saint Lucy of Beadwell.

What a curious girl she was. And what a damned waste for her to hide away as someone's governess somewhere. He was to be her guide through the British Museum, but he could happily admit he would much prefer to continue her lessons in other, more lascivious arts. He had wanted to take her in the damned garden behind Ashby's house, when she'd looked up at him and admitted how she'd felt about his kisses compared with the other man. He'd wanted to crow with the victory.

Sadly, he could not continue with those lessons. He could not afford to compromise any woman, as he could not offer any remedy for it. A governess she would be.

Bex seated himself on the sofa as he waited for his companion, and the book on the side table drew his attention. *The Governess.*

He smiled. His little governess was still conducting research.

Not his.

He picked up the book. Idly, he leafed through a lengthy preface, which he gathered articulated the author's noble purpose in penning said book. He quickly realized the book itself read as a fable—a series of cautionary tales for would-be governesses.

It was, as suspected, ridiculous. Surely, Saint Lucy found it ridiculous. Didn't she? She was too levelheaded for such tripe.

"There you are, Mr. Brantwood."

He looked up and rose as the angel herself entered, a blond pixie in a pale blue frock. "Here I am," he said. "Am I lost?"

She shook her head, and the pale wisps at the side of her face fluttered with the movement. Her smile was warm and open instead of practiced and knowing. He would not like to see her with a jaded, knowing smile.

"You are not," she said, her amusement at the question widening her smile. "I had thought you would be waiting in the hall. I'm sorry if you've been kept too long."

"No apology is warranted. I was quite occupied." He lifted her book as evidence of this fact.

"Are you mocking my studies, sir?" She crossed her arms in front of her chest and did her best to appear the disapproving governess. Thankfully, her best was not sufficient to mask the hint of a smile that hovered behind her stern expression.

"I assure you, I am not," he answered. "I admire the zeal with which you are preparing for your chosen profession."

She accepted this response with a quick nod.

"I am mocking Mr. David Simple," he said, reading the author's name from the book, "whom I have decided is as aptly named as Mrs. Teachum, the governess in his fable."

The stern expression reappeared. "I knew you were mocking me."

He walked toward where she stood near the door. "Surely, there is some better example for you than the fictional Mrs. Teachum."

She stepped closer as he approached, lifted her chin proudly. "I have found it very informative on the types of situations that may arise when I have a post."

He stepped closer still—close enough to force her face upward to meet his eyes. She could play at being offended but he knew she agreed with him. He may not know everything about Saint Lucy of Beadwell, but he knew she was not a foolish girl. "This book is ridiculous and you know it," he said. "To begin, this Mrs. Teachum is nothing like you."

She did not retreat from the challenge, instead looking up at him with defiant confidence. "We are not so very different."

His brows rose dubiously; then he lifted the book, opened it, and read aloud. "'Mrs. Teachum was about forty years old, tall and genteel in her person, tho' somewhat inclined to fat.'"

Mirth brightened her eyes even as she scowled at him. "We are similar in our purpose."

He looked down at her for a long moment, reveling in the shared humor, even when she refused to admit to it. He held her blue eyes until he was very certain he wanted to kiss her again and not certain at all that he wouldn't. He stepped away, turned his back to her, and set the book on the table. "And so we address your purpose today, do we not? By the time we return, you shall be an expert on the British Museum."

"I am fortunate indeed if my guide today is knowledgeable enough to make me an expert."

Were her words spoken more softly, or was he imagining that? He faced her again, saw the remnant of a blush fading from her cheeks. She was not for him, but he found he rather liked knowing he affected her anyway. He offered his arm to lead her from the room. "Are you doubting the depth of my expertise on the exhibits of the British Museum?"

"Not at all, sir," she said, accepting the proffered arm. She beamed up at him, as though her hair and skin and eyes glowed with their own source of pure, brilliant light. "I would not waste time wondering either way when we can simply proceed on our outing so that I can discover the truth of it."

He grinned back at her, wondering how any man could resist doing the same. "Saint Lucy of Beadwell, I declare you are the very devil."

* * * *

He was the very devil.

And Saint Lucy of Beadwell made him feel more wicked than he had ever felt.

They had done nothing at all untoward. How could they in public? The maid who accompanied them was too curious about the museum to prove much of a chaperone, but the scores of other people in the exhibit halls surely prevented misbehavior.

And still he was incapable of avoiding wicked thoughts. Even as they discussed details of various exhibits and he was returning her bright and hopeful smiles, his imagination was consumed with wolfish intentions. Even the damned dress was killing him, and it was modest enough for a schoolgirl. Every time he looked at her, he noticed the blue fabric was an exact match for her eyes. When the hell had he begun noticing when dresses matched anything?

"Mr. Brantwood, I owe you a great apology for any doubts I may have harbored," she said as they finished their tour of Greek and Roman sculptures. "Your knowledge of the exhibits here is impressive. You have proven an excellent guide."

"Are you so shocked?" he couldn't help asking.

"I will admit, it is unexpected." She tilted her head to one side and peered up at him with unveiled interest. "How did you become so knowledgeable about the museum?"

"It is no great mystery," he said, turning away from her obvious curiosity. "I have spent a great deal of time here."

"I would not have guessed you would have such an interest in antiquities."

"Not so long ago, you would have been correct," he told her.

"What drew your interest?"

"I was not so much interested in the museum as I was interested in being away from my father's townhouse." He hadn't ever voiced the truth aloud to anyone. It seemed rather cowardly, now that he'd said it. He didn't like that.

"You do not get on well with your father?" she asked, in the careful voice of one who knows she is prying.

He laughed, for the topic was not one requiring sensitivity on his behalf. "My father and I get on very well when we are not in each other's company."

"I'm sorry," she said, looking up at him with enough genuine sorrow that guilt prodded him.

"Do not waste pity on me, dear," he said brightly. "The company of my father is no great loss." *For anyone.* If only he had understood that fact earlier, his debts would not be so deep.

"What of your mother?" she asked.

"My mother remains in Surrey."

He expected her to grasp at that insufficient answer, knowing it drew more questions than provided answers, but she did not, instead asking, "Why the museum?"

He grinned. "Because parks and gardens are unpleasant during periods of inclement weather."

She seemed to consider this, her dainty brow furrowing until two lines formed between them. He sensed she had more questions but that she chose not to pry further. "Well, I have very much enjoyed benefiting from your wisdom. As there is so much to see, I hope that we can repeat the outing on another day."

"You are so dogged in your pursuit of knowledge that you will tolerate even my boorish company?" he teased, though in truth, he knew he was the sort of man she should avoid. He was a cad, whether she realized it or not. Perhaps future outings with her would not be so wise, if he could not take better control of the course of his thoughts while in her company.

"I don't find your company boorish at all," she said, with an expression so plain and honest it startled him. "I quite like you, Mr. Brantwood."

Her brazen statement was a warning. More so was his own rising heat upon hearing it. If he was witnessing her artless attempt at flirtation, he could not allow it to continue.

"You should not," he said simply.

She laughed at that. It was pleasant, but hearty—the laugh of a woman of genuine good humor. He had not realized until he heard it how tired he had grown of the affected, tinkling laughter of society women who never truly allowed themselves to be overcome with mirth. Her laugh was also frustrating. He was trying very valiantly to ward her off and she laughed.

"On the contrary, Mr. Brantwood," she said, silver lights of laughter still dancing in her blue eyes. "I believe you are ideal."

"Ideal?" he asked, fearing the answer.

"Emma will not rest until she's put me in the company of an eligible gentleman. That makes you the ideal solution."

Her statement nearly knocked the breath from him. How could he have allowed her to be so completely mistaken? "I'm afraid I disagree, Miss Betancourt. I mean no offense," he said, holding up open palms, "but I am the last man you should consider eligible." He stopped and faced her, drawing her full attention. "Do not deceive yourself that I am a gallant knight to rescue you from the bleak future otherwise in store for you. I am in no position to rescue any woman. I am also far from gallant."

Blue eyes rolled skyward. "There is no need for such dramatics. I've only declared that I enjoy your company. I am also fond of the company of a well-written novel. I am not so confused as to believe you are courting me, Mr. Brantwood. I am well resigned to the course of my future. Neither one of us is in a position to marry anyone. We may comfortably be in each other's company without the burden of expectation. That is why you are ideal."

Bex exhaled, relieved and more than a little impressed by her pragmatism.

"Besides," she added with a beguilingly crooked smile, "we've already been completely inappropriate with one another. In your company, there is no need to fear that I might blunder or appear foolish. I've already neatly gotten that out of the way with you."

Bex laughed then. "You rationale is interesting. I submit it is not what most young ladies would think."

She inclined her head to one side. "Most young ladies are thinking about finding a husband. I am not. Can we not simply be friends?"

They could, but he needed to be certain she understood the full truth of it. Bex took her arm and began walking again, his eyes looking forward, focusing on some undetermined point toward which they walked. "Much as you would endeavor to convince yourself, I am not a man to be admired or befriended. I am quite the opposite. I am a man with no purpose."

"No purpose?" She stopped abruptly and turned to him. Brow furrowed, she searched his features as though some clue to his meaning would be evident there. "But you are a gentleman. Your father is a gentleman. You must have some wealth or property or living that requires your time and attention."

"I have no living or income. I am a man for whom the clock has run out. My debts have come due."

Lucy gazed searchingly at the profile he presented. "Your debts have come due," she repeated. "Do you mean that literally or figuratively?"

"Both, I suppose." He released her arm, saving her the awkwardness of pulling it away from him when she understood the truth of his revelation. "I am a destitute man with no living and I am in debt to moneylenders for funds I cannot repay."

"But how did that happen?" She shook her head. "I understand how a man can accumulate debts, but how is it that you are without a living or income?"

"As I'm sure you are familiar, given your long friendship with the duchess, the present duke was missing for four years. During that time, my father believed himself to be in line for the peerage. He insisted we take up residence in London and adopt a lifestyle that would allow us to socialize with the upper echelons of the aristocracy. Such a lifestyle is costly. In the end, it cost our family estate."

She studied him for a long moment, her expression void of the shock and judgment he had expected to see there. For once, he could not divine her thoughts but wished he could. Her response to understanding his true situation was, for no reason he could name, significant to him.

"What are you going to do?" she asked finally.

"That," Bex said, "is an excellent question." There was very little he could do. He had no money, he had no property, and he had developed no skills.

What he had were two cards left in play. Hertfordshire and Birmingham.

To be precise, he had Hertfordshire. Birmingham was not actually in play. He had no part in it yet, nor would he have a part unless he could find someone willing to advance funds—someone other than Gibbs. Ashby had not pounced on the opportunity, but there was still a chance there.

Lucy simply needed to understand how ineligible a match he would be for her. "I am hounded by my father to marry an aging widow as resolution, or find some innocent heiress to seduce, neither of which sound particularly appealing to me."

She waved her hand. "Of course, neither of those is an honorable option, but there is no shame in finding yourself in the position of needing to make your own way." Her eyes shifted and her smile returned. "I think I understand you better than you realize, Mr. Brantwood. Perhaps that is why I enjoy your company so much. We are alike in many ways."

He glanced askance at her as they walked through priceless Egyptian antiquities of which they had studied none. "You like my company *so much?*" he couldn't help asking.

She lifted her eyes to the ceiling and shook her head. "Perhaps I spoke too soon," she said flatly.

He laughed.

"In all honesty, though, I think it's quite freeing to have no expectations of each other, as I told you before."

"My point, dear, is that I am not the man you think I am and I am even less likely to marry than are you."

She looked at him a long while. "But you wouldn't want to anyway," she said. "You told me that the game ended with marriage and then the fun was finished."

"Maybe I have been saved, then," Bex quipped. "If I were in line for a dukedom, I would have been the prey of dozens of hopeful young maidens. Now that I have nothing to offer, I am saved the trouble of fending off the marriage-minded young ladies." He grinned at her. "I am free to enjoy the company of people who know my true lack of worth and, therefore, expect very little of me."

"But that's not what I meant when I said we had no expectations of each other," Lucy said. "Of course people know your value, even if it cannot be measured in titles or income. Anyone who only measured you by those things, never saw your true worth at all."

Her sweet, impassioned speech tore at him in a way nothing else had for quite some time. He would so have loved to simply bask in the idea that this angelically wholesome creature, who was all things good and pure, found attributes in him worthy of admiration.

But he was too cynical to accept that for truth. She did not know him well enough to judge him accurately. He had been cruel and callous in ways she did not know. "Your faith in me is misplaced, Saint Lucy. You don't know enough of me to know my worth—or lack thereof. I applaud your faith in humanity, by which you presume I possess some value, but I assure you there is very little about me that is noble or admirable."

"That's ridiculous," she said, matter-of-factly rejecting his declaration. "You are not without flaws"—she cast him a speaking glance—"self-pity for one—but we all are flawed. I like you. And I want nothing from you."

"But you want a chaperone to visit your antiquities."

"I planned to have Agnes to accompany me. You are here to allay Emma's concerns."

He lifted his brows and eyed her dubiously.

"I do like you," she said. "I think you are clever and brutally honest. There is honor and kindness in so much honesty. And practicality. I am especially partial to practicality as a trait in others." She grinned up at him victoriously, as though she had won the challenge by proving he was indeed a likable person.

Yet as she smiled brightly up at him, her blue eyes glinting in the sunlit room and her hair like golden strands of pure heavenly light, he was the one who felt triumphant.

Chapter Thirteen

"I cannot tell you, Lady Constance," Lucy said, sharing tea with the comtesse after her first rehearsal with Madame Castellini, "what a great honor it is to provide accompaniment for such a monumental talent. At times, I was so caught up in the beauty of her voice, I found it difficult to concentrate on my own playing. I only hope I shall not falter during the performance."

Lady Constance waved this concern away without hesitation. "You shall be perfect, *ma petite*. I heard no falter in your music during this afternoon's practice and there shall be none on the day either, I am confident. Besides," she said, bringing the teacup to her lips, "we shall have another rehearsal on Monday next. Once you have had more time with her, you will not be intimidated. It's a pity she could not stay for tea."

"Yes, that would have been nice," Lucy said, though she could not imagine ever feeling unflustered by the dominating presence of Madame Castellini. She was tall, with strikingly dark looks. Her talent and her entire manner commanded attention.

"In fact," Lady Constance continued, "you will have another opportunity to know her better tomorrow. Are you committed tomorrow?" she asked.

"Not unless Emma requires me. I must be conscious of my commitment to the duchess, of course."

"I think the duchess is more concerned with her commitment to you, *ma petite*, as she has assured me you are free to practice as much as necessary without any concern for her own convenience."

"I see. And when did she convey this?" Lucy asked the question, but she did not doubt the truth of the woman's claim. She knew that was precisely what Emma would say, if she were present.

Lady Constance adjusted herself on the divan. "In a letter I received this morning. She thanked me graciously for keeping you entertained for her during her convalescence."

Lucy laughed lightly at Emma's choice of words. "She has painted herself as an invalid." In truth, with the exception of tiring easily and the occasional bout of nausea, Emma was very much her usual self. "Well, if Emma is so determined to have rid of me, it appears I am free as a bird tomorrow, Lady Constance. Would you like to have another rehearsal?"

She shook her head. "No. Tomorrow is for the fitting, *ma petite*."

"The fitting?"

"Why the dress fitting, of course."

Lucy was sure how to respond. Surely Lady Constance did not mean to purchase her a gown for the performance.

"Did Emma arrange for this?" she asked, as soon as the thought occurred to her. It would be entirely predictable of Emma to have decided Lucy required a new dress and to have schemed with Lady Constance instead of addressing it with Lucy directly. Of course, Lucy would have declined, and Emma would have known that.

"This has nothing to do with the duchess, *ma petite*. My arrangement with Madame Castellini stipulates that I shall provide her with appropriate attire for her performance and I shall do the same for you."

"Lady Constance, I cannot possibly allow you to purchase a new gown for me. I agreed to play for no recompense other than to be of help to you and perhaps display my abilities to prospective employers. I cannot accept such a gift. I'm sure I have something perfectly appropriate among the dresses I already—"

Lady Constance silenced her with a slash of an open-palmed hand. "I shall hear none of these objections," she said in a tone that was at once kind and entirely resolute. "There are expectations as to the caliber of entertainments I will provide and I intend for my guests to be suitably impressed by all aspects of the display, including you."

"I'm sure it won't signify what I wear," Lucy said. "Madame Castellini will be the focus of attention."

"*Ma petite*, I have been living among the French for three decades, so I am a particular authority when I tell you that what you choose to wear will always signify." Lady Constance straightened her shoulders as though imparting a lesson of paramount importance. "Madame Castellini will amaze, but you will draw notice as well. You shall be the second-most-interesting person in the room, and we shall outfit you accordingly."

Lucy smiled uncomfortably at Lady Constance. Attending an event populated with highborn lords and ladies was difficult enough. Drawing all of their attention was a daunting prospect.

There was an officious rap on the parlor door and a butler entered to present Lady Constance with a calling card on a silver tray. She examined it.

"Shall I convey the message that you are occupied, my lady?" he asked without inflection.

"Not at all," Lady Constance responded, a suspiciously merry twinkle in her eye. "Ladies always enjoy the company of a pleasant gentleman."

She turned to Lucy and winked conspiratorially. Lucy, unsure what to make of the gesture, smiled back as though sharing in the fun, but did not feel the same merriment. Any gentleman who might call upon Lady Constance would not be happy to find Lucy there to intrude upon their time.

Lady Constance might be well past the age of blushing debutantes and young bucks, but she was still a handsome woman who possessed a strong English pedigree, a French title, and—if rumors and appearances were true—a substantial fortune. She might very likely have drawn the attention of a widower or two. Surely no gentleman caller would be pleased to share her attention.

"Perhaps I should be returning to Worley House," Lucy said, beginning to rise.

"Nonsense. Sit back down, dear." The words were spoken so brusquely that Lucy obeyed. She also noticed the comtesse had called her "dear" instead of the French endearments of "*ma petite*" or "*ma chere,*" which generally peppered her speech.

The door opened again and Lucy looked up to take the measure of this gentleman caller who had put the glitter in her new friend's eyes. She had not expected the man to be young.

She certainly had not expected him to be familiar.

"Ah, Mr. Brantwood. So kind of you to take time from your busy, young life to remember a lonely, old woman."

He flashed a wide grin of white teeth that seemed less sardonic than any smile Lucy had ever received from him. She was immediately suspicious.

"You are a shameful liar and far too wicked to ever be lonely," he said chidingly as he took both hands offered by Lady Constance and beamed at her. "Benson already informed me you have another guest."

Mr. Brantwood turned to face Lucy and laughed heartily, whether at her identity or her disapproving expression, she could not be certain.

"Miss Betancourt," he exclaimed. "Aren't you a delightful surprise? And here I was worried I should have to behave for your guest," he said aside to Lady Constance. "But Miss Betancourt is practically family. She knows all my faults and tolerates me anyway."

Lucy felt unaccountably stung by his words. Was he teasing her? Telling Bex that she found him likable despite his faults had been genuinely meant. Now, he tossed her words playfully back at her as though they were of very little consequence. Yet the playfulness was not really directed at her. Oddly, his flirtatiousness was directed at Lady Constance.

Lady Constance?

"Well, Mr. Brantwood, if dear Miss Betancourt has found the good in you, I shan't question it, but I will say, for my part, I have seen nothing about you that isn't devilish." With that declaration, she beamed back at him as though she had just proclaimed him the most chivalrous of knights.

What in heaven's name had happened here? Lucy had been present when Bex had been introduced to Lady Constance. How had they become such great friends? Lady Constance, she observed, was clearly pleased and not so very surprised that Bex had called. He must have called before—on multiple occasions, perhaps.

But...

No.

A thought leapt into Lucy's mind, and she immediately attempted to dismiss it. It couldn't be. It simply couldn't be.

But the thought refused to be dismissed. Hadn't he admitted to her that his father wanted him to marry a wealthy widow to rescue their family from financial distress? She fumed. How dare he? He had taken complete leave of his senses, not to mention any last shred of decency, if he had any thought of marrying a woman so advanced in age compared with himself. He might be cynical and jaded, but he was honest—or so she had believed. There was no honesty in this. He could not possibly be fostering genuine affection for a woman perhaps thirty years his elder.

Lady Constance urged Bex to sit and bent to pour him a cup of tea. Lucy caught Bex's gaze over their host's bent head and widened her eyes meaningfully.

His shoulders lifted and he gave a slight shake of his head as though he could not discern her meaning.

Silently, she mouthed, "Why are you here?"

He gave another shrug, this time accompanied by a look of innocent confusion.

Liar, she thought; but Lady Constance lifted her attention from the teapot, so Lucy could not continue the surreptitious conversation.

"I apologize, but I'm afraid this pot is barely tepid and not fit to serve. I will have more hot water brought for you." Lady Constance looked back down at the teapot disapprovingly, as though the impertinent pot had willfully become too cold.

She rose to cross to the bellpull, so manners dictated that Bex rise as well. He moved to stand near Lucy's side. "What is it?" he hissed.

Lucy looked up and speared him with her most punishing gaze. She had very little practice with disapproving looks, but she sincerely hoped this one was sufficiently severe. "Are you actually trying to court a woman at least a score of years older than you are?" she asked, being careful to keep her voice low enough so that only Bex would hear.

Her accusation only seemed to amuse Bex, which incensed her further.

"It shouldn't be but a moment," Lady Constance said, returning to seat herself in one of the French rococo armchairs that flanked the sofa. The gilded, feminine chair seemed an appropriate throne from which the comtesse could preside over social calls.

Bex sat as well and Lucy glowered at him.

He smirked cheerfully at her.

Lucy could not entirely account for the extent of her disappointment. She had no particular visions of Bexley Brantwood as a gallant knight, but she had been thoroughly convinced of his distaste for his father's proposed remedy to his financial ills.

"Do not let me interrupt your visit, ladies. Do continue on with whatever matter you were discussing before I arrived," Bex urged.

"We were discussing a performance I am hosting," Lady Constance informed him, the excitement returning to her eyes. "Madame Castellini is an Italian soprano of international renown."

"I've not heard of Madame Castellini," Bex said, "but I will admit my tastes are generally not so cultured as to include the Italian operas."

Lady Constance smiled indulgently at this admission. "You are a heathen, and I shall consider it my personal obligation to undertake your education in the arts, Mr. Brantwood."

"I believe Mr. Brantwood is being false," Lucy said abruptly, drawing a sharp gaze from Bex. He lifted his brow. She could feel the dare in his expression. She should reveal him.

"Do explain," Lacy Constance asked, leaning forward in her seat.

"Mr. Brantwood may not be familiar with the opera, specifically, but I can assure you he is very cultured. He was my personal guide at the British Museum just two days ago and proved exceedingly knowledgeable on the various installations there." She returned Bex's curious gaze with a sweetly innocent smile. "He was particularly knowledgeable regarding the snakes and lizards."

Masculine coal-gray eyes widened but instead of seeming chastened, admiration for her teasing barb lifted the corners of his lips. She felt the beginnings of a flush, despite her present dissatisfaction with him.

Lady Constance inclined her head as though desiring a more thorough examination of Bex in light of this information. "How fascinating. Have you always had an interest in nature and antiquities, Mr. Brantwood?"

"I have an interest in spending time out of the house, Lady Constance. My father and I are often at odds."

"I believe that is expected between parents and children, is it not?"

"If that is the case, my father and I are particularly competent," Bex responded.

"My condolences, sir. How tiring. I have no children of my own, and so must pester young people belonging to other parents," she said, encompassing both Lucy and Bex in her apologetic expression.

"I don't feel pestered in the least," Bex assured her. "I find your company immensely entertaining, Lady Constance."

"You are a consummate flatterer, Mr. Brantwood," the comtesse said, appearing, despite her words, to have been thoroughly flattered.

Lucy found the entire situation abhorrent. She wanted no part in Bexley Brantwood's mercenary schemes and she was inexplicably hurt to have been so deceived in his character.

She should not be hurt. He had explicitly warned her that he was a cad, yet she had believed better of him.

She had been so certain that all of London would think her unsophisticated because she had spent her life in the country. To learn they were correct in such a judgment because she had been so easily fooled in the true nature of Bex's character smarted in the manner of lemon in a cut.

She had actually believed, for all his claims to the contrary, that he possessed a modicum of honor and integrity. How positively rustic of her.

At once, she felt an incredible urgency to be out of his company. She rose to her feet. "I do thank you for the tea, Lady Constance, and for the opportunity to rehearse with Madame Castellini, but I believe it is time for me to take my leave. The duchess is more in need of my assistance than she will sometimes concede. I hate to be gone for too long."

Bex rose when she did. He watched her closely. She thought he might say something—rather sensed he was about to, but in the end he remained silent. Surely, he would not object to her departure when she was giving him the thing for which he had come—time alone with his prey.

Lady Constance pouted at her. "If you must, *ma petite*, but mind you are awaiting my carriage tomorrow afternoon. I shall collect you promptly at half past one."

"Certainly," Lucy agreed with a nod. She turned and left the room, taking great effort to do so sedately, even though she really wanted to lift her skirts and hurry away as quickly as her legs would take her.

Chapter Fourteen

Lucy was ready, as promised, for her dress appointment at the exclusive shop of Madame Desmarais, despite voicing objections to both Emma and Lady Constance over the unnecessary expenditure on her behalf. Madame Castellini arrived separately at the modiste's shop approximately one half hour past the appointed time. When one was a renowned opera singer, one could do such things. As the appointment was not the first fitting for the opera singer, Madame Desmarais suggested she try her gown first, directing the elegant woman to a small room off the main shop while Lucy sat with Lady Constance awaiting the reveal of the garment.

"Madame Desmarais has assured me this gown will be unrivaled," Lady Constance said, delight shining through her features.

Lucy responded with a halfhearted smile. She was happy Lady Constance took such joy in the process, and certainly would have smiled *whole*heartedly, if not for her concerns. She wanted to warn Lady Constance of her suspicions regarding Bex's intentions, but how could she? Surely, the sophisticated comtesse would take offense at the notion that she could be so easily manipulated. Perhaps, Lucy thought, she should remember that as well. Lady Constance had seen a lot of society. Had she not cautioned Lucy about trusting others and mistaking true friends? Lucy very much wanted to convince herself of this reasoning, but she kept remembering how elated the woman was at Bex's arrival and how she responded to his flirtations.

Certainly Lady Constance had family who would make certain she was protected from fortune hunters, hadn't she?

With no way of asking the question outright, Lucy began more indirectly. "If I recall," she said, turning to the comtesse, "your nephew is Lord Marbury. Is he in London, then, for the session of parliament?"

"He is," Lady Constance said, but for once, she was decidedly concise.

"You must forgive my lack of fluency regarding the peerage, but where are the Marbury holdings?" Lucy asked, trying to continue the discussion.

"When my father was earl, there were holdings all through Britain," Lady Constance said, puffing with pride at the statement, "but the primary estate in is Derbyshire."

"I see," Lucy said. "Will you retire to the country with your nephew's family once the season has ended?"

Lady Constance laughed heartily at Lucy's question, bringing a hand to her chest. "What a surprise that would be," she said, her eyes bright with mischief, "if I appeared on my nephew's doorstep demanding to take up residence like some long-forgotten dowager countess."

"But surely your family…"

"It's sweet of you to think so, *ma petite*, but my nephew has not seen me in three decades and is unlikely to recall that he has ever met me at all. I am little more to him than an entry in the family Bible, I am sure."

"So you have not seen him since you returned to England?" Lucy asked, despite the fact that the question had already been answered.

"He is a very busy man," Lady Constance said. "For one so young, he has high political ambitions. He could be prime minister one day." Her chest swelled again with this claim.

Lucy admired her for it, this obvious pride in a nephew who'd not even found the time to visit his aging, childless aunt. "Have you invited him the concert?" she asked.

"Of course, but I do not expect that he shall be able to attend."

"I'm sorry," Lucy said quietly.

"Whatever for, *ma petite*?"

"It's obvious you care for him a great deal, even if you do not see him regularly. I am sorry that he has not found the opportunity to call on you."

"Ah, that was always the way. Boys never pay attention to these things and growing into men rarely changes them. His sister, now, she was always very attentive. An excellent letter writer. I received a thank-you letter for every gift I ever sent to Annabelle and a thoughtful reply to every letter. She and I corresponded quite frequently for years."

Well, at least there was a niece to pay attention for fortune hunters. "She must be very glad that you have returned to England, then," Lucy said, brightening with this better news.

Lady Constance smiled, but it was wistful and her eyes held sadness.

Lucy hesitated. She considered what she might say next. Because Lady Constance so valued plain speaking, she chose to be direct. "Is something amiss with your niece, Lady Constance?"

The lady sighed. "I do hope not."

Lucy would have asked another question, but Madame Castellini emerged from behind the dressing screen at that moment. "Do you like the gown?" the singer asked in heavily accented English.

"Ah, Madame Desmarais," Lady Constance exclaimed. *"La robe est très belle. Magnifique."* She turned to Lucy. "Isn't the signora stunning in this gown?"

"Absolutely stunning," Lucy agreed, admiring the rich gown of deep burgundy with a wide, lace-trimmed collar. Even more stunning than the color of the signora's dress was the hem. It consisted of a wide band of the same fabric, with evenly spaced slashes through which had been pulled billowed puffs of contrasting gauze net in pale coral. It reminded Lucy of the slashed sleeves she had seen in drawings of medieval gowns. "What an uncommon hem," she exclaimed. "It's very pretty."

"Isn't it?" Lady Constance asked.

"With so much decoration at the bottom of my dress, I should be afraid to walk out of doors," Lucy said.

Lady Constance shook her head in vehement objection to Lucy's observation. "No self-respecting French woman is wearing a plain hem these days. The more adorned the better, I say. If you want to appear at the pinnacle of fashion, you must emulate the French. They have a heightened sense of these things. Everyone knows this, *ma chere*."

Madame Castellini nodded sagely. "This is true."

Lucy was not included as everyone, it seemed, for she had not, in fact, known this. She always had limited funds with which to produce and adorn her own dresses, which were not great in number. She could recall with vivid clarity the many times her mother had told her, "Anything below the bust is a waste of good ribbon, dear. Draw the eyes upward." So it would seem her mother was also out of fashion.

Madame Desmarais held a bolt of pale peach fabric next to the singer in her burgundy gown. "This will be very complementary for Miss Betancourt's dress, no?"

As much as Lucy admired the rich burgundy gown made for Madame Castellini, she had known the dressmaker would not propose such a rich color for her dress. Jewel tones were for women such as the signora, whose rich coloring was complemented by the boldness of the gown. Lucy's delicate complexion was more suited to subtle colors and she had lived her life in a palette of soft hues—blush and mint and sky. She mentally added apricot to the list.

"There are beautiful ways of decorating your hem. Allow me to show you some sketches, Miss Betancourt." With that, the dressmaker lay the bolt of fabric on a table and pulled a large bound book from underneath. She spread it open in Lucy's lap, displaying the promised illustrations of various decorated hems.

In the end, the ladies decided upon an embroidered hem for Lucy's concert gown. The dressmaker quickly sketched a design of autumn-colored vines that would contrast the pale peach of Lucy's dress while at the same time complementing the richer burgundy gown of the evening's true star.

"You shall have to return for another fitting, Miss Betancourt," said Madame Desmarais. "I shall not need to see the signora again, but we are just beginning your gown. I shall need to see you in one week." She turned to Lady Constance. "Will that be acceptable, Madame Comtesse?"

"*Oui*," the comtesse responded. "*Nous avons dix jours.*"

The dressmaker smiled at her satisfied customer. "*C'est parfait.*"

* * * *

After the fitting, Lady Constance returned Lucy to Worley House in her carriage and Lucy used the opportunity to press further regarding the comtesse's family in the hopes she would find some reassurance that this woman who lived surrounded by people had someone who was loyal enough to truly look after her interests.

"Lady Constance," Lucy said, "I hope you will not find me impertinent, but I sense that your niece may be a troubling subject for you. I hope you will accept my sincere apologies for my questions earlier."

Lady Constance laughed. "Oh, Lucy, *ma petite*, never apologize for being sincere. Impertinent questions are the only ones worth asking. All the rest are just polite noise." She patted Lucy's hand. "I appreciate your concern on my behalf." She released a burdened sigh. "I suppose I am troubled by my niece."

"I should be happy to listen if you would like to share your trouble," Lucy said.

Lady Constance smiled, but there was no happiness behind it. "As I told you before, my niece and I were quite close in letters, though we met only a few times. From the time that she was twelve or thirteen, we have written frequently to each other. When she married three years ago, however, her letters became different. And less frequent. I sensed that her husband did not approve of our correspondence."

"And now," Lucy asked, "do you sense the same disapproval in her letters?"

Lady Constance turned her face to watch the sights of London through her carriage window. "I have not received a letter from Annabelle in more than a year."

"Oh, Lady Constance, I am so sorry to hear it. Have you written her, then? And she knows you are in England?"

The comtesse lifted her chin and pursed her lips. "I have written a letter to my niece every week for eleven years. This husband may prevent Annabelle from responding, but he will not keep me from writing."

No indeed. Lucy could not imagine it. Every week for a year and no reply. "Do you think she receives your letters?" Lucy asked. "If he does not approve of you, would he intercept them? Destroy them?"

"I have no way of knowing the answer to that question."

"If you don't mind my asking, why doesn't he approve of you?" Lucy asked.

Lady Constance lifted her shoulders imperiously. "I imagine if he is the sort of man who would not allow his wife to correspond with her own family, then I likely possess a great many traits of which he would not approve. I am surely too outspoken, too French, too independent. I agree with the man in one respect: If he prefers a meek and malleable wife, I should be a corrupting influence, indeed." Her color deepened as she spoke, her voice rising with her indignation. "Annabelle was a very spirited girl. I shudder to guess what measures such a dominating husband might take to quell that spirit."

Lucy could very well guess that if Annabelle shared a bloodline with Lady Constance, she could indeed be a very spirited and determined woman. How frightening, to ponder what the circumstances might be. "One always imagines the worst when there is uncertainty," Lucy said, offering what reassurance she could. "I'm sure things are not so bleak as you fear."

If only Lady Constance could be reassured of that. If only there were a way for her to know.

Lucy paused.

"Is that why you've returned to England?" Lucy asked. "To look after your niece's welfare?"

"One must always look after family, *ma petite*."

Lucy nodded silently. She thought about the gossip she had heard at the Ashbys' dinner party. How very misunderstood this woman was from what everyone believed. "Is she in London?" Lucy asked.

"She is not in London. Her husband has a small estate in Hertfordshire."

"How will you look after her if you cannot write?" Lucy pressed.

Lady Constance sighed heavily. "I had hoped, now that I am residing in England, she might have an opportunity to reach out to me. I have not been subtle in my return to society. If she corresponds with her brother, or anyone else in London for that matter, she must know I've arrived."

"But you have not received word from her?"

"No, I have not." Lady Constance pursed her lips. "She is not my child, after all, and it is probably not my place to interfere. Yet I find I am unable to let it rest until I can at least be assured he has not done her any real harm."

Lucy shook her head, wondering at the anxiety the older woman must feel in not knowing. "So what shall you do?" she asked.

"I imagine I shall just have to witness her condition in person. Hertfordshire is not far."

"You will travel to her, then?"

"The travel is already arranged. I depart the day after tomorrow and shall return the following day."

Lucy could not imagine what it must be like. Worrying for a loved one from across the channel must have been difficult, but being as close as Hertfordshire and not knowing must be torturous. She bit her lip. "What if he does not allow you to see her?" she asked, then immediately regretted the question. She did not wish to add to the woman's concerns.

"I imagine I shall have to engage in a tantrum on his doorstep. Of course, that will not likely improve our opinion of each other, will it?"

Lucy was quiet for a long moment. How disappointing that would be—to come so far only to be turned away. There had to be some better way.

She looked up at the other woman, thoughts whirling. "What if someone else were to call upon your niece, Lady Constance?" As soon as she'd spoken, she realized the flaw in this approach. "I realize a call by a stranger would be impractical, but what if she were to develop a ruse of some sort? She could be soliciting donations for the church or some other cause."

Lady Constance pursed her lips in consideration. "I very much want to see my niece with my own eyes," she said, "but I will concede your subterfuge may be more successful than my infantile tantrum." She gave a succinct nod. "Yes. That may be a very clever plan, *ma petite*. Very clever." She settled back into her seat then and reached down to smooth her skirts as though they had been discussing the weather in the park, or their dressmaking appointment. "Will you accompany me on my journey into Hertfordshire, then?"

Lucy's eyes widened. She hadn't meant that *she* should call upon the woman. "I…Lady Constance, I don't think…that is to say, I don't know…" She stopped, swallowed, and began again. "Surely there would be someone more appropriate than I to call upon your niece."

"Nonsense. You are perfect," the comtesse said, waving her hand as though the objection were a tangible thing and she could clear it away. "The idea was yours to begin with. Your father is a country vicar. You are exactly the sort of girl who might be traipsing across the countryside soliciting donations for the church or some other charitable cause. I would venture to say you've already done such a thing in your young life."

Well she had. Of course she had, but not outside of the sphere within which she was known—never outside of her father's parish. "I don't know," Lucy hedged. "I don't believe I should be very skilled at subterfuge. What if I am found out?"

Lady Constance smiled benevolently. "Well, I should think that is the point. If you are to learn anything of significance about Annabelle, you must eventually reveal that you have visited at my request. The ruse simply gets you past the threshold, *ma chere*."

Lucy felt her stomach tighten, anxiety already building at the thought of carrying out such a scheme. Although she was admittedly untested, she felt quite certain she would prove horrible at pretense. She hated the very thought of it.

But of course, she had proposed it, hadn't she? She thought of all the comtesse had already done—uprooted her life out of concern for her niece—and guilt suffused her for her cowardice. If Lady Constance could return to England after decades away, surely Lucy could manage an afternoon of playacting in order to come to her aid. Couldn't she? How much more difficult than charades could this truly be?

"I shall do it," she said with a firm nod of decision. "I will speak with the duchess, but I am certain she can spare my company for a pair of days when the purpose is so worthy."

Gratitude and relief flooded the older woman's expression, solidifying Lucy's resolve to do just as she had promised. The comtesse reached out to squeeze Lucy's hand with her own. "*Merci, ma petite*," she said, her voice quiet and wavering.

Lucy squeezed the hand in return and watched as the emotion was suppressed as quickly as it had been revealed.

Lady Constance lifted her chin and pursed her lips again. "Once I discover whether she requires my assistance," she said, spirit flashing in her ageless eyes, "I shall determine how best to provide it."

Lucy nodded. "She is very fortunate to have an aunt such as yourself."

Lady Constance smiled, and winked at Lucy, the laughter returning to her eyes. "Indeed," she said, squaring her shoulders. "We shall have a lovely concert on Friday next, but first we shall have some adventure."

Chapter Fifteen

Lucy was again waiting in the front hall of Worley House, this time her small valise by her side, when the comtesse's carriage arrived. It was a grand conveyance—not the vehicle in which Lucy had been collected for the dressmaker's appointment, but one designed for comfort on longer journeys. It was, Lucy noted, nearly as grand as those that bore the Worley crest.

It occurred to her, as she descended the steps of Worley House, that a woman soliciting contributions for a charity would not usually be traveling the countryside in such a luxurious vehicle. She considered possible alternatives to overcome this obvious complication as she accepted the aiding hand of the liveried coachman and began her climb into the vehicle.

"Good morning, Miss Betancourt."

Her eyes snapped up at the sound of the deep, male voice welcoming her into the vehicle, though she knew its possessor before her eyes landed upon him in the dim interior.

Bex Brantwood.

Lucy stumbled on the step and had to tighten her grip on the coachman's arm. Thankfully, he felt her falter and swiftly prevented disaster by placing his other hand on her back. She shot him a grateful smile.

Once safely inside, she seated herself next to Lady Constance on the forward-facing seat and looked between the two occupants. "Good morning Lady Constance, Mr. Brantwood." She smiled expectantly. Surely some explanation would be forthcoming, would it not?

When it was not immediately offered, impatience got the better of her and she looked to the comtesse. "Has there been an alteration of our plans?"

"Just a bit, *ma chere*," Lady Constance said. "I will admit I was considering our ruse for you and decided it is improbable that anyone calling on my niece and her husband to solicit contributions might be unfamiliar to them. More likely, it would be someone from the rectory, or nearby orphanage, or some other local institution, don't you agree?"

She did agree, but she didn't see where that necessitated the company of Mr. Brantwood. She shot him an accusing look.

He responded with a questioning lift of his brows.

Lady Constance continued. "Well, I decided we needed a different story for you altogether." She turned to smile at Bex. "Mr. Brantwood was kind enough to call upon me yesterday and he happened to mention he had business in Hertfordshire. It seemed too convenient a coincidence to dismiss, so I explained our purpose in traveling there and gained his cooperation." She looked to Lucy again. "I do think this shall be so much better."

"I see," Lucy said. She looked at Bex, where he sat across from her, appearing every bit the carefree gentleman traveler. Had he not earlier that week declared to her that he was a man with no purpose—that he had no business anywhere, much less Hertfordshire? His business was to prey upon the unsuspecting comtesse, she was sure of it. Had he no shame?

She looked into his eyes and wondered at the gall of the man, that he could unflinchingly meet her gaze. "And how will Mr. Brantwood be cooperating?" she asked the comtesse, though her hold of Bex's eyes never wavered.

"We have decided it is much more practical for you and Mr. Brantwood to pretend to be a married couple who encounter some difficulty, such as trouble with your carriage. It would be entirely expected for you to impose upon their hospitality while the coachman sees to the repair."

Lucy turned to Lady Constance at that revelation, feeling her cheeks warm. "You are suggesting that Mr. Brantwood and I pose as husband and wife?"

Lady Constance smiled brightly. "It's a much better story, don't you agree?"

The smile Lucy returned was considerably more tremulous. "That is clever," she said, turning to Bex as she spoke. Too clever by half.

A slow, sinking feeling began to develop in Lucy's midsection as she looked between her two companions. There was irony, she was certain, in the fact that Lady Constance was seeking out her family for her niece's protection, when the lady herself was in need of family to protect her from fortune hunters. It seemed, if that family was not of a mind to concern themselves with their aunt, the task must fall to Lucy.

She leaned back in her seat and faced the window, taking in the sights as the busy movements of town gave way to views of green spaces and leaf-laden trees.

Adventure, indeed.

* * * *

"Tell me, Mr. Brantwood," Lucy said, once they were well outside the noise of the city, "what is your business in Hertfordshire?" She suspected his business would have been in York, if that had been the comtesse's destination, but she waited politely for his answer just the same.

He looked up from the newspaper he had been studying and smiled cryptically at her in a way that made her feel at once warmed and annoyed. "Textiles, Miss Betancourt."

"Textiles?" she repeated, incredulous. That was the best explanation he could provide?

"That is correct. My business in Hertfordshire is textiles."

"I see." What she saw most was that he was a much more skilled liar than she would ever be, but still not good enough. Who was intended to believe this nonsensical explanation? "Are you making a purchase, then, Mr. Brantwood? Of textiles?" She resisted the urge to lift her eyes heavenward. He'd had all night to concoct some legitimate business. The result had been a single, vague word?

"No."

When he did not expound, she pressed, "What sort of textiles? Silk, perhaps?" She considered him. Perhaps he thought to convince Lady Constance he was not a fortune hunter by creating the appearance that he did, in fact, have business interests.

Bex folded the newspaper and set it on the seat beside him. "Cotton," he said simply.

Lucy's gaze narrowed. So he had concocted *two* words for Lady Constance, but what of her? He could not have forgotten that barely a week prior he had told her quite clearly that he was a man with no living or income. Would he lie to her face now, in front of Lady Constance?

Lucy straightened in her seat. "I wasn't aware your family had any business interests in Hertfordshire," she said, working to keep her tone light and her expression placid.

"My family does not," he said, crossing his arms over his chest and gazing at her quizzically. "That is to say, my father does not. I cannot speak for the duke, of course. I have no knowledge of his holdings. I am sure they are quite vast, but they have nothing to do with me."

Lucy pounced. "If you are not making a purchase of textiles and your family has no holdings, what precisely brings you to Hertfordshire, Mr. Brantwood?"

"I have a small, speculative investment in a weaving operation in Watford."

Lucy paused. She looked at him. His response had been surprisingly specific for a man fabricating a story. "A speculative investment?" she asked, and this time it was curiosity as much as suspicion that prompted the question.

"Indeed."

Lucy heard the sound of a small sigh to her left that drew her attention to Lady Constance. Clearly, although Lucy had been caught up in her line of questions for Bex, the comtesse had not been paying the close attention she would have hoped. Indeed, the other woman's eyes fluttered closed as Lucy watched her gradually lean into the corner, lulled into ever-deeper slumber by the steady, rocking motion of the carriage.

Lucy waited, listening for the rhythmic breaths that verified sleep, before she turned back to face the man who sat on the opposite bench. "What do you think you're doing," she hissed, quietly enough not to disturb their sleeping hostess.

He snapped to attention, his brow furrowing at her question. "Traveling to Hertfordshire?" He spoke it as a question—as though her tone had called his own understanding into doubt.

"Why are you traveling to Hertfordshire?" she whispered. "Why are you calling on Lady Constance so often?"

His mouth curved into a knowing grin and one brow arched sardonically. "Saint Lucy, are you envious for my attentions?"

"Of course I am not envious," she whispered, checking quickly to see that the comtesse was not disturbed, "particularly as I know your attentions are false."

Bex's brows rose at the accusation. "How am I being false?"

She cut him her severest look.

He chuckled softly. "Oh no, you don't. Don't practice governessing on me, Saint Lucy," he said. "Not when I've no idea what I've done to deserve a scolding."

Lucy looked to Lady Constance again, wishing he would lower his voice until she'd managed to say what needed saying. When she was certain the woman was still asleep, she turned back to Bex and did not waste time. "If your father continues to insist you play the fortune hunter, you shall have to find your prey elsewhere." She crossed her arms in front of her chest and glared at him, daring him to deny it.

He did not.

He laughed. He at least had the presence of mind to recall their companion and did so quietly, his shoulders shaking with silent mirth.

It rankled, all the same.

"You don't even deny it," she hissed through gritted teeth.

He placed his open palm on his chest as his laughter subsided. "You'll have to excuse me," he said, grinning crookedly at her. "I was too diverted to compose denials." He leaned forward, resting one forearm on each knee. "Do you really think I am advancing my suit of the comtesse?" he whispered.

She glared in response and he shook his head. "Oh, Saint Lucy, what a devil you must believe me to be."

Lucy did not see the humor in taking advantage of another person, particularly not one who had been so friendly and welcoming to them both. "You are worse than a devil if you are trying to convince her of your affection for her," she said, leaning forward herself to ensure he could hear the quietly spoken words.

A grin tugged at the corner of his lips as he asked, "Are you certain you are not envious, dear? We do have a history, you and I."

She cut him a look. "No, I am not envious. I am concerned for a friend—a friend for whom *I* have genuine affection." Lucy ignored the very clear memory from earlier that week when Bex had called upon Lady Constance. Surely the sting of betrayal she'd felt at his arrival was due to his dishonesty—not envy. They were friends, after all—at least she'd believed him worthy of friendship.

Now she didn't know what to believe about him.

She leaned toward him. "Have you no shame? She is more than twice your age."

He looked placidly at her then blinked, twice. "Are you finished?"

She pressed her lips into a grim line, considering how to respond—recovering control of her response. She took a deep breath and exhaled it. "Only if you have finished with this deception," she said primly, feeling very much like the governess he had accused her of being.

Bex lifted his hand and tapped one finger on the tip of her nose. The action was complete before she could have responded, or else she would have batted the hand away. As it was, she immediately retreated backward into her seat.

He chuckled, soft and low. "Rest easy, Saint Lucy. It is finished because it never began."

She glanced again at the slumbering comtesse. "You deny you have an ulterior motive in calling on her—in inserting yourself into this journey into Hertfordshire?"

He shrugged. "I enjoy her company because she is clever, and irreverent, and because she tolerates me despite my utter lack of good manners."

Lucy watched him, unconvinced.

"But," he added, his mouth widening to a self-deprecating grin, "I told you before that I was an opportunist. I do gain advantage from our association."

Lucy shot forward in her seat again. "What advantage?" she whispered sharply.

Bex tilted his head to one side. "I am not courting the comtesse, but where is the harm in letting my father believe it for a time if it provides me some peace?"

Relief spread swiftly through Lucy—relief that may have been disproportionate were it solely on behalf of the comtesse. She did not want to consider other possible explanations for the sudden lightness she felt, so she said, perhaps more sharply than she intended, "You are still misleading her if the reasons for your friendship are false."

"I genuinely appreciate the comtesse. I've no desire to marry her, nor would I do her the discredit of believing she would be foolish enough to marry me. I find her an entertaining woman and I appreciate her philosophies."

"But you do find advantage in her friendship?" Lucy pressed, but her ire was already fading.

"And you do not?" he asked.

"I am not using Lady Constance for anything!" she blurted, then remembered herself. She lowered her voice to a whisper again and added, "I am helping her to reach out to her niece."

Bex eyed her dubiously. "Am I correct in my recollection that you are seeking a post as a governess or a music teacher?" he asked, then leaned back with a wry smile. "How fortuitous that your musical talents shall be so prominently displayed alongside Madame Castellini at the comtesse's concert."

Lucy's finger rose in protest. "I was not the one to suggest playing for the concert."

"But still, you benefit."

Lucy sighed. She lowered her chin. "I concede, Mr. Brantwood. Gaining advantage from a friendship does not necessarily prove that is the reason for said friendship."

He grinned at her then. "Now you, on the other hand, have no reason to doubt. I gain no advantage whatsoever from friendship with you. I simply find my day to be more interesting when it includes you."

Lucy warmed at the teasing compliment. "I could say the same of you, Mr. Brantwood," she said, lifting her eyes boldly to his.

He grinned widely. "Then we are safe from duplicitousness."

Unexpectedly, he winked at her. Then he coughed very loudly, rousing the sleeping comtesse, whose eyes fluttered open while she righted herself from her leaning position.

"What were you saying?" she asked, rubbing her chin absently. "I don't believe I heard the last bit."

Bex smiled conspiratorially at Lucy as he answered the question. "I was just speaking to Miss Betancourt about my father."

Lady Constance huffed. "Idiotic man." She rearranged herself again in the seat and looked at Lucy. "Can you believe that doddering old fool wanted this one"—she pointed at Bex—"to trick me into a marriage to solve his financial troubles?"

Lucy stared at her then turned to Bex in utter shock. He had *told* Lady Constance?

Bex's eyes glinted merrily in the dim light of the carriage interior as he met her surprised gaze.

"Can you believe it?" Lady Constance asked her, shaking her head. She laughed then, her entire form quaking with it, and brought a hand to her chest as though she might calm herself. "I've been in France, not an asylum for the insane," she continued, her laughter ending on a drawn-out sigh.

"Indeed," Lucy said, not certain there was much else to say. Of course, she should have expected Lady Constance would find the entire thing entertaining.

"I wonder," Lady Constance said, mischief twinkling in her eyes, "what other sort of plots have been hatched to make use of my fortune." She pointed at Mr. Brantwood. "Your father can't be the only fool in London. I'm sure I've met at least a dozen or more and I've been in England less than three full months."

"No doubt you are correct, Lady Constance." Bex spoke to the comtesse, but his eyes were on Lucy, taking in her reaction to this development.

This time it was Lucy's turn to shrug.

Chapter Sixteen

Several hours later, Lucy realized her mistake. The revised plan as concocted by Bex and the comtesse required that their party travel to a coaching inn about an hour's ride from the home of the comtesse's niece. Lady Constance departed there so that Bex and Lucy could continue on the journey in their adopted identities as man and wife. Since she and Bex were to spend so much time alone together in a carriage, Lucy would have been safer believing he was a scheming fortune hunter. Since he was not, he was entirely too intriguing.

As Lucy always did when she was uncomfortable, she talked. Since she was with Bex, she asked him questions.

"Why were you looking for the card room the other evening, if you do not play cards?" she asked.

"I already answered that question: I was seeking a man—a man who *does* play cards—thus I thought he was likely there."

"And was he?"

Bex lifted a brow at her curiosity. "Yes, he was, despite the fact that I was waylaid in my effort to find him."

Lucy lowered her eyes. She had not meant to remind him—or herself—of that occasion. Warmth threaded through her at the memory. She coughed. "So, you are not a gambler, yourself," she said, knowing she was repeating herself, but needing to fill the void with words.

"I wager regularly."

Lucy's eyes lifted to his. "But I thought you said…"

The light in Bex's eyes changed, and she wondered at it. "There are many games on which to wager. All can draw you in and cause you to throw good money after bad."

"Have you thrown good money after bad?" she asked quietly.

"Since I borrowed the money to begin with, I don't know if it could be considered good money. I was young and drawn into the fun. I was an easy mark. I started with dice and cards, but eventually abandoned them for more interesting wagers."

Lucy was intrigued. "There are other games?" she asked. She supposed she should not be curious about the sort of games one might play while gambling. It was not very ladylike, but one of the best things about her odd relationship with this man was the fact that they seemed to have set propriety entirely aside.

"Not games, precisely. Investments. Schemes."

"I don't understand," Lucy said.

Bex paused as though contemplating how he might explain. "Your father is vicar in a small village, correct?" he asked, then at her nod continued. "Everyone in your village is probably doing what they have always done, farming and blacksmithing as they always have. The same is true for men like the duke. The gentry are living as they always have—managing their lands, posturing in the House of Lords, marrying off their children to everyone's advantage. There are others, though, who are changing. There are new machines and inventions that are allowing men, men with ideas, to become tradesmen in an entirely different way than they were before."

"You mean the manufactories. I've heard of a machine that punches buttons out of tin."

"That is exactly what I mean. There are lots of them in the north—more every day—and there are starting to be more near London as well. The trouble is that these new trades require more than ideas. They require money. How does an inventor build a machine if he cannot buy wheels and gears and wood and metal? Where does he put his machine if he has no building?"

"How do they get the money?" Lucy asked.

"They find investors—men with money who are willing to fund the enterprise now and collect their portion of profits later."

"So the men who have ideas and no money are matched with men who have money, but no ideas?"

Bex laughed. "I suppose yes, you could put it that way, although I don't know of many men who would want to be accused of having no ideas whatsoever in their heads."

"That seems like a good pairing," Lucy pointed out. "Where is the wager in it?"

"Not all men are the same. Men of means and reputation form companies. They can raise funds by selling shares in those companies on the exchange."

Lucy recalled hearing of the exchange, but she couldn't quite remember when. Perhaps the duke had referred to it. "So you buy shares of companies?" she asked.

"No."

"All right, now you have me confused."

Bex leaned forward, resting his elbows on his knees as he answered her. "As I said, not all men are the same. If a man is a blacksmith, or the son of a cook and a butler, he would not have the means or the connections to form a company and be listed on the exchange. These men start smaller, more humble operations, but they are still bringing great changes to the country."

Bex's eyes brightened as he spoke; his manner became earnest, almost urgent as he explained. Lucy couldn't help but watch him and be drawn into his excitement. "Wherever there is a need, there will be enterprising individuals to fill the void."

"What do they do?" Lucy asked. "Go to moneylenders?"

"These are not small amounts required to build machines and manufactories. There are men, however, who do the pairing you talked about. They put together contracts allowing men with ideas to receive money and men with money to wager on ideas."

"Is that really a wager?" Lucy asked. "It sounds like an investment."

"A highly speculative one. Not all ideas are good ideas," he said, his eyes steady on hers. "Some are even fraudulent."

"I see." She did not ask him if he had invested in fraudulent schemes. She did not have to ask. Hadn't he said he had wagered with borrowed funds? Losses meant no ability to repay. The debts would only grow, and his expected future income was gone. Lucy allowed the significance of this revelation to settle within her. Bex could be in a very deep hole indeed.

"I was naïve, bored with dice and cards, and intrigued by the entire process. Since I was expected to eventually inherit a dukedom, the moneylenders would give me enough credit to thoroughly ruin myself. I was drawn into the excitement in much the same way a man is unable to resist the spin of the roulette wheel. I was foolhardy." Bex shrugged as he said it, as though he had already put the regret behind him.

"So you don't wager any longer?" Lucy asked. Of course, he wouldn't, if what he had said was true. Who would take such risks, understanding the truth of them?

He smiled as though caught. "I don't recall saying that."

She looked up sharply. "You still gamble on these schemes?"

"Some wagers are pure luck. You can lose more easily than you can win. In certain games, however, the application of skill can improve the odds of winning."

She watched him warily. "And you have developed this skill?"

"That has been my aim."

The thought of Bex continuing to borrow and risk further debt on failed schemes made her sick to her stomach as though her own future were at stake. It all just seemed so reckless. "How have you developed this skill for identifying good ideas, precisely?"

"Because I have lost frequently enough to be good at it."

Now he was making no sense at all, and she told him so.

"Unlike some investors, who simply bore the news of the losses and went away empty handed, I took the time to make inquiries, to understand what had gone awry. I learned a great deal."

"So you know what an investment needs to succeed?" she asked.

"I've learned what makes an investment sure to fail. No one can know what will make one sure to succeed. There will always be unpredictable outcomes."

"What is it, then, that makes one sure to fail?"

Bex leaned back against the cushioned bench and crossed his arms in front of his chest. "A missing piece, generally."

His cryptic answers were more tease than explanation. "What *sort* of piece?"

"For an entrepreneurial scheme to have any chance of success, I've identified three necessary components. If one of the components is missing, failure is assured."

Lucy moved forward in her seat. "But what are the components?"

Bex laughed. "Does this actually interest you?"

"Of course," she said. "I am on pins and needles waiting to hear."

"Well, there must be sufficient expertise, whether that be a skilled engineer or craftsman. Little manufactories are popping up all over the countryside, but if you cannot build a machine that is reliable and effective, you cannot make a go of it."

"That seems to be common sense."

"It is, but my first investment was based on a machine that never actually worked. The idea was intriguing, but in the end, it never produced a single damned button."

"Well, someone's button machine worked. It's the one our blacksmith told my father about."

He gave her a scathing look. "How kind of you to let me know."

Lucy squelched a giggle. "What is the second piece?"

"Capital. There must be funds."

"But isn't that what you provide, when you invest?"

"I am not a wealthy man and I no longer have the credit of a future duke. The investments that I make are small. I am typically just one of many investors, but if the total investment needed is underestimated, and all of the money is spent before the enterprise produces a profit, everything can be lost."

Lucy nodded slowly, her brow furrowed in concentration as she considered this bit of insight. "I see. And what of the third piece?"

"The third piece is a sound plan—more specifically, a complete plan. There are many men with clever machines who never succeed. They haven't determined how to sell what they produce, or how to sell enough of it to repay their investors. In the most recent case..."

Bex stopped. He looked across at her and gave a sheepish smile. "But I must be boring you."

What he was doing was slowly killing her with suspense. "On the contrary," she declared vehemently. "I love nothing so much as a well-designed plan. There is something so sensibly reassuring in it."

Bex eyed her dubiously. "I don't know that our interactions have done much to convince me of your claimed predilection for all things practical and sensible."

"But you know I came to London to take a post as a governess; what could be more sensible than that?"

"Are you or are or you not currently unchaperoned with a man who is not your relation on your way to fake a carriage accident and enter the home of people whom you do not know under false pretenses?"

Lucy laughed. She smiled in exaggerated innocence. "Surely even a well-designed plan can go awry."

He laughed at her response. It was unguarded and pleasant—almost boyish. He had looked at her in many ways before—wolfish, hungry grins or wry, sophisticated smirks—but this version of Bex was the most threatening, because this was when she liked him the best. She could almost feel herself being drawn into him She took a steadying breath. "Please go on," she pressed. "What was the recent case you were going to reference?"

Bex smiled at her then, in surprise and she thought perhaps approval. It pleased her more than it should when they were alone in the carriage and only halfway to their destination.

"You really are interested, aren't you?" he asked. "I think you may be the most inquisitive person I've ever met."

"Perhaps others were just as inquisitive, but more well mannered than I."

"Not well mannered? Far be it from me to accuse Saint Lucy of poor manners," he said, the teasing light returning to his eyes and his smile.

"I am perfectly well mannered with others, but we have already established that you and I abandoned propriety some time ago. I can be as impertinent with you as I would like." She grinned across the small space at him.

He grinned back. What was more, he held her gaze, his eyes shining into hers as he whispered. "I hope that you will always be as impertinent as you would like where I am concerned."

Lucy swallowed. He was simply encouraging her questions. Nothing more. She should not infer anything more in the words. "The example."

"Oh...yes," he said, and Lucy wondered, with an irresponsible jolt of pleasure, if he had been as flustered as she. "The case. Well, there was one man, a hatmaker, and he invented a cutting tool that made the process easier—shaping the hats or some sort—but he never succeeded, because what he failed to take into account was that hatmakers, as a group, are not interested in new tools. They are interested in carrying forward the tradition and craft of the generations of hatmakers before them. They felt if making the hats became easier and faster, it would only cheapen the hat. No one wanted his perfectly good tool."

Lucy shook her head. "Even though it was a better tool?"

"Even though it was a better tool. There is no sense in inventing something no one wants."

Lucy sat back in her seat and considered this point. "But how can people know they want it, if it's not been invented yet?"

"They don't have to want the thing, specifically, so long as they recognize the need that the invention addresses."

Lucy looked at Bex—just looked. She would never have guessed that underneath all of his teasing and irreverence there was such a man of thought. And to think he considered himself a man with no purpose. How surprising and wonderful to discover that he had all of these theories and experiences with ideas and invention. More so, she was quite certain most men would not have bothered to elucidate on such with a woman simply because she happened to be curious. Yet Bex had explained everything with patience and pleasure.

She rather liked that about him.

She rather liked him. Perhaps that was not such a dangerous thing. After all, why shouldn't she be friends with the duke's cousin? He was practically family, in a way.

Bex turned in his seat to peer out the window of the carriage. When he turned back, she was still watching him. Caught, she looked away quickly.

"I think we must not be too far from the Maris farm now," he said. "Are we clear on our story, or should we have more practice?"

"I think we are clear," Lucy said, suddenly very conscious of the role she had agreed to play. "We are married and we have had a carriage accident."

"Correct."

"I should caution you that I do not lie well," she told him. In truth, she detested lying, though she could of course see the greater good in this particular circumstance. The only situation worse than lying was to be discovered in one's lie, she supposed. "Do you think they shall send a man out to inspect the carriage?" she asked, consternation at this thought causing her to sit upright. "I can't help but think this was poorly thought out on our parts."

Bex looked quizzically at her. "It's already been addressed," he said. "Of course, we cannot declare a carriage accident that is miraculously resolved by a short rest and a round of tea, can we?"

"No," she said. "We cannot. Perhaps we should reconsider our intent altogether. There must be some other way to get a message to Annabelle Maris, don't you think? I'm sure we can come up with something."

"There is no need to alter our plans," Bex said reassuringly. "I have already considered the matter and decided we shall have to tamper with the coach in a way that may be believably repaired. If they send someone, that man can assist our man in the final repair. All will be well."

Lucy's concerns regarding discovery of an undamaged carriage had been firmly replaced by her concerns upon learning that he intended to actually disable the carriage in some manner. It would not do to *actually* be stranded in the countryside. "Tamper how, precisely?"

"We will loosen the wheel. We cannot continue with a wheel that has come loose from the axle, but it can be reattached simply enough."

Lucy eyed him with uncertainty. "What experience have you in loosening or attaching carriage wheels?"

He raised his hand, one finger pointed upward. "Ah. You forget, I have not always been such a model example of genteel uselessness. Oakwood Lodge was not a grand manor teeming with servants. We were all required to be useful—even me."

Lucy considered him. She hadn't forgotten. And yet, even knowing his upbringing had been in the country, she couldn't quite envision him there. "I have only ever known you in London," she said, as though that somehow explained it. "Did you spend most of your time in the country when you were younger?"

He nodded. "I had never been to town until five years ago. My father felt we needed to establish ourselves in society."

He said the last part as though it were a rehearsed set of words, oft repeated.

"Were you not already established in society?"

"Not the sort of society that interacted with anyone in the House of Lords. My great-grandfather was the younger son of the fourth duke, which was"—he paused in mental calculation—"three dukes ago. We are several generations removed from any connection to the title. My family are simple gentleman farmers." His smile was oddly bitter. "That is to say, we *were* gentleman farmers. Now we have elevated ourselves to the status of idle gentlemen."

Lucy couldn't help but notice the bitterness in his tone.

"The salient point," he continued, the bitterness fading just as quickly as it had come, "is that I am quite capable of believably tampering with a carriage wheel."

"Very well," Lucy answered with a nod, sensing the need to continue away from the topic of his family's history. "To where shall we say we are traveling?"

He shrugged. "We are on our way to Watford from London to examine my business interest there. It's true enough."

Lucy nodded. She rather preferred the idea of a lie that was not entirely false. Then she asked, "But we are not on the direct road to Watford, are we? Shall we say we have gotten lost?"

Bex's chest puffed indignantly. "I resent the implication, wife, that I have misdirected our journey. Surely, if I have regular business in Watford, I should know the way."

She lifted her eyes heavenward and sighed dramatically. "You are too proud to admit to a stranger that you may have gotten lost, but not too proud to claim you are useless in the event of a detached carriage wheel?"

He put a hand to his chest. "No man can sacrifice pride entirely, not even in the aid of a worthy cause."

She shook her head and eyed him reproachfully. "What else would explain our being away from the direct route between London and Watford?"

He sent her a crooked grin. "My persuasive and impractical young wife desired a tour of the scenic Hertfordshire countryside."

Lucy folded her arms and tried to look imperious. "What if I don't want to be impractical?"

"My dear, if I must be ignorant of the workings of a carriage, you can be demanding and unreasonable."

Lucy leaned back in her seat. "As a couple, we sound like a pair of fools. I can't imagine we have any friends who genuinely prefer our company."

Bex laughed. "I should think that makes us a very authentic married couple. We should have them completely convinced."

Lucy could not help but laugh with him, though she retorted, "I think married people are quite nice, provided they were nice to begin with."

"As all good husbands must humor their wives on occasion, I will defer to your expertise on the subject." He made the statement with a grin and a wink and Lucy found she was rather enjoying the game after all.

"And as all good wives must placate their husbands from time to time, I will endeavor not to reveal that I only suggested touring the countryside after realizing we were already lost," she said with a triumphant tilt of her chin.

He laughed and leaned forward, resting one forearm across his knees, his bright smile filling the small space they shared. "You little minx, you wouldn't dare." His eyes twinkled with green and gold light that warmed her better than the summer sunshine. She had the sudden thought that she could be rather daring where he was concerned.

She felt herself leaning inward, her eyes shining up at him, and she saw the change in him—the moment his gaze lost its teasing light but none of the warmth that held her.

There was an officious rap and the carriage door swung open, spilling brilliant summer light into the shadowed interior of the vehicle. Lucy sat back abruptly and turned to the source of the light.

The coachman's head appeared to fill the opening. "I believe we are at the arranged location, sir." His head disappeared again and the folding step was lowered.

Lucy glanced quickly back at Bex. Whatever she had read in his expression was gone. His sardonically crooked smile had returned. He held a hand toward the door, inviting her to exit.

"I would suggest you wait inside, out of the sun," Bex told her, "but I'm afraid disengaging the wheel from the axle may cause the whole thing to tip if you are inside."

"I like sunshine," Lucy said, then chided herself for the inanely enthusiastic comment. She averted her eyes and scrambled toward the opening. The firm hand of the coachman aided her descent and she stepped out into the warm day. The carriage had halted in the middle of an empty lane bordered by a copse of trees on one side and an expansive field on the other. It seemed they were plunk in the middle of nowhere in particular.

Bex descended from the carriage after Lucy.

"We're less than a mile from Sunningham Park, sir," the man said, standing in wait of further instruction.

Bex nodded, then proceeded to unbutton and divest himself of his frock coat, leaning back into the carriage to toss it onto the cushioned seat.

Lucy coughed delicately and turned to look out into the field of what appeared to be green wheat swaying in the pleasant breeze. When curiosity dictated that she turn back—solely to understand the goings-on with the carriage, she told herself—she discovered Bex crouched beside the vehicle, his brow knitted together in concentration on his task. His shirtsleeves were rolled to his elbows, revealing strong, sinewed forearms, and his shoulders, outside the confines of his frock coat, were surprisingly substantial. The coachman—who was rather young for a coachman, she realized—crouched beside him, watchful and uncertain.

"Hold the wheel here," Bex instructed in an efficiently sharp but not unkind manner. Lucy realized she had never seen Bex behave in quite this way. He was authoritative, confident, and not at all teasing—as though he had everything well in hand.

And from the looks of it, he did. Lucy was standing a fair distance away, but she saw he had a tool of some sort and appeared to be loosening a bolt. Bex leaned further in. Both men grunted. At once, the wheel wobbled. Bex lifted a hand, closed it firmly on a spoke of the wheel, and pulled, wobbling it again. The wheel was not fully detached, but riding upon it would no doubt be perilous.

Bex rose from his crouched position in one lithe, easy stretch and brushed his hands together. "We'll walk up the road to Sunningham Park while you wait here," he told the younger man. "No doubt someone will come to assist you. When they do, you can make a show of retightening the bolts. If they ask what has taken so long, say you were attempting to determine what caused the bolts to become loose in the first place." The coachman looked uneasy, but Bex clapped him on the back with a congenial smile. "You'll pull it off without any trouble, I'm sure. I promise, we'll try to be quick about our business."

Bex reached into the now-unstable carriage and collected his frock coat. As Lucy watched him slip his arms through the sleeves of the coat and refasten the buttons, she marveled at this difference in his manner. He seemed comfortable in a way that he had never been before. From the time she had met him, he had always done whatever he pleased, but at the same time there was an edge to him, as though he were an amused and slightly jaded spectator who held himself apart from the others. She couldn't find even a hint of irony or cynicism in his easy manner with the coachman, or his handling of the coach.

Now we have elevated ourselves to the status of idle gentlemen. She considered his bitter comment from before. He did, it seemed, prefer to be useful. More than a preference, usefulness seemed to be his natural element. Bex had never displayed the slightest disappointment at the reappearance of his cousin or the fact that he would never, after all, be in line for a peerage. The loss of his more modest, actual inheritance, however, was obviously the source of considerable dissatisfaction. The basic need for an income by which to support oneself was in no way foreign to Lucy. She couldn't help wondering, all the same, as she watched Bex now, if there wasn't more to it than that. The way he spoke of being useful, the distaste with which he referred to his present idleness. He wanted more than a reliable source of funds to cover his expenses. He wanted—had expected—to have a purpose, and that purpose had been summarily stripped away, with no opportunity for him to prevent it. In that moment, she wanted it for him—even as she couldn't define what *it* was. She hoped he would have something to replace the future that would have been his, had things not gone awry. She wasn't sure what that something would be. A life, she hoped, as opposed to just a living.

"Shall we be off, Mrs. Brantwood?"

Lucy snapped from her mental wanderings to realize Bex was offering his arm for her to take, waiting for her so they could proceed with their charade and deliver Lady Constance's message to her niece. She was very aware of his strength and proximity when she took the proffered arm and proceeded with him down the dusty lane in the direction the coachman had indicated.

Chapter Seventeen

Lucy and Bex had walked for only a few minutes before they came upon a stone drive marked with a tidy wooden sign identifying Sunningham Park. They turned down the drive together, as though taking in the fine weather on a leisurely stroll through the countryside to call upon friends.

"It is so peaceful here," Lucy observed. "I have quite forgotten how quiet the country is, compared to the constant sounds of London."

"Yes," he said, smiling down at her in a way that warmed her beyond that which the temperature could explain. "Very serene."

Lucy was quite comfortable meandering up the gravel drive on the arm of Bexley Brantwood—so much so, in fact, that she thought she should not dwell upon it.

Intent upon ignoring how the sunshine illuminated in a new and attractive way the increasingly familiar features of the man walking beside her, Lucy instead looked ahead to the house they had come to infiltrate. It was quite lovely. Three stories of white-painted Georgian elegance with rows of windows like perfectly uniformed soldiers. At the front of the house, the stone drive ended in a loop, the center of which boasted a fountain of weathered stone. Tidy hedges formed neat lines below the wall of windows, and pretty pink blooms grew in evenly spaced clumps at the front of the trimmed green wall.

She glanced aside and caught Bex gazing down at her. "What is it?" she asked.

"You have the peaceful look of a woman enjoying a pleasant stroll in the quiet countryside. Much as I hate to disturb your serenity, may I remind you that we have just had a dreadful scare in our carriage and are distressed by both our harrowing experience and our uncertainty as to how we shall continue on our way?"

Lucy halted. "Oh, yes! Yes, of course." She looked again at the house. "Do you think they are looking out the windows at us even now and we've already ruined things?"

Bex laughed. "There you have it," he said. "That's quite good. You look very distressed indeed."

She tugged his arm. "Do not laugh," she hissed. "They will see you."

Bex patted her arm. "I think it is entirely believable, even if my wife is a frightened miss, that I might be able to keep a good humor about the circumstance, wouldn't you agree?"

Lucy cast suspicious eyes upward. "Are you suggesting that I play the frightened mouse while you are cavalier? I find I like us less and less as this ruse develops."

"It is not entirely unbelievable, however. Men are so often cads, don't you agree?"

Lucy tried valiantly not to return Bex's teasing smile. She truly did. "I have very little patience for women who are fluttering and fainting all the time."

"You are without question an admirably practical woman," Bex said, "but what is the fun in playacting if we cannot be someone other than ourselves?"

"This is not parlor charades, Mr. Brantwood. We must be believed or we shall be turned out before we have accomplished our task."

"You are, as always, a fount of wisdom and practicality," he said, but the gleam in his eye was a warning. "And since we must play our parts convincingly," he added, halting their progress toward the house and turning to face Lucy, "may I tell you, my dear, that it is my great desire as your loving husband to always protect you from harm or even the slightest mishap." He set his hands upon either side of her waist and gazed upon her with an expression so convincingly earnest, she had to remind herself of the game. "Though, to my great chagrin, I failed to provide you a safe conveyance for our journey, I shall not rest until I have remedied the situation." Then he leaned forward and placed the gentlest and most comforting of kisses upon her forehead.

The contact was not suggestive of passion in the least, but the featherlight touch of his lips nevertheless caused a tremor of sensation to course through her.

She stepped back. "You are being ridiculous," she accused with a nervous laugh, not certain whether she intended the admonition for herself or her coconspirator. If she were not careful, she would appear the lovesick newlywed without even trying.

"We are both in a ridiculous circumstance, my dear," he said with a wink. "We may as well embrace the absurdity."

Absurd, indeed. Lucy could no longer tell if her heart pumped with anxiety for the scheme she must commit, or the man who was her partner in committing it.

Bex's decisive knock upon the front door of the house was answered by a plump housekeeper with rounded cheeks and a kindly smile, causing Lucy to yearn even more strongly for life in the country. Imperious butlers were certainly distinguished and impressive, but formality was a bit exhausting at times.

"Good afternoon, ma'am," Bex said with a engaging smile that managed to be both charming and apologetic. "I do beg your pardon for the unexpected intrusion, but my wife and I have had a minor incident with our carriage just down the road."

The woman's gentle countenance immediately registered alarm at this news. "An incident? Oh, my. Is everyone all right, then?"

"Yes, yes. Thank you for your concern. We are quite unharmed, I assure you." He patted Lucy's hand where it lay upon his forearm. "Only a bit shaken up I would say. Our carriage, on the other hand…well, that remains to be seen."

"Well, I should think you would be a bit out of sorts after such a thing," the woman said with a vigorous nod. She stepped back from the door and ushered them inside. "Come have a seat in the parlor," she said, closing the door behind them and bustling back around to lead them down the hall. She led them to a prettily decorated sitting room with a floral-pattered sofa and ruffled drapery. "If you'll just wait here, then, I'll be off to find Mr. Maris and see what can be done."

Once alone, Lucy turned uncertain eyes to Bex. "Do you think we did all right?" she whispered.

He smiled and lifted a quieting finger to his lips.

She took a deep breath. How could he be so calm? She had been terrified from the moment the door opened. She wasn't certain she could have spoken if he hadn't done the speaking for them. It was lowering, that, after all her bluster about women who could do nothing but flutter and faint.

As though sensing her thoughts, Bex winked down at her again and squeezed her hand.

Heavy bootsteps sounded in the hall and Lucy looked up, feeling suddenly caught. Bex wrapped one arm protectively around her shoulder, making her feel small and indeed quite comforted, which was absurd given she had not actually endured any distressing carriage accident that morning.

She began to pull away, but Bex's arm only tightened around her, tugging her more firmly into the protective crook of his side.

A man of average height but substantial build strode into the room. He was dressed as one would expect of a country gentleman, but his sun-darkened features declared him a rugged, useful type and his brawn suggested a familiarity with physical labor.

He eyed them sternly. There was no call for false charm, Lucy thought, but basic friendliness would have been appropriate.

His entrance was followed closely by that of a woman with attractive brown curls, not much older than Lucy, in a lemon yellow day dress. Lucy recognized the family resemblance and immediately knew this to be Annabel Maris, niece of Lady Constance, despite the difference in age between the two women. Annabelle seemed healthy and showed no outward sign of abuse, thankfully.

"Good morning, sir, ma'am," Bex said with a nod first to Mr. Maris and then to his wife. "You must be Mr. and Mrs. Maris. I am Mr. Brantwood and this is my wife. I am dreadfully sorry for the imposition, but I'm afraid we've had a bit of trouble with our coach just down the lane from your house."

Mr. Maris's expression remained grim. His eyes traveled the length of Lucy from bonnet to slippers and back again as though he might find some excuse to simply dismiss them without offering aid.

Lucy disliked him immediately and felt a stab of pity for Annabelle Maris. In her sunny, ruffled dress, she looked every bit as soft and feminine as the parlor in which they all stood. She had positioned herself two paces behind her husband in obvious deference to his oversight of this matter.

"What sort of trouble?" Mr. Maris asked, showing more skepticism than alarm.

"With the wheel, it seems," Bex explained, giving Lucy's shoulder another reassuring squeeze. "My man is assessing the damage now to see if he's able to repair it."

It was Bex's turn, apparently, to receive the lengthy and unveiled measuring up from Mr. Maris. Judging by the man's expression upon its conclusion, he was not particularly pleased with his assessment. "I find two sets of hands are often more useful than one in these situations," he said with a speaking stare at Bex. "Of course, most gentlemen are no more able to fix a broken carriage wheel than a missing waistcoat button."

Lucy felt Bex stiffen at this obvious attack upon his masculinity. She, too, had assumed Bex would not have any particular skill in carriage repair, but somehow it was considerably more rude for Mr. Maris to say so.

"Two sets of hands are undeniably better," Bex said affably. "I would, of course, have remained to assist in the repairs, but that would have left my wife to remain waiting outdoors. I could not in good conscience allow her to wait at the roadside in her delicate condition."

Bex smiled congenially at Mr. Maris. Lucy grinned as well, in solidarity with her "husband," until his words settled upon her.

Delicate condition?

Mrs. Maris immediately centered her gaze on Lucy's narrow waist. Lucy gave her a tremulous smile before looking up at Bex in silent plea to…well, she wasn't sure what exactly.

Bex's chest rose in emulation of an expectant father's beaming pride and proceeded to remove any doubt as to his previous implication. "My wife and I have recently learned that we shall be welcoming our first child."

Lucy coughed. Somehow she managed to stay the instinct to turn and gape up at Bex. What in heaven's name was he thinking? Uncertain she could manage a verbal response through her shock, she lay a protective hand over her conspicuously trim midsection and smiled awkwardly.

Mr. Maris gave her another, even more thorough examination then nodded as though begrudgingly granting approval for Bex's decision making, now that he had been presented with all the facts.

"But you must sit down, Mrs. Brantwood," Mrs. Maris said, stepping forward to take charge of this situation, which now clearly fell into her feminine purview. "Perhaps you should stay for luncheon," she suggested with a solicitous smile as she took Lucy's arm and led her to the patterned sofa. "You should not overtax yourself, dear."

"Thank you," Lucy said, wondering how one went about behaving in a pregnant manner. Emma seemed simply a more tired version of her normal self, aside from the bouts of nausea. Lucy was *not* going to feign a stomach malady in front of perfect strangers. Fatigue seemed her only possible course at this point. She allowed her shoulders to droop slightly and leaned toward her "husband."

"I'm sure our guests will be anxious to reach their intended destination," Mr. Maris said to his wife, though his attention remained upon Bex. "Luncheon may be an unnecessary delay."

"I shall ring for tea, then," Mrs. Maris said, not missing a beat at the dismissal of her original intent. "We cannot send you off without any refreshment."

Lucy smiled gratefully. "That would be lovely. Thank you ever so much for your kindness." Then inspiration struck. "I am rather fatigued," she added.

Mrs. Maris smiled sweetly back at her then turned to her husband. "In the meantime, what can be done for their carriage, my dear?"

"I've already sent a man to have a look."

Bex stepped forward. "That is most appreciated, my good man. We are grateful for your assistance. The carriage is not far down the lane," he continued, fiercely cheerful despite the other man's lack of cordiality. "Perhaps if Mrs. Maris would be so gracious as to keep company with my wife, you and I might venture out to inspect the progress?"

"My man is competent. If the coach can be repaired, he'll have it done shortly."

"I mean no slight to the skill of your man," Bex insisted, "but now that my wife is safely in the care of another, I admit I would prefer to see for myself how the repair is coming along."

Lucy could not deny Bex was certainly the man to have as one's coconspirator in an undertaking such as this. He managed clever maneuvering of the situation and changed tack as necessary far more quickly than she could have done. On her own, she would have been a dismal failure.

Mr. Maris considered him for a long moment, then consented with an abbreviated nod.

As Lucy turned to smile warmly up at Bex in reward for his deft manipulation of the circumstances, she caught his eyes widen briefly in an almost imperceptible moment of alarm.

Then she heard it herself.

An arriving carriage.

Chapter Eighteen

"What is this?" Mrs. Maris asked. She hurried to a front-facing window and peered out. "Could your carriage be repaired already?"

Lucy's eyes sent desperate inquiry to Bex. *What do we do now?*

Mrs. Maris turned back from the window. "It must be. How fortunate that the trouble could be repaired so quickly. I wonder, what was wrong with it?"

"Indeed," Lucy said. What else was there to say? It appeared everything at Sunningham Park ran with rapid efficiency—carriage wheel reattachments included.

She cast another questioning glance at Bex.

"What luck," Bex said flatly.

Mr. Maris simply looked annoyed.

At that moment, the tea tray arrived and Lucy's sigh of relief must have been audible. Mrs. Maris crossed the room to attend to the arrival of the tea, and Mr. Maris took her place at the window, looking disapprovingly at the perfectly functional carriage that had just clattered up the drive.

Lucy looked to Bex. He mouthed something at her, but she couldn't make it out and gave a little shake of her head. With a surreptitious glance toward their hosts, he tried again.

"Do you think you could faint?"

What? Faint? She could not have understood him correctly. No, she could not faint.

She shook her head again.

He must have mistaken her denial for continued misunderstanding because he exchanged silent words for playacting, tipping his head, rolling his eyes backward, and letting his tongue loll out of his mouth like a dog.

She released a sound before she could stop it and clapped a hand over her mouth. She didn't know if it was a gasp or a laugh. Terrified, she cast a look first to Mr. Maris and then to his wife.

Thankfully, neither were looking her way. She turned to Bex and mouthed a firm "No!"

He lifted his shoulders as though to ask, *What, then?*

So it was her turn to be clever.

Drat.

She was awful at this. She required time to plan and consider, but Mrs. Maris was walking toward them. There was no time to consider. There was only time to act.

Lucy spun to face Bex, clutched both of his arms desperately, and cried, "Oh, darling, I'm so frightened. What if it happens again? How can we know it's safe?" She put a hand to her heart. "I...I don't think I could even get inside that hateful thing. We could have been...been"—she drove her voice up a full octave—"*killed.*"

Dramatics thus delivered, Lucy leaned heavily into Bex in her best emulation of a swoon. She had never actually swooned before. To that matter, she couldn't recall ever witnessing a swooning, either, but she was certain it required the support of another person.

Thankfully, Bex agreed and his arms closed around her. She detested playing such a ridiculous ninny, but there were compensations, it seemed. She whimpered for effect and pressed closer—all for the cause, of course.

"There, there, darling," Bex said soothingly. He lay a hand on her back and patted gently. "I promise, we shall not set a foot in that carriage until I have personally ensured it is sound and perfectly safe."

Lucy attempted a sob and failed. It came out as more of a gurgle, which she then attempted to disguise with a sniffle as she burrowed deeper into Bex's chest.

He released a suspiciously ragged cough.

She pulled her cheek from its place against his coat and looked up at him with wide, pleading eyes, fighting the urge to smile, as she knew he was. "Do you promise?" she asked, in much the same way a child might ask a parent to return with sweets.

"I vow it, my dear," he said passionately, mirth dancing in his gray eyes. He hugged her close, patting her back again, and spoke to the others over her head. "Perhaps, if we could impose upon you for just a bit longer, my wife could benefit from a rest and some tea while we assure ourselves of the carriage repair. Would you mind very much, Mrs. Maris, if I handed my wife into your care?"

"Not at all," Mrs. Maris replied. Lucy could not see the woman's face, as her own was still buried in Bex's chest, but she heard the hesitation in the other woman's response. Lucy would be equally uncertain as to just how to manage such a creature, were their roles reversed. The idea that she—a grown woman—would need to be handed into the care of another grown woman would be incredibly offensive but for the fact that she needed a few moments alone with Mrs. Maris.

In an action that required no pretense whatsoever, Lucy sighed and reluctantly stepped out from the warm cocoon formed by Bex's strong arms and solid chest.

Mrs. Maris stepped forward and took Lucy's arm. "Come, dear, why don't we sit and let the gentlemen inspect the carriage, shall we?"

Lucy followed mutely, allowing the other woman to lead her to a spot on the sofa where she sat compliantly. She accepted a cup of tea and attempted to appear both shaken and mollified by her husband's promises.

"Well," Bex said, brushing his hands together. "If you will excuse me, I will go have a look at the coach. Will you join me, Mr. Maris?"

Mr. Maris looked a long while at Lucy as she sipped her tea in as frail a manner as she could pretend. His lips pinched in disgust and Lucy knew he would love nothing better than to send his ridiculous guests away immediately. He must have decided a safe carriage was the quickest way to ensure their departure, for he eventually drawled, "Yes, let's see to it," and led the way from the room.

As soon as the men had exited, it occurred to Lucy she had been left to her own wits in navigating this odd scenario. Now that she had gone to such extremes to get herself here, she wasn't entirely certain what to do next.

She gave Mrs. Maris a tremulous smile.

The other woman reached forward and patted Lucy's gloved hand. "There, there," she said, in echo of Bex's words. "I'm sure everything will prove shipshape and you shall be back on your way in no time at all."

"Thank you," Lucy said. "That's kind of you to say." She wasn't sure what a complete ninny might say under the circumstances, but that seemed to suffice. She wasn't even sure she needed to continue to play the ninny, but she hesitated to reveal just how much of their visit had been a fabrication for fear of shocking poor Annabelle Maris. Of course, she could not deliver the message without revealing some part of the fabrication, could she?

"I...I should tell you that I have heard of you before today," Lucy began cautiously. "I believe we may share a mutual acquaintance."

Mrs. Maris leaned back and gave a nervous laugh. "Well, that would be a rather unlikely coincidence, wouldn't it? I can't imagine whom we may know in common. I am never in London."

Lucy straightened her shoulders. She looked into the other woman's eyes—hoped she conveyed her earnest desire to come to her aid. "I have lately made the friendship of the Comtesse de Beauchene, who I am told is your aunt."

Annabelle Maris visibly stiffened. "Well," she said tightly. "That is unexpected."

"I am so very sorry to have...surprised...you in this way." Lucy bit her lip, uncertain what to say next. She searched the other woman's eyes for some indication of her emotion at hearing of her aunt, but could find nothing but guarded watchfulness. "I only wanted you to know that your aunt has spoken of you to me."

Mrs. Maris smiled, but the expression was clipped and unfriendly. "It seems unlikely to me that the Comtesse de Beauchene would mention me at all. She and I are not in contact."

Lucy adjusted herself awkwardly in her seat and searched for some sign of warmth in Mrs. Maris, who had chosen to refer to Lady Constance by her formal title as opposed to "my aunt." She was sad for the bitterness the woman so clearly possessed—and so unnecessarily. Lucy knew then that Lady Constance was correct in her suspicions. Not only had her niece not received her letters, but it appeared she had grown resentful from the lack of communication.

Lucy reached out to the other woman, with her hand and with her eyes and with her heart. "Mrs. Maris, you should know that your aunt is very concerned about you. She writes you regularly and suspects you may not be receiving her letters."

Porcelain clattered as Mrs. Maris clumsily set her tea aside and pushed it away. "I...well...what?" she stammered. She coughed, and sat even more erect in her seat before turning accusing eyes on Lucy. "That is a preposterous claim," she hissed.

Lucy wanted to cry for the sheer sadness of it. "I assure you," she said softly, her eyes pleading with the woman to listen and understand, "your aunt *has* been writing to you. She is now back in England and wants very much for you to know that you may rely upon her for"—Lucy bit her lip, considering her words, then finished—"anything."

Mrs. Maris did not warm in the slightest upon hearing Lucy's words. Instead her eyes grew hard and her mouth more grim. "The claim that I find preposterous," she clarified, her enunciation tightly clipped, "is not whether that woman has written, but that I would not have received her letters. Are you accusing my husband of misdirecting correspondence addressed to me?"

Lucy's stomach lurched. *That woman?* All at once, understanding blanketed her with a heavy weight. Annabelle Maris had received *all* of her aunt's letters and had chosen not to reply.

Lucy waited a long moment before speaking, considering her words carefully. When she did speak, she adopted a cautiously soft tone. "I do apologize, Mrs. Maris, if I have inadvertently given offense. That was not my intent. I only meant to pass on a message of care and concern from a family member and, I assure you, that message was kindly meant."

"If my aunt had any care or concern for her family, she would have paid attention to where her loyalties should lie and she would have married a respectable Englishman."

Lucy stared at the woman. Loyalties? This was the crime for which Lady Constance was to be estranged from her family? Disloyalty to the Crown? The idea was absurd.

"Mrs. Maris," Lucy began, her cordiality waning, "you must know that your aunt has returned to England permanently and taken a place in society as a proper English lady."

"My aunt is not a proper English lady. She became a Frenchwoman years ago," Annabelle Maris said, her eyes flashing with indignant patriotism. "She chose her side. She may have known Napoleon himself."

The sharp words stung Lucy as though she were the subject of them, rather than Lady Constance. If not for the harshness of the attack on a dear friend, Lucy would have found Mrs. Maris's position laughable. "Surely your aunt could not have wielded any influence in French diplomacy and war. No more than she could have influenced the king had she stayed in England."

"The French killed my husband's own brother and many more of our fine Englishmen. It would be a disgrace to this house and to the Maris name to recognize a French comtesse as family. She represents everything that is reprehensible."

Well.

Lucy was at a genuine loss for words. She could not reconcile this angry, spiteful woman with Lady Constance's anecdotes of her sweet and affectionate niece. Lucy almost hoped that Annabelle Maris had always been hateful, for the idea that she had once been affectionate and was so transformed was truly disheartening. Lucy did her very best to see the good in all people, but she was struggling mightily to find it in this woman—particularly as she noted the yellow silk flowers that adorned the hem of the woman's day dress.

Reprehensible, indeed.

Mrs. Maris abruptly stood. She glared down at Lucy. "I cannot fathom what my aunt has promised you and your husband to persuade you to devise this falsehood in order to convey her message, but I view this entire situation as evidence that the French are a scheming and duplicitous people. We are quite better off without her corrupting influence in our lives."

Lucy gaped. She could not keep quiet at such harsh words. "Corrupting influence? That is not at all fair."

Mrs. Maris crossed her arms smugly in front of her chest. "Do you often enter people's homes under false pretenses, Mrs. Brantwood?"

Lucy's indignation faltered at the woman's use of her pretend name. "I do not," she said quietly, feeling the shame of the continuing lie.

"Well, then, she has certainly been a corrupting influence in *your* life. I do not wish to discover the likely effect upon my own."

Lucy rose, standing erect in the middle of the awful woman's drawing room, and faced her with an equally righteous stare. "Mrs. Maris, you are incorrect. Lady Constance is a genuine and caring woman, whose concern for her family is so great that she called upon her friends to aid her in taking all measures necessary to assure herself of the safety and happiness of that family. I consider my life to be enriched by the presence of such a person and would declare that she is likely the most honest person in all of London. I can only be grateful that she is not here now to witness what a shrewish and intolerant woman you have become. I do believe it would break her heart to know it."

If Lucy's words had any measurable effect on the woman's hardened heart, she did not show it. "I believe it is time for you and your husband to continue your journey, Mrs. Brantwood. I shall not confide in my husband the nature of our conversation here, as I cannot be certain as to the force of his reaction for the injurious treatment to which we have both been subjected."

Lucy met the woman's stare with equal challenge. Lady Constance deserved better than this hateful treatment. Lucy fervently wished the two would never again meet. "I understand your position quite clearly, Mrs. Maris, and apologize for the intrusion in your day. Mr. Brantwood and I will not impose upon your hospitality any longer."

Mrs. Maris turned the handle and pushed open the sitting room door. Lucy sailed past the sharp-tongued woman and into the entry hall where Bex stood with Mr. Maris, idly discussing carriages and horses.

"Dearest, are you quite well enough to be walking about?" Bex asked solicitously.

"Oh, she is quite recovered, I think," Mrs. Maris said, with only a hint of irony in her tone.

Bex strode to Lucy and gazed down at her, brow furrowed in false concern and eyes bright with genuine question.

Lucy smiled placidly up at him. "Never underestimate the restorative benefits of a strong cup of tea. I think it is past time we be on our way and allow these fine people to return to their day, don't you agree?" She clutched one of Bex's arms with both of her own. "Besides, I find I am quite anxious to arrive in Watford."

Chapter Nineteen

"What went wrong?" Bex asked as soon as they were alone inside the carriage.

"How do you know something went wrong?" she asked in reply.

"Because you do not wear the self-satisfied expression of a woman who has just righted a great wrong and reunited estranged loved ones."

Lucy sighed. "You are right. It was all for nothing. Annabelle Maris is horrid. I hate to think so ill of a person, but she has received every one of her aunt's letters and chosen not to reply."

"Really? Why?" Bex settled into the seat and rapped on the roof of the coach.

"Because she and her husband have decided that anything associated with the French is, by definition, evil. Therefore, since Lady Constance married a French comte and spent more than a score of years there, she may as well be Empress Josephine in their eyes."

Bex's brows pinched. "That's ridiculous."

"Precisely," Lucy said with another beleaguered sigh. "Sadly, Mr. Maris lost a brother in the war. She also mentioned other fine Englishmen lost."

Bex grunted. "We all knew men lost in the war, but we cannot place those losses on the head of one woman who happened to marry a Frenchman before war was ever contemplated. It's not as though the Comtesse de Beauchene took up arms against the English herself."

"Agreed," Lucy breathed, relieved to be back in the company of a rational person. "I cannot believe the sympathy I harbored for that woman. She clearly has none for others."

"She is well matched with her husband, I suppose. He was a rather surly individual, wasn't he? I'd say he was extremely put out by the entire episode and lacked sufficient manners to pretend otherwise."

"They do deserve each other," Lucy declared, lifting her chin with the finality of the decision. She could not help but add, however, "I cannot put them out of my mind. I grieve for Lady Constance. She will be devastated to learn the truth."

"She will no doubt be greatly disappointed, but she seems to be a resilient woman," Bex said easily. "Her life has taken many turns and she has adapted. She will no doubt adapt to the latest with aplomb."

Lucy looked at Bex for a long moment. He was right. It seemed an odd reversal to have Bexley Brantwood applying such pragmatic wisdom to her concerns. It was…comforting.

Lucy could not think of one other man of her acquaintance, save her father, with whom she could have such an open and frank conversation. But that had always been the way with Bex, she supposed, because of their unorthodox beginning.

"What is your business tomorrow?" Lucy asked. Bex answered with a dismissive shrug that apparently warranted the effort of only one shoulder. "It's quite likely uninteresting to you, but as you've asked, you are now forced to be polite and hear about it."

Lucy smiled. As though she were alone in a carriage with Emma, Lucy slouched indecorously against the cushions, half lying upon her side, and laughed as she told him, "I am well and trapped, sir. Please do tell me all about it."

His eyes glinted with laughter of his own as he leaned against the opposite cushions in the mirror image of her arrangement. "Very well, tomorrow shall be about the business of textiles."

She skewered him with a look meant to tell him he was being incorrigible. "Yes, you mentioned your business was textiles," she said with more pique than she really felt. "I'm only wondering what they have to do with you."

"I have an investment in a manufactory in Watford."

"So this is one of your wagers?" she asked. "What sort of manufactory?"

"A textile one," he said, one side of his mouth quirked upward.

She cut him a look.

"It is a weaving shed with new machines."

Now Lucy was genuinely intrigued. "What kind of machines?"

"Power looms," he said. "To weave cloth faster and more efficiently."

"More efficiently than by hand?" she asked.

"Originally, yes, but power looms have existed for some time. The design here is intended to be faster and more efficient than other power looms, and also to weave finer cloth."

"I see," Lucy said, leaning on one elbow as she listened. "How does it work?"

"Well, I believe I shall learn the full answer to that question tomorrow."

"Do you mean to say you don't know how it works? But you've invested in it?"

"I don't know how it works in detail," he admitted. "That's the entire point of my earlier explanation. I am not the inventor. I am merely one of many investors who hope to make a profit if the operation is successful. I know they use something called a Crompton's mule to spin the yarn, which then goes into the power loom, which is powered by steam and weaves the fabric."

"What if the machine is not a success?" Lucy asked.

Bex sighed. "That would be unfortunate."

Instinctively, Lucy had the sense it would be very unfortunate indeed. She knew she should probably not pry into his personal financial affairs, but she was concerned for him—and likely too curious for her own good. "Were the funds for this investment also borrowed?" she guessed.

One eyebrow lifted sardonically as Bex lounged upon the other cushioned bench. "You pay very close attention," he observed. He was silent for a moment following that comment and she thought he would not answer. He did not, after all, owe her an answer. The question was an impertinent one. Then he did answer her, in a quiet, grave tone, all the while watching her reaction. "There are men willing to lend funds for such an investment."

Lucy was immediately concerned. "If the investment fails, will you have to repay the loan?"

"The loan must always be repaid." His eyes were shrouded now.

Lucy sat up slowly. "That seems a very reckless risk to take. You are investing in a machine you know very little about and with money that isn't even yours. If the venture fails…" She sighed. "Oh, Bex. There could be grave trouble for you."

"I shall survive," he said, but his eyes were clouded with doubt.

Lucy stared. How could he have been so reckless? What had he been thinking? "Why, that's worse than gambling over cards," she said. "At least if you lose at cards, you have lost your own money. A cardplayer could end with nothing, but you risk ending with less than nothing. You may end with a great debt and no way to repay it."

Bex laughed. "Cardplayers can just as easily gamble with borrowed funds."

Lucy stared. "Do gentlemen actually do that?"

He nodded. "Quite regularly, I assure you."

Lucy was aghast. "That's horribly irresponsible." She looked at Bex, a new wave of concern washing through her. "What will you do?" she asked. "If the investment is lost, how will you repay it?"

"It is my strong hope that the investment will not be lost. That is why I am traveling to Hertfordshire to observe progress."

"Oh, Bex," she breathed. "I am frightened for you."

He shook his head. "There is no need to be frightened. It is not as grave as that. I will manage something."

"Manage something" did not constitute much of a plan as far as Lucy was concerned. She was contemplating all manner of dire consequences, though in truth she didn't really know—and didn't really want to ask— what might happen if he failed to repay the debt. "I wish you hadn't taken such a risk," she told him.

Bex sat up and looked at her earnestly then. "My father, blackhearted soul that he is, once told me every man must use what he has at his disposal. I have nothing—no funds, or property, or particular brilliance. What I do have is a willingness to take on risk—a willingness to allow my destitute situation to become worse—perhaps much worse—if all my investments fail."

"There are other investments?" she asked softly.

Bex nodded. He held Lucy's gaze for a long, imploring moment and she had the distinct impression that he was asking her to understand—asking her not to judge him too harshly.

She complied. There was desperation behind his recklessness. He was not idly playing a game. He understood the risks and accepted them, as the only currency with which he could barter. How could she fault him for trying any way possible to gain his independence—to become a man capable of standing on his own, as any man would hope to be?

"This one will not fail," she said vehemently. "I'm sure of it."

Bex's easy smile returned. "Well, if you're certain, then we can consider the matter already settled," he said. "I hope you won't be offended if I choose to make the visit regardless."

Lucy smiled, pleased that he was behaving as himself again. She would be so anxious if she were in his position. As it was, she was experiencing considerable anxiety on his behalf. How would she sleep, waiting to know? She looked up. "When will you know if the venture is profitable?" she asked.

Bex released a long exhale and shook his head. "That is difficult to say. Progress has taken longer than originally planned. My hope tomorrow is to discover the cause for delay and see what can be done for it."

"May I accompany you?" she asked impulsively.

"Tomorrow?" he asked. "To see the weaving shed?"

"Yes," she said, a little breathless at the excitement of the prospect, now that she'd thought of it. "I'd very much like to see it. I'm quite curious about the power looms. And now that I know how important it is to you…" She leaned forward. "Well, I'm rather anxious to see how it's working—if it's working."

Bex reached forward and squeezed her hand gently with his own. "It is very sweet of you, Saint Lucy, to be so concerned on my behalf, but we are traveling the countryside together today under the guise of being husband and wife. It would be highly inappropriate for you to continue to accompany me in places where we are known to be otherwise."

"But we should be chaperoned if Lady Constance accompanies us as well," Lucy said, unwilling to be set aside so easily. "And I am not the privileged daughter of a peer. I have spent countless hours among hardworking people. I am not frightened by low manners or ragged appearances, if that is your concern."

Bex eyed her.

"We shall see."

Lucy smiled. She was certain once they had been reunited with Lady Constance the two of them working together would be infinitely more persuasive than she would be on her own. "I am very concerned for you, you know," she said. "I was only just thinking how relaxed and comfortable we are, like family who have known each other for years. If I have pried inappropriately into your private affairs, it is only because I have become too comfortable around you to remember that I should not."

Bex leaned back on his cushion and drew one bent knee up onto the seat. "I do enjoy not having to behave so mannerly around you. It does feel as though I have known you for much longer than our actual acquaintance," he said, echoing her previous thoughts.

"I agree!" Lucy exclaimed. "It feels rather like we are brother and sister."

His brow lifted sardonically at her observation. "I'm the only man who's ever really kissed you and you describe your feelings about me as 'sisterly.' You are devastating to my ego, dear."

She laughed. "Well, that part wasn't sisterly at all."

"I should hope not."

"It was quite exciting, actually," she said, knowing it was a little bit wicked for her to say it. "In the end," she added matter-of-factly, "I can admit that you were correct and kissing you was quite nice. It was certainly more exciting than that poor man at the Ashbys' who was looking for his sweetheart."

Bex laughed. "Take care, Saint Lucy. It is wicked of you to admit you enjoyed it."

"I don't see why, really," she said, despite have just thought so herself. "There is no reason why I, as a grown woman, should not admit that it was a very pleasurable experience. We are not courting. I've no reason to play coy, though I'm not sure I could, even if I had a reason."

"I'm sure you could not. You are, as we have established, rubbish at deception."

She considered her performance earlier in the day and could not object to his conclusion, so she ignored it. "We have no continuing romantic connection to each other, either legitimate or illegitimate."

"What do you mean by that?" he asked.

"Only that neither one of us would be in a position to consider the other for a proper relationship, and we would clearly not engage in an improper relationship. The kisses are simply pleasant memories between two people who shall hopefully remain friends." She smiled at him.

"I imagine we will," he said. "But I wonder... You are correct when you say I am not courting you. I'm of no use to any woman as a husband. But how can you be so certain I do not have lustful intentions for a scandalous affair?"

"Because you know I am no more available for an affair than you are for a marriage," she said simply. "We are too practical to engage in either."

Bex laughed throatily. "While I admire your pragmatism, you do understand that usually, if a man and woman reach the point of considering a love affair, practicality is not necessarily the prominent factor in their decision."

"It should be," Lucy said. "Practicality should always be a prominent factor in one's decision making."

"You must explain how anyone might *practically* decide to engage in a passionate liaison," Bex said, his gray eyes glittering with amusement.

"Well," Lucy said, pausing to give fair consideration to the question, "if I *were* to engage in a clandestine affair, you would be the ideal choice."

* * * *

Bex stiffened. He was quite certain he had heard her correctly, but her expression as she awaited his response was so disproportionately placid, he doubted. He lifted one brow and remained carefully neutral as he asked, "Would I, now?"

"Absolutely."

And so he had been correct. His body responded even as he kept his voice calm. "Oh, please explain."

"Well, you've already kissed me—more than once—and I already know I like it. Plus, even though I've never done any of the things that lovers do, I'm knowledgeable enough to expect that the whole thing could be awkward and embarrassing rather than pleasant or exciting."

Bex stared into her pertly lifted chin and her steady, unblinking gaze and knew that Saint Lucy of Beadwell had no blasted clue just how much she was torturing him at this moment. A more worldly woman might have engaged in the same conversation as a teasing flirtation, but not Lucy. She was pragmatically discussing a hypothetical love affair with a man while alone in a closed carriage and she truly had no idea of the havoc she was wreaking. Bex shifted in his seat to ensure his frock coat covered the evidence of her effect and knew he should not allow her to continue, but he couldn't seem to deny himself the sweet torture of hearing why this pixie-sized angel would choose him for a partner in a scandalous liaison.

"I don't think that would be the way with you, though," she mused, her eyes focusing on some faraway point and her voice soft as a dream. "Somehow I feel that I could be comfortable with you in a way that I couldn't imagine being with another man. I would be so frightened and foolish with anyone else. If anyone were going to show me how to"—feathery lashes fell to land on pink-tinged porcelain cheeks—"do those things, I think I should be less frightened with you. As we've agreed, it is strangely as though we've known each other for a very long time.

"Consider this conversation," she continued. "It's horribly improper and I should be dreadfully embarrassed to be discussing any of this with you. But I'm not. Because it's you."

Her eyes lifted then and gazed at him with such sweet admiration that guilt suffused him. He did not deserve such a look from anyone.

"Aren't you a little bit frightened," Bex asked, working diligently to keep his voice steady and calm, "that all of this talk of love affairs while we are alone in a carriage together may inspire me to make decisions based upon temptation, rather than practicality?"

Bex watched as she considered the dilemma he had posed. She pulled her weight from the elbow upon which she'd been leaning and sat upright, facing him. Her wide blue eyes met his and held him, transfixed.

Those eyes. Those beautiful, expressive eyes that hid nothing. There was something gleaming there in those lake-blue pools. But it was not fear. Thank God.

It was not fear.

Chapter Twenty

Bex stilled as sweet, expressive eyes fell to his mouth in unspoken invitation. He waited.

He waited for what seemed to be a thousand years in a moment, just to be certain she was given every possible opportunity to look away, retreat, or otherwise break the moment. He knew if she did, he would be decent and noble and keep his hands and his lascivious thoughts to himself.

But she did not. She held it, as he did, leaning toward him, lips parted with the same breathless anticipation that heated him from head to toe.

When he was certain he had waited long enough, he waited just a second longer, and then he reached for her. He placed his hands on her waist and dragged her into his lap, filling his senses with the feel and scent of her. His lips found hers in a frantic search.

The kiss was not tentative. He assaulted her and she clung to him, opening her mouth for his exploration, demanding even more than he gave.

Hands.

Her hands started at the nape of his neck, pulling him more firmly into the kiss, but moved on quickly. Even through his coat, he loved the feel of her delicate fingers roaming over his shoulders, down his arms, and across his chest, as though there were not enough places for her to touch him.

There were far too many places for him to touch her—so many tempting places. With one hand over her silken curls to cradle her head, he slid the other across her slender rib cage to cup one breast through the fabric of the dress. She pressed into the touch, but it wasn't enough. He moved upward, laying his palm over the bare skin above the hem of her bodice, feeling her chest rise and fall with her excitement.

She pulled herself even closer to him, rocking in his lap in a way that mercilessly stoked his arousal.

God, it wasn't enough. He needed to touch her. Still cradling her head, his mouth still plundering hers, he leaned her back just enough so his exploring hand could smooth down her side, over the curve of her hip, and down her bent leg to the hem of her dress. Breaking the kiss to bury his face into the crook of her neck, he slid his fingers underneath the fabric and slowly upward along a smooth stocking until he felt the fabric end at warm, silken skin.

As his hand spanned her slender thigh, squeezing with gentle pressure, she released the softest, most erotic mewling sound he had ever heard in his life. That sound alone could break a man, and he hadn't even touched her yet—not really touched her.

Even as he knew it was selfish and greedy and horribly wrong of him to think of touching this angel so intimately, Bex knew with equal certainty that he was too weak to deny himself. He wanted it so damn badly and so did she. *God.* That was the part that made him give in. He felt her body hum with it. He could feel her vibrate with wanting to be touched. She strained for it. Her fingers where they clutched his shoulders, her hips where they lay warm and tempting across his thighs, and her cheek as it nuzzled against his hair—they all moved instinctually to the rhythm of what they both wanted. She was too innocent. She couldn't possibly know what she wanted, but her body knew, and he was just selfish and greedy enough to grant the dangerous wish.

He slid his hand upward, feeling her warmth, feeling her move in response to the touch. She didn't shy away. Instead, her response urged him onward and he complied, trailing his fingers slowly toward the apex of her thighs.

His hand found the slit in her drawers and traced the opening, feeling the moisture there. He couldn't imagine anything more arousing in that moment than the tangible proof that this perfect, angelic creature wanted him. He pushed the damp fabric aside and repeated the motion, this time tracing softly at her opening.

She made that sweet sound again, and he basked in the pride of knowing he produced it. She squirmed and her legs parted, inviting him to touch her again.

So he did.

He touched and traced until she pressed herself against him. He lifted his head to watch her face, transfixed by the pure eroticism of seeing her introduction to these sensations painted across her lovely features. He wanted to introduce her to everything—teach her so much more than just this first taste of passion.

It couldn't be his. *She* couldn't fully be his, but he could take this fleeting moment.

Her fingers dug into his arms and he could feel her hips undulate with rising urgency as he stroked and teased her. He dipped his finger into the hot place where he wanted to bury himself and she moaned, hips rising to meet his pressure. His thumb found her sensitive bud and stroked there.

She breathed his name.

He wanted her to be naked. He wanted to see all of her, wanted to watch her hips writhe with his touch, but he could only feel her response, feel how beautiful she was below the dark shroud of her skirts. Instead, he concentrated on her face, watching as each movement of his hand triggered some new response. Her lips parted as he dipped inside her again. Her eyes widened, then fluttered closed as he drew his thumb across her. Her head turned to the side and she bit her lip in the sweet agony of it. She had the most expressive face, and everything—every torturously sensual thing—was there for him to experience along with her. No master could have painted or sculpted a more vivid and stunning portrayal of sheer passion. He had never been so hard in his life.

"Oh, God," she breathed, clutching him. "Bex, I..." Her voice was questioning, uncertain.

"Let it happen, sweetheart," he whispered.

Her breath came in short pants until she broke, with one final moan, and her expression of release and rapture was the most beautifully erotic image he would ever know. Even as he watched it, he knew it was indelibly branded into his memory.

His hand slowly retreated, righting her drawers and sliding along her leg to her ankle. He cradled her to him with both arms around her as her breathing slowed. As he hugged her to him, he concentrated on ignoring the merciless pulse of arousal in his own unsated body. She burrowed snugly into his embrace and he closed his eyes, knowing she would recover herself shortly and the awareness would set in.

And the inevitable regret.

He held her anyway, greedily taking his last few moments until it happened.

He knew the moment she began to come back to herself. He sensed it even before she began to pull away. Slowly, she slid from his lap, bewildered eyes above pink cheeks. Silently, she reached a hand up to take stock of her mussed hair, then reached both hands down to smooth twisted skirts.

Bex waited patiently, dreading the words that would break the silence.

He did not expect accusation or censure. Those things were not Lucy's way. He did expect awkwardness, remorse, and a shift in their odd, comfortable friendship. Probably, too, there would be a stern reminder that they could not violate propriety in such a way again.

It was far less punishment than he deserved for daring to touch her. Had she been in her usual, practical state of mind, she would not have allowed it. Still, deserved or no, he dreaded seeing the regret so vividly displayed across the features that had been ripe with passion only moments before.

Lucy released a soft sigh. She looked up at him. Her cheeks were still pink, but her eyes were not shy. "I was right."

Bex stilled. He shook his head. "What?"

Then her perfect, swollen lips broke into a smile. "I was right."

He hunted for the regret in her features, but it was not there. Her eyes were bright and she was smiling at him. Smiling.

"About what, exactly?" he asked.

Then she laughed. "About you," she said, and because there was not a coy bone in the woman's body, she said, "I'm not at all frightened or embarrassed with you." She shook her head as though mystified herself to realize it. "I'm not even shy."

At her words, Bex felt a physical unburdening of his soul. He wanted to laugh with the lightness of it. "No," he said, draping his arm protectively around her shoulders, "you are not shy."

She sat comfortably tucked at his side for a long moment before she abruptly turned to face him. Startled, he looked down at her.

"I want you to show me more."

Her words were such an echo of his recent thoughts that his mind and body immediately settled upon the most lascivious interpretation of her meaning. Bex steeled himself against the dangerous train of thought and sought clarification. "Show you more of what?"

"More of this," she said, her hand coming to rest on his thigh as she made her earnest request. She lifted clear blue eyes to his and said, without any hesitation or apology, "I want you to show me the rest of it."

Desire lit through him again, like a bellows fanning the flames of a smoldering fire. "No, we cannot," he said, a bit more firmly than he intended. He was saying it for his own benefit as much as hers. He had dreaded her regret, but he could not have predicted she would request they keep going. One of them had to think responsibly. They could not, under any circumstances, continue with these dangerous games. He would have her ruined before the day was out, and what then? He was in no position to save her from said ruination.

She pursed her lips and looked at him quietly for a moment. Then she said, "But why not?"

Good lord, the list of reasons why not could rival a Greek epic in length. He opened his mouth to provide the most pressing, but she held up a staying hand and continued before he could speak.

"Just consider for a moment," she said. "I understand we aren't supposed to do...these things, but why couldn't we, really?" Her eyes drifted around the coach as though pondering her own response to this question as opposed to waiting for his.

"Because we are in a carriage, to start," Bex blurted, feeling the urgent need to catalog, for both of their sakes, precisely why her suggestion should be summarily dismissed.

At his words, she broke her mental wandering and turned to gape at him. "I did not mean immediately," she said, as though he were daft to have assumed so. "I meant at some other time."

"Some other time when we are unchaperoned and alone?" he asked, one brow raised in challenge.

"We are reasonably clever people," she defended. "Surely we could arrange for some other opportune time."

"No," he said firmly. "There can be no other time." What the devil was happening here? She was supposed to be saying these things to him.

"You don't have to worry that you can't afford a...mistress...I don't want to be a mistress, at least not in the conventional sense of a woman with a protector and a financial arrangement. That whole thing seems rather mercenary and callous and...wrong." She wrinkled her nose, as though the thought produced a tangibly unpleasant odor.

"Wrong indeed," he said. He knew as well as everyone else that calling a woman a mistress and placing her in elegant clothes or surroundings did not alter the inelegance of the arrangement. Polite society excluded such women because they were, despite appearances, paid whores. Bex would be damned before he would allow Saint Lucy of Beadwell to even contemplate such an arrangement.

"It is wrong," Lucy repeated with a punctuating nod. "That is why I would never dream of proposing a financial arrangement. I am simply proposing a different sort of friendship. You've made me see the possibility."

Bex nearly choked. "I have made you see the possibility? That was not my intent, I promise you." At least, he would not admit to such an intent, even if the prospect was damnably tempting.

"Of course you have," Lucy said.

Bex released a heavy sigh. "I am sure you will explain."

"Certainly," Lucy said with a pert nod. "We have just engaged in highly inappropriate conduct." The color rose on her cheeks.

Finally. Sense. "Agreed, and you have my regret and sincerest apology."

Lucy laughed. "But I don't regret it. It was..." She bit her lip. "It was very nice."

There was that word again. He should begin a campaign to have the word eradicated from the English language.

"It is just like you said about our first kiss. It's only a scandal if someone knows about it," she said.

"You should not listen to me so closely," he said miserably. "I am considerably less wise than I pretend to be."

She laughed again, and the light sound filled the interior of the coach yet only managed to make his mood heavier. Five minutes before, he had dreaded her declaration of regret; now he was actively trying to convince the woman she did not want to become his lover.

He was mad. Barking mad.

"But you were correct. The rules of society only matter to society. When there is no one involved save you and I, our judgments are the only ones that matter. If we are discreet, no one else need know."

"What of your husband?" Bex blurted. "If you are ruined, he will certainly discover it." His words were harsh, but he needed them to penetrate.

"We both know I will never marry," she said quietly, eyes cast downward. "I am going to be a governess. I am already past the age most women marry and I will spend the next several years hidden away in some family's schoolroom, preparing their daughters for marriage. My prospects are already dismal now. They will not improve with time."

"You cannot be certain of that," Bex said, but it felt like a lie, so he tried again. "There are too many reasons why not and only selfish, irresponsible reasons to proceed."

Lucy reached out and lay a gentle hand upon his arm. "Please listen to me, Bex," she said, her voice softening to a plea that tugged at his heart in a way he found decidedly uncomfortable. "I will never be a wife. I will never be a mother. Can I not, for a brief time, know what it means to be a lover?"

Her eyes were so blue and bright with entreaty. She was small and vulnerable, and damn him, but he wanted to yield to this heartbreakingly sweet request. She would make it so damn easy for him to convince himself that he was being somehow noble and generous to give her this one thing she so greatly desired. Because her reasons, irresponsible though they might be, were not selfish. How could he call a woman selfish when she must sacrifice everything and she asked to keep only one small thing?

Because it was not a small thing, that was bloody why. It was a monumentally sized thing. How could they be assured of discretion? What if she regretted it and hated him? What if he hated himself?

What if he crushed the tender heart of another innocent woman and the little bit left of his broken soul was lost forever?

"No, Lucy. It cannot happen. The idea is as tempting for me as it is for you, but when you have had more time to contemplate, you will be grateful that one of us had the strength to ignore this impulse."

"I understand." Her voice was barely a whisper. Her eyes were wide with hurt, and he hated the way she retreated back to the opposite seat. She very clearly did not understand, but she would. Once she truly considered what she had proposed, she would realize how close they had both come to disaster.

Chapter Twenty-One

Lucy had never cared much for uncomfortable silences. She usually avoided them in the simplest way—by making conversation. It was quite simple to find topics of general interest that would not be offensive to others, and she found most people were as relieved as she to be freed from the awkwardness.

The half hour that Lucy spent alone in the coach with Bex following his resounding rejection of her proposal was not one of these occasions. She found she much preferred the silence in this instance. She could not converse with him. She preferred to avoid looking at him. She hated that she had to blindly repair her damaged coiffure while he sat across from her, and she said a prayer of silent gratitude that he chose to close his eyes and be silent as well.

She did make a valiant effort not to feel too deeply rejected by his vehement dismissal of her proposal. He had, after all, referred to her offer as tempting. He had even implied his refusal was for her own good. Therefore, she should not feel ridiculous.

But of course she did.

She felt like a child who'd become carried away, or a simpleton who'd carried a jest too far. Perhaps she had been carried away, but she had truly believed in their friendship and their undeniable attraction for each other. She had only proposed the continuation of activities *he* had initiated, after all. Yet he'd responded as though the suggestion had been completely unexpected and entirely preposterous.

Had heightened emotion caused her to abandon common sense? Lucy could not deny the power of the sensations caused by Bex's touch, but was she rendered nonsensical?

No. She did not believe she was. Had she abandoned propriety? Yes. Common sense? No.

And in the end, sensible or no, the rejection still stung. That was the worst part. Her mother had always said, where there is a will, there is a way. Lucy had discovered, too late to save her dignity, that her offer was not tempting enough to create sufficient will as far as Mr. Bexley Brantwood was concerned.

Lucy had never offered herself to any other man. She couldn't imagine she would again—certainly not after learning the cost to one's pride to have such an offer declined.

She had even said please.

She did her best not to visibly cringe at the thought. It was not precisely begging, but still...

Lucy released a quiet sigh and belatedly hoped *he* had not observed it. Now that her own girlish fantasies had been dashed, she must go and break the heart of a dear friend. Not only would she be prevented from immediately escaping Bex's company upon their arrival at the coaching inn in Watford, but she must maintain her composure in front of Lady Constance while conveying the very troubling news that her niece, though happily unharmed was, in fact, a shrew.

This day only illustrated that Lucy was not born for a life of adventure. She had forgotten briefly, but the heavens had swiftly conspired to correct any misapprehension in that regard. How had she reached a point of such recklessness? Bex had predicted she would be grateful for his better judgment. She could not imagine any woman in such a predicament feeling gratitude for having been rejected. That said, however, she could see that it was the best outcome, in the end.

This situation only proved what she had always instinctually understood. Recklessness did not suit her.

She should count herself lucky that none but one man knew of her foolishness. She snuck a glance at the man in question, noting he was most certainly not looking in her direction, either. Whatever else he had decided, she did not believe he would tell tales.

* * * *

Immediately upon arrival in Watford, Lucy felt guilty for her own foolishness and her preoccupation with what was, in the end, a minor embarrassment when compared with the heart-wrenching news Lady Constance was about to receive. The lady had transplanted herself from

France to England for the love of a niece who was nothing more than a shrew and who cared not a bit about her aunt. That was a rejection worthy of heartbreak.

"There you are," Lady Constance said, rising the moment Lucy crossed the threshold into the shadowed public room of the timber-frame building. She bustled toward them, taking Lucy's hand. "You must both come and sit with me and tell me what you have discovered." She paused, then looked critically at Lucy's appearance. "You do look rather disheveled, *ma chere*. I understand you were enacting a carriage accident, but you may have overplayed it a bit."

Lucy raised a self-conscious hand to the wayward strands of hair that hung below her bonnet and brushed her neck.

"Never mind, it is done now, isn't it?" Lady Constance continued, ushering Lucy to a small round table set with three places. She turned toward a young serving girl who hovered in the corner of the room. "You may bring the supper, please."

With a nod, the girl scurried off. Lucy took the seat to which Lady Constance had led her. Once the ladies were seated, Bex took the chair to Lucy's right. She averted her gaze, but it was a small table and she could feel the warmth and substance of his too near presence.

"Now, my dears, you must inform me completely of everything you discovered. Did you see my niece?" The lady leaned forward in anticipation.

Bex answered first. "We did, my lady, and can assure you she appears to be in robust health."

Sharp eyes narrowed at Bex as he spoke. "You are delaying the unpleasant portion of this report," Lady Constance said. It was not a question, but a statement of fact.

Lucy sighed. She lifted her chin and faced her friend. "I had the opportunity to speak privately with your niece, Lady Constance. I am afraid she is changed from the girl who once wrote to you so devotedly."

The comtesse's lips formed a grim line. Her gloved hands rested, clutched together, atop the weathered table.

Lucy reached her own hand out to lay upon them. "I am sorry to say that Annabelle has received your letters and chosen not to reply."

Lady Constance swallowed heavily. "I see," she said quietly. "Has she given a reason for this choice?"

"She has," Lucy said, wishing she could somehow soften the hurt her words were causing. The serving maid returned then with three low bowls of hot stew and a plate of bread. Once she had laid the food on the table and departed, Lucy continued. "Mr. Maris's brother was killed in the war and as such, he and his wife do not approve of the French."

"*He* does not approve?" Lady Constance asked.

"Mrs. Maris was quite clear in communicating her own disapproval, though I cannot say to what extent it is attributable to her husband's influence. Mr. Maris does appear to be a…" Lucy searched for the words. "A strong personality," she finished.

Lady Constance released a burdened sigh and lifted her chin. Her elegant features had lost the bright light that usually illuminated them, allowing her age to show more readily than it usually did. "So I am to be condemned for my disloyalty to the Crown in marrying a Frenchman," she said without rancor.

"It is grossly unfair," Lucy said, unable to show as much calm resignation as Lady Constance. "No rational person could blame you for the death of English soldiers simply because you were married to a Frenchman. I am so sorry that she has taken this unreasonable position. I am afraid I was entirely unable to convince her how insupportable it is—the very idea that you would bear culpability—"

Lady Constance lifted a staying hand. "Now, dear." Her smile was wan. "Prejudice is not born of reason. You cannot fight it as though it were."

"How do you fight it, then?" Lucy asked.

The older woman looked steadily at Lucy, the usual shine of mischief notably missing from her ageless blue eyes. "In this case, you do not."

She donned a brittle smile and looked back and forth between Lucy and Bex. "Well, our little adventure was successful, then, as we have our answer. In the end, I am just a silly old woman filled with imaginings of false conspiracies. I am happy to know that Annabelle is well and well matched in her marriage."

Lucy thought she might weep.

Bex cleared his throat to speak. "If you will pardon me for speaking frankly, Lady Constance, you may be the least silly woman of my acquaintance. I respect the loyalty you have shown your family and I respect the lengths to which you have gone to assure yourself of their well-being. All families should be so fortunate to have an advocate such as yourself."

"Mr. Brantwood, your flattery is accepted and appreciated," Lady Constance said, her eyes brightening with emotion at his words.

"It is honest admiration, nothing less, I assure you," Bex said. "You have my great respect, madam."

She nodded graciously. "And you, mine, Mr. Brantwood."

"There is the flattery," he said with mocking admonition.

"You discredit yourself, Mr. Brantwood," she said. "Your way may not be clear as of yet, but you will right the ship, I am certain of it." She punctuated her words with an almost imperceptible wink, and Lucy wondered if Bex had confided in the woman regarding his financial affairs, or if she was perceptive enough to have divined on her own the basic truth of his circumstances.

Lady Constance rose then, prompting Bex to do so as well. "Miss Betancourt and I shall have a long journey to London in the morning. I suggest we all retire. I do thank you sincerely for your assistance in my business here, Mr. Brantwood, and wish you success in your own business on the morrow."

"If you have an interest, why don't you accompany me to the weaving shed tomorrow," Bex proposed, much to the surprise of both ladies.

"The three of us should be a rather unusual party, don't you think?"

He shrugged. "It would not be so unusual for you, as a widowed woman of means, to be considering an investment in the textile industry. I could introduce you as such. And since you are traveling in the area with a companion, clearly she would accompany you."

"My, my," Lady Constance said, looking askance at Lucy before face Bex again. "One false carriage accident and you are a regular Shakespeare, Mr. Brantwood."

He shrugged. "It is not so far from the truth. Besides, both you and Miss Betancourt have demonstrated a curiosity about the process. I don't see any harm in satisfying it."

The lady's eyes turned sharply to Lucy. "You are curious as well, Miss Betancourt? I don't doubt it. You have a sharp mind, *ma chere*. You are far too intelligent to pretend disinterest in business pursuits simply because they are the traditional domain of men."

Lady Constance turned back to Bex. "Well, as we are all so curious, we will accept your offer, Mr. Brantwood, and look forward with great interest to seeing your weaving looms."

Chapter Twenty-Two

"Has that building been erected *into* the hill?" Lucy asked as soon as their carriage approached the weaving shed. She sat, her small form leaning toward the window, looking toward their destination with the enthusiasm of a child and somehow torturing Bex as though applying the wiles of a temptress.

He felt horribly wronged. Apparently the heroic restraint he had shown in denying himself the pleasure of thoroughly ruining Saint Lucy of Beadwell was not to be rewarded, but punished. Every time he looked upon her, he did so with the knowledge that all of her secrets had been within his reach and he had declined.

Declined because he would have hated himself for accepting her, but damn, he hated himself anyway.

"Yes," he explained, determined to remain intent upon the topic of the day. "Weaving cotton requires a damp climate that is more prevalent in the north than here in Hertfordshire. Building the shed into the side of the hill draws the moisture from the earth to produce the required humidity."

"Really?" Lucy said, staring raptly out the window. "It's very large," she added.

"It is, isn't it?" Bex mused, peering over her head to view the sprawling weaving shed.

"Have you never seen it before?" Lady Constance inquired.

"Only in drawings," Bex said. "Investments were secured before the building could be constructed."

"There are practically no windows," Lucy observed. "It must be horribly dark."

"There are supposed to be windows in the roof," Bex explained.

Lucy's turned sharply to him, blue eyes wide. "In the roof?" She turned swiftly back to peer out the carriage window, not bothering to wait for confirmation. "How very intriguing," she murmured.

She was so interested. So curious. She had been curious about him, damn it, and he very much wanted to appease that curiosity.

"Have you not been invited to visit before now?" Lady Constance asked, and Bex turned to her, grateful for the distraction from his futile thoughts.

"I have not been invited to visit at all," he answered. "I have insisted upon it, much to the dismay of Mr. Sheckler."

Lucy turned from the window, again. "Mr. Sheckler?"

Bex nodded. "The engineer and man in charge. The improvements to the power loom and the plan to locate it nearer to London were his ideas. He is the man of business. I am simply one of his many sources of funds."

Lady Constance sniffed. "And he does not expect that you will oversee the use of your funds?"

Bex sighed. "No. My desire to do so is apparently unique. There are often large numbers of investors, rounded up by men in London. You are expected to pay your share then wait and see. It's all rather speculative. My contribution is not significant enough to grant me any influence. I simply choose to remain informed and attempt to exert influence where I may."

"Your investment may be very significant to you, even if you are not significant to them." Lucy said it quietly, not as a question, but a realization.

He felt an oddly misplaced pride at her perceptiveness. Put that way, it did seem rather unbalanced, but so did any other wager. "That is often the way with games of chance, is it not?"

"I would presume so," Lucy said. "I have never gambled myself."

Haven't you? He didn't give voice to the thought, but he rather considered her proposal to him yesterday a considerable gamble—one that carried catastrophic risk for her.

"Will this man in charge, Sheckler, be willing to receive us?" Lady Constance asked.

"I have written," Bex said. "We are expected. I cannot say that we will be happily received, but the presence of a potential new investor may improve our welcome."

"Well," Lady Constance said, adjusting herself more squarely in her seat, "then I am happy to be of assistance."

"And I promise I shall behave as a proper companion," Lucy said, pulling her gaze from the window and arranging her hands primly in her lap. "I shall squelch my curiosity and refrain from asking impertinent questions. It shall be useful practice."

Bex did not believe for one minute that Lucy would remain quiet or restrain her curiosity.

"Nonsense," Lady Constance snapped. "It is never useful for a woman to practice appearing unintelligent."

Bex chuckled at her vehement response. "By all means, Miss Betancourt, pose any question you would like."

"Well," she said, "I do have a question."

Then she bit her lip.

Bex was transfixed. She quickly tucked her lower lip between her teeth, then slowly released it, allowing it to slip from the hold, plump and red from the pressure she'd applied. He could not look away. The surge of desire was immediate and powerful. It was as though he had been condemned to a purgatory in which his sentence was to envision her every action, however innocent, as though she were doing so in his bed. Without her dress.

"If the climate is better in the north, why didn't they simply build it there?" she asked finally.

He stared for a long moment before he even comprehended her question. He coughed. "Oh. The north. Well." He cleared his throat again. "That is the interesting bit. All of the other weaving sheds are in the north."

"Because of the climate," she added helpfully.

"And because the raw cotton imports arrive in Liverpool," he explained.

"All the more reason to build there," she said. "Why here?"

"Yes, that is a very clever question," Lady Constance contributed. "I should like to know the answer as well. If I am going to play the investor, I must know these things."

Bex delivered his answer to Lady Constance, as he found it easier to maintain his concentration while doing so. "Improvements in power looms are happening quickly and are very competitive. Some inventors with clever improvements have fallen victim to spies and had their ideas stolen before they could see them to fruition. Building far away from the others protects them."

"Such intrigue in the weaving business. Who would've expected that?" Lady Constance said.

"There are also other advantages to Hertfordshire," Bex added. "The raw cotton must travel further because it arrives in Liverpool, but once the cloth is woven, it is closer to London. Watford is ideal because of its location on the canal and because there is already coal coming in for the paper mills."

"What is the coal for?" Lucy asked.

"The looms are steam powered," Bex explained. "The coal runs the boiler that makes the steam."

"It all sounds very complicated. You are very knowledgeable," Lady Constance commented.

"Mr. Brantwood insists on a detailed understanding of pertinent information before investing," Lucy said to the older woman.

"A lesson learned only through the pain and expense of numerous uninformed investments," he said, denying himself the undeserved praise inherent in her words.

"There is no shame in learning a lesson through experience," Lucy said.

He looked to where she sat, chin raised, valiantly defending him against his own censure, but she quickly averted her gaze.

It pained Bex to know that their comfortable rapport was somehow broken. It pained him nearly as much as the physical ache of wanting her, yet he had intentionally denied himself that very thing.

Damn. He hated the greater good. At once, he could understand her recklessness in making the proposal, for a lifetime of sensible decision making seemed bleak indeed.

* * * *

Lucy tried very diligently to appear the demure companion when their small party entered the weaving shed, but she was simply not capable of it. The space was enormous. And there really were windows in the roof! They were able to light the cavernous space because there was no ceiling, just exposed timber joinery supported by tall cast-iron columns, open all the way to the windowed roof.

When Bex had discussed the machinery, he had referred to power looms—in the plural—but she had expected three or four. There were hundreds, maybe a thousand, in neat rows on either side of a central aisle. She longed to see one in operation, to hear the sound it made. It must be deafening if they were all running at once. Did they all run at once, she wondered. None were running now.

Lucy snapped to attention when they were approached by an impatient-looking man in a stained waistcoat and rolled-up shirtsleeves.

"Good morning," he clipped. "You are Mr. Brantwood, I presume?"

"I am," Bex answered. "And you are Mr. Sheckler?"

The man nodded and looked at the ladies with a narrow, questioning glance.

"This is the Comtesse de Beauchene," Bex provided. "And her companion, Miss Betancourt. The comtesse is interested in learning of potential opportunities for investment, so I took the liberty of inviting her on my visit. I hope that is not too much trouble."

Mr. Sheckler looked at Lady Constance with considerably greater interest and gave an awkward partial bow. "No trouble. Welcome, my lady."

"Thank you, sir," Lady Constance said with more imperiousness than Lucy had ever seen her display. "You should know that Miss Betancourt is not only my companion, but my secretary as well. I rely heavily upon her good judgment and expect that she will have numerous inquiries."

And that, Lucy decided, was why Lady Constance was one of the best people she had ever known. She lifted her chin proudly and allowed herself to be subjected to the man's dubious perusal.

Finally, he nodded. "Ask what you will. Let me show you what there is to see."

There was, as it happened, a great deal to see. He walked them through the cavernous shed where he clarified there were exactly twelve hundred of the power looms in question. He introduced them to men presented as tacklers, beamers, pirners, and loomers. As Bex did not request clarification, Lucy could only assume he already understood their functions. She resolved to inquire later as to the specifics of each role. Though she had lingering discomfort at the thought of a lengthy conversation with Bex, she did not want to pose a question to Mr. Sheckler that exposed her total ignorance.

He took them to the boiler house where the steam was raised, and the engine room, where the steam engine provided power for the looms. Their party was presented with so much information, Lucy barely had time to digest it all, much less consider inquiring as to additional facts. There was one question, however, that seemed ever more pertinent as their tour continued.

Finally, Bex gave voice to it. "Everything seems very much ready and in order, Mr. Sheckler. Why aren't the looms in operation?"

Mr. Sheckler's mouth tightened into a grim line. "There's been a delay."

"Another delay?" Bex asked. "There have been too many delays already. What is the cause of this one?"

"We don't have the raw cotton yet. We heard from our man in Liverpool and he needs more time."

"More time for what?" Bex asked, his voice rising.

Mr. Sheckler shook his head. "It's all up to the brokers."

"What do you mean by that?" Bex demanded.

"Look," Mr. Sheckler said, backing away from the menace in Bex's expression. "Every bit of cotton in Liverpool is sold by a broker. Every spinner who gets any of that cotton buys it with a broker. The brokers decide who gets it and how much."

"Was this surprising news for you, Mr. Sheckler?" Bex's voice had calmed, but Lucy knew his frustration was simply more veiled.

"We knew what we needed. We had a man with us who was a broker for one of the importers and he assured us he would be ready with what we needed. Now he says he needs more time." Mr. Sheckler threw up his hands as though absolving himself of responsibility for the entire matter.

"Why?" Bex asked.

"He doesn't say. Only that he needs more time."

Bex was silent. Lucy could feel her heart pounding. She knew how critical the success of this investment was for Bex and how quickly he needed progress to be made. The delay must be a devastating blow. She couldn't keep silent.

"But Liverpool is so far," she said. "Can you not buy cotton grown nearby?"

Mr. Sheckler just stared as though she had spoken in another language.

Bex sighed and leaned down to speak privately with her. "The raw cotton is not grown in Liverpool," he said with quiet patience. "It is grown in America. The ships arrive in Liverpool."

Lucy's eyes fell. She had displayed her ignorance after all. "Well," she said, "if there is a problem in Liverpool, can't the ships arrive in a different port?"

Mr. Sheckler laughed derisively at her last question. "Well, blimey, she's solved it. I'll just pen a letter to the Americans and tell them where to sail their ships. I'm sure they'll sail right up the Grand Union Canal and drop it right at our doorstep." He grunted, turned his back on them both, and walked away, mumbling something about bringing women in the first place.

Lucy glared after him.

Bex lay a hand on her arm. "Never mind him," he said. "He's as much frustrated with his shipment as he is with you. Truth is, we can't tell the ships where to arrive. They arrive in Liverpool and that's that."

Lucy crossed her arms in front of her chest. "He could have simply explained that, instead of mocking me so rudely."

"I agree," Bex said. "I'm certain he is not accustomed to inquisitive women."

"There is nothing wrong with an inquisitive woman."

Bex smiled at her rationale. "You'll have no argument from me, I assure you," Bex told her, palms up in supplication. He stepped forward and stood too close to be entirely appropriate—close enough that Lucy had to tilt her head up to meet his eyes.

Involuntarily, her heart tripped.

"I have learned I rather prefer inquisitive women," he said softly.

Just when Lucy thought perhaps she would recover from his devastating rejection, he would do something like that and wreak devastation all over again.

Chapter Twenty-Three

Lady Constance was not a woman who pursued anything in half measures.

If any doubt of that fact had remained after the trip to Hertfordshire, it was cleared away when Bex arrived at the comtesse's London residence later that week for the much-anticipated performance of Madame Castellini. When she had referenced an intimate concert, he had envisioned considerably fewer people in attendance. He could guess credit for the event's considerable attendance was at least in part due to continued curiosity about the comtesse, but then he had never had a particular preference for the opera. Perhaps the others did.

Bex had not come for the music.

Or rather, Bex had not come for the singer. The invitation provided him the opportunity to further his cause with Ashby, but he would have come regardless. Were he a deaf man, he could not have kept himself from coming to watch the musician at the pianoforte this evening. Lucy had occupied every shadowed corner of his mind from the moment she'd proposed they become lovers.

Lovers.

What a captivating lover she would be—inquisitive Lucy, with her torturously expressive face and incapacity for artifice. He was plagued with visions of her in his arms and in his bed. The desire consumed him, even as he endeavored to set it aside—to remember the reasons he'd had no choice but to decline and the reasons why his attentions much be focused elsewhere.

Ashby. Birmingham. They were ever more important now that Hertfordshire grew less promising by the day. Those should be the focus of his attention. Vowing to force it so, he scanned the grand parlor, brightly lit as clearly no expense had been spared in illuminating the performance. The room was crowded with faces, but Ashby was tall and Bex spotted him quickly enough.

He had already begun to move in Ashby's direction when he noticed the man's companion. *Damn.* He could not very well approach Ashby when he was conversing with Worley. Bex did not want his cousin involved. The duke would only demand to know more. He was not a gambler and would not approve of the scheme. More importantly, Bex had declined his aid—dramatically so. He did not want the duke to know he took it anyway through their mutual connection.

Bex altered his direction and faced another unwelcome surprise.

"Father."

"Bexley."

Though Bex loved Lady Constance as a dear friend, he cursed her in that moment. She had been entirely too thorough in extending invitations. Also relevant was the fact that Bex's father was a scheming ass—a fact that their hostess well understood yet evidently chose to ignore.

A satisfied gleam lit the old man's eyes. "You've done well, getting yourself invited here," Edward said. "Well done."

Thank you seemed an inappropriate response when Bex had so many more colorful and satisfying things he could say to his father. He shrugged and let the old man believe what he would.

Edward leaned in then. "You must work quickly to secure her affections before some other man beats you to it."

Bex considered his father with an oddly distant abhorrence. He was, in the end, a shallow, petty, conscienceless man. The realization had come gradually to Bex—too gradually—and he'd followed his father's lead for too long, to the detriment of himself and others. Now Bex resented even pretending to consider his father's distasteful schemes.

Was sleeping in a comfortable bed, shielded from the elements, really worth pandering to this man—allowing him to believe he had won? Was he foolish enough to expect his son to obey even as he had failed in every obligation and duty as a father?

"Do you know, Father," Bex said, suddenly feeling the need for clarification between them, "I don't think you will have to worry about the pace of my courtship."

"Mr. Brantwood!"

The comtesse herself prevented Edward from responding, calling loudly even as she beamed at Bex, her eyes bright with merry mischief. "How long have you been here without seeking me out?" She feigned a pout.

"I shall have you punished, *ma chere*, for neglecting me. What good is a gathering if one cannot gather handsome young gentlemen?"

Bex's brow lifted curiously at her enthusiastic greeting.

She turned to Edward then, her voice and personality having drawn the attention of everyone nearby. "And you must be Mr. Edward Brantwood. I am so happy that you accepted my invitation. I admit I am positively consumed with curiosity about you, sir. One always wants to know a good friend a little better, and how better than to know from whence they come?"

Understanding dawned. Lady Constance had not chosen to ignore his father's schemes. They were precisely the reason she'd invited the man. She intended to toy with him. Her effusive declarations of friendship had brought a gleam of victory to Edward Brantwood's eyes and she saw it. She had put it there, the teasing minx.

"Lady Constance," Bex interjected, smiling at the woman because he could not begrudge her the play. "You are too complimentary. You appear entirely taken in by me, and my father will know you for either a liar or a fool."

She brought wise blue eyes, shining with laughter, to face him. "*Pas du tout,* Monsieur Brantwood," she said with a dismissive wave of her gloved hand. "I am never a fool."

Bex grinned at her. "But possibly a liar."

She winked at him, her secretive smile confirming for all observers the rumors of her scandalous French tendencies. "One must always remain mysterious, *ma chere*."

He gave a slight dip of his chin and tried not to laugh aloud at her antics. "Indeed." He had noticed her tendency to behave mysteriously always increased when she was among society, as though she were performing for an audience. His father was certainly a rapt audience. He supposed he could allow her the fun, even if his father took temporary pleasure in it.

With all the expertise of sophisticated flirtation, Lady Constance turned the full brilliance of her handsome visage toward Edward Brantwood. "Do you enjoy the opera, Mr. Brantwood?" she asked, leaving doubt in Bex's mind whether she intended to convince Edward she was interested in the son or the father.

It was extremely effective. Edward practically leered back at her.

Bex knew his father cared absolutely nothing for the opera, but would not want to appear provincial. That had been the entire reason for their relocation to London years earlier, had it not? True to expectations, he responded, "I enjoy all forms of high culture, Lady Constance, and as I'm sure you have seen, I have instilled that same appreciation in my son."

Bex nearly snorted at the elder Brantwood's attempt to play the proud father.

"Of course you did," Lady Constance nearly squeaked, so high had her voice risen. She cast Bex an amused glance before returning to his father, all gravity and seriousness. "All parents should be so attentive to the education of their children."

"I am beyond fortunate," Bex said, unable to muster the necessary enthusiasm to validate the statement.

He was rewarded with a warning glance from his father for his lackluster tone, but the warning was quickly replaced with a simpering smile for the comtesse. "I have paid considerable attention to Bexley's education, my lady. I have complete trust in his ability to manage all our family's affairs."

It was a lie. The only affairs left for their family included avoiding bill collectors and begging for charity. It amused Bex to know Lady Constance could recognize the lie as well. She already knew precisely *how* Edward expected Bex to "manage" the family's financial affairs.

Still she smiled at Bex with a twinkle in her eye. "Your father confirms my suspicions, Mr. Brantwood, that I am clever to call you my friend."

"Too clever by half," Bex told her, sending her a warning that she had played enough.

"*C'est ridicule*," she said, slicing one dainty hand through the air. "One can never be too clever." With one more brilliant smile for both men, she gathered her skirt in one hand. "Now, I must not neglect my other guests. Do enjoy the performance." She directed the words to both gentlemen, but a light touch on Bex's arm as she spoke gave him the distinct impression she meant the message for him.

She was far too clever, and observed too much.

"You have made more progress than I realized," Edward Brantwood said in a low tone, stepping closer. Others might not have heard his words, but anyone who observed his calculating smirk could have guessed there was naught but mischief in his message.

Bex did not bother to respond. He could find humor in entertaining the comtesse, but not in further encouraging his father. He scanned the room again. Ashby was standing alone with his wife in the far corner, and he could not squander the opportunity. "Enjoy the evening, Father," he said, and walked away with no more than a curt nod.

Bex crossed the room with purposeful strides and considered for the thousandth time exactly what to say to Ashby when he reached him. The ironworks in Birmingham had the best prospects of any investment he'd yet seen, but he could not benefit from that success without funds to participate. His patience for living in his father's company and under the duke's charity was wearing thin. He needed a winning hand soon; otherwise, he would be forced to consider more drastic alternatives. Sadly, he hadn't even devised more drastic alternatives.

Bex was direct in his path toward his quarry, but did not hurry, as he did not wish to appear desperate or overeager. He eyed others nearby as he went, ready to prevent some other distraction from reaching Ashby before he could.

The distraction came from behind him. *Damn.*

"My lords and ladies," Lady Constance called. She clapped her hands loudly to secure their collective attention. "My lords and ladies," she repeated. "Thank you, thank you. Do come and sit and we shall begin our performance."

Damn and damn. Ashby and his wife were inching toward the rows of chairs with everyone else in the room. Trying to reach him now would be impossible. Damn his father for even being there.

Bex delayed joining the shifting crowd, allowing most of the chairs to fill before he moved to do the same. In a stroke of good fortune, Ashby did not sit with his wife, but selected a seat in the back row, as though to slip away unnoticed during the performance. If he did so, Bex could intercept him. He chose a seat nearby.

"My dear friends," Lady Constance said, addressing the group from the front of the room where she stood in a space cleared of furniture save an ornately carved pianoforte. "I am so thrilled for us all that we shall enjoy this special pleasure, a private performance by the brilliantly talented Madame Castellini."

The group returned her announcement with restrained applause.

"This evening," she continued, beaming under the undivided attention of her guests, "musical accompaniment for Madame Castellini shall be provided by my dear friend, the lovely and gifted Miss Lucy Betancourt."

More polite applause sounded from the group, but Bex paid it no attention. The announcement of Lucy's name had him craning to see if she had yet appeared. He had known she would be there and still her name had sent a spike of heightened awareness through him.

Madame Castellini swept into view, tall and dark and bold. With olive skin, hair nearly ebony, and rich, dark eyes, she cut a striking picture in a deep burgundy gown. She immediately held the audience captive—all except Bex. His attention was caught by the diminutive figure who had quietly—almost surreptitiously—entered the room and stood waiting in the background.

She was as pale as Madame Castellini was dark. Next to the singer's rich, sultry beauty, Lucy was light incarnate. Her gown the softest pink, or perhaps peach, it was still not as light as her alabaster skin or her halo of silver-blond hair. She gave the impression of delicate, untouchable porcelain. If Madame Castellini was a dark mystery, Lucy was a dream—a heavenly, fragile dream to be coveted from a distance.

Only, she had offered to remove that distance—to allow herself to be touched by him.

And he had declined.

She curtsied to the assembled lords and ladies when Lady Constance introduced her again. She did not look directly at the audience. She was nervous. He willed her to look his way so that he could reassure her—send her some sort of signal that might relax her—but she did not. She took her seat at the pianoforte. It was the largest he had ever seen and she looked very small seated there, in front of the grand instrument, in front of the grand assemblage of aristocracy.

His. She could be his. His body hummed with the knowledge of it.

She began to play, and the room was overtaken with the melodic sounds. She played with fluidity and economy in her motion and her posture, all of the flair reserved for the music she produced. For those first few bars, all in attendance watched Lucy—his Saint Lucy of Beadwell. He noted the looks of several in the audience: appreciation of her obvious skill. He swelled with pride for her.

Then Madame Castellini began to sing, softly at first but gathering in power. All eyes were on the singer from her first note.

Except his own. The Italian opera singer was gifted and her song transcendent. Lucy was the vision that complemented the song—an angel of light and music. He watched the line of her slender back and her long neck as her head bent over the keys, more intent than he'd ever seen her. The soprano's voice seemed to envelope her, only exaggerating her ethereal beauty—making her seem even more heavenly and out of his reach.

Of course he could not touch her. She was poised for the recognition she deserved. If he gave in to the thing he wanted so badly, the price would be the loss of everything for her. Her beauty and her musical gift that so moved them all and threatened to outshine a renowned opera singer—it would be forgotten. Her cleverness, her inquisitiveness, and the delightfully pragmatic way in which she viewed the world—they would never be discovered. She would only be a ruined woman, nothing more.

He had done the right thing.

Damn.

He should do the right thing for himself and stop thinking of her, stop obsessing over a gift he could not accept. He needed to direct his attention away from torturous thoughts and in the direction of progress. He wanted out of his father's house and out from under the duke's charity.

He looked to Ashby and cursed again. His seat was empty. The man had already slipped away.

* * * *

Lucy was grateful when the performance was over. She had never been comfortable on display and, even with Madame Castellini the focus of attention, the performance had been nerve racking. Playing had not been the difficult part. She had always been able to lose herself in concentration to the music. The introductions had been uncomfortable, with so many pairs of eyes watching her. The end had been a little better, simply because she had known the performance was done and she'd not made any grave mistake. The applause had been raucous—for Madame Castellini, of course. The best part was that Lady Ashby had smiled at her directly and given her an approving nod. It was a positive sign. She should feel better about it. Becoming a governess and music teacher may not be the life for which little girls dreamed, but she was not a little girl. It was a sound plan—a practical plan—but somehow practicality had begun to seem less appealing than it had before.

When the applause was finished and the people had drifted away, Lucy looked into the rows of chairs and found only Emma sitting there. She went to her friend and sat next to her, taking her hand in hers. "Madame Castellini was splendid, was she not?"

Emma nodded. "She was. Quite." Her response was not as enthusiastic as Lucy had expected.

"Lady Ashby nodded at me after the performance," Lucy said brightly. "I think she approved."

Emma patted her hand. "How could she not, dear? You are wonderful. And I have already spoken to her about you—about your plans."

"You have? Thank you."

That was unexpected. Was it the reason for Emma's melancholy?

"Please don't be sad for me," Lucy said, still holding Emma's hand in both of hers, looking down at them as she spoke. "This is the best path for me just now."

Emma nodded. "I know this is your choice, Lucy, and I mean to help you. I am not sad. I simply don't feel well."

Alarm coursed through Lucy. "You don't feel well? Why didn't you say so immediately? What are you feeling, precisely? Where is the duke?" She stood, scanned the room for him. When she did not see him, she returned her attention to her friend. Emma was rather peaked. How could she have been so self-involved as to not notice? She sat again and searched Emma's face. "Tell me exactly what the trouble is, dear."

Emma patted Lucy's knee gently with her gloved hand. "I am only tired and a little queasy," she said, "and I should like to go home and lie down. It is nothing that rest will not cure."

"Are you absolutely sure it is only that?" Lucy asked. "Should I call the physician? The duke may insist we send for the physician."

Emma's smile was wan. "I do not require a physician. I require my pillow."

Lucy was on her feet in an instant. "And you shall have it," she insisted. "Do not move, I shall return with the duke."

Emma laughed, showing a little more spirit. "Do not go anywhere, Lucy. John only went to get me something to drink. He shall return momentarily. Sit. Be calm. All is well."

Lucy did as she was instructed.

"You played beautifully," Emma said on a sigh. "I only wish I could be more enthusiastic in my praise, for you deserve it. You are gifted and a joy to watch when you play."

"Thank you. I love you for coming to support me, but I suspect it was a mistake. The evening has been too taxing for you."

Emma inclined her head. "A bit, maybe, but I am glad I came." She smiled again. "I am also glad to be going home."

"A brilliant performance, Miss Betancourt," the duke said, approaching them with two water glasses. "Very well done."

Lucy stood as he handed one glass to Emma. "Thank you, Your Grace, but you should know that the duchess is ill. I think it is time for all of us to take our leave."

The duke's brow knit as he lowered himself to the chair on the other side of Emma. "Is it worse, darling?" he asked, all solicitation and concern.

Emma smiled. "It's a bit of queasiness, nothing more," she assured him. "I am grateful to have such diligent caretakers, but I am in no danger, I assure you. I am simply ready to return home, if that is no great bother."

"Don't be ridiculous. Of course it is not a bother," he told her. "You and our child are the most important people in the world. Making sure you are well will never be a bother." He stood. "I will have the carriage brought around from the mews. Lucy will stay with you." He glanced to Lucy to gain her confirmation of this statement, and she nodded.

"Thank you, dear," Emma said. "I shall be glad for Lucy's company while I wait, but she must not return home with us."

"Nonsense," Lucy declared. "Of course I shall."

Emma shook her head, then stopped and held her temples, as though the vigorous motion had been a mistake. After a pause, she said, "You cannot leave, Lucy. You played brilliantly. You must stay and allow Lady Constance to present you to her friends so that they may adore you. If you shall truly be a music teacher, you cannot squander the opportunity to make connections with those who have seen you play. It is too important."

"You are important," Lucy said.

"I am simply tired. Accompanying me home will accomplish nothing other than ending your evening earlier than necessary." She looked up at the duke. "Tell her, John," she said. "Tell her she must stay."

"Who shall see her home?" he asked, glancing from Lucy to his wife.

"Lady Constance shall make an arrangement. She will have her own carriage bring Lucy home if need be, I am sure." Emma turned to Lucy and took her hand. "You must stay, dear. Do not worry a bit about me."

Lucy was torn. She wished she could tell if Emma truly was only tired, or if her friend was attempting to be brave in the face of feeling much worse. "Are you absolutely certain?"

Emma nodded and took her husband's hand. Lucy looked at the duke. There was nothing Lucy could do for her friend that he could not. "All right," Lucy acquiesced. "I shall ask after you when I return, so leave a message with Agnes if you have need of me."

"Of course." Emma released her husband's hand and watched as he left them to see about the carriage. She sighed again and returned her attention to Lucy. "Lady Constance will not allow you to be shy," she said. "She will be a good chaperone for you this evening."

"You know I would prefer a warm fire and a book over a room full of strangers in fine clothing."

"Be brave, dear," Emma said. "You shall enchant them all."

Lucy's eyes narrowed. "No one expects to be enchanted by their governess, Emma. Are you suggesting I stay to meet employers, or unmarried gentlemen?"

Emma gave a halfhearted shrug and a sly smile. "Where is the harm in either?"

Lucy shook her head. "Even ill, you are incorrigible."

The duke returned then and announced that the carriage would be brought around forthwith. "Are you ready, darling?" he asked, holding out an arm to assist his wife in rising.

She took it with both of hers and managed to pull herself from her chair, although less gracefully than she might otherwise manage. She turned to Lucy before they left. "Do enjoy your evening, Lucy," she encouraged. "In between everything else, try to enjoy yourself."

Lucy nodded and watched the duke and duchess as they left, his arm protectively around her, ignoring all but his wife.

And then she was standing alone among the empty chairs, as everyone else had returned to the grand parlor. She sighed, wished a little that she was departing for home as well, and then set off to find Lady Constance.

* * * *

Lady Constance found Lucy first.

"There you are, *ma petite*," she called. "I have been looking for you."

Lucy turned to the comtesse to see that she was surrounded by a small group, including, to Lucy's great discomfort, Bexley Brantwood.

She noticed him immediately, as though she had an extra sense that existed solely for detecting his presence. She had hoped to avoid him this evening—had even thought perhaps he would feel as awkward as she and choose not to attend. Alas, that was not the case.

Lucy moved to stand near Lady Constance, aware of holding the attention of all nearby.

"We were just discussing how beautifully you played," the comtesse said with a proud smile.

"I can't imagine anyone noticed the accompaniment at all, with such a moving performance by Madame Castellini," Lucy said with a hesitant smile. "It was an honor to play for her."

The men and women surrounding the comtesse responded with approving murmurs and nods of support before returning to their individual conversations, leaving her the attention of only Lady Constance—and Bex. Lucy studiously avoided looking to him. She wanted too badly to have his approval. She was so desperate for his praise above the others that she would not allow herself to look at him, as to do so would be to ask for it. He had the uncanny ability to divine her every thought.

"Come, Miss Betancourt, have you been introduced to Lord Danvers?" Lady Constance indicated the gentleman on her immediate right who turned upon hearing his name. He was a tall, smartly dressed man with dark looks—he was every inch the dashing, rakish gentleman.

At the slight shake in Lucy's head, Lady Constance turned to him. "Lord Danvers, allow me to present Miss Lucy Betancourt. She is a longtime friend of the Duchess of Worley." She then turned to Lucy, waving one hand to indicate the gentleman. "Miss Betancourt, I present Lord Danvers. He is an exceedingly pleasant gentleman unless you are playing whist, in which case he is an unabashed cheat."

Lucy looked to Lord Danvers to assess his reaction to this unconventional introduction, but he only threw his head back and laughed heartily at the description. "I am indeed," he said through an amiable smile once he had recovered himself, "and it is a pleasure to make your acquaintance."

"Likewise, my lord," Lucy said with a slight curtsy. He had been a good sport, and she was always pleased to meet someone of good humor. It was easy to return his smile, but the expression became strained when she sensed a presence at her back.

Bex.

Why was it that she could feel him? How was it that he affected her so?

Lucy tried to ignore how his proximity awakened awareness and heat throughout her body. She swallowed. "Do you enjoy the opera, Lord Danvers?" she asked, attempting to participate in their polite conversation.

"I do," he nodded, and she noted a slight lift of his brow. "Do you enjoy the opera, Miss Betancourt?"

Too late, Lucy realized it was precisely the sort of question a woman might ask were she angling for an invitation, but she had not meant it in that way at all. She was not attempting to flirt with Lord Danvers. She felt her cheeks grow warm. She had only meant to discuss the evening's entertainment, nothing more. She tried to clarify. "I do, my lord, but then, I don't know how anyone can bear witness to an amazing talent such as Madame Castellini and not become an enthusiast. I have been to the opera twice with the duke and duchess, but I don't think I have ever seen anyone quite of Madame Castellini's caliber."

She was doing it again. Just as always, she was filling an awkward moment with incessant speech. She couldn't seem to stop herself.

She felt a staying hand come to rest at the small of her back, and Bex's deep voice came from behind her, warming her more deeply than his simple nearness had done. "Lady Constance, you must tell us of opera on the Continent." The pressure of his hand was gone just as she was becoming accustomed to its reassuring presence.

He knew. He knew she'd been rambling toward social idiocy and he'd prevented her from continuing. He knew better than most in what sort of situations she could find herself if she spoke first and thought second.

"Italian performers are superior, of course," Lady Constance responded, with the authority of one who had spent most of her life on the Continent, "but I find the quality of the London productions to be quite good."

As she spoke, Lucy sensed Bex moving from behind her to stand at her side. She reminded herself that the movement was not possessive. He was simply drawing himself into the conversation.

"I am glad to hear we have not been subjecting ourselves to a poor man's substitute for good opera," Lord Danvers said lightly. "Now if you will excuse me, I should find my sister. Once can never trust the rogues that lurk in London ballrooms." He cast a quick glance toward Bex, and Lucy had the distinct sense that the look was not the first in a silent conversation between the two men.

When Lord Danvers left, Lucy took a deep, fortifying breath and turned to Bex. "Good evening, Mr. Brantwood." She tried diligently to exude friendliness without too much familiarity—to behave as though his rejection had not altered their rapport. She was fairly certain by the tilt of his lips and the amused glint in his eyes that she had managed to communicate her trepidation instead.

Could a woman have no secrets?

"Good evening, Lucy."

He clearly had no compunction with familiarity. Lucy glanced to Lady Constance, but the comtesse seemed to think nothing of his use of her given name. She supposed the lady did know they'd traveled the countryside posing as man and wife.

Still, Lucy cut Bex a look. "You shouldn't be so familiar here," she said quietly. "No one will want me as their governess if they think I am fast."

Bex said nothing but lifted his brow, eloquently pointing out the absurdity of her admonition. She could hear the unspoken words. *If allowing your given name is fast...*

"Appearances are important," Lucy said, unable to keep a healthy bit of pique from her tone.

Lucy turned to apprise Lady Constance of her need for conveyance home at the conclusion of the evening, but found when she did so that their group had grown to include Lady Ashby, along with a younger gentleman and another young woman. Lucy stepped guiltily away from Bex's side and cast him one last warning glance, praying he would behave in Lady Ashby's presence.

Lady Ashby's greeting for Lady Constance was effusive, as everyone's seemed to be. Lucy could understand why she was so universally liked. She played the game very well, knowing with whom she could be irreverent and with whom she should adhere to propriety. Lady Ashby seemed to be the latter.

The comtesse smiled prettily and greeted her with a gentle squeeze of the other woman's hands. "Lady Ashby, I am so looking forward to hearing your thoughts of the performance. Did you enjoy yourself?"

"Oh, immensely," she responded, beaming back at the comtesse. "Such a moving performance and that voice"—she shook her head as though she could not quite believe it even now—"positively transcendent. We may all stop entertaining this season for fear we cannot meet the standard you have set with this triumphant evening."

Lady Constance accepted the praise graciously. "You flatter me, Lady Ashby, but I cannot claim credit for Madame Castellini's gift. I am simply pleased that you so enjoyed it."

Lady Ashby nodded and turned to Lucy. "And you, Miss Betancourt. I am impressed with your playing. Very impressed."

"Thank you, my lady," Lucy said.

Lady Ashby turned to her companion. "Don't you think she did exceptionally well, Mariah?"

Lucy stiffened. Hot embarrassment shot through her.

"Oh, yes," the girl responded enthusiastically, coming forward to meet Lucy.

"This is Lady Mariah Randhurst, my brother's fiancée." Lady Ashby indicated the man who accompanied them. "My brother is Lord Renleigh."

Lucy swallowed. She stared a moment at Lord Renleigh, who stood back from the group of ladies, but listened politely and nodded upon hearing his name. She had kissed him. *Kissed him.* Of course he would turn out to be Lady Ashby's brother—her *engaged* brother. Whatever would Lady Ashby think of her if she knew? She said a silent prayer of gratitude that no one could possibly know it had been she in the garden with him during the Ashbys' dinner party.

No one save Bex.

Lucy wished she could suppress the thought. She dare not look in his direction.

"I'm pleased to meet you, Lord Renleigh, Lady Mariah." The words felt thick and uncooperative, but Lucy pushed them out anyway. "My felicitations on your coming nuptials." She stole another glance at Lord Renleigh, tried to find something about him that seemed familiar, but nothing was. She caught herself looking at his mouth and immediately turned to look elsewhere. Perhaps there had been another Mariah at the Ashbys' dinner party?

It seemed unlikely. She swallowed. She could feel Bex's eyes on her—knew they would be full of amusement. If she met his gaze now, she would either die of mortification or collapse in laughter herself. Neither behavior would recommend her to Lady Ashby as a sensible and respectable governess.

"Thank you." The girl smiled brightly then cast an adoring look at Lord Renleigh. She was small and pretty and looked not much older than eighteen. Lucy felt a stab of guilt at having stolen what should have been Mariah's kiss—with her husband-to-be. It occurred to her that if she became a member of the Ashby household, she might continue to encounter both Lord Renleigh and the future Lady Renleigh. She cursed her impetuousness.

"I told Ashby that I must come congratulate you on your performance," Lady Ashby said. "The duchess said you were musically inclined, but I did not understand how gifted you are."

"I am humbled by your praise, my lady." Lucy mustered the courage, then, to steal a glance at Bex. She did not find the mocking glance she expected. Instead, he seemed to be watching Lord Renleigh intently, an unreadable expression on his face. Sensing her attention, he turned to meet Lucy's gaze. That was when she received the amused wink she had been expecting. She felt her flush brighten.

"Following that performance," Lady Constance said, "I should think a great number of ladies will feel the same. I predict musical instruction by Miss Lucy Betancourt shall become a valuable commodity."

"Indeed." Lady Ashby nodded, looking not entirely pleased with the comment from the comtesse.

"The duchess has told me of your situation," Lady Ashby said quietly to Lucy, as though the predicament required discretion. "My eldest, Elizabeth, has already shown a keen interest in music."

"I would encourage any young woman toward music, my lady. It has been a source of great joy and comfort to me throughout my life."

Lady Ashby nodded approvingly at her comments. "I am very busy just now with my brother's pending nuptials. With our mother gone, so much of this falls to me, you understand." She leaned conspiratorially toward Lucy. "But following his wedding in a fortnight, I shall be dedicating myself to the task of engaging a governess for my three girls. I should like to meet with you the following week, to discuss it, if that would be acceptable to you?"

"Of course, my lady. Thank you so very much for the compliments, and I shall be available at your convenience. I look forward to discussing your wishes for your daughters' education."

"Two weeks, dear," Lady Ashby said, raising a finger to stress the importance of her message. "Do not commit yourself before then."

Lucy nodded. "No, my lady. I would not consider it. Thank you."

Lady Ashby looked upon Lucy with the satisfied smile of one who knows all the details have fallen into place, then turned to her companions. "Renleigh, Mariah, should we not go see what Ashby is up to?"

Lord Renleigh did not respond. He was occupied whispering into the ear of his fiancée, who blushed, wide eyed, at whatever he was telling her.

"Renleigh," Lady Ashby said more sharply, finally catching the younger man's attention.

He stood erect and coughed. "Yes. I agree," he said, and Lucy was quite certain he had no earthly idea to what he had just agreed. Mariah's blushed deepened.

"How very touching," Bex said as they walked away. "To see such a love match. Why, they are so smitten, I wouldn't be surprised to learn they are sneaking off into darkened corners or private gardens."

"Of course they should," the comtesse said, with a surprisingly nostalgic smile as she watched the couple. "Love is only new once. Let them enjoy it."

Lucy gave serious consideration to driving the heel of her slipper into Bex's toe, but chose to restrain herself.

Lady Constance turned her attention back to Lucy. "Now, where is our favorite duchess? She will be tiring by now. She must come and sit by me. I shall have Benson bring chairs."

Lucy lay a staying hand on Lady Constance's arm as she raised it to gain the attention of her butler. "I'm afraid she is past tired, my lady. The evening away from home proved too much for her. The duke took her home immediately following the performance."

The comtesse's brow knit. "Oh, no. Is she quite ill?"

Lucy shook her head. "She said she was only tired and queasy—nothing concerning. I am afraid, however, that I shall have to impose upon you for a means of returning to Worley House this evening."

The lady's slender hand sliced the air between them. "Of course, *ma chere*. I will take you home in my own carriage."

"There is no need for you to be out at such a late hour, Lady Constance," Bex said, stepping forward into the conversation. "I am capable of accompanying Miss Betancourt to Worley House."

Lucy shot him a look of alarm. She couldn't leave with him—unchaperoned.

He only laughed. "You cannot plead scandal, Saint Lucy, when we spent hours together in a carriage in Hertfordshire."

"I am not frightened of you, Mr. Brantwood," she said, stressing the use of his surname, "only of the damage to my reputation if we are seen leaving together unchaperoned. I am certain Lady Ashby will require a governess with an unimpeachable reputation."

"Lucy is correct," Lady Constance declared.

Lucy could not resist lifting her chin in juvenile triumph at winning the point. She also could not fathom spending the time alone in a carriage with Bex, nor could she understand why he should want to do so.

"You shall have to wait until the last of the guests are gone before departing," Lady Constance continued. "Then no one will know that you have left together."

Bex looked victorious.

But why? Why would he want to orchestrate time alone with her? He'd declined her proposal. If a man had any designs on compromising a woman, surely he would accept the direct offer to do so when given.

Wouldn't he?

Lucy sighed inwardly and accepted that she was wasting her time pondering these questions. Clearly she knew the least of anyone when it came to the reasoning of men—particularly Bexley Brantwood.

Chapter Twenty-Four

Bex had gravely miscalculated. Why had he insisted he see Lucy home in the comtesse's carriage?

He knew exactly why.

Possessiveness.

He'd just felt so damned territorial when she'd spoken to Danvers and then to Renleigh. He'd been absolutely unable to conquer his preoccupation with the fact that Renleigh had kissed her. She had said it was merely nice. Renleigh hadn't even known whom he was kissing. Neither one of those facts seemed to matter a damn to his sense of male pride. Besides, what kind of man couldn't tell when he was kissing his own woman? Bex would damn well know it if he were kissing Lucy.

But she was not his woman. She had offered to be, if only for a time, but he had nobly declined the offer.

Noble deeds were grossly overrated.

And therein lay the difficulty in accompanying Saint Lucy of Beadwell, alone in a carriage, to Worley House in the dark of night. It was as though he had consciously chosen to add torture to self-deprivation. Perhaps it was not she who qualified for sainthood after all. He seemed to be pursuing it with dogged determination.

Well, if this was sainthood, he wanted none of it.

He had to get control of himself; otherwise, he would pull her onto his lap, tell her what a fool he'd been to decline her precious offer, and explore every place on her body, inch by inch—with his tongue.

No.

No. No. No.

"Did you enjoy the concert?" she asked, unaware of the precipice on which he stood.

"Yes. You played very well." It came out more stiffly than he'd intended, but as he was, in fact, stiff in certain areas, he couldn't much help it.

"Thank you." Her response was soft. He could just make out her slight smile in the moonlit interior of the coach.

"You looked beautiful," he added, before he thought better of it.

"Thank you," she said again, then somewhat awkwardly returned the compliment. "You looked very handsome."

He released a strained laugh. "I am not trying to be courtly, Lucy. You are lovely this evening."

She looked up at him then, wide eyes shining in the moonlight, like a hunted animal caught in the night. "I...I had a new dress."

It was not the new dress. She could have worn a rag and he would have been just as hungry for her.

"Lady Constance insisted," she continued. "I could have worn one of my other dresses, but she was purchasing Madame Castellini a new gown and insisted I should have one as well."

"That was very generous of her."

"It was, wasn't it? It was needlessly so in my case." She tilted her head to one side as she considered. "Though I can understand that someone the caliber of Madame Castellini would expect or even demand certain compensations to appear for a private performance."

Thank heaven for Lucy's habit of filling silent voids. Bex had only to provide the occasional prompt and she would carry the conversation, rescuing him from the burden of doing so himself when he was...preoccupied. She was so much more interesting when she was relaxed, animated, as she was now—gesturing and telling him about dresses—rather than worrying about subdued, ladylike behavior.

"Madame Castellini's gown was stunning, was it not? I think she looked as beautiful as she sounded. I thought her gown was gorgeous from the moment I saw it at Madame Desmarais's shop."

"Didn't you like your dress?" he asked.

Her eyes widened. "Oh, yes, of course. I was very pleased with my dress. It was exactly the right sort of dress for someone like me. To compare it to Madame Castellini's dress doesn't even make sense."

Bex leaned closer in an attempt to better view her expression in the dim light. "Someone like you?"

Lucy laughed as though the answer to his question should have been obvious. "Well, someone *not* like Madame Castellini. Of course *she* can appear in a richly decorated burgundy gown. She is a famous opera singer. She is…mysterious and sultry. I am a small, pale vicar's daughter from the countryside. If I wore a dress like Madame Castellini's, I should look like a child playing with costumes."

Bex was immediately assaulted with a vision of Lucy in a gown similar to the one they discussed, and he did not find the vision to be childlike in any way. "You do not think you could wear a red gown?"

She pursed her lips. "Well it wasn't red, precisely. I would call it claret or burgundy, even maroon, perhaps. I suppose it was not aubergine, really, as that would be quite purplish, wouldn't it?" She shook her head. "Anyway, it was quite spectacular, if a gown can be so."

"You did not answer my question."

"Oh. Well, of course not. I already said I should look foolish. I am more suited to modest, pastel colors."

"But do you like them?" he pressed.

"Of course. I like to look good and those are the colors that look good on me." Her eyes drifted downward as she spoke, and he wondered if she truly believed it. Like everything else in Lucy's life, she was convinced of the colors she was supposed to wear, but had she even bothered to give consideration to which colors she would like to wear?

Even as he knew he shouldn't—recognized it for the mistake it was—Bex leaned even closer to her and used two fingers to lift her chin. He stared into her certain gaze for a long moment before he asked softly, "Don't you think you can be sultry and mysterious?"

Lucy's head drew back. "No, I do not, but I do not endeavor to be, so it doesn't matter." She stared at him for a moment, then released a nervous laugh. "I thought we were making idle conversation about dresses. As it is, this dress is not very practical, as I shall not have much use for it as a governess. Something more serviceable would have been better, but I do appreciate the gift. It was very kind of Lady Constance."

Bex thought it would have been kinder of Lady Constance and her French dressmaker to make Lucy feel as though she were equally beautiful. It was a damned shame, in fact, that they had not.

Chapter Twenty-Five

"Your mother has written."

Bex looked up from the newspaper and regretted his decision not to find some outing away from the house that morning. The uncooperatively wet weather had encouraged him to believe he could avoid his father while remaining at home, but he had clearly been incorrect.

He sighed. "How touching to learn that you still correspond with your wife."

"You will shut your disrespectful mouth and listen to me." Edward's face was mottled with purple.

Bex arched a brow in silent question.

"Your mother has written that there is unrest among the tenants. Word has reached them of the sale and they are causing trouble." He pressed his lips together in annoyance at the complication.

"How inconvenient," Bex observed, "that the tenants might be troubled by the fact that their farms and their lives have been handed over to a new landlord who is unknown to them and their current landlord has not even seen fit to inform them. It seems awfully selfish of them."

Edward glowered at him. "You may keep your impudent opinions to yourself. My point is that I am required in Surrey. I expect when I am gone that you will further your courtship with Lady Constance. We must each do our part, Bexley."

Bex sighed. He could allow his father to presume his directive would be obeyed—but he found he couldn't do it. The frustration of self-denial over the past week had made him just cantankerous enough that he couldn't pretend to abide by his father's wishes.

He told the truth instead. "I will not attempt to trick Lady Constance into marriage. She is by far the most interesting widow of my acquaintance and I consider her a friend, but I will not masquerade as a lovesick suitor for a woman who feels more a favored aunt."

His father snorted derisively. "Your righteousness won't feed you, and if you refuse to be rational, neither will I."

"I will not treat her so callously, nor myself. I have not abandoned the possibility, Father, that I may yet regain for myself that which you so reprehensibly squandered. If I do, I may one day be in a position to marry. I will leave open this door to my own happiness."

His father sneered. "Happiness? With that damned nobody? That vicar's daughter? She has nothing to recommend her but a pretty face and a friendship with the duchess. That friendship may win you a seat at their table now and again, but what sustenance will it place on your own table?"

Bex eyed his father warily. "I do not speak of anyone specific. I speak of the future. The far distant future."

"I have warned you before not to play games with me, son," Edward said. He rounded the settee to stand in front of Bex and glared menacingly at him. "I saw you with her after the performance, hovering at her side all evening like a foolish lovesick swain. Ridiculous."

Bex gritted his teeth as he listened, vowing not to rise to his father's bait.

Still, the man's diatribe continued. "You have nothing. She has nothing. Together, the two of you would have nothing still. How long do you think moon-eyed love lasts when one cannot afford basic necessities? Where would you live? How would you eat? Even if she is impetuous enough to disregard those things and actually accept you, how long will that affection last in the depths of poverty? And what do you think Gibbs will do when you cannot pay? Do you really think he will leave you in peace and forget what he is owed?"

Bex stood and faced down his father's contemptuous stare with equal fire. His chest rose and fell with the exertion of keeping his rage in check. He would strangle his own father if only he were not prevented from doing so by the last shreds of decency he had retained. He spoke deliberately and enunciated clearly when he spoke. "It is by your actions that I have nothing to offer as a husband, and I will not impose that circumstance on any woman, whether she be of your choosing or of mine."

"You are too entrenched in your own youthful stupidity to behave sensibly. That tart is not your future."

"Do not speak of her that way again."

"It doesn't matter what I call her, she can do nothing for you."

"She is none of your concern."

"Nor should she be any of yours. I will leave Friday morning for Oakwood Lodge and will return four days later. I expect to learn when I return from Surrey that you have spent your time wisely—with Lady Constance."

Bex nearly snorted at his father's command. He was not in a particular mood for wise choices, whether by his father's measure or anyone else's. He knew precisely with whom he would prefer to spend the next four days. In point of fact, he decided he did have an errand out of the house that morning after all. He folded the newspaper and tucked it under his arm. "Safe journey, Father," he bit out, then he quit the room.

Chapter Twenty-Six

Lucy's life in the vicarage was busy. There was always some project or parishioner that required attention. As such, Lucy usually reveled in those peaceful moments to herself when she could read, write letters, or simply gaze out a window in quiet repose. After the excitement of the prior week, however, several days in a row of nothing in particular to do had exhausted Lucy's capacity to enjoy solitude.

Emma was increasingly tired and had taken to the habit of lengthy afternoon naps. Lucy had written to her parents, completed *The Little Academy*, and had recounted in her mind numerous times her foolish offer to Bex.

She was so desperate for any distraction, she was grateful for the knock that interrupted her thoughts, even when it was only Agnes who opened the door at her summons.

"Yes, Agnes?"

The girl's eyes were bright with excitement. "There's a package delivered for you, miss."

"A package?" Lucy repeated. Now, that had potential to break her monotony, but she was not expecting anything. "Well, bring it in and let's see what it is."

Agnes stepped into the room, her arms carrying a box wrapped in plain brown paper and tied with simple string. It was large enough to be intriguing. Lucy took it from her, feeling it. It was weighty, but not heavy, precisely.

She set the package on the bed and considered it. She could not think of anyone who might send her a parcel. Perhaps it was some sort of thank-you from Lady Constance? Lucy didn't feel she deserved thanks, but if Lady Constance felt strongly about it, a simple note would have sufficed.

This parcel was more substantial than a note. It felt decidedly present-like, despite its plain wrapping.

"Do you know who delivered this, Agnes?" Lucy asked, as she worked at the knot at the center of the parcel.

"No, miss. It was brought upstairs to me by one of the footman. I didn't make any inquiries."

Of course not, Lucy thought, finding the knot particularly stubborn.

The knot finally released and the rough string fell away. She peeled back the folded brown paper to reveal a box marked with the scrolled letter *D*—the signature of the dressmaker Madame Desmarais. It was too much. Lady Constance had already provided the dress for the concert. Already composing in her mind the thank-you letter she would immediately dispatch to the comtesse, Lucy lifted the lid on the box. Its contents were wrapped in raw muslin. She lifted one corner of the muslin and saw a patch of rich, deep red. Her pulse skipped. She lay the fabric back down, safely covering the bold color again.

"Close and lock the door, Agnes," she commanded brusquely.

"Yes, miss." Agnes hustled to do as she asked, then sidled toward Lucy, her curiosity no doubt piqued.

Lucy took a deep breath and peeled back the raw muslin a second time, feeling her temperature rise as she glimpsed the red fabric again. She spread the covering wide and gazed down at a scarlet silk bodice trimmed with jet beads.

She heard Agnes gasp.

"Who knows this parcel was delivered, Agnes?" she asked, her eyes still focused on the contents inside the wrapping. She was afraid to touch it.

"I don't know, miss," Agnes said, taking the question as an invitation to step forward and peer over Lucy's shoulder. "I think it's a gown," she whispered, her voice thick with astonishment and wonder. "It's red as blood."

It was indeed. Red as sin.

Lucy reached down and fingered the row of jet beads. They winked at her in shiny blackness against the silky red of the fabric. Gently she ran her palm across the dress. It was smooth and chilly against her warm hand. She swallowed. Gingerly, she took one shoulder of the dress in each hand and lifted it slowly.

"Oh," Agnes breathed.

The gown was beautiful—wickedly beautiful. It was richer and bolder than anything she'd ever seen, much less owned. It was scandalously low cut. The sleeves were barely more than wide-set wedges of spare silk.

"Who would send such a dress?" Agnes asked, her voice hushed and reverent.

Who indeed.

Lucy felt warm everywhere. Surely her skin must nearly match the dress for how hotly her flush burned. She did not answer Agnes's question. She knew—oh, she knew—but she did not answer.

"Is it a gift?" Agnes pressed.

A gift. Lucy smiled to herself. This dress was no simple gift. It was an invitation.

No.

He was not sending *her* an invitation. He was accepting the invitation she'd already given.

Had she really meant it? Could she go through with it? She stared at the dress and knew what accepting it meant. Had she been in earnest? Did she really want a love affair with Bex Brantwood?

"Will you try it on, miss?" Agnes asked.

"Do you think I should?" Lucy felt an exhilarating panic at the thought of actually wearing the dress, even if only in her bedroom and only in front of Agnes.

"Don't you want to?"

Lucy lay the dress back onto the bed and turned to the maid, who was staring at the garment in wide-eyed reverence.

Yes. She did. She very much wanted to try it on. And besides, it would be cruel to disappoint Agnes, wouldn't it?

"I…I suppose I could try it on," Lucy said, running her hands over the fabric again. She couldn't keep herself from touching it. "I'm sure I could never actually wear it, but"—she gazed down at it—"someone must have worked very hard to make it. It seems a shame to not even try it on."

"Oh, yes." Agnes clapped her hands together. "Let me help you." Agnes dove forward, grasping at her chance to handle the garment. She lifted it completely out of its wrapping and draped its full length across the bed.

Lucy gaped at it. It was very, very red. It was loud as a scream against the coverlet of pale green and pink flowers.

"There's another piece," Agnes said.

Lucy turned as Agnes lifted another garment. It was a chemise. Lucy reached forward and touched it. It was the softest, most delicate chemise she had ever seen.

It was dyed the same blood red as the dress.

Surely, no respectable woman wore a dyed red chemise. She had never heard of such a thing. Red undergarments? Should she try it on? She looked at Agnes in indecision.

The girl bit her lip and shrugged, still holding the wisp of red up for them both to see. "It does seem to be made for the dress," she said into the shocked silence.

Lucy nodded slowly. "I…yes…it rather does, doesn't it?"

Agnes lay the chemise onto the bed and riffled through the box again. "There are slippers as well. And stockings," she said. Then she lifted a scrap of paper with a wide, triumphant grin. "There is a note."

With a shaking hand, Lucy took the note from Agnes and read it. It was brief and cryptic.

Tomorrow. One o'clock. Number 27 Inverness Terrace.

She stared at it for a long moment then released a sigh that became a nervous laugh on exhalation. Well, what was a scandalous liaison without a scandalous dress? She blew out the rest of her nervous air in a determined rush. "Agnes, I am going to try it all on."

The maid nodded; her expression was the picture of neutral acquiescence, but her eyes twinkled in anticipation. She lay the chemise back down and quickly set to work on the buttons at the back of Lucy's day dress.

Once Lucy was stripped of all but her plain white chemise, Agnes laid Lucy's half corset next to the dress. Both women could clearly see the dress was cut so wickedly low and wide in both the front and the back that the half corset would not be fully covered by the gown.

"The skirt is awfully narrow as well," Agnes said, hands on her hips, considering the garment.

Lucy investigated, holding the skirt at its fullest width. "Well, we shall see. Perhaps it is too small."

In the end, Lucy tried on the gown with nothing underneath but the matching red chemise.

Agnes finished fastening the short row of buttons at the back of the bodice and stepped to Lucy's front to take in the full effect.

"Oh, my," she breathed.

Lucy looked down and realized she could see an incredibly generous portion of her own breasts. She swallowed. "Do you have the glass, Agnes?"

"Oh. Yes. The glass." The maid turned in a fluster and picked up the mirror. She stepped back and held it up, tilting it slightly to position it for Lucy's full view.

"Oh, my," Lucy said, echoing the maid's reaction.

Lucy felt as though she were staring at someone else's reflection. The fabric of the dress was opaque silk, thick and rich. Nothing could be seen through it, but it draped so closely across her skin it was as revealing as if the dress were, in fact, sheer. And the bodice…

Well.

Lucy had never been particularly well endowed, and especially would not expect to appear so without the lift of her stays, but the clever bodice of this dress accomplished more than her stays ever had. The band immediately below her breasts hugged her so tightly as to squeeze her upward, and the cut was so low, there were barely a few finger widths of fabric that could really be called a bodice at all. It was a decidedly daring display of skin.

Even flushed, her skin looked as white as a ghost's next to the crimson silk.

Lucy knew nothing of mistresses and paramours, but surely this was a dress to be worn by a temptress. No respectable woman could be seen in such a dress, any more than she could be seen out in her nightclothes.

Of course, this dress was not for a respectable woman. It was for Lucy, who had boldly offered herself to a man who could not marry her.

"Where did it come from?" Agnes asked, still gaping at this transformed version of Lucy.

Lucy ran her hands over the silk another time. "Well, Agnes," she said matter-of-factly, "I would presume it has come from the same dressmaker as my concert dress. Who else would have the measurements to create a gown that fits me so…so…"

"Snug?" Agnes suggested.

"It does fit rather closely, doesn't it?"

"Quite," Agnes agreed.

Lucy ran her hands over the snugly fitting band of silk that ran below her bust.

"Someone must have ordered it made," the girl pushed.

"Yes," Lucy said, toying with the row of tiny jet crystals. She took a deep breath and lifted her head, facing her reflection again in the mirror. Agnes straightened, adjusting the glass. Lucy drew back her shoulders, lifted her chin, and looked. Just looked.

She would never have imagined herself looking as she did now. No one would. No one who had ever known Lucy would possibly envision her as a bold, womanly seductress.

No one, that is, except Bex.

He had envisioned her exactly like this, because *he* had ordered the dress.

She thought of him as he must have been, describing his vision to the dressmaker, choosing colors, feeling bolts of fabric, selecting this very silk, all the while thinking of her. Did selecting her dress make him feel the way she did now, short of breath and tingling with anticipation? Making the offer to Bex had not seemed so frightening as it did now, standing in the dress he had made for her. The idea seemed very tangible all of a sudden—dangerous and irrevocable.

Lucy stared in the glass again. She looked dangerous. He had done that. Bex was the first person in her life—the only man—who had ever seen her as a bold temptress. No one had before, and likely, no one would again.

"Yes, Agnes," Lucy said on an exhale of air. "Someone ordered the dress. It was a man. He sent it as an invitation. You must tell no one." She took another deep breath. "I will need you to deliver a message, because I intend to accept."

Wide eyed, Agnes nodded.

Chapter Twenty-Seven

Lucy alighted from the hackney cab and stared down the line of stately, narrow row houses, like a regiment of distinguished soldiers, polished and awaiting inspection. She felt oddly as though she were charging forth across a battle line of sorts, taking command of her own life.

There were very few people on the quiet street, but still she kept her eyes lowered. She clutched the long, hooded cloak more closely around her throat. She had borrowed the cloak from Agnes. It was well worn—threadbare in places—and thus more likely to go unnoticed. She could not have asked Emma for the loan of a cloak, but even if she had, any garment from the duchess would be far too conspicuous.

The desire to remain unnoticed mingled with the shivers of anticipation Lucy felt—both sending her hurrying toward number twenty-seven. She ascended the steps quickly and rapped gently on the knocker.

She experienced a moment of panic as she realized she had not considered what she might say to the servant who answered her knock. Who should she say she was? What would the household staff think?

Her concerns were alleviated when the door opened and she looked up at Bex himself.

"You came," he said, gazing down with a mixture of desire and wonder that seemed to warm her very soul.

"I came," she said softly.

With a quick glance to assess the activity on the street, Bex urged her inside. Lucy obeyed and, for the first time in her life, entered a man's residence without the benefit of a chaperone. It was not lost on her that the very reason for having never done so was to avoid even the appearance of precisely what she intended today. Crossing the threshold into the home of

Bexley Brantwood felt like the most significant steps she had ever taken in her life thus far.

She took them without hesitation.

Bex closed the door behind her and enfolded her in his strong arms. He pushed back the hood of the cloak and placed a gentle, lingering kiss on the top of her head. "I am afraid I have exhausted my ability to resist you, Saint Lucy," he whispered, his breath soft against her hair.

She burrowed her face into his broad, unyielding chest. "I don't want to be a saint anymore," she mumbled against him.

"You will always be a perfect saint," he said, then held himself away from her and looked into her eyes, "but I want you like the very devil."

Bex's storm-gray eyes seemed to darken with heat and promise. They were devouring and powerful and they held her in such a vise she could not have pulled her own gaze away if the entire house crumbled around them.

He held her there, captured in his gaze for what could have been a moment or an hour for all her awareness of time, and then he crushed her to him again, holding her so tightly she could barely breathe.

"I still cannot believe you are actually here," he said.

Gently, she pulled back from his grasp and he released her, just enough so that she could look up into his face. She smiled shyly. "Now that I am here, whatever shall you do with me?"

Bex's knowing grin sent delicious shivers through her. "You've gotten a bit brazen, haven't you?"

She had felt very bold—until he'd pointed it out. Belatedly, she looked around to verify their privacy, knowing it was ruining the effect of her boldness. "Have you sent everyone away?" she asked.

"Not everyone," he said with a light laugh. "We can't leave ourselves entirely helpless."

"I'm not without practical skills," Lucy said.

"Of course you aren't," Bex said, drawing her in to hug her closely again. "I am sure you lay claim to all sorts of skills that can be called practical, but you won't need any of those today."

She swallowed. "So only some of the staff are here?"

"Yes. And I have assurances of their discretion."

Lucy must have looked doubtful, for he laughed again and said, "My father is not particularly well liked. I think they are happy to occasionally keep a few secrets from him."

Lucy nodded.

"Why don't you come with me," he said, taking her by the hand. Still enrobed in the borrowed cloak, Lucy followed without hesitation as he led her up the stairs at the end of the hall and up two flights of stairs. He guided her to a door at the back of the narrow hall, and opened it into a tidy bedroom with a large bed, two tall windows covered by simple brown drapes, and a comfortably worn corner chair. It was a simple, masculine room shrouded in shadow from the pulled drapes.

Lucy stood on the threshold, unsure what she should do. Then Bex took her hand and smiled down at her with so much sweet patience that all of her uncertainty ceased to matter. He didn't care that she didn't know what to do. He did, and she trusted him.

He gave her hand a gentle tug, and she stepped forward into his bedroom. He closed the door behind her and reached up to untie the fastenings of her cloak. Lucy stood compliantly while the sides of the garment fell loose, revealing a slash of the scarlet fabric underneath. He pushed the two sides of the cloak apart and over her shoulders. It fell away and pooled in a heap at her feet.

Chapter Twenty-Eight

Bex stared. She was not beautiful. She was ethereal and wicked at the same time. She was so soul-alteringly lovely, it caused him physical pain.

"That dress is its own scandal," he breathed.

Because it was.

Even as he blessed his unbelievable fortune for the gift of seeing her in it, he vowed no other man ever could, for his own sanity. The alabaster skin of her slender throat, her long arms, and the tantalizing curves of her breasts glowed in the dim room as though from their own source of light. The luminosity was only extinguished where it was shrouded in crimson.

The scarlet silk cupped her breasts and lifted them up to him as an offering. It skimmed neatly down from her bust and teased so closely over her curves, it tempted him like a clue to a secret. With a motion he could not have halted if he tried, his hand reached forward to stroke the smooth silk down her side, from the swell of her breast to the curve of her waist and the round of her hip. He felt like a thief fingering a prized ruby, poised in indecision of whether he should close his fist and take it, giving in to his consuming lust for the forbidden jewel.

When he spoke, he barely recognized the rough and unsteady voice as his own. "We have yet to do anything that can't be undone," he told her. "You can still change your mind." A little piece of him died to say it, but she had to know she had a choice—up until the deed was done, she would have a choice.

She lifted liquid pools of silver blue that threatened to unman him. Holding him with that gaze, she slowly shook her head. "I'm not afraid, and I'm not unsure." Her words were soft but unwavering. She lifted her hand to his face and stroked his check with a featherlight trace of her fingertip. "Please don't send me away."

Oh, thank God.

He gathered her up and nearly lifted her from the floor in his desire to reach her. His mouth slashed over hers as all of his hunger and need were unshackled by her words. He felt her arms encircle his neck and she clung to him as fiercely as he plundered her mouth. He was overcome with the compulsion to experience her in every possible way, to consume her fully before the mistake of fate that put this woman within reach was corrected and she was stolen from him.

But no. He would not overtake her. He drew back, pulling his lips from hers, even when she involuntarily leaned toward him, chasing the contact he'd broken. He pulled her close, feeling the rise and fall of her chest, knowing she struggled to regain control just as he did. He placed a kiss on top of her soft hair. "We have hours, my angel. I don't plan to spend a single minute in clumsy haste." He splayed the fingers of both hands across her back and stroked them slowly downward, cupping her bottom and drawing her snugly into him. He closed his eyes and sighed at the feel of her softness pressed against his tight, straining need.

"You don't have to offer me an escape. I don't want to leave," she said, her mouth moving against his chest. Then she pulled herself back and looked up at him, her delicate features set with firm resolve. "And you don't have to offer reassurances of how it will be. I trust you. That's why I asked you."

She slid her hand to the nape of his neck and teased her fingers into the locks of his hair there. He sighed with the pleasure of it. She lay her forehead against his chin and whispered, "My life will be useful and respectable and sensible, but I don't want to feel any of those things right now. I feel like there is a candle inside me that is melting everything into a tingling liquid. It's moving everywhere and making every single place on my body beg to be touched. Please, give me that gift. Please don't send me into my practical, predictable future without first knowing that touch—your touch—in every last place." She pressed herself more tightly to him, and he felt the tension radiating from her.

Christ.

She was killing him and he could have wept with the sweetness of it. Who was seducing whom here?

He set her from him and looked down at her in that fire of a dress. "I promise," he said huskily, his eyes boring into hers, "I will worship you. Not one single inch of you will want for attention when I am done."

He felt the shiver run through her.

With the discipline of a Spartan warrior, Bex turned away from her. He stripped down to his shirtsleeves, draping his coat and waistcoat across the corner chair. He untied the collar of his shirt and pulled it over his head, tossing it atop the other clothing.

Then he returned to Lucy.

Sweet Lucy. She had taken off her slippers. He smiled.

He came up behind her this time. Burying his face in the crook below her pinned-up hair, he pressed kisses along the back of her neck, across her collarbone, and up to her ear. His hands slid around her pixie-sized waist to splay across her stomach and traveled upward. They closed over her breasts, pushing them upward until they nearly swelled out of the wickedly low-cut dress. He pulled her full length hard against the front of him and continued to knead her pert breasts until, through the fabric, he could feel her pebble in response to his touch.

"Here?" he asked, his lips and tongue teasing her earlobe. "Did you want me to touch you here?"

She nodded wordlessly and, with eyes closed, leaned her head back against his chest. Her hands reached back, and he felt her grip the sides of his thighs for support.

"Where else do you want me to touch you?"

"Everywhere," she breathed. "Show me. Show me where I should want you to touch me."

Slowly he spun her to face him and covered her mouth again with his, taking advantage as her lips parted to taste her and deepen the kiss. She mewled, and the sound made him so hard for her, he thought his skin might rend.

"My God, Lucy," he said when he pulled his mouth from hers. "Do you have any idea what you are doing to me right now?"

She tentatively placed one hand, palm open, on his bare chest. It was warm and teasing. After a moment, the other hand followed and she began a bold exploration of his torso, from his stomach to his shoulders. Once she had satisfied herself, running her fingers nearly everywhere within reach, she slid them around his waist and spread warm palms across his lower back.

"Tell me," she said, her lips moving against his naked chest, her breath teasing in his hair. "Tell me what I'm doing to you."

She was sweetly invading every piece of his soul, but he could not tell her so.

Instead, he took her hand and guided it to where his erection strained against his breeches. "You are turning me into a green boy," he said, nearly groaning at the pleasure of the contact.

She looked down where her hand touched him, not shying away from the moment, and he decided her bold curiosity was more seductive than the most skilled courtesan. She had asked him—begged him—to touch her and, God help him, he wanted it more than she did.

In one easy motion, Bex swept her into his arms, dress and all, and laid her gently back across his bed, a slash of pale skin and bold fabric against his drab bed linens. Her passion-filled eyes were alert, curious, as he'd known they would be. His inquisitive little angel.

She was not his—not truly—but she was his today. She had given him that, and in exchange he was determined she should be the recipient of the gift for which she had so sweetly asked. He vowed to show her passion so thoroughly that all of her curiosity would be satisfied. And from a dark, vain place inside his soul, he vowed that if another man ever made love to her, the act would not compare to the memory of this first perfect taste of passion.

He wanted everything for Lucy. He wanted a lifetime's worth of adoration in one afternoon.

"Where shall I begin?" he asked softly, placing one knee on the bed to hover over where she lay. "Should I begin here?" He dipped his head to lick at her earlobe, worrying the tiny nib with his tongue and teeth. "You have tiny, perfect ears," he whispered, feeling her shift beneath him as his warm breath tickled her neck. He moved his mouth to kiss that place where his breath had warmed her. She turned her head away, instinctively granting him greater access.

"Has anyone ever kissed your shoulder, sweetheart?" he asked, knowing the answer. He touched his lips to the base of her throat then pushed aside the band of fabric that formed the narrow sleeve of her gown. His lips lingered on the smooth round of her shoulder.

"You," she said, breathless. "You're the only one who's kissed me there."

"We cannot have you neglected." He trailed a row of kisses across her collarbone toward the opposite shoulder, while his hand slipped the other sleeve of her gown over the smooth curve. He pressed his lips briefly to this newly exposed spot, but did not linger there. Without the support from her sleeves, the row of jet crystals at the hem of her bodice draped ever further down the curve of her breasts, sagging slightly, so the line of beads rose and fell over the peaks and valley.

He placed a soft, lingering kiss at the top of one creamy swell. She arched to press herself into the contact, and his lips curved into a smile against her skin. Still supporting himself above her on his knee and one hand, he used the other hand to slip his finger inside her loosened bodice, cupping one warm and weighty breast and lifting it free of its red silk cage. He lowered his lips to it, kissing gently around the soft skin then closing his mouth over the tightened peak and suckling there.

She arched and mewled.

God, he loved that sound. He could spend the rest of his wasted life working to elicit that very sound from this woman.

She whispered his name and threaded her fingers into his hair, pressing him to her, pressing herself into his mouth.

Slowly, he released his hold, blowing gently over the dampened peak and watching the shiver course through her.

"Bex," she whispered again. "Please."

"There's too much of you, sweetheart," he whispered. "There's so much more." With those words, he pulled the ruby fabric down, revealing her other, equally perfect breast, and proceeded to apply the attention it deserved—she deserved.

Finally, he pulled his mouth from her, whispering against her flesh, "You are so beautiful."

She pushed upward, trying to rise, but he halted her. "No, sweetheart, I am far from finished." He took her mouth again, unable to resist the torture of pressing his bare chest against the peaks of her breasts. He felt her melt back into the mattress as she responded to his kiss, more feverishly this time. More urgently.

He teased and nipped at her lips, whispering to her in quiet breaths of her beauty, her seductiveness, and how her sweet, eager innocence was torture to him. His free hand slipped to the fabric of her skirt, drawing it inevitably upward. Feeling his way, he ran his hand along smooth stockings and thin drawers, warm from her building heat. His hand skimmed the place at the crest of her thighs and her hips shifted, responding to the tease.

At once impatient, Bex tore his mouth from hers and lowered his weight to stand next to the bed and roughly push her skirt fully up to her waist. Checking his desire for haste, he removed first one and then the other silk stocking, rolling each one down the creamy limb it covered with enough care to cradle porcelain. Then he smoothed his hands back up each naked leg to meet in the middle and remove her thin drawers.

He looked down at her then, spread across his bed, her breasts freed from her bodice and her skirt pushed up to her waist revealing her nakedness. With her eyes closed and her lips parted, she was both wanton and innocent, like a vision from the most sensual dream he could ever have conjured.

Her eyes fluttered open as he watched, and he grinned wickedly down at her. "Stay right where you are, angel."

* * * *

Lucy was certain she could not have moved if the building were aflame. Given the heat building inside her, she could set an incinerating blaze herself.

And still she would not move.

She would not interrupt Bex's sweet, thorough attentions for anything. The more he touched her, the more she knew she needed him to keep touching her—to never stop touching her until she grasped that elusive thing that her body seemed to crave with ever-greater urgency.

Bex would give it to her. She knew with more trust and certainty than she'd ever known anything that this need, this ache inside her, ached for him. He knew how to answer it, and in that moment nothing and no one mattered more than the answer—his answer—to the question her body asked.

"Please," she asked again, knowing—not caring a whit—that she begged him as the starving begged for food. "Please, Bex."

"You are so beautiful," he whispered again, his breath tickling the sensitive flesh at the inside of her thighs.

Lucy didn't feel beautiful. She felt sultry and free. If she only knew what to ask, she would find the air, despite her breathlessness, to ask for every wicked thing—to beg for every wicked touch.

"Bex…I…"

His hand stroked higher on her thigh, then covered the mound at her center. Involuntarily, she pressed herself upward into the touch. "Please…I…"

Just touch me. Show me what I want.

He lifted his hand from her, and she mourned the loss like a death. Her hips squirmed in protest. He placed a kiss at the very top of her thigh. His tongue darted out in a teasing stroke and a new course of shivers chased through her.

She spread her legs wider, shameless, no piece of her wanting to hide from him.

He rewarded her, trailing a finger along the place that cried most urgently for his touch. "You are the most perfectly sensual woman, sweet Lucy. You are so ready for me."

"Please," she urged again, wanting more of the same, more of the rest. "Take me," she whispered. "I will die if you do not."

"You will live a little longer, my angel. I cannot yet. Patience." His finger stroked along her core again, then he lowered his head and his tongue licked along the same path. Lucy stilled, letting the heady sensation of this new touch wash over her.

Was he supposed to be doing that? Did people *do* that?

He licked again and, God save her, she didn't care if it was supposed to be happening, she just hoped he would not stop. He kissed and teased and licked her until she gripped the bedsheets in tight fists and could not even call his name through the building urgency. He slid a finger into her heat as his mouth moved over her, and she gasped at the pleasure of it. He tortured her with pleasure until she could do nothing but crave it, even as it happened, letting the sensations consume her until she quaked with a final intensity and shouted his name.

He retreated slowly. When she had recovered enough to open her eyes and look at him, she found him hovering above, watching her. The intensity of his expression gripped her. It was full of so much naked truth—desire, possession, victory. She reveled in the heady sensation of bringing a man—this man—to a point past artifice where all that was left to feel was primitive and transparent.

"We can stop here," he said, his voice thick and deep.

"No." She answered without hesitation. There was more and she would have it. "You promised," she whispered.

His gray eyes closed briefly then opened, darker and more primal.

"Show me the rest," she instructed, emboldened by his response, and he did her bidding. He was gone only a moment to shed the last of his clothing, then he was over her again, taking the peak of one breast roughly in his mouth, dragging his teeth across the sensitive tip. Her hands threaded into his hair then clutched at his shoulders.

He lifted his head again and looked down at her. He inhaled and exhaled slowly. "Are you certain?"

At her nod, he positioned himself between her legs, and she felt the pressure of him at her opening. He slid one hand under her buttocks, lifting her as he entered, easing himself into her core. He stilled then, filling her while her body adjusted to the invasion, tensing first then relaxing.

She considered the sensation, feeling tight and full in a place she had never felt empty before. Instinctually, she knew she would feel empty when he retreated. Without thinking, she pushed against him, drawing him deeper to fill her more tightly, and she liked the feeling. She pushed again.

Bex groaned and buried his face in the crook of her neck. "I'm trying to be still and let you get used to me," he said in the same thick voice as before.

Lucy didn't think that sounded right. The need to move, to squirm under him, only grew as he remained inside her. "I don't want to be still," she whispered, and as though to give credence to her words, her hips moved involuntarily and her insides tightened.

He groaned again. This time he withdrew partway. Just as she opened her mouth to object, he filled her again and it was the movement she'd been seeking. Her hips rose to respond to it. He withdrew and returned again, in the same taunting motion, and she met the thrust again, drawing her hand around his back to hold him as they moved together.

He repeated the wicked pattern, slowly at first, then more quickly and more forcefully as she clutched herself to him and felt her intensity building all over again.

He whispered every name he had for her with each escalating movement—Lucy, angel, sweetheart. His words, his movement, his scent all melded to one heady reality—him—that consumed her senses and drove her need ever higher before she clung to him and felt the quaking overtake her again.

"Lucy." He called her name in astonishment and she knew, even as it happened, that he was feeling her body as it quaked and she didn't care.

No. She did care. She wanted him to feel it. She held on and let the feelings shake them both.

"Oh, God, Lucy."

He filled her with one final thrust, deep and satisfying, and then she was empty again and his weight fell on her, steadying her through the last of the shudders that coursed through her body. She felt a shiver run through him and he said her name again, a whisper this time.

Lucy released an uneven sigh, consciousness returning, unwelcome and comforting at the same time. She stroked her hands slowly up and down his back until she felt his weight lift from her.

The shock of air drew her attention to a spot of dampness on her abdomen and she realized he had spilled his seed there, after he had left her. He pushed himself off the bed and retrieved a cloth from next to his washbasin. He returned to her and wiped his seed from her skin.

Lucy was startled to realize he had considered the possibility that she be left with child. She was even more startled to realize that she had not. It was a significant detail, that.

He had shielded her.

Even in the heat of passion, he had safeguarded her from the consequences of their choice.

Bex stretched out beside her, pulling her skirt back down over her legs, and pulled her against him. She huddled, small and tight, in the cocoon of his arms and had the inexplicable feeling that he had rescued her from a greater danger than a child—a danger so fresh that she still clung to him from the fear that lingered.

Chapter Twenty-Nine

"I can feel your disapproval upon me, Agnes."

The maid looked up, her eyes wide, all innocence and confusion, as the two sat together in the hired carriage, returning to Worley House after Lucy had collected Agnes from an afternoon of errands.

"Oh, don't pretend, Agnes. I know you disapprove. I also know it is out of concern for me and I thank you."

Agnes lowered her round, chocolate eyes. "It wouldn't do for me to be forming opinions on where you go and what you do, Miss Betancourt."

Lucy sighed. "You are worse at lying than I am, Agnes. You may as well look me in the eye and tell me what you have to say." Lucy wasn't sure why she pushed the maid to offer commentary—wasn't even certain if she should be seeking censure or understanding.

Agnes lifted her gaze to Lucy. She wrung her hands and bit her lip before saying, "It's all very exciting, but I wonder..." She paused, her face pinching with the awkwardness of the conversation. "Do you think he'll marry you...in the end?"

Lucy looked steadily back at the woman, who was likely very near to her in age. Her question was precisely the question that any one of Lucy's friends or family would immediately ask if they knew what she had done.

Of course, he would not marry her. She had known that he would not. That was not the answer Agnes sought, with her wide, hopeful eyes. Guilt stabbed Lucy. She should have considered that, before involving the poor girl. Of course Agnes would hope for a marriage. A marriage would mean absolution for all of them, wouldn't it? Lucy sighed. She would like very much to ease the maid's guilty conscience, but she could not lie to her.

"I do not," Lucy said softly. Disappointment weighted the girl's shoulders as the hope drained from her eyes. Lucy lay a gentle hand on her arm. "He has not played me falsely, Agnes. There was never any expectation of marriage."

This revelation drew Agnes's interest anew. She stared at Lucy in wonder and something akin to respect. When she spoke, it was in a whisper, despite their decided lack of company, as though the thought were too scandalous to be spoken aloud. "You never thought to marry him?"

Lucy straightened her shoulders, feeling her cheeks warm slightly at the shock in the maid's expression. "I do not expect to marry him, or anyone else for that matter. I will shortly be taking a position as a governess." And as they were being so frank with each other, she added, "So long as it does not become public, my ruination shall never matter to anyone."

To anyone, save myself.

Agnes nodded slowly, but Lucy sensed the other woman did not truly understand. Lucy could not look back over the past few hours and see the sin in what she'd experienced. She could not remember the way that Bex had touched her and the way that he had made her feel and believe for a moment that he had mistreated her. Didn't she deserve this adventure?

I will worship you.

The memory of his words sent warmth snaking through her even then. She had felt worshipped, cherished—not used or wronged. If the truth were revealed, however, that is how she would be seen. As surely as she would be considered ruined, she would be considered a victim as well—a weak, defenseless woman who lost her soul to a devious man. Just as Agnes pitied her now, so would others pity her, even as they refused to accept her.

She was not ashamed of her choice. She did not regret it.

How could she, when she knew that Bex had given her the gift of an experience she would never have had without him? He said his father would be gone for three days. These few days were a brief respite of adventure and excitement in an otherwise practical and miserably sensible life.

Well, that wasn't fair.

She was not miserable. She appreciated sensible people. She preferred them. Practicality was always the preferable choice.

Except when it wasn't.

Practicality reduced complications, but some experiences justified complicating things. Lucy could barely comprehend what had happened that afternoon, but she knew wholeheartedly she would accept a great number of complicating details in order to experience it again.

What luck, then, that she and Bex had two more days.

Just two more days.

* * * *

Lucy did not notice the burly gentleman when she first alighted from the hired coach in front of Worley House. She did not notice him until he was near enough to touch her.

"Pardon, miss," he said, and she nearly cried out at the surprise of the sound so near to her ear. Her head snapped to face him at the same time that she instinctively sidled away from the words.

He was dressed as a gentleman, but had the marked face and brawny build of a ruffian. She looked toward the house to see that Agnes had not heard the man and continued toward the door. Lucy considered calling out to the maid.

"Pardon, miss," the man repeated, eliminating any doubt that he had been attempting to gain her attention. "Please," he said gently, backing away a step as though he knew the movement would reassure her, "I mean no threat to you, Miss Betancourt."

He knew her name. Curiosity warred with instincts to flee to the safety of Worley House, not fifteen feet away. Its proximity made her bold, perhaps, for she asked him. "Who are you? How do you know my name? What do you want?"

"My name is Archibald Gibbs, miss, and I make it my business to know as many names as possible. I also make it my business to take care of my friends. That is why I am here."

"You are not my friend, Mr. Gibbs, nor do I imagine we have any friends in common."

"As it happens, we do have a common friend," he told her with a sigh. "I have considerable business with Mr. Brantwood."

And there it was. "Business" no doubt referred to unpaid debts to be collected. She recalled Bex mentioning at one point that he may be followed by his moneylenders. Was this man following him? Was he now following her? The way he watched her—it was careful, wary, but not sinister. She did not have the sense that he meant her harm, but neither did she consider it particularly benign to approach her on the street in such a manner.

She stepped toward the house. "If that is the case, your business is not with me. I bid you good day."

"Please, Miss Betancourt," he said, halting her departure. "I believe we can be of help to each other."

Even as she knew she should not, Lucy took the bait. Because if there was some way—some chance—that she could help Bex in his predicament, she would do it. "How is that, Mr. Gibbs?"

He shrugged, looked into the street for a moment to watch a passing carriage, then turned back to her. "I would venture a guess that your friend, the duchess, isn't aware of where you've been spending your afternoon."

So he was following her. That observation didn't seem particularly helpful. Her eyes narrowed. "Are you threatening me, Mr. Gibbs?"

He stepped forward, palms raised in supplication, and shook his head. "I am not. I am only encouraging caution. If I know where you've been spending your time, Miss Betancourt, it stands to reason others may as well."

"Thank you for your concern, Mr. Gibbs, but as you do not know me, I should think my reputation is none of your concern."

"I beg to differ, miss," he said, and oddly, his eyes looked kind, despite all the signs that she should be threatened by him. "It is my business to know things, especially regarding men who are important to me. Men who owe me a debt are very important to me. I have been paying attention to Mr. Brantwood and have come to understand who might be important to him."

"I think you misunderstand my importance to anyone," Lucy said, her spine straightening. "But even if I were, as you say, important, what would that mean for you? What is it you want, Mr. Gibbs?"

"I have no interest in threatening you, Miss Betancourt. You seem like a good enough girl. I only hope that you will consider the circumstances. Mr. Brantwood is a man who bears the weight of debts. To a man with no living, the weight of those debts is heavy indeed, but to another man, these same debts may not seem so insurmountable. A duke, perhaps, might find the amount insignificant."

Lucy eyed Mr. Gibbs closely, cautious to keep her expression unrevealing. Bex did not want the duke to pay his debts. She knew that. She did not know if this man knew that, but she sensed informing him would not benefit Bex's circumstances. She waited silently for the man to continue.

"If our friend were to engage in conduct of which the duke disapproves, it seems to me Worley would be less likely to offer his help. As Mr. Brantwood's friend, I would not want to do anything to close that particular door for him."

Lucy regarded him. "As Mr. Brantwood's creditor, you mean."

Mr. Gibbs shrugged. "Can a man not be both? I will tell you that Mr. Brantwood's debts are considerable and there are other measures I could take in an attempt to collect. I only suggest you think about it."

He held a calling card out to her then and she took it. He waited while she read it. *Archibald Gibbs, Proprietor, No. 22 King Street, St. James.*

"I am more friend to Mr. Brantwood than you realize, miss. As a friend, my advice is for you to be more careful so that neither one of you is harmed."

Lucy tucked the card into the pocket of her cloak and nodded. "I shall take it under advisement, Mr. Gibbs."

He nodded to her then and stepped away, continuing down the street as though they had never spoken. She glanced around to see who might have noticed, but the square across the street was empty save for two women, backs turned, walking the opposite direction. When she glanced again toward Mr. Gibbs, he was gone.

* * * *

When Lucy reached her bedchamber, Agnes informed her that Emma was much revived following a day of rest and the family would dine together. She had just enough time to change and ready herself for the evening meal.

Agnes helped remove the scarlet gown. As Lucy hid it away, her mind spun at this new, previously unconsidered, consequence of her actions. Hadn't Bex said the duke was paying the lease of the house he shared with his father—the house where she had just been? Her stomach clenched at the thought of the evening meal. Would they know? Would she be somehow changed in a way that would be discernable by her dearest friend or by her clever and observant husband?

She was changed, of course—irrevocably so. Yet oddly, nothing was different. She was still a vicar's daughter from Beadwell with no dowry or prospects. She was Emma's friend and companion. She was Lord and Lady Ashby's soon-to-be governess. Nothing about the course of her future was altered in the slightest, yet somehow everything had shifted. She felt oddly as though her path forward remained unchanged, but she now viewed it from a perspective several feet to one side.

Lucy shook her head. She was making no sense at all. She sighed heavily.

"Is everything all right, miss?" Agnes asked.

Lucy gave her a kind smile. Agnes knew everything was not all right. It was awful and wonderful and, despite Mr. Gibbs's warnings, Lucy knew she was going to commit the same transgression the next day and the one after that. "All is well, Agnes," she said, because she knew it was what the maid needed to hear. "Thank you for your help."

Lucy wasn't sure if she meant with dressing, or with the entire drama, but Agnes nodded in acceptance and left her. Lucy walked to her dressing table and lifted a hand mirror, surveying her appearance. In her pale blue dress and prim knot, she was herself again, and already the events of the afternoon seemed the stuff of dreams and fancy.

* * * *

"I'm sorry I've been such a pitiful hostess," Emma said as soon as they were seated in the dining room. "What did you do while I was sleeping today, Lucy?"

Lucy looked across the table at her friend and belatedly realized the difficulty in facing Emma and the duke would not be in their intuitive sense that Lucy had changed, but in their direct questions regarding how she had spent her day. She did not want to lie to Emma. If anyone might understand her choice, surely it was her dearest lifelong friend.

But she couldn't confide in her now—not in front of the duke. What if the duke blamed Bex? What if the duke ceased his support of Bex and his father and they were cast out without a home?

"Agnes and I went out," she said, concentrating on swirling her spoon in her soup. She did not want to look Emma in the eye when she lied to her. "We had a very long walk and browsed at a bookshop."

"Was the weather warm, then?" Emma asked. "I'm afraid I entirely missed the day."

"It was quite nice. How are you feeling now that your time is getting closer?" she asked, hoping to redirect the focus of their conversation.

"There is no difference, really," Emma said, dabbing daintily at the corners of her mouth with her napkin. She indicated with a wave, and her soup bowl was whisked efficiently away, barely touched. "I am tired and continue to be queasy. I am told I should experience some changes at the end that will signal the baby is readying to make an appearance."

"Yes, well," the duke drawled, "you were also told the sickness would not persist past the first few months. I'm not certain my confidence is high in the guidance we've received." He leaned back in his chair and regarded his wife intently. "I think we should be prepared for the fact that there may be no signs at all."

"That sounds wise," Lucy agreed and immediately felt a stab of shame that she intended to be away a significant portion of the next two days. It was, she realized, the final sign that she could not continue. "I shall cancel my outing tomorrow," she said, and immediately the events of the afternoon were pulled even further into a place that seemed more imagination than memory.

"That's nonsense," Emma declared. "What plans?"

Lucy swallowed and realized her mistake for voicing the decision aloud, thus necessitating another lie. "I was going to return to the museum with Mr. Brantwood—with Agnes, of course." It was the plan Bex had devised before she left him that afternoon. He was going to collect the two women from Worley House, rather than leave them to find their own way again. "I shall simply send a message postponing the outing."

Even as she offered it, Lucy grieved for the loss. It would not simply be postponed, of course. It would be over.

"Nonsense," Emma said again.

"Don't be stubborn, darling," the duke said. "Miss Betancourt is correct. The museum isn't going anywhere. She can visit any day in the next score of years. Your well-being is the most important thing." He turned to Lucy then. "I shall endeavor to be home as much as possible over the next several days, but I do have some commitments that cannot be canceled. I will be greatly comforted knowing my wife is in your care."

"Of course." Lucy couldn't not suppress the reminder of her outing to Hertfordshire. The duke's words were so similar to Bex's when he persuaded Annabelle Maris to care for her. She could not help smiling that Bex's impression of a doting husband had been a rather authentic interpretation.

"I am pregnant," Emma said, frustration in her tone. "I may not be spry, but I am perfectly lucid. I do not require a keeper. If I have need of anyone, I am surrounded by a house full of competent staff who shall gladly come to my aid."

"It's no use arguing, Emma," Lucy said. "The decision is made." And it was. She would send a message to Bex. She was already considering the words in her head. She must convey her regrets for canceling their plans, but sending one's regrets was just the polite form used in every cancellation. How could she convey that *her* regrets were real—that she was bereft over the forfeit of her two additional afternoons, and so very grateful for the one she'd had?

"If you would like to pen a note after dinner, Miss Betancourt, I shall see it delivered to my cousin first thing in the morning."

Lucy turned to the duke. "Thank you, Your Grace. That is very kind."

Her concerns over wording were all for naught. The note would convey none of the things she wished, unless she wrote it in code.

Chapter Thirty

Bex sat in the small breakfast room and read the letter again. Guilt and frustration chased through him, leaving him empty of nothing save the defeat.

He lay the letter on the table and stared, unseeingly, at the opposite wall. His hopes for Hertfordshire were dashed. The broker had still not procured any raw cotton. The overseer had released all the weavers and tacklers and everyone else. The weaving shed was to be shuttered—a thousand looms having never woven a single bolt of cloth.

That was that. He had nothing, and now, no remaining cause for hope. Hertfordshire was dead and he had not yet secured a backer for Birmingham. Lucy would return this afternoon and he had planned to talk with her about their future, but how could he with this news? He had nothing to offer her yet.

Bex had watched her from the upstairs window the previous afternoon, hurrying to the waiting carriage. She had pulled the hood of her cloak over her head to hide herself from prying eyes, and it was like the dousing of a bright light with a candle snuffer. Guilt had torn through him then, and sliced ever deeper now.

He had deflowered her. He had taken sweet, pure, saintly Lucy and turned her into a scandal, sneaking about under cover of cloak and hired carriage. She, who deserved more than any other to be offered all that is pure and honest and good. He had no ability to offer her those things and he had greedily taken away her hope of having them from anyone else.

He had ruined her.

To marry her now would only ruin her more completely. What could he offer her but poverty? What sort of position could he even find to support her? He was trained for nothing but to be a gentleman farmer and his father had done his best over the past several years to cure him of even that. Besides, what was a gentleman farmer with no farm? There was no estate. There was no income. There was nothing but homelessness for Bex and his father as soon as the duke's generosity was exhausted.

Lucy had thought she wanted this with him—she had called it a gift. Since her life would be one of service and spinsterhood, she wanted to experience a romantic affair rather than live her life never knowing. And she had wanted him to be the man to show her these things. He had greedily grasped at the opportunity without ever letting himself dwell on what he knew to be true—her rationale had been horribly and devastatingly flawed.

She had not been doomed to a life of governessing and loneliness—not before she came to him. Then, her life could have taken any unexpected turn. She could have married, could have met a man worthy of her.

But he'd taken all of that away. He'd not given her a gift, as he'd so greedily let himself believe. He'd sentenced her to a life of atonement. He'd stolen her hope right along with her virginity.

She had not been his to take, but now that he had, she was his to protect.

He didn't know how he would do it, but Bex knew in that moment that, with or without a marriage, this woman was his responsibility for the rest of her life. He would not allow her to pay for his weakness.

"Good morning, son."

The voice jolted Bex from his thoughts and he sprang from his chair, turning to face his father. Just before he spoke, he caught himself and stopped. He released a long breath and spoke with outward calm, wary of his father's game. "You have returned early, I see."

Edward peered at him and pursed his lips as though considering Bex's reaction to his return. "Yes. Yes, I have. What have you been doing in my absence?"

Bex returned to his chair, his mind already drafting the missive to Lucy that their afternoon plans had been quashed. "Not much of note. How could I when you've barely been gone two days."

Before Bex could prevent it, his father reached over him and snatched from the table the letter he had placed there.

Edward studied the page, then, with a dismissive toss, returned it to the table where it landed atop the butter. "Ridiculousness," he spat.

Bex's jaw tightened. "It's none of your concern."

"You forget yourself. I will decide when I speak to you and you will listen."

Bex rose and faced his father with an eerie calm. "No. You have no authority over me. I won't listen to your tirades and I will not do your bidding."

"No?"

"No. I will manage my own financial affairs."

"With these ridiculous schemes?" Edward snorted derisively. "You are as foolish as the gamers who believe they will make their fortune at cards or dice. There is only one fortune made at the Birdcage and that is the one belonging to Archibald Gibbs."

Bex had exhausted all stores of tolerance for his father's lectures. "As my future will not rely upon any contribution from you, I will proceed without regard to your wishes."

Edward stepped forward. "What about regard to your dignity? To your family name?"

Bex stared at his father, incredulous. "You accuse me of sacrificing my dignity?" Of all the accusations his father could have leveled at him, he could not have predicted such an absurd, hypocritical conclusion. The man was living off the charity of his cousin and could no longer support his family due to his own greed and shortsightedness.

Edward pointed at him. "You are descended from a duke. Your family are peers and landed gentry. You would lower yourself to tradesman and forfeit your right of birth?"

Bex shook his head in disgust. "My family used to be landed gentry," he spat, glaring at the man he once sought to emulate. "They are now impoverished beggars with no right to hold themselves above any man able to support himself without charity from others."

Edward's eyes narrowed. "You could have changed our fortunes. You had opportunities. Real opportunities, not these silly schemes."

"Do you mean Lady Constance? Yes, all of your problems would be solved if I would just marry a rich widow." He crossed his arms in front of his chest. "Well, I will not. You should know once and for all, Father, that I will not be a fortune hunter to support you. I never will."

Edward lifted his chin in challenge. "I knew you wouldn't. You have been chasing that vicar's daughter, instead. That is why I've washed my hands of you."

Bex paused. His father looked victorious. Too victorious.

"You've received a letter this morning," Edward said tauntingly. "I intercepted it as I arrived." His father produced a small, folded square of paper and held it aloft.

Bex glanced briefly at it. He wanted to grasp it from his father's hands and learn what it said, but he was clever enough to understand the more he wanted that letter, the more power he would grant his father.

He did his best to ignore the letter instead. "What do you mean?" he asked, his eyes narrowing. "How have you washed your hands of me? Have you done what you threatened? Are the servants tossing my possessions into the street as we speak?"

Disregarding the letter proved a successful tactic. His father tossed it to the table. "It's a letter from that chit. She was a mistake. You should have listened to me."

A slow, sick churning began in Bex's stomach, but he worked very hard not to show it. He desperately wanted to read the letter, to know what it revealed. "You didn't answer my question," he observed flatly. "How have you washed your hands of me?"

Edward smirked. "I know you've been sniffing around Lord Ashby, trying to get him to fund one of your schemes. I don't expect he will be doing so after all."

How had his father even known about Ashby? He stepped forward, unable to maintain his outward reserve. "What did you do?"

If his father was having him followed, if he'd read Lucy's letter, then he knew everything. He knew too damn much not to ruin them all.

The twisting in Bex's stomach stopped and sank instead as a dead weight inside him, chilling him from his core. He lunged forward, grabbing fistfuls of his father's foppishly tailored coat, not caring that the man was his family, not caring if he harmed him, only needing to know the truth.

"What did you do?" he demanded again.

Edward's initial shocked expression gave way to a slow, sinister spread of lips and teeth. Even as Bex held him in a vice of strength fortified by fury, the man smiled and Bex had his answer.

Bex hated him then. He hated that they shared a name. He hated that his blood was this man's blood. He tugged harder, bringing his father's face to within mere inches of his own and glared, letting loose all the venom and hatred boiling inside him. He needed to hear it still. "You will tell me now what you have done, or I will tear each appendage from your body, one by one, until you do."

"You are a waste of a son," Edward spat.

"Now," Bex thundered, pulling upward until his father's feet began to lift from the floor and his face registered genuine alarm. Edward Brantwood had been strong in his youth, but he was no longer a young man. Bex was, and he had spent years on an estate farm, sometimes working alongside tenants and stable hands. Bex would have no difficulty in causing serious harm should he choose to do so, and his father knew it.

"I knew you wouldn't do what needed to be done. I knew you would make our situation worse because you refused to make it better. You gave me no choice but to go to Ashby."

Bex's voice barely escaped, low and thick, through his clenched teeth. "What did you say to him?"

"I told him I had lost control of you. That you are a disgrace to the family. That I could not, in good conscience, allow him to lend you funds when you had taken his children's intended governess as mistress."

Bex threw him then. Through his rage, he did not know where or how the bastard landed and did not care. If he'd held a knife, he'd have used it.

He snatched Lucy's letter from the table and left the room, unfolding the paper as he went.

Mr. Brantwood,

While I am sincerely grateful for your offer to accompany me to the museum, I am afraid I cannot leave the duchess as she nears her time. Regretfully, I must postpone any such outings indefinitely. Please know that I am sincere in my disappointment, as you have proved to be a most knowledgeable guide.

Your pupil,
Miss Lucy Betancourt

Chapter Thirty-One

Lucy awoke to a knock on her bedchamber door and looked up to see Emma stealing into the room and closing the door quietly behind her. Lucy was immediately disoriented. What time was it? She didn't usually oversleep. She shook her head to clear her bleary mind and focused on Emma.

Emma was still in her night rail and wrapper.

Lucy sprang from the bed in a single, clumsy motion and rushed to her friend. "Is something the matter, Emma? Is it time? Should I get the duke?"

Emma shook her head silently in response, but her lips were pressed tightly and her eyes were troubled. Something *was* the matter.

"Emma, sit, please," Lucy said, guiding her to the bed. "Tell me what the trouble is."

Emma's hand reached out and gripped Lucy's arm with surprising strength. "You should sit," she said firmly. "The trouble is yours."

Lucy's eyes flew to Emma's, saw the betrayal there, and knew already. She sank to the bed and sat. "You know," she said quietly.

"Is it true?" Emma asked.

There was so much Lucy wanted to explain—to clarify. She wanted to ask exactly what Emma knew and correct any misinformation, but in the end, the details were unimportant, so she said, "Yes." She could not stop herself from adding, "I'm sorry."

Emma sighed. "I wish you had confided in me, Lucy. I blame myself."

She turned to see Emma's golden brown eyes bright with tears. "No," she said, taking Emma's hand. "You should not be feeling guilt. I am the guilty one. You should be angry and disgusted with me. I should have told you. You should have found out…"

A small thread of panic wound its way through her. "How did you find out?"

Emma closed her eyes. She sighed heavily before opening them again and turning to Lucy.

The duke knows. Somehow the duke knew and Bex would be homeless and it was all her fault.

Emma squeezed Lucy's hand reassuringly before breaking the news. "From Lady Ashby."

Lucy shot up from the bed. "What?" She shook her head. "That can't be right. How could she? I don't understand."

"It's true." Emma's voice was steady and calm, while Lucy's heart raced.

Panic unfurled inside her, eclipsing everything else save the last remnants of her denial. "How can that be?"

"According to Lady Ashby, her husband was approached by Mr. Brantwood regarding an investment. He was cautioned against it by Mr. Brantwood's own father who claimed his son was a man of loose morals who had taken as mistress the very woman the Ashbys intended to hire as governess."

Lucy stared. "How could he?" His own father? It couldn't be true. She threw her hands up. "I am not his mistress," she shouted, as though somehow that signified, which she knew it did not.

"So, it's not true?" Emma asked, brow knit in confusion.

"No. Yes. Oh, God." Lucy collapsed back onto the bed and covered her face with her hands. "I am an idiot," she said into her palms. "And I have ruined everything."

"I think you had better explain it all to me, Lucy. We shall decide together what to do next."

Her quiet words, spoken firmly, penetrated Lucy's lament, and slowly Lucy lowered her hands. *Everyone will someday test the loyalty of their true friends.* How wise Lady Constance was. Lucy was unfairly testing Emma's loyalty now, but here Emma was, offering quarter, remaining by her side.

Lucy's eyes lifted to Emma's. She saw the love there before her own vision blurred with tears. "I believe, Emma, you are the dearest person who has ever lived."

She felt another reassuring squeeze at her hand as Emma said, "Tell me everything."

And she did. She told her all of it, from the very first meeting, and apologized profusely for every time she'd been too ashamed or too frightened or too selfish to confide in her.

"The absolute worst part, Emma, is what I've done to Bex. If the duke refuses to help him, he'll be without a home. And I didn't know he had approached Lord Ashby, but I knew he needed funds for his investments and I've ruined that as well." Lucy buried her face in her hands again. "I convinced him to do this and it cost him everything," she said miserably.

Emma's hand ran soothingly back and forth across Lucy's shoulders. "You care very deeply for him, don't you?" she asked gently.

It was a pointless question. She loved him. Of course she loved him. She had for some time and she'd known it, but it didn't matter when they couldn't be together. It surely didn't matter now that she was responsible for destroying him. "I care enough that I regret the harm I have done," Lucy said, knowing it was not the confession Emma sought, but she could not voice it, not when the emotion was so foolish and so wasted.

Emma sighed. "I will concede his chances with Ashby are lost, as are yours, but John is not an ogre. We shall discuss this, all of us, and decide what is to be done." She rose then. "I don't think you will be calm until we've settled this, dear, so we should not delay. Dress, compose yourself, and come to my room. We shall talk there."

"Thank you, Emma," Lucy said, and because she was overwhelmed with the need to do so, she threw her arms around her friend and hugged her the best she could despite her protruding middle. Emma returned the hug and left with her best attempt, no doubt, at a reassuring smile.

Lucy released a tremulous breath into the empty room and said a prayer of gratitude for the gift of Emma in her life. She donned a dress quickly and went to the dressing table for her hairbrush. She spied the ecru card there for Mr. Archibald Gibbs. He had been right to caution her. He had been a friend to Bex, after all.

But he had been too late.

Her recklessness had already ruined Bex's chance to gain an investor. She picked up the card and toyed with it as she considered. Why hadn't Bex confided that he did have a plan beyond the weaving operation in Hertfordshire? She supposed he may have kept it from her because she'd demonstrated such an aversion to his risk taking. Gaining an investor in Lord Ashby would have provided funds, but not ensured success.

But these calculated risks—these opportunities to change his fortune— they were his purpose. And she had taken that away. She had cost him an investor.

A thought took hold of Lucy. She *owed* Bex an investor.

She looked at the card in her hand. Clearly Archibald Gibbs would not be extending any further credit.

* * * *

"Well," Emma asked when the three of them were assembled in her chamber, "what shall we do?"

Lucy swallowed. She looked to where Emma sat upon her bed, her husband standing beside her. "Please allow me to apologize for my reckless behavior and the tarnish it has brought on your household."

Emma shook her head. "You are not here for a scolding, Lucy. You are a grown woman. We are here to discuss what can be done."

Lucy nodded, appreciating her friend's continued support, but she looked next to the duke, not expecting to see the same absence of censure.

"I agree," he responded, much to her surprise, but then added, "I will deal with my cousin another day."

Lucy shook her head. "No, please, there is no need. He has been punished more than he deserves already."

"I had thought better of Bex Brantwood," the duke said, his expression darkening. "I suppose I knew enough not to expect better of his father."

Lucy fumed at the mention of the man who had ruined his own son. "Edward Brantwood is an awful, scheming man. Why do the Ashbys believe him?"

"He is the man's father," Emma said. "And even if he is wrong, there are other investments and other governesses. The Ashbys will not embroil themselves in scandal, and their decision will guide the view of many others."

Lucy sighed. "So I am ruined."

"It depends upon your definition of ruination," Emma said with a weak attempt to appear hopeful. "Even a hint of scandal means you will never be a governess, sadly, but many a tarnished reputation has been resolved with a firm denial and a well-timed wedding."

Lucy shook her head. "There are no marriage prospects for me."

"I will provide a dowry," the duke said. "That will alter your prospects."

Lucy did not want prospects. She wanted Bex, and he would not want her with the duke's charity. He might not want her at all, now that her recklessness had destroyed his plans. "No," she said. "I will not marry just to save myself. My reputation is insignificant. I will return home to my parents." She turned to direct her entreaty to the duke. "My future plans were not the great loss in this circumstance. Bex...Mr. Brantwood had very few avenues by which to reverse his ill fortunes, and I have taken those away from him. I have...stolen his purpose."

"I don't see that *you* are the one who has stolen from him," the duke scoffed.

"No," she insisted, rising from her seat, tears of frustration pooling. "Why will no one understand? Why do you insist upon declaring me the victim, as though I do not know my own mind? My liaison with Mr.

Brantwood was my own choice. More than that, it was my proposal, and when he refused, I persisted. I have ruined him."

The duke quieted in response to her outburst. He watched her for a moment before looking to his wife, his expression softening as he reached to take her hand. "I can understand," he said finally, "that a pair could be so overcome with affection for each other that they could be moved to recklessness."

Emma lifted their joined hands to hold his to her cheek.

"But if you must take ownership of your own choice, Miss Betancourt, then so must he claim responsibility for his."

Lucy straightened her shoulders. "Then we shall bear joint culpability, Your Grace, but if I am in a position to repair the damage, I should like to do so."

"Bu you said the cost to Mr. Brantwood was the loss of Ashby's investment," Emma pointed out. "How could you be in a position to change his mind?"

Lucy exhaled. "I cannot persuade Lord Ashby, but I could find another investor." She looked to the duke.

He pressed his lips into a grim line before he answered. "I believe we have already established Mr. Brantwood's unwillingness to accept charity from me."

"This would be an investment," she reasoned, but even as she argued, she knew the duke was correct. Bex would view it as charity. She bit her lip and considered. "What if it were not only you?" she asked. "What if you were one of a pool of investors?" Bex had invested that way, hadn't he? He certainly didn't consider that charity.

The duke stepped forward to lay a hand on Lucy's shoulder. "Your affection for my cousin is very clear, Miss Betancourt, and I do admire your determination to come to his aid." He sighed before continuing. "But given the fresh scandal, even I would be hard pressed to persuade many gentlemen to consider an investment with Mr. Brantwood at the present. I am sorry, but Mr. Brantwood may need to puzzle out a solution to his own financial affairs."

Lucy's head and heart fell. If even a duke could not assemble a group of investors…

She lifted her eyes to the duke. "What if someone else could?" she asked. "Could assist me in assembling a group of investors?"

The duke looked dubious.

"But who else could that be?" Emma asked.

A smile broke—her first of the day. "I believe I know just such a man."

Chapter Thirty-Two

Bex sat at a table in the corner and sipped scotch. He had been there every night for a week. He had come to the only place from which he was reasonably certain he would not be thrown out.

Of course, it would not be long before Gibbs knew all the sordid details and concluded there would be no forthcoming payments from the duke on Bex's behalf. Perhaps then he *would* be turned out.

If Lucy were there, she would tell him he should have some plan for that eventuality, but she was not with him. She would never be with him. He could not imagine a scenario in which he would likely ever be in the same room as Saint Lucy of Beadwell again.

Besides, he did have a plan. Eventually, he would return to the townhouse and collect his things.

There. He lifted the glass to his lips again. He had a plan.

A shout rose from the hazard table. He glanced idly in that direction, but couldn't muster the curiosity to go see what the fuss was about. To be honest, it was best he did not. He was just angry enough that if some fool managed to bump into him, he would punch said fool in the mouth. Since the hell was crowded, he was safer in his chair.

There was a murmur of activity at the entrance, so he allowed his attention to wander listlessly in that direction instead.

And regretted it.

Damn.

He shook his head, certain either his drink or his melancholy was playing tricks with his eyes.

He looked again. They were not.

He rose, slamming his glass to the table as he did.

She was there. She had walked into the Birdcage in that flame of a dress—*his* dress—on the arm of Archibald Gibbs. What the hell was she doing there? What the hell was she thinking to be anywhere in that dress?

He had covered half the distance between them before he even realized he was charging at her, but he did not slow. He wanted to level every single man he passed—every man who gaped at her—but it would only slow him down, so he did not.

He knew the moment she saw him. Her eyes grew wide.

"Bex."

He was not close enough to hear his name on her lips, but he saw it there. Then he was close enough, and he grabbed her arm from Gibbs. "What in hell are you doing here?" he barked at her. Didn't she realize how foolish and dangerous it was for her there?

Her arm twisted in his grasp. "Bex, you're hurting me."

He relaxed the strength of his grip but did not let go. He turned to Gibbs. "What is this about? Did you do this?"

Gibbs surveyed the attention they were garnering. "Perhaps we should have this discussion in the back."

Bex agreed. He wanted Lucy out of that room. He hated that she was there. He hated that she was in that dress. It meant only one thing, and it was a thing he could not even contemplate without pouring his rage onto everything, human or inanimate, that crossed his path. "Lead the way," he commanded to Gibbs.

Their walk through the hell felt like a damned parade—a Lucy parade in which every ass in London felt entitled to ogle her. He glowered at all of them, rushing her through the crowd to the door Gibbs held open for them. He shut the door behind them, then left through a different one, at the side of the room, leaving them alone.

Leaving him alone with Lucy.

Bex knew his anger was too high. He gave himself a count of ten before he spoke, but it still came through gritted teeth. "No," he told her. "You will not do this. I forbid it."

Lucy stared at him. "You forbid it? Do you know why I'm here?"

"Of course I know why you're here," he spat. "Why else would you be here dressed like that?" He shook his head, tried to shake the anger out of it, and looked at her, pleading. "You don't have to do it, Lucy. This is not your only option. One transgression does not define who you are." Didn't she know that? How could she not? Whatever had possessed her to make such an extreme choice? Had the duke and duchess turned her out?

Lucy eyes grew startlingly large. "Define who I am?" She released an incredulous huff. "You think because I...with you...that I am here to..." Her voice fell to a scandalized whisper. "You think I am here to find a protector, to become someone's mistress? You think because I can no longer be a governess, I have decided to become a paramour?" Betrayal mingled with disgust on her features.

"What am I to believe? Why else would you be here? What the devil are you doing in that dress?"

She crossed her arms in front of her and turned, presenting him a profile of her hardened jaw. "I will wear whatever dress I please and go wherever I choose."

He worked to quiet his temper so that she would hear his words. He began again, more softly. "You do not have to do this. Just because my father has set out to destroy your reputation, there is no need for you to aid his cause. If the duke has turned you out..."

"No one has turned me out." She turned then. Her head was high and her voice was steady when she responded. "I may be guilty of ill-advised indiscretion, but I have no intention of turning such behavior into my livelihood." Her eyes bore into him, her ashen face a painting of so much quiet dignity and devastation. "I may have lost the good opinion of polite society, but it does not necessarily follow that I have lost my own sense of self-worth. Whatever line I have crossed in the view of others, I will continue to answer to my own conscience and my own sense of decency."

Bex felt a flash of guilt. Though she had not said it, the accusation was present between them. *She* may not have considered falling to such a fate, but *he* had believed her capable of it.

"Then why are you here?" he asked.

"It is not to barter myself, I assure you," she said softly.

"Then why are you in that dress?" Seeing her in it—displaying it publicly, to other men—it was too much of a betrayal for Bex to bear.

"Because it is a fitting costume for what I have come here to do."

"Which is what?" he demanded. She was daft if she thought he was going to send her back out into that den of iniquity dressed as she was.

"Play music, for a start."

"For a start?" he asked. "What else have you arranged with Gibbs?"

She cast him a speaking glance. "Mr. Gibbs is only interested in my *musical* talents. My other business is with Mr. Thistlewaite."

"Who the devil is Mr. Thistlewaite?"

"The Mathematician," she stated simply, her expression ripe with censure for his failure to know the man's true name.

"Why do you require the Mathematician's talents?"

She exhaled in a huff and glared up at him, placing one clenched fist upon each side of her waist. Her head tilted, taunting, to one side before she answered. "Presently, I am not entirely certain. I may have changed my mind."

"Good," he declared. "I'll send for your cloak and we can remove you from this place."

"I'm not leaving."

Ridiculous. He was getting nowhere with her. He strode to the door, yanked it open, and hollered to the first staff person who happened by. "Bring me the Mathematician."

"I'm not leaving," she repeated quietly.

Bex walked to where she stood, her tiny frame rigid with red-draped resolve. "Whatever your intentions are, you know precisely what others will assume when you appear here." He shook his head. "What do you think to accomplish? Why do this?"

Lucy looked up at him with round blue pools of sorrowful resignation. Her voice was soft, timid even, when she spoke. "Why? I suppose because the end seemed to justify the means. Now if you will excuse me, I have an obligation to fulfill."

She walked away.

He couldn't stop her. He wanted to stop her. If she had looked up at him with anything other than that haunting look of devastated betrayal, he would have dragged her out of this place, declared his intention to marry her, and happily lived out the rest of their days, starving and dressed in rags. Society could be damned. They could be disgraced and destitute for all he cared, so long as he could have her. He should have made the decision days ago. He should have protected her from all of this, and from his own jealousy-driven judgments. He should have done so when she still looked up at him with longing gazes and sweet admiration. But he had failed her. The way she had looked at him today proved he had closed any door to her heart that had once been open.

So he couldn't stop her. He watched her progress across the crowded room filled with people unworthy to touch her—unworthy to even look upon her. With her head held high and with the unhurried pace of the perfectly dignified, she crossed the room. Her pale hair caught what light the room possessed and shone unnaturally above the deep scarlet of the gown that draped her form and trailed in her wake. A silver angel engulfed in the flame of sin.

She reached the far side of the room and slowly lowered herself, spine rigid, onto the painted bench before the pianoforte. Her face was placid, her sea-blue eyes intent and focused as she arranged her sheet music and ran delicate fingers across the instrument's bone-white keys. Her chest rose and fell with a deep breath, and she turned. She faced the room, with the full attention of its occupants, and bestowed upon them all a smile so blindingly brilliant he wanted to possess it for himself alone.

They applauded her. She hadn't played yet, but they applauded her beauty, the promise of the performance to come, the grace of her presence.

She nodded in acknowledgment of this warm welcome into the world for which she was too good, too pure to belong; then she turned back to the instrument, bowed her head, and began to play.

She was magnificent. The music was beautiful. It rose above the din like a hymn over Babylon.

She was a perfect fallen angel.

He was a perfect ass.

He had brought her to the fall, and not only abandoned her there, but judged her in her lowest moment.

Bex felt very much his father's son. He hated both men in that moment.

"You sent for me, sir."

The voice pulled Bex from the trance through which he watched her, and he pivoted. The Mathematician stood tall and ghostly in the doorway.

Bex beckoned him forward. "I understand you have made an arrangement with Miss Betancourt," he said when the man was close enough to hear him despite the low tone in which he spoke.

No reaction registered on the man's face. "Mr. Gibbs has struck an arrangement with Miss Betancourt. I will be aiding Miss Betancourt in my capacity as an employee of Mr. Gibbs."

"It is the same damn thing," Bex bit out, possessing no patience for meaningless details.

"I prefer precision in all things, Mr. Brantwood."

"Understood, Mr....Thistlewaite. What is the nature of the aid you will be providing to Miss Betancourt?"

"Miss Betancourt has asked that I assist her in evaluating figures and drafting documents of agreement, sir."

Bex waited. When no further explanation was forthcoming, he asked, "Figures and documents pertaining to what?"

"Investors, sir. Miss Betancourt wishes me to assist in forming a consortium of sorts."

"For?" Bex prompted.

The man gazed questioningly at Bex as though deciding how much he would divulge, but eventually replied, "To fund a business venture, sir."

"What business venture is that?" Bex peppered back.

"Whatever you decide, Mr. Brantwood."

Bex stared at him. Was the man confused? "Whatever I decide? What the devil does that mean? What did she tell you…precisely?"

The Mathematician gave a satisfied nod as though, finally, Bex had posed the correct question that would allow him to elucidate. "Miss Betancourt explained in great detail to Mr. Gibbs and myself her fervent belief that you would have no great success continuing to gamble on the business plans of others, but rather that you have acquired sufficient understanding and perspective such that others should invest in a venture of your own oversight." He paused, considering, then continued. "I believe her exact words were that you understood the necessary ingredients and should be allowed to concoct your own recipe, sir."

"My own recipe?"

"Indeed."

For him? Bex reeled. Was Lucy truly here pursuing some sort of project for *his* benefit?

"I am to draw up documents that confirm the value of your expertise and oversight, thus granting you with an equal share of profits until investors have been repaid with interest, after which you will retain full ownership of the business enterprise."

The end seemed to justify the means.

He was stunned at the depth of Lucy's faith in him. And terrified by it. "Just who is supposed to be finding these investors?"

"She is, sir."

"How would she do that?"

The Mathematician glanced toward the source of the music. "I believe she currently has the attention of several, sir."

"Does she really believe she could secure investors? That they would be convinced by a woman—a woman who could offer no details of what would be done with the money?"

"She has already secured two investors."

"Two investors?"

"His Grace, the Duke of Worley, and the Comtesse de Beauchene."

Oh, God. Bex thought his heart had already fallen to the lowest reachable depth, but he had been wrong. It plummeted even further. They had *all* placed their faith in him. Lucy had sacrificed the last shreds of her reputation for him.

He had no ideas in which to invest, no theories or notions to be implemented. Had she not understood? He was a man with no purpose. Their funds and their faith were wasted on him.

He could do it—he could grasp at the money and use it for a time, but to what end? Only betrayal. These people had come into his life determined to like him. After all he had done, they had chosen to extend their support instead of their blame. They were the last people in his life willing to stand by him even when he didn't deserve it.

He would not take their money.

He would not take their money when all he could offer in exchange were false promises and failure.

He stood quietly and listened to the sound of the piano music, intermittent notes finding their way to his ears despite the number and strength of competing noises. He stepped to the doorway and watched her. She was intent upon her performance, deep in concentrating and unaware of the men drawing ever nearer, like a pack of circling wolves.

Birdcage, indeed.

Bex left the gaming hell without a word to Lucy. He could not fathom what drove her belief in him and he knew without a doubt he did not deserve it.

* * * *

"What do you mean, he declined the money?"

Lucy stood in the back room of the Birdcage and stared at the Mathematician, her mind unable to process this revelation, though her heart understood. The weight of disappointment—disillusionment—had already settled around her shoulders. She had worked so hard to be convincing. She had spoken with so many men. Two had even pinched her backside, but at least they had contributed. After all she had done, he declined?

"Precisely that, Miss Betancourt. I am to communicate that he appreciates your efforts on his behalf, but he declines to accept the contributed funds and kindly requests that they be returned to the contributors."

"Are you sure?"

"Quite sure."

"But...why?" The decision made no sense. The funds were precisely what he needed to put all he had learned to use.

"He did not elaborate, miss."

Pride. What other reason could there be? He was too proud to accept charity. Only this was not charity. This was investment—a demonstration of faith in his abilities. And she was his friend. She was—or had been—his lover.

Until it had ended. Then he had assumed she was a harlot, and now he rejected her attempts to help him. Stupid, prideful, hurtful man. Tears stung. She closed her eyes in an attempt to stave them off. She pressed her closed fist to her lips.

The Mathematician coughed. "I am sorry, miss, for your wasted effort."

Lucy opened her eyes, tears and all, in time to see the reedy man tentatively reach one arm toward her. He patted her shoulder three times and quickly withdrew.

She ought to thank him—show appreciation for this attempt to comfort even when doing so obviously brought him a good deal of discomfort—but she could not. She was too frustrated and angry.

"He is a fool." She snapped her head higher, blinking away the tears. "Do not return the funds."

He eyed her skeptically. "Do not return the funds?"

"Not a penny."

* * * *

The door of the townhouse occupied by the Misters Brantwood was opened by a middle-aged manservant who made no effort to hide his consternation upon finding an unchaperoned young woman standing in the rain outside his door.

"I beg your pardon, miss. You must have the wrong address."

Lucy pushed her way inside, taking advantage of the man's inability to anticipate this action. She stepped, dripping, into the foyer and pushed the hood of her cloak away from her face. "I do not have the wrong address," she clipped. "I am here to see Mr. Brantwood—the younger Mr. Brantwood—and I'm not leaving until I do."

The man's eyes grew wide. "I…miss, I don't think…that is…"

She lifted a staying hand. "I don't care what you think. I only care that you inform Mr. Brantwood that I am here and waiting for him."

He stood, frozen with indecision, for a time before eventually recovering his wits. He gave a curt nod, mumbled some form of agreement, and hurried off.

Lucy released a great breath. He was home. She would see him. She would tell him what she had come to say.

What *had* she come to say? Perhaps she should have taken the time to consider that before she arrived. She knew what she wanted to say. She wanted to scream at him to accept the investments, to build something for himself, to use it to find his purpose. She longed to ask him to build something for her—build a life for them both that would allow them to be together.

But she could not ask for those things. He had never wanted those things and she had known that from the beginning. His words echoed in her memory. *Nothing ruins passion so well as a marriage.*

What they had shared was passionate and, more importantly, their brief affair was what she had offered and he had accepted. She would not regret it, even if it had left her aching for something she could never have.

Someone she could never have.

Footsteps sounded on the landing above. She swallowed, straightening her spine, and waited for him to face her.

He came into view at the top of the steps and paused there, meeting her eyes. His lips formed a grim line. He was unhappy that she had come. Even though she had expected it, the realization devastated.

* * * *

Bex looked down into the foyer at a wet and bedraggled Lucy, patron saint of the betrayed and disappointed. She met his gaze unwaveringly. He broke the contact first, making his way down the staircase to stand in front of her.

She spoke first, so much anger and frustration spilling out in a single, burdened word. "Why?"

He shook his head. "Lucy, I am grateful for the lengths to which you have gone to help me, but I cannot accept funds from these people."

"Why not? Some of 'these people' are your friends."

Why not? Because he could not fail them all again. Because he could not have Lucy connected to yet another of his misguided and self-destructive pursuits. Because he had wreaked enough havoc to ruin them both several times over and he would not do it again. He would not take the money she had collected on his behalf and make her a liar with his own failure.

"Because you misunderstand," he said. "I speculate with investments in businesses. I am not a man of industry myself. I understand it was well intentioned, but you solicited contributions under the false pretense that I would be conducting business of my own. I will not. I have none. Therefore, the contributions must be returned."

Her eyes were cold, accusing, and he hated it. Her question was sharp. "Why will you not?"

He wanted to. He wished desperately that he could. He couldn't tell her so, because she would only encourage him. She would waste more of her faith—more of her life—believing, waiting for him to make something of himself, to become a man capable of providing security and protection. He was not greedy enough to subject her to that.

"Because it is not who I am."

She shook her head. "I don't even know what that means. 'Who you are' is a man who has been given an opportunity—one born of the faith of others, which is the most precious kind—yet you choose to throw it away."

"I do not throw it away. I politely decline."

A fire lit in her cold eyes. "Politely decline?" she asked, her voice rising to an incredulous pitch. "You reject the faith of your closest friends and family, squander the opportunity they've given you, and call it polite? It's asinine, that's what it is."

Bex's control slipped. "What opportunity?" he asked, splaying his hands wide with the question. "How, precisely, do you envision me putting these funds to use? What enterprise am I funding, Lucy? I don't design machines or invent new things."

She stepped back, retreating from his anger, and guilt nipped at him. "I...I don't know." Her brow knit. "You are the one—you—who has seen all of these new enterprises. You are the one who has found the...the ingredients. You."

Him. Yes, he had boasted to her, hadn't he, that he knew the ingredients to the recipe? He had forgotten to tell her of the most vital component—an idea. He was not a man of ideas.

He looked at her for a long moment, resolved to what he must do. Her life was in an uproar, all her plans destroyed at his hand. She had critical decisions to make just then—all her future plans must be redefined, because of him. If he allowed her to hope, allowed her to put her faith in him, she would make decisions based upon those expectations—fatally flawed expectations.

"I am decided, Lucy. There is no point in further discussing it. I assume Gibbs paid you for your performance?"

Her eyes flashed with blue anger. "He did. One pound, three shillings."

Bex steeled himself against the look she cast him. "Take that and whatever else you have and leave London. The gossip will not follow you. Go back to your parents. Travel north. If the duchess provides you a reference, you will find a post. Nothing needs to change for you."

Her expression hardened, her pale jaw set as though carved from marble. "What will you do?"

He looked down at the carpet, not wanting her to catch the truth in his eyes. He had no bloody idea what he would do. He would not burden her with that. He sighed and looked up again. "I know what I will not do. I will not prey upon others."

She stepped toward him then. "How do you prey on others if they willingly offer support?"

"You don't understand, Lucy."

The indignation fell from her expression, leaving only wounded eyes and an unearthly pallor. "That is the first thing you have said today with which I can wholly agree." She opened her reticule and pulled from it a folded square of paper. "Mr. Thistlewaite has prepared this list of contributors to the consortium with their respective amounts. Your contribution of oversight and expertise has been assigned a monetary value and included on the list. Do with it what you will."

He took the paper, and her hand fell listlessly back to her side. He saw the resignation and disappointment in her ever-expressive face and hated himself for putting it there. The hurt she bore encircled his own heart and squeezed, tightening in his chest and interfering with his very breath.

He could go to her and tell her he would do as she asked, that he would accept the money. Nearly every part of him wanted to tell her he would do it. Every part except the memory that he had been faced with this dilemma once before. He had rejected her, despite the heartbreak it had caused, denying her what she wanted because he knew it was not what she needed. And then he had yielded to temptation and changed his mind despite his better judgment, causing irreversible damage.

Steeling his resolve, he vowed not to succumb this time. "Lucy"—he closed his eyes, breathed deeply, and amended his statement—"Miss Betancourt. Please know I hope, most passionately, for your future happiness."

She only stared at him in response. She did not need to say the words. He could see them as clearly as if she had written them down for him to keep.

I don't believe you.

Then she turned and left quietly, all the determination and fury with which she had arrived gone from her posture, as though she'd left it behind for him to burden his memory.

Bex looked down at the paper she'd given him and unfolded it. A list of misplaced trust, with his own name at the bottom. How fitting. His eyes did not linger long on his own name, for another on the list caught his attention.

Miss Lucy Betancourt—one pound, three shillings.

Chapter Thirty-Three

The mood at Worley House was somber and Lucy knew it was her fault. In the past few weeks they had received neither callers nor invitations. Emma insisted it was due to nearing the end of her time, but Lucy knew the truth. No one wanted to extend an invitation that might include the unfortunate scandal the duke and duchess had in their house. Emma and her duke would be fine once she was gone. They were, after all, a duke and duchess. Lucy had wanted to return to Beadwell immediately, but Emma had insisted she stay until the child was born.

Emma rested often and they were quiet days, waiting for the birth. Eventually, Lucy admitted to herself that she was not waiting for only the baby. She was waiting for word from Bex—some indication that he had relented, or even just that he was thinking of her—but there was none.

Lucy read often, or tried to read. She often found herself staring sightlessly at pages of books or at walls or windows. It was for this reason that she happened to be standing at the drawing room window, looking down over the street and square below, when she saw the man walking up to Worley House. She knew him by his posture and his gait, even before she could make out his face, and her heart skipped. Bex.

He had come.

He had finally come for her.

Perhaps he had come to tell her he would use the money after all. Perhaps he had not and would still refuse it. She didn't care.

It was true. The realization came quickly, but not entirely as a surprise. She did not care a whit if he used the money—only that he had come for her. She didn't care if they were poor, if they could be together. She didn't care that love was impractical, so long as they could have it.

She waited and watched as he disappeared into the house and out of her view. She turned to the door, expectant for the knock of the butler, announcing his arrival.

She left the window and stood at the sofa. She lifted a nervous hand to her hair, smoothed her skirts, and tried to exhale her anxiety. When no knock came, she went to the door and opened it. She walked into the hall and, from the shadow, peeked down into the foyer below.

She watched as the butler led him to the duke's study.

Lucy returned to the drawing room and sat on the sofa, unsure of what to make of this. Why hadn't he asked to see her? Did he see the duke as a surrogate guardian? Was he asking the duke's permission to speak with her?

She waited what seemed an interminable amount of time and then worried she had been waiting too long. Had he gone without speaking to her at all? She rose and went to the window again.

She stood sentry there for long minutes, but could not stay. She went to the hall again and watched over the foyer, waiting.

* * * *

"Your Grace, I know that you contributed to the consortium Lucy devised." One brow rose on the duke's otherwise expressionless visage and Bex amended. "That is, Miss Betancourt." He cleared his throat and continued. "I have been delinquent in not extending my gratitude. After all that has happened, it is more than I deserve and I thank you."

The duke was assessing, his unreadable blue eyes penetrating into Bex as though seeing into his very soul. "You may thank Miss Betancourt and my wife. They advocated quite determinedly on your behalf."

"I will not insult you with platitudes or ineffective apologies for my lapse in judgment. I will only give you my word, Your Grace, that I will not bring any further pain or ruin into Miss Betancourt's life. She is not deserving of it, nor any of the harm that I have caused."

"Won't you?" the duke asked with an inscrutable expression.

"I will not."

"What will you do?" he asked and relaxed ever so slightly into his chair. "I assume you have not come only to thank me."

"Not only for that reason, no." Bex cleared his throat. "It was my original intent to return the money, Your Grace, as I could not, in good conscience, accept your investment when there was nothing in which to invest."

"Your *original* intent."

"Yes. You see, once I had discarded any idea of accepting the contributed funds, I was left with nothing but my existing investments. The most promising of these was a weaving shed in Hertfordshire."

The duke leaned back in his chair and crossed his arms. "In Hertfordshire?"

"Yes. It was intentionally located away from other weaving operations to shield the improvements in the power loom from prying competitive eyes and nearer to London in order for the cloth to be quicker to market. Watford sits on a newer branch of the Grand Union Canal."

"I have never heard of a weaving shed so far south."

Bex leaned forward in his seat. Now they were getting to the crux of it. "For good reason, Your Grace. Raw cotton from America arrives in Liverpool. A broker there had assured the Watford shed a share of the imports, but in the end, he was unable to fulfill his promise. I suspect pressure was brought to bear and the broker could not risk his regular customers for the chance of new, especially one so far away that the others could not keep watchful eyes."

"So the location of this weaving shed had proven to be not only its brilliance, but also its fatal flaw."

Bex nodded, pleased to see the duke was at least intrigued by the tale. "I believed that to be the case, but a simple comment Lucy—that is, Miss Betancourt—made stuck in my head. She asked why the raw cotton couldn't arrive in London instead of Liverpool. I dismissed the idea as naïve and impossible, but perhaps it is not, Your Grace." Bex straightened his shoulders. "What if a merchant—a fledgling, newly funded merchant, with a cousin who'd lived in Boston for four years and worked as a shipping clerk—what if he—if they—could bring raw cotton to London?"

The duke studied him for an interminable moment, his intelligent eyes steady, even as the thoughts circulated behind them. Finally, he spoke. "You want to be a shipping merchant?"

"I do, Your Grace."

"That is a highly speculative venture. There is a risk of loss while at sea, and risk again when you arrive in England and cannot sell your goods for a profit."

Bex nodded. "You are correct. Very few men have the capital or connections to even consider such an enterprise." He straightened. "But I was fortunate enough to meet an intelligent and resourceful woman who believed in my capability to undertake an endeavor such as this. By her efforts, I have a consortium of investors who have seen fit to provide that funding. If I can fund a single voyage with a shipment of raw cotton, I am guaranteed to sell all of it. I have a waiting purchaser who is desperate for it."

The duke's brow furrowed as he considered this explanation. Then, slowly, he leaned forward, bringing his hands together on the desktop. "So you begin your own career as a merchant and manage to save your Hertfordshire investment at the same time?"

"That is my hope, Your Grace, but I will require your assistance to do so, in particular, your connections in Boston."

"You understand, I was only a clerk in Boston?"

"I do, but you are a duke now. Certainly that raises your stock a bit, even to the Americans."

The duke inclined his head in acceptance of this truth. "I will write a letter. I cannot promise what will come of it, but I can write the letter."

Relief drained the tension from Bex's shoulders, making him want to slump into his chair, but he held himself erect. "Thank you, Your Grace. You have my word, if you will accept it, that I will repay all that my family has taken from you, as soon as I am able."

The duke's eyes narrowed. "What of Miss Betancourt?"

Bex swallowed and met the man's gaze. "The investment is not the only opportunity I have nearly squandered, Your Grace. If this endeavor is successful, I will be in a position to offer marriage to her, if she will have me. That is a greater inspiration than the repayment of my debts."

"And if it is not successful?" the duke asked.

"I will be much as I am now, unable to offer her anything. I am determined to succeed, but I understand I may not. I cannot speak with Lucy until I am assured of providing her security. I will not have her wait for me." A smile tugged at his lips as he thought of her. "She would understand the need to be practical."

* * * *

So much time passed before Lucy saw him—saw Bex—that she started when he appeared. He left the duke's study and walked directly to the front door, purposeful in his direction and not even looking to see that she was there.

All the fear and panic that had been building inside her congealed into a thick, heavy weight.

He was leaving.

She couldn't believe it. He was leaving. What if the duke had told him to leave?

"Bex." She called his name before she could stop herself.

He halted immediately and turned, his gray eyes lifting to where she stood on the landing, gripping the banister, unable to do anything but stare down at him in devastation and pleading. She had hoped to see joy, relief in his gaze, but she saw only trouble and regret. Her throat constricted. She opened her mouth to speak again, but nothing came. What more was there to say?

If he had not come for her, what more was there to say?

She was the greatest fool that ever lived. All of his words came back to her in a rush. *I am a cad. I am a man with no purpose.* How many times had he cautioned her against expectations? How many times had she insisted she understood?

She stared down at him still, arrested, unable to voice the questions she knew he read on her face—in her wounded expression.

He stood as still as she, as though time had stopped for them both, because it could do nothing but move forward into an unwanted place.

He moved first. It was not a dramatic motion. He simply closed his eyes. They closed only briefly, but it broke the spell that trapped them.

Then he opened his mouth as though to speak, only he didn't. He said nothing, but turned his back to her, placing his hand on the doorknob. He turned it, opened the door, and walked out.

Betrayal stabbed through her even as she knew it for a lie. He had not betrayed her, because he had made no promises. He had not abandoned her, because he had not offered to protect her.

Her ability to move recovered, she sank to an undignified heap on the top step. She gripped the rails of the banister and stared in abandoned horror at the empty foyer. Tears washed over her cheeks, unchecked and spilling onto her dress.

This, she realized, was ruination. It had nothing to do with rumors or reputation or practicality or purpose. It was the loss of one's life, because somewhere deep inside a light she didn't know burned had gone dark.

She leaned her forehead against the carved wooden rails and sobbed.

She almost didn't hear the knock through her grief, but it became more insistent and penetrated through the lament of her mind.

Her head lifted and she stilled.

Knock.

Yes! Hope coursed through her. He had changed his mind. *He had changed his mind.*

She rose in an instant and scurried down the steps, nearly tripping in her haste. She finally reached the door and flung it wide.

Chapter Thirty-Four

Lady Constance peered disapprovingly at Lucy from the front step of Worley House. "Hmmm. It is worse than I thought. Invite me in, *ma chere*. We cannot have people on the street seeing you like this."

Lucy blinked. She moved aside to allow Lady Constance inside, then stepped over the threshold to the place Lady Constance had occupied. She looked up and down the street.

He was gone. Her hopes once more dashed, she came inside, determined that she would not allow them to be resurrected. It was far too painful.

"Take me to the drawing room, *ma petite*, and order me tea," the comtesse said, as though somehow sensing Lucy, in her state, required basic instructions to function.

She obeyed, and the two found themselves seated in the drawing room, a tray of tea and cakes between them.

"You shouldn't be here," Lucy told her simply. "Ruined reputations are like fever. If you come too close, you may catch it."

The comtesse dismissed this with a wave and a shake of her head. "The French are so much more realistic about these things, *ma chere*."

"Are they?" Lucy asked. She wondered if perhaps she should go to France.

"Is this what you have been doing?" Lady Constance asked. "Moping all the time? And why are you waiting at the front door? Have you been standing sentry waiting for him to come to you? Should I assume, then, that he has not come?"

"He was just here," Lucy said, choosing to answer the last of the list of questions, as it seemed the most significant at the present.

The comtesse leaned forward. "Really?

"He was not here for me," Lucy explained. "He saw the duke; then he left."

"He did not ask for you?" Lady Constance asked.

"No."

"Did he know you are here?" She shook her head. "Disregard my question. Of course he knows you are here."

Lucy swallowed, working valiantly not to cry. She failed. She could feel the tears on her cheeks. "He knows. He saw me, on the landing. He… he didn't have anything to say."

"Is that so?" she asked, pursing her lips in disapproval.

Lucy nodded.

Lady Constance huffed and changed positions in her seat. She changed subjects just as abruptly. "You should know that I've decided to retire to the country at the close of the season, after all."

Lucy lifted her head at this. Had Lady Constance's nephew finally found the decency to invite her? "You have? Where will you go?"

She gave a delicate shrug. "I've let a country house. In Hertfordshire."

In Hertfordshire? Lucy tried to gauge the other woman's thoughts, but her expression was the same relaxed mien with which she discussed all things, significant or meaningless. "Will you be near to Annabelle?" she asked.

The comtesse looked at her directly then, her smile turning nostalgic and perhaps a bit sad. "We cannot give up on those we love, *ma chere*, simply because they are fools. Sometimes we must force wisdom upon them, even as they resist."

Lucy felt an unlikely smile form at Lady Constance and her philosophy. Did she truly believe she could overcome her niece's prejudice with sheer persistence? If anyone could, she supposed, it was this woman. "I hope that you are right, Lady Constance, and your niece will change her mind."

The comtesse sighed. "If she does not, it will not be for want of effort on my part." She reached a hand out to hold Lucy's. "You should come with me when I go."

Lucy shook her head. "You don't need a paid companion, Lady Constance."

The comtesse drew her hand back in affront. "I did not offer to pay you, child. I was inviting you as my guest. You need to leave London. The whole thing will settle down if you are away, and you are not well enough known, or of high enough rank that the scandal will spread far."

It was precisely what Bex had told her to do. Only Bex had not offered to go with her. Tears threatened behind her eyes and she blinked, keeping them at bay. "Thank you, my lady, that is very kind of you to offer." Perhaps she should do it. She had decided to return home after Emma's child was born, but somehow the idea of home didn't seem comforting in the way that it should. Perhaps she needed a change. And perhaps she needed several more doses of Lady Constance and her particularly pragmatic wisdom.

"Pardon me, miss."

Both women turned to see Agnes in the doorway of the drawing room, urgency in her expression.

"Her Grace is asking for you. I believe her time has come."

Her time? The baby! Lucy leapt from her seat and hurried toward the door, belatedly remembering the comtesse. She turned back. "I'm so sorry, Lady Constance, but I must go. May I consider your offer?"

The comtesse had risen as well. "Of course, of course." She made a motion as though to push Lucy toward the door and Lucy did as she was bade, rushing from the room.

"Are you coming as well, my lady?" she heard Agnes ask.

Lucy paused to look over her shoulder. Lady Constance had followed her into the hall and was not descending the steps to the foyer, but following her to the second-floor landing leading to the bedchambers.

Lady Constance winked at her. "Well, I'm certainly not leaving now that things have taken an exciting turn."

Lucy didn't take the time to remind the woman that Emma might not, in fact, desire the presence of the Comtesse de Beauchene at the birth of her child. She only raced up the steps, hurrying to reach her friend.

The duke had reached Emma first. When Lucy walked into the duchess's bedchamber she was in bed, propped comfortably with pillows into a seated position. Lucy rushed to her side. The duke stood at the opposite side, holding one of Emma's hands, a look of sheer confusion and panic painted across his usually certain features. His confusion deepened as he faced the new arrivals.

Emma, who appeared considerably more serene than her husband, attempted to pose the question evident on the duke's face. "Lady Constance, how did...that is, what is...er." She exhaled. Her brow furrowed. "Hello."

"Hello, Your Grace," the comtesse said cheerily, pausing just inside the bedchamber door. "Don't mind me at all. I am only here comforting Lucy."

Emma's eyes darted to where Lucy stood at her side. "What is wrong? Has something happened?"

Lucy's answer was interrupted when her hand was squeezed in a grip so tight it threatened to break her fingers. She watched helplessly as Emma's face contorted with a seizing pain. Alarmed at the extent of her friend's discomfort, her eyes went to the duke's.

He was no less concerned. "Has the physician been called?" he barked to no one in particular.

"Yes, Your Grace." The housekeeper bustled into the room followed by Emma's lady's maid and Agnes. The women carried a basin of water, clean linens, and a small tray of bread and barley water.

Emma's grip on Lucy's hand released, and Lucy looked down at her. "Are you all right?" she asked, knowing the question was a useless one. She knelt at the bedside so that she could look directly at Emma. "How long have you been having the pains?"

Emma exhaled slowly, recovering from the passing pain. "All day, I suppose. I wasn't certain of it when it began this morning, because they were so mild. By midday, I could tell it was happening, but I also knew it would be quite some time and I didn't want to alarm anyone."

"Not alarm anyone?" the duke asked, throwing his arms into the air incredulously. "You have been suffering all afternoon and said nothing?"

Emma patted his arm. "It's fine, dear."

"It is not fine," he blustered. "How can we care for you if you don't tell us what is happening? You cannot be so stubborn, Emma."

She waved a hand at him and turned back to Lucy. "Why is Lady Constance comforting you, Lucy?"

Lucy shook her head. Anything troubling her was unimportant in the face of this momentous occasion. "It was nothing," she insisted. "Lady Constance was simply visiting to tell me about her plans after the season. They are not important now."

Emma studied Lucy with sharp, knowing eyes then turned to the comtesse and asked without preamble, "Is she lying to me?"

Lady Constance was equally frank. "She is, dear."

Emma lifted a staying hand and lay the other on her rounded belly, exhaling slowly as she was gripped with the beginnings of another pain.

The duke fell to his knees at her side. "Is there nothing we can do to make this less agonizing?" he asked, his voice plaintive and impatient.

"The pains are preparing her," the housekeeper said calmly, still folding and sorting her linens. "She must open for the child."

Helplessly, Lucy allowed Emma to painfully squeeze her hand again, while she used her other hand to rub Emma's back, cringing as her friend curled forward around the pain.

The duke barked at Agnes. "Go and wait for Dr. White. Bring him up directly when he arrives."

Wide eyed, Agnes nodded. "Yes, Your Grace." She hurried from the room to do his bidding.

Emma exhaled again and settled back into her pillows as the seizing passed. She lay her head back and closed her eyes. They were still closed when she spoke. "I shall hear the truth now, Lady Constance."

"Surely none of that matters just now," Lucy objected.

The duke rose. "I agree. Emma, you require our full attention."

Emma opened her eyes and faced her husband. "There is nothing you can do for me now except provide a distraction." She turned to Lady Constance and nodded.

"Lucy was distraught by the visit of Mr. Brantwood," the comtesse said, and Lucy cringed.

Emma looked to her, surprise and hurt on her features. "Mr. Brantwood came to see you and you weren't going to tell me?"

Lucy shook her head. "No. He didn't come to see me." Tears threatened again, and she hated them. Of all the meaningless things to be worried about at that moment. She felt so selfish and horrid when Emma was in such pain.

"He saw the duke," Lady Constance clarified.

Emma turned accusing eyes to her husband then. "You? Mr. Brantwood came to see you?"

The duke looked to Lucy. "How did you know?" he asked.

"I saw him arrive," Lucy said softly.

"Why has no one seen fit to apprise me of anything that happens?" Emma demanded.

"He only just left," Lucy insisted. "Lady Constance arrived almost immediately afterward and then we were called here."

Emma's brow knit in confusion. "He didn't see you at all?"

Lucy's eyes lowered. "He saw me, on the landing, but he didn't speak to me. He had not come for me."

"What did he want?" Emma asked, this time directing her question toward her husband. "Why did he come and why didn't he ask for Lucy?"

The duke knelt again, stroking Emma's hand as he spoke soothingly to her. "Surely none of this matters now, darling. Do not worry yourself. You need to rest between the pains. Keep your strength."

Emma snatched her hand back. "I am not exhausting myself by conversing," she snapped. "And if I am worried, it is because my husband will not answer my questions."

The duke's mouth opened and shut silently, so nonplussed was he that his attempts to be soothing to her nerves achieved the opposite effect. "I...only...you are..."

"Here is Dr. White," Agnes announced, hurrying into the room with a gray-haired gentleman of slight build and kind features. He smiled widely, and he was the only one in the room, save Lady Constance, who did not appear near to panic.

"Good afternoon, Your Grace," he said to Emma.

"Good afternoon, Dr. White. Thank you for coming so quickly. I believe I shall be having a child today."

"Excellent," he said, beaming with approval at her. He removed his coat and crossed the room to the washbasin, rolling up his shirtsleeves as he went. He was still washing his hands when Emma was gripped with another pain. He did not alter his pace.

"She is having another pain, Doctor," the duke ground out.

"Yes, when was her last?" he asked, taking time to dry his hands on a clean cloth that the housekeeper provided.

"Just before you arrived," Lucy offered, glad to be of some little help.

The doctor came and stood at Emma's bedside, calmly observing her in the throes of her agony.

"Can you do nothing to help her?" the duke demanded.

"We shall help her deliver a baby, Your Grace. That will stop the pains."

Lucy didn't quite care if the doctor applied calm and common sense. Her friend was hurting and he only watched. "Is there some position that would be more comfortable or something we can do to hurry it along?" she asked.

"The duchess can move as she would like," he answered, still as calm as though he were there on a social call. "Whatever position she finds best."

Emma sighed again in the signal they had all come to recognize as the waning of the contraction, and Dr. White moved closer to her. "I should like to examine your progress, Your Grace, if that is acceptable to you."

Emma looked up at him with sharp, clear eyes and asked, "Will I likely deliver a child in the next several minutes, Doctor?"

His mouth quirked into an amused grin. "No. I imagine you will not."

"Then the examination can wait," she clipped. "My husband and I were having an important discussion."

One brow arched in curious surprise, the doctor receded, allowing the duke to step forward and face his wife's ire.

"Emma, this is not the time…" he began.

Her hand sliced into the air, cutting off his objection. "You said you want me to be calm. Tell me what is going on, and I shall be calm."

Lucy could not deny the simple logic in her friend's words, nor could she deny her own burning curiosity to know what Bex's purpose had been in meeting with the duke. She watched, anticipation building, as the duke considered Emma's request. When his shoulders slumped in defeat, she knew he had decided to tell. Her own posture stiffened.

The duke glanced briefly at Lucy before he answered his wife, and Lucy knew the look meant the visit affected her somehow. She had expected as much, but the confirmation twisted her stomach nonetheless.

Lucy felt a hand on her shoulder and turned to learn its owner. Lady Constance had come to stand at her back, intuitively understanding how difficult this was for her. The simple act of support had Lucy reconsidering her resistance to heading into Hertfordshire with the comtesse at the end of the season.

"Well?" Emma prompted, hours of discomfort having diminished her stores of patience.

The duke glanced at Lucy again. His mouth formed a grim line.

"We are here, dear!" Lady Ridgely, Emma's beloved aunt Agatha, rushed into the room and directly to Emma's bedside. "How are you, dear?" she asked, motherly concern dominating her features. She did not wait for the answer, but turned to the physician. "How is she, Doctor?"

"I've not examined her yet," the doctor replied matter-of-factly.

The countess's eyes grew large and round. "What? Why not?"

"That is enough," the duke interjected. "Everyone out. The doctor must examine my wife."

"Fine," Emma snapped, "but then you will answer my question."

"What question?" Lady Ridgely asked.

"Later." The single word from the duke ceased all further discussion on the matter.

Wanting to shout her objection at the delay, Lucy allowed herself to be ushered from the room with the others. Only the duke and Lady Ridgely remained with Emma and the physician.

Her bottom lipped tucked firmly between her teeth, Lucy paced in the hall outside the door. What if the duke answered Emma's questions before she returned? Lucy knew she could not ask the duke to tell her as well, and could not ask Emma in the middle of childbirth.

Immediately, she felt horrid guilt at her selfishness for putting her own curiosity over her friend's childbirth. She shook her head in disgust at herself.

"Let's go have a sit, shall we?" Lady Constance said. Her voice was gentle and soothing as she spoke to Lucy, then clipped as she turned to Agnes. "Could you bring tea and biscuits to the drawing room please? Plenty of biscuits."

"Yes, my lady." Agnes nodded and hurried off to follow the instructions of the comtesse.

Lucy did the same, allowing Lady Constance to lead her to the drawing room, where they discovered Lord Ridgely, Emma's uncle, pacing that room in much the same manner Lucy had been pacing the upstairs hall.

"Is everything all right?" he rushed to ask as they entered the room.

"The doctor is examining her now," Lady Constance said, her even tone contrasting the earl's urgent one. "He will gauge her progress." She walked to the sofa. "Why don't we all sit. Tea is on the way."

Lucy started toward the sofa to do as the comtesse suggested, but halted as voices filtered up from the hall below.

"Sir, I do not believe now is a good time," she heard the butler say as she changed direction and headed to the door instead of the sofa.

"I saw a physician arrive."

Bex. Her pulse quickened.

"I saw Lady Ridgely nearly fall out of her carriage and run up the steps," Bex insisted from the foyer below. "She *ran*, I tell you. The woman ran. I demand to know what is happening."

"Bex." Lucy said his name from the landing where she had watched him leave.

His eyes flew to her, and he took the steps two at a time. "Is it the duchess, then? Has the child been born? You are not hurt or unwell?" He reached her and took her hands in his, studying her from head to toe as though assuring himself of her well-being.

"I am fine," Lucy said. "The baby has not been born yet, but Emma is laboring. The doctor is here. Everything is fine so far." She bit her lip. "I think. The doctor is examining her now."

"And you are well?" he asked.

"I am fine." She was better than fine. He was worried for her. Had he come back for her? Why? Why had he left? There were too many questions not to voice them. "Why are you here? Why did you leave?"

He shook his head. "I never left. I've been sitting in the square across the street."

Lady Ridgely's voice echoed through the halls of Worley House. "Lucy," she called. She found them then, on the landing. She glanced at Bex and at their joined hands before looking to Lucy. "The doctor has finished his examination. Emma would like you to join her now."

Lucy nodded. "Yes, of course." She looked at Bex and pulled her hands from his. "I should go to her."

He nodded in agreement. "Go."

She left him then, and went to Emma, not knowing why he had come, or if he would be gone when she emerged.

Chapter Thirty-Five

"What did the doctor say?" Lucy asked immediately upon reentering Emma's bedchamber, now bright with sunlight streaming through pulled-back curtains and opened windows. Her eyes fell on Emma and she knew, of all the questions spinning in her mind, that was the only one that mattered just then.

The duke provided the answer. "She is progressing normally, but he feels it will be some time yet. He prescribes rest to the extent she can be restful."

As though to belie his words, Emma groaned and curled forward into the pain of another contraction. Struck again by her uselessness, Lucy rushed to her side.

The housekeeper bustled into the room, this time directly to the open windows. She began closing them and pulling the drapes, sending the room back into shadow.

"What are you doing, woman?" the doctor demanded, turning from where he riffled in his bag of implements.

"This room is all wrong," the housekeeper said indignantly. "It must be warm and dark."

"Nonsense," the doctor said. "We do not sweat the child out. It must be clean and fresh. Open the windows."

The housekeeper placed a hand on each hip and glared at the gray-haired physician.

"Do as he says," the duke barked, injecting himself into the standoff.

With this order from her master, the housekeeper begrudgingly tied the curtains back again and unlatched the windows, pushing them open to once again saturate the room in sunlight and open air. With a watchful eye on the doctor, however, Lucy saw her move next to the fireplace, stoking up the fire to heat the room. The doctor turned, discovering her intent, and shooed her from the room. She left, grumbling as she went.

Emma released a light laugh and Lucy turned at the sound. She lowered herself to sit on the edge of the bed and spied the perspiration on Emma's forehead. She reached for a cloth and wiped her friend's brow, thinking the doctor was right to demand the cool air. "Has the pain passed for now, Emma?" she asked gently.

Emma nodded.

"You should close your eyes and rest between the pains as the doctor said," Lucy told her.

"First you must hear from John," Emma said, squeezing Lucy's hand. "I am too tired to recount the tale. Tell her, please, John." Emma lay back and closed her eyes then, trusting her husband to do as she asked.

The duke sighed and looked down at his wife with so much love and exasperation. "She will not rest until I've explained," he said, his eyes still on Emma.

"I am listening," Lucy prompted, trepidation rising at what she would hear.

"Mr. Brantwood came to discuss a business arrangement," the duke said, finally looking up to meet Lucy's gaze. "He has decided to use the funds after all."

Her anxiety dissipated as she digested this news. Her heart swelled. "He has an idea?" she asked. He hadn't given up on himself, she realized. He was going to *do* something.

"He claims it is your idea."

That gave Lucy pause. "My idea?"

"Mr. Brantwood is going to use the funds to sponsor an entire shipment of raw cotton from America to arrive in London harbor instead of Liverpool."

Involuntarily, Lucy's mouth widened to a foolish grin. "Raw cotton," she repeated, bemused. "Brilliant." It was brilliant. It was perfect. What a perfectly clever plan. "So he will profit from his venture *and* save the weaving shed from failure." How ridiculously simple—so brilliantly obvious.

She shook her head. He had done it. He had found his purpose and begun to forge his future. In a small way, she had helped. Joy filled her heart at his success, for surely he would have it. His future. His purpose.

And then Lucy recalled his face as he had left. He had not looked up at her with triumph, but regret. He had not run to her to tell her of his plan or declare his feelings or ask *her* to be a part of this new future he forged.

She felt the tears stinging behind her eyes again and was not sure that she could keep them at bay this time. She closed her eyes and exhaled.

When she spoke, she knew her voice was revealingly unsteady. "That is wonderful news for Mr. Brantwood."

Emma's eyes fluttered open. "Tell her all of it, John. Don't torture her."

Lucy looked to the duke, and she knew he could see the desperate hopefulness in her expression. She had no way of hiding it.

The duke sighed. "Mr. Brantwood has decided he will wait until the shipment is a success to ask for your hand. He did not want to ask you to wait for him when he could not be assured of succeeding. If it fails, he will have nothing to offer."

Lucy stared at the duke. Her hand? Wait for him? She closed her eyes and let this revelation settle into her. He intended to ask her to marry him. She waited for the joy, the relief, the bliss of certainty to overtake her.

Only it didn't come. Suspicion came instead. She shook her head and looked at the duke in accusation. "Why did he come to you with his plan?" she asked.

"He wanted an introduction to the shipping company in Boston and I am able to provide it."

"Does he need it?" she asked. "To proceed with his plan?"

"He does," the duke said.

Her heart fell once more. She looked down at her friend, peaceful in rest, with no outward sign of the excruciating pain that had gripped her moments before, nor the one that would come again any moment. What a falsehood her peace was. How tempting it would be to accept it for what it appeared to be, but it would be false. How tempting to accept Bex's plan to offer for her, when that was a falsehood as well. Her eyes rose to the duke. "What was the price for your aid?"

The duke shook his head. "I don't know what you mean."

Lucy sighed heavily, exhaustion settling onto her in a way it had not ever before that she could remember. She was tired of this city, of life in society. She was equally tired of fantasies and practical plans. She was tired of trying so hard to make sense of anything and everything. She was tired of when life did make sense—so much sense—as this did. Her smile for the duke was wan and there was no happiness behind it. "You love your wife, Your Grace, and I am her dearest friend. And I am ruined. You were only thinking of her happiness, as you should, because you love her."

"What the devil are you talking about?"

"Was the part about asking for my hand *your* condition for the bargain?"

The duke's brow furrowed. "What?" But his attention was drawn away just as quickly when Emma groaned again and clutched her belly, seized by another pain. She would have gone to her, but the duke was already there, taking her hands in his and whispering calming words. Lucy watched the tableau and, once again, found herself envious of her friend's discomfort. She did not like the feeling. It was borne of her selfishness and disappointment and her own poor decisions. She did not blame the duke for the bargain he had struck. Of course he would do whatever was necessary to bring peace and comfort to his Emma.

She left them then, husband and wife.

* * * *

Bex paced the drawing room in the wake of Lord Ridgely, who was unable to remain seated despite the regular requests to do so by both his wife and Lady Constance.

"I am better when I am up and about," Ridgely had insisted, and Bex had agreed. He was too anxious to remain still. He hadn't spoken to Lucy yet. He hadn't explained. He had realized the second he walked out the door that his decision to wait had been a mistake. He had convinced the duke it was the right thing, but it had been wrong. He had thought it was a kindness not to ask her to wait for him, but it was worse to leave her with no assurances at all. He was the worst kind of cad.

And then she was there. She appeared in the doorway, her eyes settling immediately on his. There was hurt and exhaustion in her sad blue eyes and he was impatient to clear it away. He crossed the distance between them with long strides. "Lucy," he breathed, reaching to take her hands.

She let him, but her hands lay limply in his and her expression remained unchanged.

Bex was keenly aware of their audience, but he did not care. What he needed to say to Lucy could not wait. "Lucy," he said, "Love, I am so sorry for not speaking earlier."

"No." She pulled her hands away. Fire lit in her blue eyes, replacing the sadness. "Don't call me that. Not now. We've never been false with each other."

"Lucy, no, you don't understand. I am not here to lie to you. I am here to explain."

Her chin lifted. "I've had the explanation from the duke. I'm fully apprised of the arrangement."

"Then you know?" he asked, studying her face for some reason behind her coolness. "And you're not pleased? It's what you wanted. I'm going to use the money to build a future." He reached for her hands again. "For us, if you'll have me." He smiled down at her, waiting for her to realize everything it meant.

She snatched her hands back again. "I won't do it. I won't allow the duke's aid to be my dowry, nor will I marry a man who does so for his financial security. I will speak with the duke. I will ask him not to rescind his commitment to help you, but I will not marry you."

Bex stepped back, stricken at her words. She would not marry him. "What do you mean the duke's aid is your dowry?" He could feel his voice rise, even as he tried to stop it. "What the devil does that mean?"

She advanced on him, the light in her blue eyes becoming darker, more fierce. "Do you think I don't understand the arrangement you have with the duke? You need his help and he has a ruined woman living in his house. Did you think I would not understand how both problems managed to be resolved in one happy conversation?"

Bex gaped at her, finally comprehending what she believed.

No.

No. No. No. No.

How could he ever convince her that wasn't the way it happened? He had to try. "Lucy, I swear to you, you are wrong. The duke never asked me to marry you. *I* told him I intended to marry you. It was my idea to wait until my literal ship had come in, but it was a stupid, stupid idea. I hated the way you looked at me when I left earlier today. So much so that I couldn't go home. I crossed the street and sat in the square, berating myself for a fool. When I saw everyone, I came back. I was worried you were hurt." He shook his head. "I should have known it was the child, I just...I wasn't thinking sensibly."

Lucy's voice was small but unwavering. "I wasn't thinking sensibly earlier, either, but I am now. I know that you do not want to marry me."

"*That* is the falsehood," Bex insisted, determined to make her believe. "I would have offered for you a thousand times before now if I'd been able to offer you any kind of security or future. You have to believe me. I love you, Lucy." His eyes closed and he knew he begged, but he did not care. "Darling, please, you have to believe this."

He looked down at her and saw the liquid begin to pool at the rims of her clear, bright eyes. He desperately hoped the emotion there was a sign of her faith in him. He knew she loved him. He knew it. She had gone to such lengths. She had wanted everything for him, when she had nothing left for herself. "Please, Lucy," he said again, his fingers spearing through his hair.

The tears never fell. Her expression hardened. "Mr. Brantwood, you should go. We are in the midst of a family event and you are intruding."

Bex reeled. She didn't believe him. She wasn't going to believe him. And she sure as hell wasn't going to marry him. God, he'd done worse than take her virtue. He'd destroyed her trust in him.

All of a sudden, he felt like a prize fool. He looked at the others in the room, at the quiet shock on their faces. He was, indeed, intruding. With a curt nod for the onlookers, he turned and walked out.

Chapter Thirty-Six

"Come and sit, *ma petite*."

Lucy did as Lady Constance directed, tearing her eyes from the door through which Bex had walked away. She would choose ruin over marriage to a man who had been forced to offer for her.

"Well, that was unexpected," Lady Constance said.

"Quite," Lord Ridgely agreed.

Lucy sighed. "*I* should have expected it," she said. "Of course the duke would feel honor bound to intervene in some way. He is good to help his cousin, but compelling him to marry me… I just wish he had considered my feelings before doing so. You may all think me romantic and irresponsible, but I do not wish to marry a man who does not love me."

Lady Constance patted her arm. "Do you recall, *ma petite*, what I told you this afternoon about my niece?"

Lucy looked up at her. "That you still hope to change her mind?"

The comtesse nodded. "Precisely, dear. We cannot give up on the people we care about simply because they behave foolishly."

Lucy sighed. "You are right, of course. I know the duke's intentions were good and on top of that, he may not have been at his most sensible, given his heightened concern for Emma." She would forgive him, of course. She would not be forced into marriage, but she would forgive him.

Lady Constance smoothed her skirts and straightened her shoulders. "The duke is not the foolish one in this scenario, *ma petite*."

Lucy looked up then. "What are you saying? Are you referring to Bex…I mean, Mr. Brantwood?"

Lady Constance shook her head. "No. As I said this afternoon, sometimes, for their own good, we must force wisdom upon those who cannot seem to find it. You, my girl, are being a fool."

Lucy stared at her. "What?"

"That boy," Lady Constance said, indicating with a nod the door through which Bex had left, "has been in love with you since the first time I met you both." She clasped her hands together in her lap. "If there is one thing the French know best, it is love."

* * * *

Bex should have hurried away. He should have put as much distance between himself and Worley House as quickly as he could, because the farther away he got, the less likely he would be to turn around and make more of a fool of himself than he already had.

It was done. He had offered for her and she had declined.

Still, she had only declined because she didn't believe him.

He halted in his path. Could he make her believe him? But how?

He began walking again. The duke was his only witness. If the duke had led Lucy to believe the offer of marriage had been part of some mercenary bargain, he had no proof to convince her otherwise—nothing but his own word, which was worthless to anyone.

Damn. Why had the duke done it?

"Bex."

The soft voice stopped and spun him as firmly as though a strong hand had gripped his shoulder. "Lucy?"

She was there, out of breath, her cheeks flushed with exertion, looking very much as though she had run after him. Hope tugged at him.

"Bex, stop," she said unnecessarily, for he'd stopped the moment she'd said his name the first time and would not have moved for anything—save her command.

"Lucy, I…" *Damn.* He had another chance—maybe a last chance—but he didn't know what to say. He was too afraid of squandering the opportunity.

She walked up to stand in front of him, close enough that his arms could close around her. He wanted to reach for her. He wanted to grab her and hold her to him until she believed him, but he didn't want to scare her away. He had never felt so powerless.

"Bex," she said, "I love you."

And all the power returned to him. He felt as though he had the strength to hold back a battalion of men, but he only needed to hold her. He did.

His arms closed around her and he was enveloped with the scent of sweetness and sunshine.

She clung to him for a long moment, then pulled back. "I am so sorry," she said, tears brightening her eyes. "I was so desperate for you to mean what you were saying, but I was too afraid to believe it. I didn't think it could be true."

Bex reached for her again. "Oh, Lucy, it's the truest thing I've ever said and loving you is the truest thing I've ever done. This ship may sink in the Atlantic and I will still want you to be with me. I know I shouldn't ask it of you, but I want you by my side even if we are starving."

"Oh, Bex, I want that more than anything."

He held her back from him then, looking down at her in disbelief.

"Well, I don't mean the starving part. I don't want that more than anything, but if I am starving, I'd like you to be starving too." She shook her head and released a frustrated breath of laughter. "Oh, you know what I mean. I love you."

He bent down and brushed his lips to hers. "I love you too, Saint Lucy of Beadwell," he whispered against her mouth. "No matter what happens next, I love you too."

And he did his best to show her that—right there, in the middle of Grosvenor Square in the bright light of a summer evening.

Epilogue

May 1819

"Aren't they splendid?" Lucy asked, gazing out over the veritable armada of white-sailed ships that filled the view from the London Docks.

Her question was answered by William, Viscount Brantwood, who pointed a chubby finger toward the vessels and proudly declared, "Hip."

Lucy hugged the infant closer. "Yes, darling, ships. Which one is ours, do you think?"

To this new query, William's answer was similar. He jabbed again with his outstretched finger and repeated, "Hip."

His insistence elicited a laugh from both Lucy and William's mother.

"I think he would like to claim them all," Emma said, stepping forward to stand next to Lucy at the quay's edge.

"Do be careful," called a stern voice from behind the women.

"There is no need to fret, dear," Emma assured her husband.

Despite her reassurances, the duke stepped forward and collected his son from Lucy. William was quite pleased with the improvement to this elevated vantage point as he was settled into the arms of his father, and he giggled in appreciation.

"Please do step back from the edge, ladies," the duke requested, doing so himself. Lucy imagined if he could have scooped both his wife and his son into the protective cocoon of his arms at that point, he would have done so.

"I know you are protective, but we shall be perfectly all right," Emma insisted, nevertheless complying with his request. Lucy did the same.

The duke glanced about at the rocking ships and scurrying dockhands with pursed lips. "The docks are not generally a place for genteel ladies."

Emma's smile was indulgent as she faced her husband and patted the arm that encircled their son. "We are far from delicate. We are well accompanied and it is the middle of the day."

"We couldn't possibly have missed this," Lucy added. "And besides, little William loves the sailing ships, don't you, darling?" She widened her eyes while poking a finger toward him, and he rewarded her with a shriek of giggles.

No, Lucy thought smiling in satisfaction, she would not have missed this. She was here to see Bex's ship. *His* ship. The first two shipments of raw cotton for the weaving operation in Watford had been sponsored by the newly established Brantwood Trading Company, but the ship itself had been owned by another merchant. Now that the weaving shed was in full operation, Bex had put profits from that endeavor and the first two cotton shipments toward the purchase of his very own ship at auction. Lucy could not wait to see it.

"We are impatient to see this grand vessel," the duke said, echoing her thoughts. "Where is your husband, Mrs. Brantwood?"

"I am here," came a call from farther down the quay, and Lucy spun, involuntarily, at the sound of her husband's voice. Joy filled her heart as it always did when Bex was near.

He raised a hand in greeting to their small group and Lucy swelled with pride at the confidence in his stride and the excitement in his handsome visage. She resisted the urge to lift her hem and hurry toward him. When he reached her, he took her hand, placed a kiss on her forehead, and said, "Come, darling, she's just this way."

Bex led her down the quay to the prow of a double-masted ship that loomed massively in front of her, as though the masts pierced the very clouds. He released her hand and stepped toward the ship, arm outstretched in presentation. "My dear, allow me to introduce the *Lady Claire*."

"Oh, she's beautiful," Lucy breathed.

"Yes, she is," Bex said softly, and when Lucy faced him, she saw that his attention was directed at her, not his ship. Her cheeks warmed under his appreciative gaze.

"She's a grand lady," the duke declared, reaching the front of the ship with his small family.

"I cannot believe you are the owner of this massive ship," Emma declared. "It's so large."

"She's a brigantine, ma'am. One hundred and ten feet, rigged for speed."

The group turned to attend to the tall man with sun-streaked hair and weathered features who had stepped forward to make this declaration.

"Allow me to introduce Captain FitzHarris," Bex said. "New captain of the *Lady Claire*."

"I am pleased to meet you, Captain," Lucy said, and the others greeted him in kind.

The captain smiled broadly in return. "Would you like to come aboard and see her?"

Emma looked toward her son in her first display of uncertainty since they'd arrived at the docks.

"You may have your tour with FitzHarris," Bex insisted, reaching to take William from his father. "I've already been aboard and I will stay here with the boy."

"Yes, you go first," Lucy added with an encouraging wave to Emma and her husband. "I shall stay with Bex and have my tour next."

Lucy watched Emma blow a kiss to William before taking her husband's arm and following the captain to board the *Lady Claire*. Then she turned back to Bex, unable to keep the wide, satisfied grin from her face as she gazed up at him, child in arms.

"She is beautiful," he said, looking out over the boat and the harbor.

"You love her already and she's been yours less than a week," Lucy pointed out with a laugh.

Bex's brow lifted. "I loved you before you were mine," he said, "so you've no reason for jealousy."

"I'm not envious," Lucy said, gripping her husband's free arm with both hands. She lay her cheek against his shoulder as the two of them looked out at the brigantine, rising majestically above the harbor. "I think I love her as well."

"With so much love, she could be the mother of an entire fleet of merchant ships, don't you think?" Bex asked.

"Oh, I do," Lucy declared. "I know that she will be."

Love the Brides of Beadwell?

Keep an eye out for

THE CHASE

Coming soon

And be sure to read

THE REUNION

Available now

From Lyrical Press

ABOUT THE AUTHOR

Sara Portman is an award winning author of historical and contemporary romance. In addition to being named the 2015 winner in the Historical Category of the Romance Writers of America® Golden Heart® contest, Sara has been a finalist and winner in several other writing competitions. A daughter of the Midwest, Sara was born in Illinois, grew up in Michigan, and currently lives in Ohio. In addition to her writing endeavors, Sara is a wife and mother in a large, blended family.

Visit her at www.saraportman.com.

Printed in the United States
by Baker & Taylor Publisher Services